"Well," Riveroma said. "...
You know, Jak, if I were ...
you. He's been taking a ...
less continually since yo...
less stunt. And I think ...
trying to save your own hide. Now that he's seen you as
you are—and since your entire record shows you don't
care in the slightest for or about Dujuv—this whole
process will go so much more quickly."

Bex Riveroma is a slick liar, the master of Principle
204, Jak kept reminding himself. He always tells the lie
that gets in under your skin and that's hard not to
believe. He gives your own worst thoughts back to you
and makes you believe them.

He hoped that Dujuv was remembering that too.
He looked down. A simple roll forward would send Jak
into a long enough fall to die instantly on impact.

"Barnes plays with old-fashioned space opera in this
far-future SF adventure....This is a fun romp."
    —**Locus** on *The Duke Of Uranium*

PRAISE FOR JOHN BARNES'S
MOTHER OF STORMS

"Astonishing speculations combined with brilliant
extrapolations."   —*Kirkus Reviews*

"Sheer storytelling power."   —*Booklist*

"A tour de force of a fascinating future."   —*Locus*

ALSO BY
JOHN BARNES

Orbital Resonance
A Million Open Doors
Mother of Storms
Kaleidescope Century
Encounter with Tiber (with Buzz Aldrin)*
Earth Made of Glass
Finity
Candle
The Return (with Buzz Aldrin)
The Merchants of Souls
The Sky So Big and Black

JAK JINNAKA NOVELS
The Duke of Uranium*

*available from Warner Aspect

A PRINCESS OF THE AERIE

JOHN BARNES

ASPECT®

WARNER BOOKS

An AOL Time Warner Company

WARNER BOOKS EDITION

Copyright © 2003 by John Barnes

Cover design by Don Puckey/Shasti O'Leary
Cover illustration by Matt Stawicki

Warner Books, Inc.
1271 Avenue of the Americas
New York, NY 10020

Visit our Web site at www.twbookmark.com

 An AOL Time Warner Company

Printed in the United States of America

First Paperback Printing: January 2003

10 9 8 7 6 5 4 3 2 1

For Jes Tate.

"Yeah, of course, Jak Jinnaka was my friend. Or at least I was his. Several times. Lots of different circumstances. I suppose I could say that I was the heet who knew him best, but he confided in women more than he did in anyone male. Although toktru, he didn't really ever tell anyone what he was thinking or why he did anything. I knew, because I asked him a few times, that he didn't follow the Wager, really, but he pretended to, and he'd quote Nakasen's <u>Principles</u> when it suited him, which usually meant when he could manipulate someone or get something he wanted. Which, come to think of it, was pretty much when and why he did anything.

"I guess he didn't always feel that that was what he was doing or the way he was. But then, he was the kind of heet who lied just to stay in practice, masen? Anyway I was his tove and pizo, almost his brother. Later I was more like his accidental comrade. Now and then, I was good and mad and trying to kill that spawn of a viper. And having known him for ninety years, I'd have to say that everything he ever thought or said was for his self-interest. I'm sure he'd tell you different. Like I said, he'd lie just to stay in practice, masen?

"I'd rather talk about a lot of other subjects, you know. This new generation of slamball players, or my old career. What it's like out by Vega. My years with the Spatial, or how the Socialist Party might do in the next elections. I've known a whole big bunch of very great people, in a long life, and I'd rather talk about <u>any</u> of them than about this one very famous one. Weehu, I'd rather talk about recipes for beefrat, or the new fashions, masen?"

From "Jinnaka's Oldest Tove Talks!" <u>Reasonably True News,</u> vol. 1042, Story 412, page 3, open distribution at standard terms, 92 hours viv, 65 hours movepics, 31 hours holo, 546,324 stillpix, of Dujuv Gonzawara available at additional charge (subsid. fees to Solar Slamball League, Socialist Party, Provo Spatial, quoted on request), see catalog for over 1 million Jinnaka stillpix

CHAPTER I

Not Just Any Sacred Orgy

Jak Jinnaka sat in the Dean of Students's office, in the waiting area. It was one of the lightest offices in the whole Public Service Academy, way up in the administrative levels, so the gravity was only about five percent, and the ceiling was high, so to burn energy and avoid boredom, he was pushing off from the central bench with his hands, drifting toward the ceiling in the lotus position, then drifting back to the cushions below.

He held his breathing even and focused on the lecture replaying in his earphones. "The practice of diplomacy is always extremely delicate, but it is most delicate in dealing with allies," Teacher Postick was saying, "for with enemies, it's mostly a matter of occasional bribes and threats and some ordinary cooperative matters like prisoner exchanges, declaring open stations, and moving fighting away from civilian areas. With allies, not only must one bribe and threaten constantly, but one must also appear not to be threatening at all, and to be giving bribes out of warm affection."

Jak's buttocks touched the bench. He pushed up again and drifted toward the ceiling. This far up in the Hive—most of the way to the surface, more than a thousand kilometers above the central black hole—gravity was so low that each bounce and drift took a full minute, and he was going almost all the way to the ceiling each time. He was listening to the review lecture from "Fundamentals of Diplomacy" for the fourth time in two days; he had an exam in an hour and a half.

Jak had mumbled, so the recording hadn't picked up the question from the room, but Postick always repeated a question. "The question was, 'Will there be questions about ethnography?'" Postick said. "Jak, you win the Stupid-Question Sweepstakes for today." That was about as nice as Teacher Postick ever got; usually he was far more sarcastic. "Every negotiation problem is riddled with ethnographic considerations. Diplomacy without ethnography would be algebra without numbers or literature without sex and violence. Now, of the many hundreds of possible ethnographic issues—for all of which you might be held responsible—I would pay special attention to the following—"

Jak fast-forwarded. He specked if he had to listen to it even one more time, he'd die. Ethnography was the subject he liked least. He left the recording on pause and pushed off the cushion extra hard. Floating gradually upward, he applied the Disciplines, slowing his heart rate and breathing.

He was confident as ever that he would be able to talk the Dean of Students into forgetting this latest uproar. Jak's best tove, Dujuv, was in there right now and had been in there for an exceptionally long time. Dujuv was goalie on the PSA's slamball team, so Dujuv usually got more slack than Jak did, but punishment never took Duj off the slamball team or Jak off the Maniples team.

It was odd that this was taking so long.

Jak dove deeper into his meditative state, becoming very calm and clear, as if he were actually running the katas of the Disciplines, and considered Principle 128: "Since your emotional state rarely affects anything, always have whatever one you like, and never worry about what it is." He added to that Principle 171: "Courage is fear without consequences."

All his life people had told him how much peace and confidence they derived from following the Wager, that the seven-hundred-year-old wisdom of Paj Nakasen helped them endure adversity and triumph over it. Jak dakked it was soothing to re-recite old phrases he knew by heart, but specked that he would have gotten the same confident, calm feeling by concentrating his mind on any phrase he'd learned in childhood, such as "with a quack quack here and a quack quack there." Nonetheless, he did feel calmer.

His head thumped on the ceiling. He let go of the lotus position, flailed, and tumbled slowly back down to the bench, kicking and waving. The lecture got turned back on somehow, so as he descended, Postick talked about all the different tribes and cities of Mars and how many different kinds of negotiating problems could arise out of their local customs and beliefs. Jak, to his surprise, didn't die.

When the seat cushion came within reach, Jak pulled himself around to plant his feet, and switched off the lecture. He was really hoping that no one had seen that, especially not the Dean of Students.

Jak started to play through the recording one more time, realized he could recite most of it, and, with a sigh, touched the reward spot on his purse, the blue fingerless glove, worn on the left hand, that contained a microsupercomputer. Most people would rather be without their clothing than their purse, but Jak had never really learned to like them. Still, his purse had been coaching him well. It was hardly the device's responsibility that Jak wasn't learning quickly, and Jak wanted it to continue coaching well in the future, so he touched the reward spot twice more. He felt, more than heard, the purse's little cheeble of pleasure.

"All right, check content of what I say next against that review lecture I've been replaying. Ready?"

"Ready."

"Negotiations are always difficult and negotiations with allies are more difficult than negotiations with enemies. Masen?"

"Correct but general."

"Negotiations with allies are more difficult because— um, you have to act like you like them, and—"

The door from Dean Caccitepe's office dilated and Dujuv airswam into the waiting room. He was a panth, a breed that the genies had made into extraordinary natural athletes, with ultrafast metabolisms, very high muscle mass ratios, sharper than normal vision and hearing, perfect balance and kinesthetic sense, and extraordinary reaction times. This had necessitated some compromises; panths were notoriously not bright, test pilots rather than engineers, line sergeants and not staff officers.

Also, though they could sit silently for hours and rest as relaxed as a cat, usually they bounced with sheer exuberance of life. Dujuv was airswimming in a straight, businesslike line—no rolls, kips, or tumbles. Not good.

Jak and Dujuv's private code was signed with the left hand. As he airswam, Jak's toktru tove reached slowly out with his left, giving Jak a clear view: thumb straight—*good news*. Three fingers curled under—*extremely mitigated*. Not suspended or expelled, but the emotional weather on the other side of that door, today, wasn't toktru happy.

Dujuv airswam out. Jak waited to be called. Duj got away with everything short of murder partly because administrators, teachers, and pokheets viewed Jak as the leadership of every operation, and partly because Duj was the star goalie of PSA's slamball team. Jak was pretty good at Maniples (third singles for the PSA's club, and only in his sophomore year), which helped him, but not like slamball helped Dujuv. Whatever Dujuv's grim portion had been, Jak was about to get it with seconds and some to take home.

"Jak Jinnaka," a voice said. "The Dean will see you now."

Jak airswam into the Dean's inner office. Dean Caccitepe was an ange, a breed with very long faces, and long slender limbs. Even for an ange he was tall, but since he was older—probably about 225 years old, to judge by the coarse brown facial hair and weary expression—and didn't seem to get much exercise, his body was a pudgy sphere at the center of all that leg and arm, like a spider from a children's cartoon. He gestured Jak to the guest perch in front of the desk, then airswam into his own chair, facing Jak.

He folded those long, long arms on the desk in front of himself and leaned far forward, looking deep into Jak's eyes with utter sorrow. "First of all, let us be clear. You are a Hive citizen admitted as a special favor to a foreign government, and we expect you to behave like and as a Hive citizen. Don't hope for clemency just because Psim Cofinalez likes you."

Jak nodded. "I'm aware, sir." Jak and Dujuv had not actually had the test scores to get into the PSA, but two years ago, just after graduating from gen school, they had gotten mixed up in a complicated business that had involved, among other things, a kidnapped princess, a duke in disguise, control of most energy sources in the solar system, and blackmailing one of the most dangerous people alive. In a series of improbable accidents, Jak and Dujuv had come through it all as good friends of Psim Cofinalez, who had shortly after become Ducent, and then Duke, of Uranium.

As a reward, or to get them out of the way (most likely both), Psim had enrolled them at the PSA as foreign students—and made it clear that staying in was up to them.

Worse yet, Psim had explained this to the PSA's administration, so his name could not even be used in a successful bluff.

"Now," the Dean went on, "we prefer that none of our students have wars named after themselves, at least not until after they graduate."

"A war? Over some amateur pornography?"

The Dean had stopped smiling. "Is *that* how you intend to describe yourself and Dujuv Gonzawara's having penetrated security for the Venerean delegation, placed hidden cameras, and recorded a Venerean sacred orgy—and not just any sacred orgy, but specifically the Joy Day orgy?"

Jak refrained from shrugging and tried to look innocent.

"The innocent look is not going to work, Jak Jinnaka. Joy Day is the most sacred of all the Venerean orgies. It was a major concession for the Venerean delegation even to meet with us when it meant being away from home over the Joy Day holiday." The Dean stared down his long nose at Jak, as if considering pecking out his eyes, and said nothing further.

At last Jak ventured, "I suppose most of them would want to be at home with their families."

The Dean's eyes became hard and cold as metallic hydrogen. "Why do you think that a crude ethnic sex joke will help?"

Jak wondered what he had said. Apparently something else that would offend Venereans.

"Pro forma," the Dean said, "since anyone who chose to

be so offensive can hardly have done so out of ignorance, but pro forma, because we are supposed to assume that ignorance may be the problem, let me tell you what you should have known, and known thoroughly, since you were ten. Venereans do *not* practice incest. Incest is defined as 'prohibited intercourse with a family member,' and since what Venereans do on Joy Day is *required,* and in any case they do not recognize consanguinity as a basis of familial affiliation, no such thing happens at the Joy Day orgies, and, to repeat the point, *Venereans do not practice incest.*

"I refuse to believe that you did not at least learn *that* in the required Solar System Ethnography unit on 'fighting words and how to avoid them.' You should have had that three times in gen school—it is on the list of basic things to be remembered, always, in dealing with people around the solar system. And apparently pretty nearly everything about Venus must have failed to register—" as Jak had feared he would, Caccitepe looked down, and then looked up again; the smile was not back, but there was a trace of a smirk that was no more reassuring. "Aha. But I see I failed to dak just who and what Jak Jinnaka is. You've failed Solar System Ethnography *twice.* A required course that everyone knows is easy."

"Actually, sir," Jak said, trying for a diversion, "what Dujuv and I were thinking was kind of like this. I mean, we dak, we toktru dak, that Venus is an important ally and all that. And especially since there have been some problems, the last few years, and some tensions, I guess you could call them, well, we were hoping that this might improve relations."

"Am I going to hear the same silly explanation that Dujuv gave me?"

Jak put on his very best expression of wounded inno-
cence. It had no perceptible effect on the Dean.

Jak went ahead, anyway. "Sir, maybe Dujuv isn't very
good at explaining things, and maybe he got a little mixed
up trying, but I'm just as sure that he was *trying* to tell you
the truth. Will you let me?"

Caccitepe's eyebrows tried to scale his high forehead.
Still, he gestured for Jak to go on.

"Well," Jak said, "just think of it this way. Almost all of
the population of Venus is resourcers, and everyone knows
that they're a pretty strange lot. I mean, how could they not
be? They live their whole lives in the giant crawlers, no sky,
no stars, always high grav, and instead of pure clean vacuum they live at the bottom of a boiling chemical hell, in a
tin box full of noise from gigantic treads, huge engines,
heat pumps that keep them from baking, and the hell-wind
against the hull. They're all half-deaf and full-crazy.

"But the djeste of their freedom makes them the symbol
of liberty to young people all over the solar system. I mean
you just can't get any more open and democratic than the
way they live, toktru they have their feets, it just singing-on
resonates for everyone young, not only here, but in the
Aerie, and in all the minor stations too." (If only the Dean's
facial expression would change—Jak was without a clue
about how this was going over.) "Well, sir, young people do
feel like the high price the Venereans charge for resources
is unconscionable, and it chokes back growth, which hits
the youngest generation hardest. Among people up to age
seventy or so, Venus looks greedy at our expense, and it's
toktru resented. But at the same time, they're a symbol of
freedom. So if people had a chance to see all these old, dig-
nified diplomats doing all that wild stuff—well, of course

nobody's going to get all excited or anything, but it's sure going to remind them why Venus is the lightest planet—"

"It has the second highest gravity of anywhere inhabited," the Dean said. "Is this the quality of your research?"

"I mean light the way kids use the word, sir. Fun. Fashionable. Exciting. New. Something you want to be associated with. Like rich people with style. Not like some pathetic loser gweetz with a job and bills and no future. Like that."

The Dean smiled as if he were about to torment a small animal. "Oh, yes, oh, yes, I should dearly love to try to sell *that* story upstairs, if I had to, which (glory to Nakasen) I won't." He brought his feet up onto his perch, still chuckling, bracing his hands on his knees. "And you did manage to keep your preposterous tale straight, much better than Dujuv. Did you consider how the Venereans might feel about it?"

"Well, sir, my concern was the Hive. That's where our loyalty is supposed to be, after all. So I probably wasn't thinking about the Venereans at all."

"Do you see a pattern here? Because I do. And not a good one. You seem to think that the Hive is all that matters, and that all your superiors will, or should, feel that way as well. In fact you seem to think that consideration for the different feelings and ideas of the citizens of other nations is somehow a weakness or a failing in someone working for the Hive."

Bewildered, Jak dakked what he was being accused of, but not why it would be an accusation. What was good for the Hive, so far as Jak could see, was good, regardless of what it might mean for the perverts of Venus, the miserly miners of Mercury, or the surreal tribals of Mars.

"Jak," Dean Caccitepe said, "you know that I'm not

going to try to appeal to your moral sense. I'm not that big a fool. But if you think ignorance is a mark of patriotism, we have a problem. And I think that's how you actually feel. Why else would you avoid and/or flunk, constantly, a not-at-all difficult required class? Certainly it's consistent with your cover-up story. I know perfectly well that you and Dujuv were merely trying to finance an end-of-year slec party. But even if I didn't, I'd have known that your entire story was nonsense. Now, can you tell me why?"

Jak shrugged, looked down, and mumbled, "Because you're smarter than me."

"*No,* Jak. I *am* smarter than you—many people are—but that is not the reason your lie failed. Almost anyone could have seen through it. Now, why? This is important, Jak. If, in just a few years, we are going to have you out there lying on behalf of the Hive, with the security of a billion people dependent upon your lie's being believed, then you had better be able to tell a good one (and more importantly avoid telling a bad one). Now—again—why was it that *anyone* could have seen through that lie?" The question was clearly serious. "I'm still waiting for an answer," Caccitepe said.

"I don't know. I don't have any idea," Jak said, possibly for the first time in his life.

"What is Principle 204?"

"I don't—"

"Just recite it."

Jak drew a breath, blanked his mind, and let the familiar words tumble out. " 'Principle 204: Always make your lie the lie that your listeners want to tell themselves.' All right, sir, I sort of see *that* it has to do with the case, but I don't see *what* it has to do with the case."

"Hmm." The Dean frowned. "Either that was a real question or your act is improving. Either of those is a good thing, of course. Hmm." He tented his fingers under his jaw, seeming again to look for something to peck at on his desk. After some thought, Caccitepe said, "Well, then, here's what I've decided. Mind you, if you don't like it, you can always appeal through official channels."

Jak shuddered.

The Dean nodded a few times to himself, his sharp face and small head bobbing on his long neck. Jak tried not to think of it as stork-like, because he was already feeling like a bite-sized frog. When the Dean spoke again, that smile was back. "Now let me tell you what you did. You had exactly the effect you're claiming to have intended—in the Hive. Millions of our younger citizens accessed those illegal recordings and were fascinated. Venerean diplomats are getting fan mail from pornography buffs. Interest in and affection for all things Venerean surged—we're predicting dozens of best-selling entertainments with Venerean themes soon. Intrigue and adventure vivs, vids, and novels for the next few years will feature many Venerean sidekicks, love interests, or other important secondary characters, and there are going to be practically no Venerean villains for the next six or seven years. You truly have made the Venereans the lightest of the light, Jak.

"You've made them deeply angry, too. The average Venerean likes us less than ever, and the anti-Hive parties and organizations are growing fast.

"When you pulled your little trick, we were in secret negotiations for a more equitable trade treaty. You've just strengthened their hardliners and our accommodationists— so guess what you've done to the negotiations? Guess who will be making concessions and who will be accepting them?

"Now, you don't have to *like* Venereans, Jak, but if you

don't want to give the store away to them, you have to know who they are. Can I make that any clearer?"

"No sir."

The Dean's smile had become very, very deep and strangely warm. He settled back, letting his back straighten so that Jak became aware that Caccitepe was actually well over two meters tall, and beamed down his long nose at Jak. "No doubt you are well aware that the time is almost here to set your Junior Task."

Jak tried not to hold his breath. All students were given a task to be completed by the end of the junior year. Caccitepe was one of the dozen or so administrators who set Junior Tasks . . . and he was legendary for setting difficult tasks, sadistically aimed straight at your weaknesses.

"Jak, we have to maintain your independence and your talent for improvisation while finding a way to harness them. There are two kinds of people that can't be trusted with any important job—those who always follow directions and those who always tear them up. Before you graduate, you *must* be able to completely understand directions, intentions, and context, and then do the right thing, which is *often but not always the thing you were ordered to do.* Am I making myself clear?"

"Toktru clear, sir. I dak."

"Well, then. Right now, you are compulsive about not following directions, which makes you as much their prisoner as any robot, and you willfully refuse to understand any point of view other than the most narrowly chauvinistic one, which means you can't modify the directions intelligently. By the end of your junior year we will have fixed all this completely."

Jak felt a cold chill up his spine, but he nodded and said, "Yes, sir."

The Dean smiled at him, very kindly and warmly, and the chill became a vast glacier of frozen helium. "So. First of all, you will continue on the Maniples team and you will not be on academic suspension."

He relaxed a little.

"You will be under a much tougher condition. Every term while you remain here, and via correspondence during Long Break, you will repeat Solar System Ethnography, regardless of how many times you pass it, *until* you actually earn top rank in the class, after which you will repeat the optional class in Advanced Ethnography until you earn top rank in that class. If you insist on being a fool and a boor we cannot fix that, but we can make sure that it's a choice, rather than a matter of ignorance."

Jak breathed a sigh of relief; this wasn't so bad. He would still be on the Maniples team, and if he was sentenced to perpetually take the course he most disliked, well, at least with all that exposure to it, he should be able to speck some detection-proof method of cheating.

"Now those are the preconditions for your staying. About your Junior Task." The Dean seemed to be glowing with joyous bonhomie, like one of the medieval gods— Buddha or Santa Claus or Satan, Jak could never keep them all straight. "You will take on an independent project to be graded by me. It must be a situation exactly like those you will encounter as a field operative: the directions must be vague, the goals not entirely clear, the situation one in which you have to interact extensively with people who are not Hive citizens and do not share our goals. It's a shame that that little adventure of yours a couple of years ago— when you rescued Princess Shyf, put Psim Cofinalez in line to be Duke of Uranium, and acquired a number of cross-cultural friends, including one Rubahy—isn't coming up

now, because it would have been perfect. You have one
week to tell me what your project will be. Questions?"

"Er, well, none right away sir, but—"

"Then goodbye, and good luck on that exam you have
forty minutes from now. If you're quick, you can probably
review all the ethnographic material just before you go in."
The Dean winked so merrily that Jak might almost have
mistaken it for friendly.

Unable to think of anything else to say, Jak got up and
airswam through the door, which closed behind him
silently. An instant later he heard bellowing, joyful laughter. Jak resolved not to mention that to anyone. Already, his
story would be disbelieved by every other student, when he
got to the part where the Dean smiled.

CHAPTER 2

I Don't Need You to Kill a Man

So apparently the first thing I have to do is come up with a project," Jak said to his best tove Dujuv, as they sat down to share a plattcr of Whole Steamed Beefrats in a private booth in the Old China Cafe, their favorite booth in their favorite place of many years, in Entrepot, a vast shopping area tens of kilometers across, far down in the lower decks of the Hive, not far above the industrial service decks, so far down that the main floor was on the .76 grav deck. The Old China had a proletarian-jock tendency to big portions, heavy sauces, and strong flavors, especially to sweet-and-sours.

Since his allowance was generous and his Uncle Sib was rich, Jak was probably among the Old China's wealthicst customers. Not the wealthiest, though. That had to be Sesh.

The greatest shock of Jak's life had occurred two years ago when he had discovered that Sesh Kiroping, the girl who had been his sweet, amiable, pleasant demmy for his last years in gen school, was in reality Princess Shyf Karrinynya, or more formally, Her Utmost Grace the Princess Shyf, Eleventh of the Karrinynya Dynasty of the Kingdom of Greenworld, by the Blessed Choice of Mother Gaia. Greenworld, a vital ally to the Hive, was in the Aerie, the other giant space station in the solar system.

Discovering Sesh's real identity had led Jak, and later Duj, into wild adventures, caused Sesh to return to the Aerie, and gotten Jak and Dujuv into the PSA not as Hive citizens, but as special favors to the Duke of Uranium, Psim Cofinalez, one of the hundred or so most powerful people in the solar system.

Jak thought of that adventure as the best weeks of his life, living like a hero in an intrigue-and-adventure viv: plots, rescues, counterplots, affairs with beautiful girls, high adventure with good toves. Since then he had mostly spent time in class, or socializing with Fnina, his current demmy, who had the looks of a model, the clash-splash-and-smash of a viv star, and the perspicacity of an unusually naive brick. She had been attracted to Jak by Mreek Sinda's best-selling documentary about him, a grossly distorted version of his adventures, and Jak really thought that in two years Fnina had not yet noticed that he was not the heet in Sinda's show.

He still practiced the Disciplines daily, and was if anything better at them than ever, but there was no one to fight with, and sparring had lost some of its pleasures; he still consumed intrigue-and-adventure vivs, but couldn't help noticing how much less interesting than the real thing they were. For that matter, during his brief period of adventures, aside from his sex life with a passionate, beautiful, horny princess, he'd also had a tender love affair with a crewie girl on the sunclipper on which he traveled—her first, and he still dreamed of how sweet and affectionate it had been. Comparatively, Fnina was merely compliant and proficient, and within a few months, anyway, his fame would have at last worn off and she'd find someone else.

Everything in the last two years was nothing compared to those few weeks. That wild set of adventures had begun with a casual conversation, right here, in this booth. Jak suddenly hoped that this booth was lucky.

Dujuv's attention was where it usually was, on his plate. Jak had often heard him say that beefrats were the real triumph of the genies—without beefrats, there'd be no hamburgers or meat loaf in space; cows were just too big and inefficient. A beefrat would eat pretty much anything and turn it into so much juicy, tender steak on each tiny body that, when full-grown, they looked like thick cylinders garnished with a whippy long tail, tiny little head, and four pink hands.

Dujuv was gobbling down beefrats at his usual pace—hands, tails and heads came off in a single blinding motion, into the bone bowl to his right; then the beefrat torso in his left hand whirled as he stripped off the outer layer of meat with his teeth. After ripping them apart with his hands to get the sweet hidden bits between the bones, he plopped the skeleton into the bone bowl at his left even as his right hand grabbed another steamed beefrat and the process began again. Duj had once said, casually, that he'd never really known how to enjoy beefrat until he'd dakked you needed a bone bowl for each hand.

Jak watched the process in some awe, as always. A plate of Whole Steamed Beefrats was twelve of them; Jak had accounted for three, probably a quarter kilogram of meat. But then Jak, unmodified as he was, didn't have the speeded-up metabolism of a panth.

Dujuv at last came up for air. "So did Dean Caccitepe give you any ideas for where to find a project?"

"Not even a hint. So what's *your* Junior Task? Score four knockbacks the next time we play Nakasen University?"

"Four knockbacks is one more than the school record." Dujuv dragged a foreleg through his teeth, getting the last succulent bits. "I could eat these fat little bastards all day. Hmm. Well. The Junior Task for me is actually harder than getting four knockbacks against Nakasen, I think. I have to go along on *your* project, and help you out, which is not necessarily hard at all, except that I'm also supposed to keep you out of trouble, and I ask you, *can* anyone? Is that a fair assignment?"

Jak gaped. "So your project is to be my pizo?"

"Singing-on, tove. I'm to be your *responsible* pizo. Dean Caccitepe's exact words. It's that little adjective, 'responsible,' that makes the whole job so tough, masen? So, you go save the universe; I come along and help. Any idea what I should pack?"

"No idea at all. But it's only been a few hours. I'm still recovering from that test—which might as well have been an ethnography exam. I can't believe that he did that to us. Every question had some condition like, 'Bearing in mind the implications for the Fertility Festival of the Booga Booga Nation' or 'Without reviving historical memories of the Second Civil War in Beriberistan' or 'assume that *machismo, gimu,* and bloody-mindedness are all relevant.' I mean, it's supposed to be a negotiation class, and that test wasn't about negotiating *anything*—it was all about respecting some rule that you can't pick your nose with your pinkie on Tuesday. It's as if they gave you a test on how to be a goalie and all the questions were about fast and slow surfaces and which team had the most left-handed power slingers, and none of them were about stopping the ball or whipping out."

Dujuv looked thoughtful as he plucked the head, hands, and tail of the next beefrat. "You know, stops and whipouts are the things you practice all the time, of course, I mean, they're basically what they hire a goalie to do, but to do them at the right time, in the right way, so that your team scores and theirs doesn't—and to set you up to score on a knockback . . . hunh. Well, for that, you really do need to know things like the speed of the surface and how many lefties they have."

"It was just an example."

"But see, that's what's interesting, that you picked that example. Because those things *would* be relevant in a goalie class. And look, I'm never going to take any negotiating class, or anything else academic that isn't required—nobody wants me for my brain—but what kind of deal are you going to get if you don't dak the other heet?"

"Anyway," Jak said, sick of the entire subject, "I'm going to talk with Uncle Sibroillo about coming up with some kind of project. I'm having dinner with him tonight." Jak had never known his parents, and had been discouraged from asking questions about them; Sibroillo was the only relative he knew. Jak had moved out of Sibroillo's home after graduating from gen school, but they still saw each other a couple of times a week. "He's a silly old gwont but he does have ideas, sometimes good ones."

Dujuv shrugged. "You'll think of something, Jak. How long have we been friends?"

"Since the second day of gen school, so I guess about ten years."

"Well, then, in ten years, I've never known you to actually fail to think of something."

Jak raised his left hand and spoke into his purse. "Time check."

The purse replied, "Fifteen twenty, standard. Sibroillo will pick you up in one hour ten. He's going to surprise you with a pricier, fancier place than usual, and he hopes to catch you not dressed for it and thereby make you feel like a gweetz. If you want to get a shower and change into something nicer beforehand, we should leave in the next five minutes."

"Thanks. Pay the bill here. Leave a tip thirty percent over average."

"Done." The little lighted square in his palm went out.

"Well, you heard the gadget," Jak said. "Guess I'd better run, tove."

"Yeah. You want to take a beefrat with you?"

There were two left of the plate. "Naw, have 'em all."

"You paid for 'em."

"Well, I have the money, you have the appetite. It's a specialization of labor. Gotta move, tove."

Dujuv nodded, his face already down in another beefrat.

Jak spoke to his purse. "Get Pongo to the nearest station."

"Done, off."

With a final nod to Dujuv, whose mouth was still much too full to talk, Jak pushed the button to slide the private booth door open, and walked out past all the mostly-closed booths, through the front door and across the courtyard to the little spur of track between the walls of an alcove. After a short wait, both walls dilated into doors, and Pongo emerged from the left and grounded.

"Right here," Jak said to his Pertrans car, which, recognizing his voice, turned on a green okay light and popped open its canopy. Jak jumped in, fastened his belt, and said, "Okay, close up and get me there."

The canopy closed, the inducers lifted Pongo half a centimeter off the tracks, and they shot off in a series of high-acceleration lurches and bobs. They couldn't go as fast back to Jak's place as Pongo had come by itself—Jak couldn't take forty g—but Jak had set up a standing funds authorization for extra energy, shortcuts through the high-priced tunnels, automatic payment of misdemeanor tickets—all the costs of speed. To go through the Hive in a hurry, Pongo had to bounce from one space between Pertrans cars to another, jinking in and out of tubes, speeding or slowing to match speeds with each successive hole, calculating a hundred dips and bobs ahead as traffic entered and left the tube system. Jak loved it; Uncle Sib called it "being shaken like a rat," though just why anyone would shake rats was beyond Jak.

At ten minutes till arrival, Jak had his purse call ahead to have his house start drawing a bath. Since Pongo docked inside his living quarters, Jak undressed in the Pertrans car. When the car grounded and popped its canopy, Jak walked straight to his bath, dropping his purse onto the recharger on the bathroom counter.

As he settled into the warm sudsy water, the purse said, "Mail from Princess Shyf."

"Bring it up, on the screen I can see from the tub."

The purse said, "I am requested to point out that this message came in through the purely personal channel, one of your encrypted back doors, and she used a back door that hadn't been used before. So this arrives in the highest confidence."

"Interesting," Jak said, meaning he was fascinated. "Put it up." He settled back into the suds to see what Sesh had to say to him. Two years ago; when he had just performed a daring rescue, and with so much conspiracy and counter-conspiracy in the air, setting up the back channels had seemed like a good thing to do just in case. Now, she'd activated one.

The screen swirled for a half second as the decrypter worked. Sesh's image appeared. She was almost as tall as

Jak, and thin. Her ancestry owed much to the gracile breed, and her blazing red hair, deep blue eyes, coffee-with-cream skin, and fine bone structure still mesmerized Jak. There was something sad and wary in those fascinating eyes.

"Hey, Jak, weehu, it's been a long time since I messaged you." Her smile deepened, suggesting that he ought to forgive her; he did, of course, instantly. "I guess I'm doing all right at this stupid princess job, I mean I speck I'm at least an average princess, maybe a little better than that, and I'm sure I can be way above average by the time I make queen. Get queened, queenify, queen out? What *do* you call it, and why hasn't anyone ever told me? Anyway, you know what I mean."

She leaned forward, close to the camera. The view down her cleavage brought back fond memories, so Jak tried to focus on her face, but then he was lost in those eyes again. "Jak, I'm finding that more and more I need services that I can't get officially. The whole Royal Palace is one big snake pit and I need at least one snake on my side. I can't tell you what it is that I need in this message—it will be decrypted and read here, and in the Hive, and probably twenty other places too, soon. I need some things done quietly and unofficially. I think your Uncle Sib will guess what kind of things, so you should show him this message.

"Anyway, it's nothing terrible—I don't need you to kill a man or carry a secret message to my lover or anything like that. But I need a good friend that I can trust to do it, and I know from that time you rescued me, you're good at the kind of stuff I need done, and you've had all that training from your uncle, and I know your Long Break is coming up, so I have arranged a fast passage over to the Aerie.

"When you get here I'll pass you off as a visiting school friend, set you up with a room here in the Royal Palace, and . . . well, mostly we'll party and hang around and enjoy life here, which *is* pretty enjoyable I must say, but also while you're here you can do a few things for me, and I know that you might be a lot more interested if I mention this, so let me add that some of those things are, um, kind of wild and edgy and a little crazy and dangerous.

"Also, here's something else I'd like: bring along Dujy, and while you're at it bring along Myx. Neither of them is essential but it would be so fun just to have the four of us together again. And of course in the event of trouble, Dujuv is so good . . . you know, a panth, and a loyal friend, and all of that . . . not that I expect that you'll be in a fight or anything, but then, I can't say that I wouldn't expect there to *not* be fighting, either, masen? Weehu, that was another one of *those* sentences. Well, anyway, I hope I'm making some kind of sense all the same.

"I expect that sending this by back channel with so little real information will probably at least pique your curiosity. So here's what you do. The Hive Spatial has CUPV slots open for you, Myxenna, and Dujuv, for the next cruise of RHBS *Up Yours,* and its very first port of call happens to be the Aerie."

Jak smiled; she knew how he liked to travel. He'd been a CUPV before, three times, all on merchant sunclippers. A CUPV was "Crew, Unpaid, Passenger Volunteer," a fancy way of saying a paying passenger working on the ship to have something to do; it counted for union points, and it was more interesting than the viv, the gym, and reading, which were most of the amusements for passengers on sunclippers, and tended to become boring in a few days—a major problem since getting between the worlds on solar sails and gravity assists took many weeks even in the lower solar system.

During peacetime, the Spatial took passengers. Warships, with their quarkjet engines, traveled on direct trajectories much faster than the solar orbits in which the sunclippers moved, and charged less than the super-fast private quarkjet liners. At half the cost of a quarkjet liner, it was often worth it to administrators to be able to move bureaucrats and corporados around in a quarter or less of the time a regular sunclipper would take, and transporting needed, high-ranking workers on Spatial ships would not threaten the social order, for no one was going to acquire a taste for luxury while traveling on a warship.

Furthermore, the Spatial's passengers, like any other passengers on a union ship, were eligible for CUPV status. Jak had never been on a Spatial ship—and *Up Yours* was a battlesphere, the biggest and second-fastest class of deep space warship. So whatever it was that Sesh wanted him to do at Greenworld, just getting there was going to be a wonderful opportunity.

"*Up Yours* will be leaving just after your final exams. It took me a few good tricks to get access to those CUPV slots, let me tell you, but I did, and the three of you need only claim them—just call on Lieutenant Creyamanen on *Up Yours,* anytime down to a week before it boosts. As a CUPV you can even pick up some union points, just in case you're still interested in that funny-looking short-haired girl."

"Phrysaba," Jak said. "Phrysaba Fears-the-Stars." Besides Sesh, Phrysaba was the other person whose letters Jak's purse was supposed to announce immediately.

"I'm not *toktru* insecure on that point, I mean, look at her, who could be? But anyway, give it some thought.

"Now, the important last detail: *don't reply.* I worked up a few things all on my own to get one good back-channel message out. There's just the slightest chance that nobody on Greenworld has detected this message, so let's not risk their detecting your reply. Just show up. You at least, with Dujuv and Myxenna ideally." She gave him the big warm happy smile that had always melted him, and said, "I still miss you a lot."

He played her message twice more as he finished his bath.

CHAPTER 3

I Have a Feeling That Your Troubles Are Over

And that's the project he's requiring, Uncle Sib," Jak said, unhappily staring down at his pasta. It was superb, but he was full, and he rarely ate in so light a place now that he had his own apartment. "Vague directions, unclear goals, and a chance to use my nonexistent ethnographic skills. And I have to find it for myself. This is like having to find the rope to hang yourself with." He managed to eat a couple more small, perfect mussels and a twirl of linguine, for manners' sake; perhaps, if he sat and picked long enough, he might get up the will for dessert.

He couldn't help thinking, enviously, that Dujuv could probably have eaten all this, finished Sib's, and then consumed three desserts.

Sib nodded. "It doesn't sound especially easy. I might have some thoughts on the subject."

"Actually, I have one very large thought on the subject. We should discuss it privately." Now Sib would change the subject, but Jak and he would have a conversation, soon, away from listening devices. Practicing basic security was automatic to both Jinnakas; Jak had been brought up knowing that his uncle's business must not be discussed in public.

"I'm assuming that this idea will turn out to have involved some actual thought, knowledge, and attention?" Sib didn't sound entirely hopeful. During his brief adventure two years ago, Jak had learned that Sib and his long-term demmy Gweshira were members of Circle Four, a notorious and powerful zybot (a social engineering collective trying to covertly reshape human society and history), and that Sib and Gweshira had always hoped (to their frequent disappointment) that Jak too would want to be involved in public affairs, political intrigue, and sedition—categories which overlapped heavily if you were in Circle Four. All zybots were supposed to be illegal, but Circle Four was often useful to the Hive and so it was tolerated, as long as it stayed quiet.

"Well," Jak said, "I admit I never used to pay attention to the news or politics. But I've changed, at least somewhat. I'd attribute it to my classes at the PSA, and Gweshira's influence." Jak looked down at his plate, mentally counted off ten seconds, and looked up to see his uncle, as he'd expected, about to explode with rage. It was a funny sight and Jak laughed aloud. "And most importantly, *your* influence, you silly, sensitive old gwont. I was just having fun with you."

"I was thinking of something else," Sib said, staring into Jak's eyes with utter sincerity.

"You were so annoyed that you were ready to wet yourself. And rightly so. You put a lot of work into waking me up to the larger world around me, Uncle Sib, and you deserve full credit. I was just teasing. Sorry if I went too far."

Sibroillo tried to hold his expression of wounded dignity for another moment, but failed utterly and began to laugh. "Gweshira always says that when she teases me, I look like a furious toad."

"With the goatee," Jak said, "more like an angry terrier."

"Ahem." The word was more whistled than spoken, from directly behind Jak. He turned. At the table behind him, a very senior Rubahy warrior (to judge by the darkness of the patch on his right shoulder, and the shape and size of his enormous teeth), more than two meters tall, had turned all the way round at hearing the hated slur. His feathers were already fluffed and his rage spines were extending from his back.

Jak got out of his chair and made the kneeling single-knee bow: deep apology. "I deeply regret the offense, but I assert by my honor that I am blameless. I was saying that my uncle resembles, somewhat, the type of dog called a terrier. I meant no slur upon your species and was not thinking of the Rubahy at all. Still, saying that word in a public place was obviously careless and foolish, for I have angered a noble warrior whose respect I would much rather have. I ask his forgiveness and mercy."

"And you receive it in abundance." The Rubahy's rage spines sank back into his back, and his feathers smoothed; the huge, flat, flexible lips extended to cover the monstrous slicing-teeth. He extended a three-fingered, two-thumbed hand; as was proper, Jak gripped it lightly and stood. "You have a courteous way of speech. Have you known other Rubahy?"

"I have known one well," Jak said, thinking of Shadow on the Frost, from whom he occasionally received inexplicable mail and to whom he would then reply with whatever random facts about his life he happened to think of, always being told that the message had brightened Shadow's day. "But he lives in exile in human service, and he has many enemies, and so I hesitate to speak his name."

The Rubahy made a standing bow. If the name of Jak's

unknown friend were revealed, and it were an enemy of this Rubahy, with a misunderstanding so recent, anything from a snub to a duel might follow, depending on the exact degree of enmity. "I am glad not to know his name, then, for his teaching courtesy to you has made me think of him favorably, which is superfluous for a friend, improper for an enemy, and dangerous for an unknown (since it might someday lead me into a quarrel on an outnumbered side)."

Jak nodded. "Then let it suffice that, yes, I was taught some courtesy, and by a Rubahy."

"And so you honor your teacher." The Rubahy and Jak shook hands. The insult was now better than forgiven, making them bond-acquaintances; if either were attacked in the other's presence before leaving the restaurant, the other would be morally required to come to the aid of his bond-acquaintance.

The human and the Rubahy turned their backs and resumed their conversations. Jak only then noticed that they had been surrounded by waiters and bouncers with tranquilizer guns. Knocking both of them unconscious would have been much cheaper than the cost of cleanup and repairs (not to mention the lawsuit by Jak's surviving kin.)

"You would not have handled that at all well a few years ago," Sib observed.

"Well," Jak said, "that was the-friend-whose-name-I-can't-speak-here's influence, of course." *A good tove and a loyal friend, even if he looks like what happens if a tyrannosaur mates with a sasquatch and the children all marry chickens,* Jak added mentally, mindful of the Rubahy warrior behind him.

Shadow on the Frost now served in the special Rubahy bodyguard corps for the Duke of Uranium. Sesh was a princess, Psim was a duke, his old crewie friends were

downbound, coming back from a shakedown voyage to
Jupiter . . . and Jak was back in school in the Hive. He suddenly, deeply, fervently hoped that the Dean's assignment
and Sesh's message would shake him out of this miserable
rut and get things moving again in his life. "Want to go
back to my place for a nightcap?"

"Sounds good, old pizo."

As Sib and Jak entered Jak's apartment, he raised his
purse to his mouth and said, "Full check, please."

There were hums and beeps as the watcher-watchers activated, swept, and checked. Bursts of Jak's recorded voice,
saying trigger combinations like "king assassinate, pluto-
nium sell Rubahy," and "Hive imperialism," came from a
dozen loudspeakers, and the watcher-watchers listened
across the whole electromagnetic spectrum for any outgoing signal triggered by them, or for any recording device
tucking them away for future reference. After almost two
minutes of these checks, during which Jak and Sibroillo
stood stone-silent, Jak's purse said, "All clear."

Sib smiled. "Weehu, I can see you've been tinkering
with your bugfinders. Anything get planted here much?"

"Just random police checks, I think. I did the enhance-
ments as part of a class project and just left 'em in afterwards."

Sib nodded. "Good project and a clever approach. All
right, what is it you've been so mysterious about?"

Jak played Sesh's message.

"Believe it or not, Uncle Sib, I really would like your
opinion."

"Now I know the world is ending. I'll have to watch it
again before I *have* an opinion."

He listened all the way through a second time. "Well,
that *is* interesting. Certainly you'll be able to get your Dean

to take this as the project for your Junior Task. It's almost too perfect. You've done the standard authentication checks?"

"And all the premium ones that I can access and afford," Jak said. "I did pay some attention to you, growing up."

Sib grunted with satisfaction. "Well, we should keep in mind that a really good fake can spoof them. Authenticators are just big fast smart AIs, and a singing-on good fake will fool them more often than not, but a bad or average fake won't, so this message is either authentic or a much-better-than-average fake. But that said, I think I know what's going on."

Recognizing a prompt when he heard it from a heet who was always willing to write a check, Jak asked, "What do you think is going on, Uncle Sib?"

His uncle hesitated for a moment. "Er, I know you're fond of her, so—you're not a prude, are you? You do realize that aristos pretty much go at it like dogs in the park?"

"Sure," Jak said. "It's one of their most attractive qualities. But a sex scandal wouldn't be a problem for Sesh. A young good-looking princess with a hot sex life would just make the porn gossip media more often, and maybe get a few nasty sermons preached at her by the Tolerated Faiths. If she were pregnant by the wrong person—" he thought "—no, she'd just get an injection like anyone else, before anyone knew. Since as far as anyone knows she agrees with her father about everything, she could have just turned over anything political to regular government security.

"And all the other possibilities seem much more far-fetched. She could be secretly married to a commoner and need me for some part of the cover-up. She could be secretly pregnant with a child from a rare genetic line—say a purebred gracile or a schiz-free leo—and afraid to be charged with criminal gene loss." He ticked off other possibilities with his thumb against his fingers. "Or, addicted to a psychosis or retardation-inducing drug, maybe *xleeth* or dreamballs. Or, so deep in shopping debt or gambling debt that she's used shares in her kingdom as collateral and a rival house bought the IOUs. Or, secretly engaged to Psim Cofinalez—every message from her she talks about what a toktru fine heet he is, and half the solar system would go to war to prevent a marriage between them. But she said she didn't need me to run a message to her secret lover. What am I leaving out?"

"Try not to hate me but it's ethnographic."

"The whole universe seems to be ganging up to make me learn everyone else's social customs," Jak grumbled.

Sib looked thoughtful and pulled at his goatee for a moment. "You know," he said, "you're righter than you think you are, pizo. The whole universe *is* ganging up to make you do that. Eventually you'll figure out that you can't fight them. Anyway, I think she's a target of republicans—perhaps they've gotten hold of something *they* regard as a sex scandal—and she needs to do some unofficial suppressing."

"Uncle Sib, why do you always say 'republican' with that tone of voice? I mean, the Hive is republican—we don't have an aristocracy."

"Jak, there's republican and then there's *republican.* The Hive is a republic because it was built as part of the first development of the Wager, and Paj Nakasen designed our society, and he thought a republic was a better idea than a monarchy. (Who knows why he thought something stupid like that?)

"Now, as for me, I moved to the Hive ninety years ago and I've never ceased regretting that we don't have a king, but at least the Hive is goofy but livable. Most of the solar

system's republicans want to eliminate hereditary aristocracy because they want to reintroduce the sort of social de-
generation that made such a mess of Earth in late medieval
times, just before the big leap into space. Especially in
places like Greenworld, where people are used to preserv-
ing whatever stupid traditions came down from their stupid
ancestors.

"They have this silly thing called a bill of rights, a bunch
of arbitrary limits on what the government can do, which
had to be left in place as a concession when Rufus Karrinynya conquered the place and established his dynasty.
Believe it or not, Greenworld republicans think that bill of
rights, written on Earth by people who thought they were
going to seriously worship Mother Gaia, should take precedence over a right of conquest eleven hundred years old.
That's what makes me furious! The abstract right of words
against the commonsense rights of a bloodline. There were
Karrinynyas on that throne before the Bombardment fell,
and if Circle Four has anything to say about it, there always
will be Karrinynyas—bright, brave, and beautiful to everyone, cruel and deadly to their enemies, loyal, generous, and
kind to their friends, and understanding power politics the
way a hawk understands thermals. Those are the kind of
people you want running a nation."

"Well, obviously," Jak said, "you do. The rich important
families of the Hive are the same way, and they—"

Sib charged on; having achieved a high haranguing
orbit, he would now go on forever, or until he collided with
something to stop him. Jak braced for more lecture.

"Look at the republicans: ratty little schoolteachers and
teacher's pets, unsuccessful business boors, army officers
with stalled careers and delusions of grandeur, idiots with
plans for utopia, all full of rules of conduct for their neigh-

bors. They will nearly all consider it somehow wrong that your ex-demmy enjoys spending vast amounts of tax money on herself. And they don't see that to be ready to rule, she needs vital contacts and connections in the aristocracy, which she gets spending time with them—shopping, getting drunk, partying, taking drugs, dancing, attending lavish displays of wealth, and so on. Honestly, what better way to get to know each other than to learn exactly how best to lick each other's genitalia—"

"Um," Jak said, trying again, "obviously people need an emotionally bonded network. I mean, I toktru dak why hereditary aristocracy works so well—"

"Oh, anyone as bright and clearheaded as you would. But it's not so obvious to republicans. They have these ideas about who-has-the-best-ideas and who-is-best-qualified, as if life were school. (It's the sort of folly one gets into by allowing oneself envy and resentment just because one wasn't born to a crown.)"

"Um, yeah, all right, Uncle Sib, so these republicans get precessed about sex—"

Sib was deflected but not stopped. "Well, of course, because one of the most important strengths of a monarchy is the way that your feelings about your parents are the model for your feelings about the king and queen, and nobody likes to think about their parents having sex. (Look at how you react to Gweshira and me—)"

"Yuck, Uncle Sib. Okay, I get it. So you think republicans have gotten hold of Sesh's recreational recordings, or something, and they're trying to blackmail her?"

"Blackmail, or more likely they're just planning to go public with it, as a way to embarrass her. Greenworld has a big nest of republicans, and because of that bill of rights nonsense, the princess can't just call up a government agency and have them suppressed. She needs someone out-side the government to do it. So she might need you and Dujuv to destroy a video facility, or hack and wipe under-ground text media, or just beat the shit out of some dissi-dents. Possibly she wants to set up a small secret police unit, consisting of Myxenna to do the intelligence work, Dujuv for the strong-arm stuff, and you to supply creativity.

"Now, I could be completely wrong. But if I had to bet, I'd think . . . young beautiful princess, Greenworld's puri-tanical republicans, can't just send the pokheets . . . I guess that's what I would be thinking."

"And thugging for Sesh—do you think the Dean will buy that as a Junior Task?"

"I'm sure he will. One of the oldest Hive policies is to provide personal assistance to friendly monarchs. Or, as we used to put it when the Dean and I were in the same of-fice—I'll tell you all about that some other time, if you're not good—"

"I'll be good!"

"Insolent puppy."

"Old gwont."

They both laughed; it was good to be getting along so well. "Oh, well, what we used to say was, Hive policy is that if it's a king and it's an ally, we'll shine his shoes. Roughing up a couple of too-sincere student leafleteers, or destroying the data of some meddling historian, on behalf of one of our oldest and most important allies, would fit that policy perfectly. I think the Dean will be very pleased with this; I have a feeling that your troubles are over."

Jak had never before known the Dean's office to be such a friendly place. Caccitepe had greeted them at the door and shaken their hands, steered them onto three perches facing his desk, and given them each a bulb of coffee. But as the Dean airswam to his perch, Jak and Dujuv were still nervous. Who could say how long it might stay friendly? Myxenna Bonxiao, on the other hand, was wonderfully relaxed, as she was in any situation that involved people. Jak found himself sitting between her and Dujuv, wishing he either had Duj's stolid stoicism, or Myx's lively warmth, or any seat other than the one directly opposite the Dean.

"Let me first say that I'm very pleased," Dean Caccitepe said, bringing the bulb to his mouth and taking a little sip. "I really must congratulate you on finding such an advanced and interesting project so quickly. Jak will have to exercise all sorts of judgment and discretion to do well at it, it will call upon Dujuv's courage and discretion, and it will engage many of those social skills that we've felt so strongly are Myxenna's gift. I would say it plays to everyone's strength while offering a solid challenge to everyone. Furthermore, I had already accepted the job of finding and supervising the Junior Task for Myxenna"—he nodded to her, smiling warmly—"and I'd had no idea what would be an appropriate challenge for her, since she does so well at everything."

As happened often around Myxenna Bonxiao, Jak suppressed a flash of envy. Myx really was good at everything, and so great-looking, in a completely sexual way, that it made you ache.

After enjoying smiling at her for longer than Jak would have thought strictly necessary, the Dean went on, "So of course I expect great things of you all."

The sinking sensation in Jak's intestines grew stronger.

Dean Caccitepe's face was in perfect bliss. "This is exactly the kind of thing that all three of you will be doing in your early years working as operatives in public service, and hence, as I said, perfect, and so, as I said, I congratulate you. Any questions?" He said it flatly and carelessly, not really a question.

"None at all, sir." Dujuv's tone was level, even, as careless as the Dean's.

Myxenna said, "I'm looking forward to it. I had been afraid the Junior Task would be something for the office of air conditioning or the post office."

Jak, never sure how long any favorable situation could hold together, said, "No questions. It's toktru a lot clearer than most assignments, sir."

A few minutes later, the three of them took a table together in the Public Service Academy commons, a big drum that tumbled slowly to provide enough grav in the booths to keep drinks in cups and papers on tables. Myx sat at Jak's side, Dujuv across. Both stared at the wall.

"Weehu," Jak said. "Toktru I don't want to referee between you two. First of all none of this was my idea and I think Sesh was out of her mind, or way too sentimental, which might be the same thing, when she specifically asked for the two of you. I know perfectly well that you are *not* together, and haven't been mekko and demmy for a long, long time."

"One year, seven months, and three days," Dujuv said.

Jak ignored that. "I know that you avoid each other and that neither of you wants to know anything about what the other one is doing."

"True for one of us," Myx said.

"And I know that the two of you are never, never, absolutely never, ever, going to be mekko and demmy again, and you both know I normally wouldn't even ask either of you to be civil to the other one. So I am not looking forward to sharing a vague open-ended mission with you."

Dujuv stared at the wall and said, "I can behave. Just don't expect me—"

"You're *not* behaving." Jak was exasperated. "You're acting like you're about to attack or maybe hide in a storage compartment and cry."

"I'll talk to you later." Dujuv leapt to the top of the booth wall and launched himself into the center of the drum, where the grav was only about five percent. He airswam out a service entrance, snagging and consuming two desserts off an incoming robot dessert tray. The service door swung shut as two empty plates caromed off the dining deck, making people in other booths jump.

Myxenna looked sideways at Jak and raised an eyebrow. "So are you going to give up and just let him behave like a silly barbarian pig, or chase after him like a gweetz and spend hours trying to soothe him? You know what they say about panths. They were created for the old Martian emperors, and if you're going to raise a biologically-enhanced Praetorian Guard, of course you make it super-loyal. Probably they copied imprinting off baby ducks, mixed it with devotion off big dumb dogs, and set it to develop at adolescence. So poor Dujy bonded to his first real demmy, and now he can't feel right unless he's being loyal to her.

"Well, I'm not a panth, and nobody bred me to have all that stupid doggy loyalty, and I can't return his feelings. It's tough on him to *have* those feelings, of course, but unless he'd bonded to a panth girl he'd never have found anyone who would accept all that devotion—except, of course, some aristo who would have used him as an expendable resource. I'm not a panth and I'm not a queen, so he's stuck." She brushed her thick jet-black hair away from her face, wet her lips, and focused the blue stars in her green irises directly into Jak's eyes, her smile coaxing his smile out to join it.

She was fascinating in an utterly different way from Sesh. Jak knew, having found out on a few occasions which had toktru precessed Dujuv, that her pale skin, spattered with small freckles, was soft and delicate but that Myx liked a firm grip and deep pressure when touched; he knew that when you were in bed (or up against a wall, or in a freefall room, or a Pertrans car . . .) with Myx, she seemed to guide you singing-on into what you had always dreamed of doing. "It's been a while," she said, smiling, "and Dujuv can't possibly get any more precessed than he already is, you know." She tugged her top tighter and sat up straight; for such a small woman, she had very big breasts.

"Assuming this won't bother Fnina," she said, "or that she won't find out."

Jak smiled. "Or that I don't care if it bothers her. Besides, she never knows anything that's going on unless Mreek Sinda makes a viv out of it—my demmy is that media-gweetz's number one fan. Sure, let's go back to my apartment."

Afterward, as Jak and Myx lay comfortably naked on his bed, idly touching, Jak said, "Sometimes I speck you're the only person who feels like I do about sex and friendship and so on."

She kissed him lightly. "You mean, sex is good, friendship is good, sex with friends is really good? And that's about all?"

"Something like that."

She rolled over onto her belly, letting him admire her perfect back. "Hmm. Well, of course, that was always Sesh's attitude, too, masen? Except I don't think she cared much. She could always buy all the sex and most of the friends she wanted."

"Kind of a cold thing to say about a friend."

"Just realistic. You didn't notice a lot of things about her. Not being male, I wasn't hypnotized by the high firm tits, or the long legs. Or that cute little sweet smile, which I'd watched her practice in the mirror when we were both fourteen. She's cold inside. All her life people have been fun to hang and dine and fuck with, but toktru disposable. Now, maybe she's sentimental, the way people are about pets. Maybe she was trying on the feelings of friendship and loyalty just to see if she liked them, the way she used to try on feeling in love or being proud or being horny. Maybe I'm completely crazy and just projecting everything backward.

"But still . . . this whole deal smells weird, Jak. Toktru. Sesh wants her old gen school toves for a secret mission? She could hire two or three top-end private ops or mercs for a year out of her monthly shoe budget. And besides, if she's not as 'aristocratic' as she always seemed and she actually *can* form real, close, personal friendships, then wouldn't she have one or two by now, maybe among her ladies, maybe in her guards, that would be better on the job than we would? Since they would know their way around the Aerie, and around Greenworld?

"So I don't know about all this, Jak. Of course it would look fine to Dujuv—she's a friend to him because once a friend, always a friend. And it would look good to your uncle and to the Dean, because as far as they're concerned, it doesn't really matter what Sesh actually wants, it's a chance for someone from the Hive to do some big favors for the Karrinynya heir. But I'd rather know what the other players are playing for, *before* they deal me in to the game."

"But you're going."

"Weehu, yeah, I'm *bored*, Jak."

"Me too, Myx." Jak turned toward her and found himself lost in the green and blue star patterns of her eyes. "Toktru, sometimes I think I'm just bored stiff being here, bored stiff with being an ornament in Fnina's social life, bored stiff with all the things in my life that weren't those few weeks of adventure a few years back. Just plain bored stiff."

Myxenna smiled and turned on her side; Jak stroked under the curve of her full breast. "Mmm. Well, I do know something that will get you stiff, besides being bored. Do you want to think or have more sex?"

"How about one then the other?"

The second time was slower, gentler, with more laughter. When they were both sated and happy, lying in each other's arms, Myxenna traced a finger down Jak's sternum and said, "So it's in your liver."

"Unh-huh. Uncle Sib wrote that down on the agenda for that mission, back then. Deliver the sliver in the liver to River. Not that anyone actually calls Riveroma 'River.' He's not the kind of heet who gets nicknames—I speck that Sibroillo just figured that if word of it ever got to him it would precess him. Imagine two petty ten-year-olds who hate each other—that's Sibroillo Jinnaka and Bex Riveroma."

Myxenna sighed. "So the sliver is still in there?"

"'Fraid so. I'm safer with it than without it. No one would ever believe I'd had that little sliver of silicon removed, and if I'm ever captured by Riveroma, or by Triangle One, or by any of a dozen other malphs . . . well, chances are they'll just kill me and pick through my liver at leisure, but they might speck that the sliver might be booby-trapped or that I might have some value as a hostage. If there's no sliver, they've got no reason at all to keep me alive—and at least one thing they're going to be toktru pre-cessed about. So no matter how you look at it, I'm better off with that sliver."

She shuddered. "I hate the idea of anyone cutting into your body. Or anybody's body. If you left it up to me we'd all spend our three hundred and fifty years eating and making art, dancing and telling jokes, and fucking. Especially fucking." She kissed him just at the base of the sternum, feeling and savoring his skin with her full, soft lips. Her hand gently pressed his thighs apart. The tip of one finger brushed gently up and down until it found the singing-on place to flick, quickly and lightly. "If only Shadow on the Frost hadn't rescued you—if he'd known about the sliver—"

"But he didn't know," Jak said, squirming from her airy touch, "and he's Rubahy. Honor-bound to protect an oath-friend. Shadow's honor and loyalty make Duj's look mild by comparison."

"And by comparison to Dujy, you and I have none at all," she whispered. "Don't you love that?" Before he could answer, her tongue was deep in his mouth.

CHAPTER 4

Outranked By a Toaster

Swift as death itself, the Republic of the Hive battlesphere *Up Yours* shot through the dark between the worlds, toward the Aerie, just half a day away. Though *Up Yours* was two kilometers in diameter, with the volume of a medium-sized mountain, it was nearly invisible in war mode. Nothing protruded above the spongy black vacuum gel armor. Trillions of microfiberoptics carried starlight from each point on the ship to a distribution of millions of points on the other side, so that it did not occlude stars for any observer farther away than about a thousand kilometers (which the ship itself traveled in less than five seconds). Radar that entered the snarl of tunnels in its absorbent surface never emerged again to reveal its position; perfect insulation left its heat traces apparently as cold as the dark between the stars, and if necessary *Up Yours* could store all waste heat inside for more than a year. No exhaust of mass or energy betrayed the battlesphere's position; the ship ran ballistic after each brief eight-g burst of acceleration from its quarkjets, in an almost straight line, much faster than solar escape velocity, to its destination, where it matched orbits with a similar burst.

Within five minutes of thrust shutdown, the vacuum gel armor regrew over everything, and the ship vanished from all but the most sophisticated and subtle detectors. It could be spotted, sometimes, barely, by faint radar bounce back (if it was nearly on top of you), by a probe with a sensitive gravimeter (if the probe happened to pass close enough), by the scintillation of starlight passing through it (which lasted only a fraction of a second), or when it crossed the disk of a planet in a telescope (which, in most of interplanetary space, would happen about one ten-thousandth of one percent of the time). In battle, its quark-soup exhaust itself jammed many detection systems. Otherwise, in war mode, the ship was invisible.

Up Yours ran in war mode most of the time, for the solar system swarmed with enemies of the Hive, and battle-spheres—the pride of the Spatial—were prime targets. Beneath her self-healing foam of vacuum gel, practically her whole surface was either thrust nozzles or weapons.

Yet though a battlesphere was the most concentrated collection of destructive force ever to carry a crew, and though the solar system was always at war, their presence inspired no fear. The Aerie's seventeen arms were each long enough to reach across the Pacific Ocean, it was home to a full two billion people and more than four hundred independent nations, the biggest manmade object of all time, yet *Up Yours* could have torn the entire Aerie to pieces no more than a meter across in less than ten minutes. *Up Yours* was allowed to approach, not because there was no danger of war, but because, all thanks to Paj Nakasen's Principles, war was not the danger it had been. Humanity, after millennia of slaughter piled upon slaughter, had at last admitted to and studied its own vicious and bloody nature, painstakingly worked out a few rules of war, and made them stick. Foremost of these were Principle 174 of the Wager: "Every habitat must stay habitable," and Principle 209: "When the common interest is survival, individuals must gang up or be ganged up on."

Wars were fought with little weapons where there were people, or big weapons where there were not, and to violate that principle was to be hunted down like vermin. Any nation or corporation that seized or destroyed a neutral sunclipper faced an immediate and total embargo on food, water, power, and air; a nation attacked while taking its turn patrolling the approaches to Pluto could count on thousands of allies, including the Rubahy themselves; tyrants and madmen could seek power by means as cruel as ever, but if they took one step that might make any human habitat unfit for life, their own forces would turn to slay them.

Thus though war was endemic, a warship able to rip civilization off the face of a planet, or to reduce a planet-sized station to rubble, could approach the solar system's biggest population center, defended by an equally awesome set of weapons, with no fear on either part. Such was the power of the Wager.

This was the lecture playing to the three CUPVs as they worked their way down the auxiliary accelerator tube, replacing panels as they went. When *Up Yours* needed to sacrifice stealth for speed, it could gain about 10% more acceleration by recycling the stray quarks from the synthesizers that drove the main jets. Here in the tubes, quarkplasma condensed into a demon's-goulash of subatomic particles, whipped around in opposing directions to collide at the foci of the auxiliary propulsion dishes, creating a powerful secondary thrust.

On merchant sunclippers, where Jak had worked before, a work crew selected music for its work area. On a battlesphere, the public address system ceaselessly broadcast political/philosophic/religious lectures, to keep crewies loyal—to the Wager, to Nakasen's vision, to the Hive, and to Nakasen's vision of what the Wager meant to the Hive. Thus Jak, Myx, and Duj airswam after their sprites (which looked like stage tinkerbells) through the tunnels, replacing panels as they went, in a constant drone of lecture.

Jak had learned to tune it out; he had no idea whether Myxenna or Dujuv listened to it, because as CUPVs they were temporarily members of the Spatial—subject to punishment for seditious remarks. On a battlesphere, microphones and cameras, like the political officers who monitored them, were ubiquitous.

Jak had CUPVed on the sunclippers *Spirit of Singing Port* to Earth, and *Promeithia* back to the Hive, on his single mission two years ago, and spent most of his first Long Break the year before as a CUPV on a short-hauler, *Lakshmi's Singing Joy,* on a Hive-Mercury-Venus-Hive voyage. He was almost halfway to a full-fledged union card. His experience had mattered not at all. The Spatial put CUPVs on any old job that had to be done but was normally a waste of a good crewie, and kept them there till there was reason to move them.

Physically, Spatial ships were far more comfortable than sunclippers; there was more room and more energy available, so the facilities were more extensive.

But socially, it was quite another matter. This voyage was helping Jak to realize that he'd rather take a sunclipper anytime he wasn't in a hurry or going to a war. Even though *Up Yours* was going directly from the Hive to the Aerie in seventeen days (a sunclipper would have taken four months and at least one flyby of Venus or Mercury), it was seventeen very long days. Plenty of work but no griping (except within your skull). Plenty of time off and exercise facilities, but no locker room socializing. Plenty of pizos but you'd better bring your toves with you. Myxenna might have added plenty of midshipmen and ensigns but no fraternizing; Dujuv might have added plenty of food but no variety.

Jak spent his spare time trying to pass the correspondence version of Solar System Ethnography, or asleep, or in brief, necessary bouts of peacekeeping between Myx and Duj.

They went on replacing panels in the tubes. The lecture on the Principles and war law ended, and was followed by short interlude lectures before the next long one.

Jak had rather enjoyed the two-minute interlude of ship's history, at first, but it played at least twice per shift, and now he knew it by heart.

It was intended to make sure that you dakked why it was an honor for a crewie to serve on a battlesphere in general and *Up Yours* in particular. *Up Yours* was a *Nuts* class battlesphere, almost five hundred years old, one of the largest warships in the solar system, though it lacked the sheer speed and better ablative armor of the more modern *Like So Not* class battlespheres. Fourteen battlespheres in all, a quarter of all those existing, made up the main line of the Hive Spatial.

Up Yours had been named, like all battlespheres, for a message of defiance from an important historical human commander, in this case Ralph Smith's message to the Rubahy during the desperate fighting on Titan. She was the third battlesphere of that name, the first having gone completely dead to communications at far above solar escape velocity, and continued ballistically up out of the solar system, never to return, too fast for any ship to catch, presumably with its crew unable to get the quarkjets back on.

The second had instantly become white-hot plasma in the suicide crash of a Rubahy fighter pilot during the Sev-

enth (and so far last) Rubahy War. After a respectful few
centuries, a Hive Spatial orbicruiser had been named after
the fighter pilot, and *Tree Bowing to the Storm* was now re-
garded as a "good luck" ship, though traditionally it never
served in the same fleet or task force as *Up Yours*.

Jak followed his sprite down the poorly lit tube, swimming in the thick gas that had been injected to make maneuvering easier. *I always wondered why Spatial crewies
couldn't wait to hit port and stayed off the ship as long as
possible. I thought it must be the harsh conditions, and now
I speck they just wanted to get away from the loudspeaker.*
That was seditious; good thing that Jak never talked in his
sleep.

He fitted yet another panel into yet another square, passing the old pitted one back to Dujuv, who airswam away
with it. Tube maintenance was to spaceships what painting
had been to sea ships; you didn't get done, you just got to
do it somewhere else. Crewies on sunclippers rotated
through a variety of jobs to provide cross-training and ward
off deadly boredom, but crew on *Up Yours* spent weeks or
months of the same duty every shift. This might not be a
bad basis for the required paper in his Solar System
Ethnography course; merchant crewies were a recognized
ethnic group, and one possible paper topic was to compare
a recognized ethnic group with a similar, identifiable sub-
category of people within the Hive.

Jak turned and handed off another rough panel to Myx,
accepting a smooth one in return; he placed the smooth one
carefully, released the special grips from it, and let it self-
fasten into place. The soft glow of light in the tube was
pleasant, and the swimming gas, designed to be sticky and
thick, made maneuvering easy in free fall. Since the panels
couldn't be exposed to any gas that wasn't inert, workers

had to wear rebreathers, but they were lightweight and comfortable, and the air they supplied was pleasantly odorless, unlike ship air.

"How long till shift end?" Duj asked.

Jak turned his left hand up to check his purse. "Sixteen minutes. Time for three more panels."

"This was challenging when we started but it's kind of routine now."

Jak chuckled. "I'm glad you retain your gift for understatement."

The constantly-on lecture switched over to an account of the history of the Aerie, which toktru Jak needed anyway as a review of background for his next exam. The frustrating part of trying to learn it, though, was that it was too simple at the abstract level and too complex at the detailed level.

In broad outline, he only needed to know that after the Bombardment and the attempted Rubahy invasion, there had been thousands of surviving space habitats all over the solar system, most of them centuries old. Though they had mostly begun in orbit around Earth or Mars, fifty years of the Bombardment and ten years of Rubahy surface raids had made planetary orbits dangerous; by the end of the war the planets were really just vast high-gravity refugee camps anyway, so there was little economic reason to move back. So the energy-poor habitats had gravitated economically, as much as physically, to the stable Lagrange libration points in the solar system, where an object would stay in place without expending energy to station-keep, and the concentration of those stations into tight nests created free trade zones, which developed rapidly and made the decision to move to a libration point more and more inevitable for each successive station. Since most of the free-floaters orbited between Earth and Mars, and the Mars libration points are much weaker and hence less stable positions, the cheapest stable libration points to reach were the Earth-sun L4 point, sixty degrees ahead of Earth in orbit, or the Earth-sun L5 point, sixty degrees behind.

At L5, Nakasen's Wager had led many of the habitats to pool resources, fuse themselves into a single design, go to the enormous expense and effort of constructing a small black hole for a central waste sink and power source, and create the Hive. Over four hundred habitats which chose not to give up their independence clustered at L4, where, to reduce the risk of collision, they had all tied in permanently to a gigantic common docking body; the hundreds of stations on long arms extending out from the docking body now formed the Aerie.

But though the broad outline of Aerie history was easy, it was doubtful that any human being could really have comprehended the whole detailed history of the Aerie. Hundreds of nations each had an origin, a history before the Bombardment, a history free-floating in deep space, a migration to L4, a period of free-floating in the cluster, a reconstruction during tie-up, and finally a history since complete conversion into a unit of the Aerie.

The lecture didn't hesitate to point out how neat and coherent Hive history was by comparison; all the 723 founding nations had been abolished and mutually assimilated into the new culture of the Wager. The nations of the Aerie were simply disorderly, something which they could easily have fixed if only their Confederacy charter didn't prohibit the annexation or colonization of habitats in the Aerie by the Republic of the Hive. Jak wondered why the Confederacy charter did that; all he could remember was that for his teachers it was a matter for indignation. Had he missed something or was it one of those things not to be talked about?

Their earphones told the three CUPVs that they were done for the day, and they gladly airswam back to the gaslock.

Moments later, in the corridor, Jak could finally pull back his rebreather hood and wipe his face. Duj's hairless scalp shone with sweat; Myx was running a hand through her sodden hair with disgust. "Thank Nakasen for a shower before final acceleration," she said. "And a clean dress uniform still left."

Dujuv stared at a spot on the wall, not admitting that Myx was there.

Jak shrugged, keeping up his personal pretense that he was on good terms with both the other CUPVs. "I'm just looking forward to no duty for a while. They work you hard on Spatial ships, compared to sunclippers."

Sesh had saved money by booking the three of them into a "three-passenger suite," as the Spatial called a closet-sized space with a toilet/shower and three adjoining coffin bunks. As Myx showered and Duj sulked and waited, Jak pretended to read ethnography.

Dujuv obstinately insisted that he was not jealous, angry, or upset with Myxenna, and maintained that he toktru had never liked her. Myxenna, for her part, was happy to be friends with anybody, and lovers with anybody attractive, but she was absolutely not about to try to deal with any of Dujuv's emotions. On Jak and Myx's last night together in his apartment, when she had sneaked in after Jak had seen Fnina for quick sex and the obligatory romantic public passionate farewell scene, Myx had said, "All right, there's a medical explanation for Dujuv. But it's not a compliment to have someone devoted to you like a codependent Saint Bernard."

The shower turned off. "You can have the next one," Jak said to Dujuv, who silently rose, grabbed his towel and shower things, and floated patiently by the door till Myx emerged wrapped in her towel. He airswam in.

The moment the door closed, Myx gave Jak a big smile, took off the towel, made sure he took a good look, winked, and airswam into her bunk to dress.

It probably helped her feel attractive, but it ruined Jak's concentration on solar system ethnography. Today's topic was *Unit 15: The Mars Origin Cults and the Eleven Martian Nations with MOC Beginnings, Part 1: Four Nations that Still Maintain MOCs.* Privately Jak still thought of the topic as "the four dumbest gangs of savages in the solar system, and how to humor them," but he had at least learned to suppress such thoughts while taking his exams, and had a passing mark on all six of them so far, with three to go.

This time, he reminded himself. Then only six more times through the whole course before graduation. Unless he finished at the top of the class . . . he smiled. He had finally thought of something to make himself laugh.

The acceleration alarm sounded all clear, and instantly the enormous weight that had been crushing Jak down into the safety couch turned off, and he returned to near-weightlessness. The last, hour-long burst of the quarkjets had been the worst, not because the acceleration was any greater, but because it had all become extremely familiar and there had been nothing to do about it. The gray-sleep drugs, the painkillers, and the breathing assister all helped, and making sure you peed before lying down really helped, but eight g is eight g, and an hour of it feels just like lying on a bed with seven of yourself stacked on top of you. And after five previous one-hour bursts, with an hour break between each, as *Up Yours* zigged and zagged its way down to orbital velocity to match the Aerie, the knowledge of what was coming and how it would feel had settled into Jak's bones.

Beside him, Myxenna sat up, groaning, and even Dujuv looked pale and tired. The one consolation about their utter unimportance to the ship was that they didn't have any immediate duties after any of the acceleration bursts, and therefore they had a few minutes to stretch out the kinks before anything else came at them.

As they all floated, stretching, in their small cabin, trying not to bump into each other, a subtle force caused them all to drift toward the wall of coffin bunks. "Cold jets," Jak said, "they've started the last course corrections."

The speaker in the room beeped once for attention, and then said, "CUPVs, be prepared for muster out processing in your quarters in forty-five minutes."

As *Up Yours* slipped between the whirling arms of the Aerie, only the minute, ever-changing accelerations from her hundreds of cold jets, poking through her fuzzy black skin like the spines of a sea urchin, indicated that anything unusual was happening. The crew were all singing-on where they were supposed to be at every instant, *more* spit-and-polish and by-the-book than ever—the Aerie was every crewie's favorite port of call. No one wanted to draw one extra second of on-ship duty during a stopover there.

So wherever you looked, every possible regulation was being conspicuously obeyed, yet the overwhelming feeling was of carnival just erupting. On the muster deck where the

B&Es were doing final check-and-stow, gear whipped from hand to hand and slapped into place with the speed and precision of an ecstatic tapdancer. Unaccustomed camaraderie swept the engine room as engineers throttled back the Casimir reactors and walked the synthesizers through cooldown. The chief officers in the worryball were as singing-on precise as ever about keeping more than four hundred million tons of battlesphere moving at several kilometers per second from crashing into densely populated human space, during an approach that had to be singing-on to the centimeter in its last few kilometers, but with a disconcerting sense of fun. Everywhere on board the letter of every rule was respected reverently, but the rules as a whole were stretched like shrink-wrap, barely containing the roiling spirit of joyful impending anarchy.

In their passenger suite, a deeply bored ensign, who clearly wanted to be anywhere else, took forever about mustering out the three CUPVs, making sure everything was done Spatial-style (i.e., officially, punctiliously, and with no sense of proportion). Yet even Ensign Petrawang was smiling shyly as she checked off information and took voice prints.

Finally she said, "All right, as far as I can tell, I've put you through every single procedure I'm supposed to put you through. You can stay here, or hang out on one of the observation decks, but either way since there're no windows in the ship, what you'll be doing is watching a screen. Most of us crewies on board prefer to use the goggles because you get a holo view and you can hop from camera to camera to give yourself a real djeste of what's going on.

"But whichever you do, make sure you make it to Muster Deck A in plenty of time. The Captain always does his farewells in order of rank, starting from the bottom up, which means you're first—so it would sure be noticed if you weren't there or weren't ready." She smiled again. Jak thought that if Petrawang hadn't been depilated for the Forces, and if she had been wearing something more flattering than a shapeless coverall, she might have been pretty.

Dujuv smiled back and said, "Thank you for the warning and thank you for reminding us where we stand around here."

"My lieutenant would have wanged me good if I hadn't warned you. If you precess the Captain one millisecond before you're off his ship, he can brig you till you die of old age. So be on time, and be serious—the Captain's all right, but he's still a captain, and if captains have senses of humor, maybe I'll see that when I'm a captain, but not much before.

"And as far as where you stand goes, CUPV, that's singing-on, what I said, you go first because you're at the bottom, and that's what your standing is. If we were also dismissing a toaster, a vacuum cleaner, and the ship's cat today, you'd still be first in line. Now enjoy the view, be *where* you're supposed to *when* you're supposed to, and remember to be grateful when you're a civilian again."

After she left, they pulled on visors to catch the view. By now *Up Yours* was well within the whirling seventeen arms of the constantly precessing Aerie, each arm a string of twenty-five habitats, each habitat a flat disk two hundred kilometers across, separated from its neighbors above and below by a little less than five hundred kilometers of space.

As Jak clicked from camera to camera, sometimes crossmonitoring in two different eyepieces so that he could get a wide-angle stereo view, he saw the many habitats moving slowly in their turning, bending columns, and the little fires on their edges of quarkjets coming on to adjust position.

The cables between them were too thin and dark to see, so the dozens of disks, each covered with cities and forests and farmland, appeared to be flying in formation against the black of space. Near ones would sometimes all but fill the sky and even the farthest ones were still almost twice the size of the Moon seen from Earth. In edge on view, you dakked that the disks were truly wafers, only a few hundred meters thick with roofs not more than a kilometer above their surfaces. Passing between the cables to go through an arm—a procedure that the guide-recording assured Jak was safe—gave him a momentary glimpse of a wide landscape below, low-g forests retinated with streams and falls and dotted with what could only be castles, each on a hill surrounded by a broad lawn. The near side of the battlesphere was only about five kilometers above the clear roof, perhaps six kilometers from the treetops; from this close, you could see that it was a world, or at least a big fragment of one, and somehow the term "habitat" felt wrong. Slowing as they were for landing, they were moving at only about eight thousand kilometers per hour, and it took almost two minutes for the landscape to roll past beneath.

Jak checked with his purse. The place was called Scadia, and it was position ten on branch three, population seven million, deliberately with only five small cities, principal products handicrafts, gravity averaging 13.7 percent with 30 percent variability, average temperature twenty-two Celsius, the locally defined principal social groupings are—

He switched back to the general channel. For one awful second he'd almost been exposed to more ethnography. Now that he thought of it, Scadia was one of Greenworld's allies in the Confederacy of the Aerie, part of the blocking coalition that kept the Aerie from merging into a single large polity with the potential to threaten the Hive's hegemony. So besides the pretty castles and park-like land between, they were toves. If he had to know what table manners to follow on a visit there, he could always look it up. Comfortable with being exactly as ignorant as he wanted to be, Jak went back to watching *Up Yours* approach the docking body.

As they approached, the arms were closer together and they saw habitats more full on and less from the edge, so that the habitats in Jak's view became an ever greater part of the sky. Finally *Up Yours* coasted on her cold jets a bare few kilometers above the wide metal plain of the docking body, a sphere six hundred kilometers across, to which all seventeen arms of the Aerie were tied. From the ship's cameras Jak could see five inward facing habitats, each as wide as an eighth of the sky and separated from its neighbor by a gap of star-filled sky.

Jak was so lost in the view through his goggles, sitting on the suite's sofa next to Myx, that he actually jumped from surprise when *Up Yours* dove through one of the fifty-kilometer-wide docking entrances on the inner sphere, dipping into the dark below the metal surface, extending her docking pylons to meet the linducer track on the inside of the huge sphere, and at last settling into maglev contact with the barest of discernible accelerations. "We have turned off the helm," the captain's voice said, "and we are decelerating normally on the linducer track. Relative to the inner wall of the docking body we are moving at about six hundred kilometers per hour; we will be matched to local surface velocity and secured in our berth in about twenty minutes. Final crew rendezvous and dismissal for off-ship leave will be ten minutes after we reach our berth and will begin at that time exactly."

Jak pulled off his headset and saw that his two toves

were doing the same. "How about we get to Muster Deck A? That ensign sounded serious."

They were there in plenty of time, and because no one wanted the dismissal to run one second more than necessary, a lieutenant came by to make sure the CUPVs knew what to do, though for some reason he made Ensign Petrawang give the actual instructions.

"All right." Petrawang looked about as bored as was possible while keeping her eyes open. "Stand here. Salute when the Senior Techny shouts 'The Captain,' and make sure the knife edge of your palm cuts across your sternum, singing-on forty-five, have your thumb in line with your palm, and you want your left arm behind you at a ninety degree angle that you could use to navigate with, fist squared and rolled *tight*. Hold the salute till the Captain says 'Rest position.' Then stand in rest position till he approaches you. *Do not look around, not even a little bit.* That's one of his particular precessors.

"Salute again as soon as you can see him in your peripheral vision. Hold the salute while he makes small talk with you. Agree with everything he says, appear to be pleasantly surprised by all of it (and look like none of it ever occurred to you before), and do your damnedest to convince the whole world that you enjoy it.

"The techny walking behind the officers will tell you when to go back to rest position. Stand in that until the Senior Techny shouts 'Captain going out,' then move to salute, hold that until the Senior Techny shouts 'Per captain's instructions, you are dismissed.' And at that magic moment, you get to turn and walk off the ship; your bags will be in the receiving area; and once your back foot leaves the gangplank, you are no longer auxiliaries in the Hive

Spatial, and you can resume your normal lives." She turned to the lieutenant. "Shall I ask the CUPVs that question?"

"Absolutely."

"Why did you put in for CUPV? Passenger fare is the same, and you'd only have had to stay in your cabin. As a CUPV not only did you spend all your time on tube maintenance, but if a war had broken out with us in flight, you'd have been in for the duration. I haven't been able to speck what you were thinking, or if."

Myxenna answered. "We're PSA cadets all headed for the special branches. Union points are useful, since we may be called on to join the ASU, and we're supposed to get as much different experience as we can."

The officer supervising Petrawang spoke. "So you're going to be spies or agents of some kind?"

"If we pass, sir," Dujuv said.

"And you're on some kind of training mission now?"

"That's as close to the subject as we're allowed to go, sir," Jak said.

"You see, Ensign Petrawang? There *are* at least three people on this vessel with a more absurd job than yours. Under the terms of our bet, you owe me all I can drink tonight."

"I do, sir." The lieutenant airswam away, clearly pleased. As Petrawang pushed off after him, she said, quietly, over her shoulder, "Think seriously about taking a merchant ship home."

The general attention siren whizzed twice, and the Senior Techny shouted "The Captain!" The CUPVs jammed their feet into the parade straps on the floor and snapped into salute.

Once the Captain began small talk, it became immediately apparent why Petrawang and the officer had gone out of their ways to prepare them. The captain was an ange, like Dean Caccitepe, but even taller and at least two hundred fifty years old, maybe three hundred. When the Captain stooped to talk to him, Jak noted how deep, wise, and kind the Captain's eyes seemed to be, and tried not to note the faint whiff of gin and citrus.

The Captain cleared his throat. "So you three were CUPVs on this mission."

"Yes, sir," Jak said, since the Captain was looking at him.

"And that was as part of something you were doing for the PSA, I understand?"

"Yes, sir," Dujuv said, for the Captain had moved down the line.

"And the PSA is the Public Service Academy, is it not?"

"Yes, sir." Myx managed not to sound puzzled or surprised, and Jak silently gave her points for that, since he wasn't sure he could have managed.

"Well," the Captain said, after a very long pause and stepping back to look them all over, "the Public Service Academy is a very fine thing. It encourages public service. I hope that all you young people will seriously consider going into public service."

He wandered on up the line; a few seconds after he was out of Jak's peripheral vision, the techny who had been the last in the little party of ship's officers said, "Rest position, CUPVs, and keep it neat."

After a very long time, during which there was plenty of time to meditate on the ever-softer and more distant drone of the Captain's voice talking to each of the higher ranks, the Senior Techny shouted 'Captain going out,' and Jak and his toves went back to salute position. Jak had read somewhere that the salute originated a thousand years ago in the old Martian Empire, as a signal of submission, indicating that you were willing to cooperate in either your own torture or your own execution.

Jak spent some no-time mentally in Disciplines meditation before the Senior Techny shouted, "Per Captain's instructions, you are dismissed." Muster Deck A rang with a sustained cheer and the three toves were nearly bowled over by an extremely orderly flying stampede. In the docking body, grav was less than one percent of standard, and airswimming was fast and easy. The crewies, officers and enlisted alike, all moved fast and stayed close but gave way to the person on the right or of higher rank, so quickly and neatly that there was hardly any turbulence or drag to the flow of thousands of bodies; they went through the big main doors like water swirling down a drain.

Since Jak and his toves were somewhere below a toaster in rank, they were quickly swept to the back of the flow by the tremendous tide of precedence, but the overall flow was so swift that still it was less than three minutes before they made their last touch on the gangplank and bounced into the receiving area to claim their luggage—civilian once more.

CHAPTER 5

Weird-bad

Dujuv asked, "Well, now what? Do we just take the gripliner out to Greenworld, go to the Royal Palace, knock on the door, and say 'Hi, we happened to be in the neighborhood?'"

Myxenna wrapped her bags in a cargo tow and grabbed the sling. "I suppose it would be politer to call first. There must be some public access terminals around someplace? Speck you shouldn't call direct on your purse, Jak, security and all that."

They airswam down a long shopping corridor that appeared to be mostly duty-free liquor stores; Myxenna airswam close to Jak and whispered, "I know somebody who will be shopping here soon."

Jak made a little raspberry and snickered. "Yeah, I was wondering if anyone else noticed."

"I suppose the job must be mostly ceremonial, in peacetime."

They found a Pertrans stop before they found public access terminals. "Well, they'll have them for sure at the gripliner station," Jak pointed out. "Let's just go there."

The docking body of the Aerie was less than a fifth the size of the Hive, and because it did not have a black hole enclosure at its center, routes could be much more direct. The Pertrans whisked them right across the big metal sphere to Station Eight, where gripliners came in from Arm Eight, in about five minutes.

It was an icy five minutes. Myx and Dujuv stared out windows in opposite directions, despite the fact that all there is to see out a Pertrans window is either the tunnel wall or the instantaneous flash of a passing window. Jak could see no way to get them to even start being civil to each other. He was beginning to miss the imposed courtesy of the battlesphere.

Near the ticket counter in the gripliner station, they found some public access terminal booths. All three of them piled into a large booth and locked the door; then Jak told his purse to get Sesh on a fresh back channel.

The woman whose image appeared on the screen was *very* not Sesh. She had pale beige skin, big prominent teeth, and little green piggy eyes that glared at them around the nose of an unsuccessful ex-boxer. Her hair was that mud-gray color of age familiar from old photos, but Jak had never seen it on a living person before. Perhaps she was a follower of one of the Tolerated Faiths, rather than the Wager? According to the Solar System Ethnography class, many of them prohibited anti-aging treatments.

"My name is Jordesta Mattanga, and I need to know immediately why you are attempting an unauthorized communications access to Princess Shyf. I also need your names and citizenship."

"Myxenna Bonxiao, Hive." "Dujuv Gonzawara, Hive." "Jak Jinnaka, Hive. Uh, we're her friends, and we came at her specific request—"

Mattanga looked annoyed. "I have no record of any such request."

"I don't know if you necessarily would," Jak said; "because I don't know your communications and security arrangements, but the Princess requested us through back channels, and she specifically asked that we not recontact her till this point in the mission, for security reasons. I am unaware of who else she might have told."

"I see. One moment." The screen froze, leaving Jordesta Mattanga's image glaring, one big lumpy gray eyebrow raised like a caterpillar crossing something that hurt its feet.

Of course, their camera was still on, so they couldn't do anything without being observed. Down by Jak's knee, Dujuv's hand signaled, *Weird-bad . . . weird-bad . . . weird-bad. . . .*

There was a clanging noise as the overrides barred the booth door. Mattanga's image began to move again. "Talk to Princess Shyf. She has graciously agreed to give you an exact two minutes of her time. You had better persuade someone that this is not the stupidest youthful prank ever pulled, because if we don't like what we're hearing, we will send out security agents to bring you here by force and jail you all till we hear answers we like. You have two minutes."

Sesh came on the screen. "What are you three idiots doing here? I know Jak has to be the idiot-in-chief, but how could either of you be stupid enough to follow him? And Jak, I know you're not the brightest thing that ever put on trousers, but this is dumber even than I'd have expected from you. Didn't you get my message?"

"That's why we came," Jak protested.

"How could you be that unbelievably stupid? Didn't I say not to communicate in any way? And how in all of Nakasen's theorems could you have afforded to get here anyway?"

"You paid our passage," Dujuv said.

Sesh stared at him as if he'd really gone mad. "Is that what Jak told you?"

"It's true," Jak said. "You arranged CUPV passage for all three of us—"

"Ridiculous!"

"And you specifically asked us to come and not to call you till we got here."

Sesh's eyes were flashing fire. "A one-minute message that said I didn't want to hear from you, ever again, and not to try to contact me—how could—"

"It was almost twenty minutes long, Sesh—"

"I am Princess Shyf. You will address me as 'Princess Shyf,' or as 'Your Utmost Grace,' idiot boy."

Jak fought down his own rising temper and said, "I have a copy of the message. On my purse. Security stamped and everything. Let me send it over and you look at it. This is the last message I ever got from you, till now."

"Send it," the Princess snapped.

"Do it," Jak murmured to his purse, which said, "Sending last message from Princess Shyf over current com link, fully secured version."

Then the screen froze again, this time with an image of Her Utmost Fury glaring out from it. The door remained locked. Dujuv's left hand had stopped signaling *weird-bad* and was now just signaling, *Weird . . . weird . . . weird . . .*, more tic than communication. An hour went by. Jak wished that he had stopped off at a restroom earlier.

Jordesta Mattanga returned to the screen and said, "I am commanded to communicate apologies from Princess Shyf for the tone of her remarks. The message copy is clearly authentic in that its internal evidence shows it was received by you when and where you say it was. It is, however, an extremely good fake. This obviously raises grave questions about the Princess's personal security. We would therefore like to invite you to come and stay at the Royal Palace for at least a brief period, to talk to our security people. We're negotiating with Hive Intelligence, since you were nominally working for them, to see if they will cover the cost, one way or another, of getting you back home in a timely way." Then she allowed herself something that seemed almost like a smile. "On the purely personal level, thank you for your patience in dealing with this mess. It was not of either of our making, to be sure, but apparently it will take both your efforts and ours to clean it up."

There was a clank and thud as the booth door unlocked.

"Now, if you will just stay somewhere in Station Eight, Kawib Presgano, of the Royal Palace Guards, will be coming up to the gripliner station to escort you here."

"Thank you very much," Myx said. "Please extend our thanks to the Princess for her courtesy."

After a necessary rush to the restrooms, they regrouped on the main floor of the gripliner station. The view was inverted from what they were used to. On the Hive, with a black hole at its center, gravity is *inward,* constant, and increases as you approach the center; on the Aerie, whose "gravity" is the centripetal force of its complicated, constantly-adjusted precession, gravity is outward, varying, and decreases as you approach the center. Thus on the Hive a gripliner out to the Ring comes and goes through the great domes in the ceiling, and the destination is "up." Here, gripliners rose through the floor, and in the low grav, the three toves hopped and bounced across transparent sections. Below them, the nearest habitat spread a vast green, blue, and white blur of clouds, lakes, parks, and shining cities across the starry sky beneath their feet.

Myx checked her purse. "That's Hiawatha, eighteen million people, lots of lakes and canals, main businesses aqua-culture and truck farming."

As they watched, Hiawatha dimmed to darkness, and Jak pulled the earpiece connection from his purse and asked it to give him a quick review of the numbers about the Aerie. On the average (no two rotations were quite alike—only constant precessing under power kept gravity close to con-stant), the Aerie turned over in about three and a half hours, too short a natural day for comfort, especially with about a quarter-hour eclipse every noon. Hence the transparent top of each habitat could be opaqued at will, the undersurface of each habitat was one vast light collector/projector, and fibers carried incoming sunlight from the backs of habitats, where it fell uselessly, to shine from the backs of other habitats, from which it shone onto land otherwise dark; op-erating the Aerie required four thousand quarkjet engines (*Up Yours* had four) scattered around the habitat edges, thir-teen trillion light apertures any one of which could send or receive light from any other, and controlled opacity on a total area of smart glass as big as North America. It also needed half of humanity's total computing capacity to make millisecond decisions in controlling all the engines, net-working all the apertures, and changing opacity on every square centimeter of smart glass.

Jak specked that he had never really known what the word "awesome" meant, before.

"Anybody hungry? I could really use something to eat," Dujuv said.

After they had found a booth in the snack bar's cen-trifuge, Myxenna and Jak talked it all over while Dujuv shoveled noodles and beefrat chunks into his mouth and lis-tened. Mostly they tried to convince themselves that Sesh hadn't meant to be so unpleasant.

Dujuv sighed, pausing between gulps. "Still . . . old toves, masen? I mean I dak, toktru, that she has another life and better things to deal with, but we are her old toktru toves, and we're the people that busted her out when she was being held in Fermi, masen? Seems like having been toves once ought to count for more than it does."

"Sometime," Myxenna said, sourly, "you toktru ought to discuss the djeste of that with your ex-demmy. That being old toves ought to count for something and that maybe people ought to behave accordingly, if maybe you speck what I mean?"

To Jak's surprise, Dujuv said, "You know, you're right. Let's talk pretty soon about it."

"I'd like that."

After the silence had become thoroughly awkward, Jak tried changing the subject. "Far as I know, I'm the only one with an enemy outside the Hive," Jak said. "So one real possibility is that this was some way for Bex Riveroma to lure me out of the Hive, to get that sliver from me. But the Hive's pretty wide open. He could have knocked me on the head anytime there. Then taken me in for ten minutes with a surgeon, grab that sliver, and everybody's happy except me and the heets from Maintefice that find my body."

Myxenna held up a finger. "Maybe he wants to talk to you personally for some reason or another?"

"It's at least one hypothesis."

Myxenna nodded, her dark hair bobbing around her face. "All right, now, next question—is Jak right, Dujuv? Do you and I have no enemies off the Hive?"

Dujuv shrugged. "There are maniacs who want to kill all the breeds and go back to 'pure human stock,' and some of them are violent. But why import a panth to assault? There're plenty here. How about you?"

"No political connections, I'm a lukewarm follower of the Wager the way that most of the solar system is, no deep personal hatreds, nobody in my family ever killed anybody except maybe my big brother in the Army. And except for my brother and me, my family is all mids—middle class, middle aged, middle management, and they live midlevel on the Hive. The most ordinary, conventional people you could ever meet. Toktru no."

"Maybe something to do with Circle Four," Jak said. "I'm never sure what might be stirring out in my uncle's web of connections, but I don't think he'd have shopped me without telling me. Or if Circle Four did, why would they also shop both of you?"

"Maybe it's a reunion," Myxenna said, smiling slightly. "Now Phrysaba and Piaro are about to come walking in here, along with Shadow on the Frost. . . ."

Dujuv chuckled. "Well, if they do, I'm going to jump out of my skin. Glad as I'd be to see any of them again."

"Just so Mreek Sinda isn't following them," Jak said. "I still can't believe the bizarre djeste she made out of what really happened."

"No one else believed it, either," Dujuv pointed out, "and it did get you laid regular, by someone great-looking. What have you heard from Fnina, anyway?"

"In the first few days, she sent me five long messages full of undying passion, at about twelve hour intervals, then dumped me for a heet in a slec group."

"Heart broken?"

"Not even dented."

"Thought so." Smiling, Duj took another big bite of the food, and said, "Weehu."

"What?"

"Normally all I notice about food is whether there's

enough of it. That's what a base calorie demand of six thousand a day will do for you. But this stuff tastes *good*."

"You're comparing it with a couple of weeks of ship food," Jak said. "It's amazing, a Spatial ship has ten times the kitchen space a merchant sunclipper does, and can get offship ingredients fresh, usually every month or so, but still the food is so much better on a sunclipper, and a lot less monotonous."

"Toktru," Dujuv said, through another mouthful.

Quietly, Jak put his purse down on the table and said, "Record the next conversation, stop when the subject of conversation changes."

"I'll check before I assume it's changed," the purse said.

"Good." Jak stroked its reward spot. "Now, old toves, I have to do a report for my Solar System Ethnography course, and the topic I got approved is 'comparison of merchant and Spatial crewie societies.' What did you all notice about the Spatial?"

"No sense of humor!" Dujuv said, through a mouthful of noodles. (Jak assumed that was what "Nofenf avumer" meant.)

Myxenna added, "They look down on anyone who shows any interest in comfort."

"Lousy place for a panth. They're all very proud of being the brainy service, so they all pat me on the head. It's funny because first it got me thinking about how much I didn't like being treated as stupid, and then about the fact that I get treated as stupid all the time, it was just more consistent on the Spatial ships, and then I got to thinking that, you know, I'm not glib like Jak or brilliant like Myx but I'm not stupid at all. I'm like most panths, normal intelligence, maybe better. That *really* made me think."

Jak nodded. "On the ship, you couldn't even talk to us about any of that. So you've been thinking *a lot*."

"I always think a lot. I just do it kind of slow."

Myxenna said, "I knew you thought a lot. You used to be kind of ashamed of it, I thought."

"I was, I guess. I was getting plenty of attention for being a good-looking goalie. That also meant people were watching me all the time. Why risk getting attention by opening my mouth and maybe saying something stupid?"

Jak said, "You don't let me get away with treating you as if you were dumb. Rightly so, masen?"

"Hey, I expect my best friend to know that I'm *playing* dumb."

"Your demmy always did know," Myx said.

Dujuv looked up, and for one moment the warmth that shone in his eyes made Jak wonder why Myxenna didn't just melt at the sight of it. "I know," he said. "Why do you think I bonded so tight that I can't let go? Because you were kind to me, and panths grow up so hungry for human contact, masen?"

"I have noticed that," Jak said. "I thought it was just part of the genetic programming."

"Naw, it's because we're all lonely kids. We have to be. We're dangerous to other kids. We get muscle and coordination much earlier than unmodifieds, but intelligence and empathic sense much later. That's why we have to be in a special crèche instead of dev school—when I was four, by unmodified standards, I was emotionally two but physically ten, with panth reflexes. Don't either of *you* ever say this because it's offensive as hell, but what we say among ourselves is that up till gen school, panths don't need parents, we need zookeepers."

It was so unexpected that Myx blew tea through her nose.

"Now *that's* like old times," Jak said.

Myx tried to grab and tickle him, but she was giggling too hard, and then Dujuv bounced across the table and got into it—on both sides, as he always did, in the interest of fairness—and they were all tussling around and laughing like crazed children when the privacy door slid open and there was a young man standing there in uniform. He coughed politely and did a terrible job of hiding a smile. "Er, the directory said you would be in this booth."

"Assuming we're who you're looking for, it was singing-on," Myx said. The young heet was tall and broad-shouldered, with light caramel colored skin, tan-patterned in the leopard-print style that was supposed to be the heliopause of clash-splash-and-smash nowadays. His uniform was dark blue and so loaded with piping, epaulets, medallions, badges, superfluous buttons, straps that connected nothing to nothing, and other decorations and baubles, that he looked like an escaped drum major trying to pass as a Christmas tree, or perhaps a magnetized doorman who had run through a costume shop. He had a long hawk-nose, big round dark eyes, and an expression fighting to be serious.

"Well, I'm Kawib Presgano, of the Royal Palace Guard of Greenworld, and I was sent out to pick up three unexpected visitors who came in on *Up Yours*. You are Jak Jinnaka, Dujuv Gonzawara, and Myxenna Bonxiao?"

"We are," Jak said. "You, um, caught us at an awkward moment."

Kawib smiled and raised an eyebrow. "Now why is it that people would rather be caught panhandling, or naked in public, than just having fun?"

"What if that *is* your idea of fun?" Myx teased.

"I wouldn't know, I've never panhandled. If you all have finished eating and wrestling, we should probably go. The Princess is not noted for her patience, and the order originated with her."

They walked up the steps and airswam out the exit. The three toves headed for the main gates, but Kawib said, "No, this way. We're taking one of the palace's hoppers. Have you ever ridden a hopper before?"

The craft that Kawib led them to, in the private garage off the station, was about eight meters long by five at the broadest part of the beam. An upper glass ellipsoid formed the canopy over a lower, larger ellipsoid of silver-blue metal studded with dozens of cold jet nozzles and four linducer grapples. On its side it bore the traditional fist-and-pine-tree of Greenworld, and on its nose the sword, chain, and crown of the Karrinynya Dynasty.

Kawib said "Recognize voice and open" and the canopy irised into the main body. Towing their bags, they all airswam into it, Kawib sitting down in the pilot's chair. "Everyone have everything? Good. Close up." The canopy slid closed over their heads as easily and silently as it had opened, closing with no visible joint.

"All right, let me finish power-up, and I'll get us in motion," Kawib said.

"You *hand-fly* this?" Dujuv asked.

"Would you like to move up to the copilot's chair and watch?"

Dujuv didn't need a second invitation.

Kawib's checkout seemed to take about twenty seconds. The basic controls looked to be a stick, rudder, and throttle that might have been familiar to any Late Medieval pilot. "You can stow your bags in any of the lockers in the sidewalls," Kawib said, "and make sure you strap in—we won't be doing any high accelerations, because this thing really can't, but the acceleration does change a lot and it can be startling. Any questions before I call in a clearance and we go? I may not be toktru conversational once we're in motion."

"Is it *that* complex to fly one of these?" Dujuv asked.

Kawib chuckled. "I ought to pretend it is, to impress you all, but the fact is that I could just tell it to take us home, and it would do it all automatically, like any other AI-flown ship. Might even do a better job than I'm going to do. But I would like to try to break a personal record for hand-flying this thing from the docking body to Greenworld, and that's where my concentration will be."

Dujuv grinned. "So we're racing!"

"Well, yeah, but only against a personal record."

"That's okay, tove, I just got off a Hive Spatial battle-sphere. Where fun is not done. So the fact that you're doing anything at all just because you'll enjoy it—well. Glad to be aboard, Captain."

"Technically," Kawib said, "I can only be a captain while this thing is off the cable, which is only at intervals. At the moment I'm the driver at best. Anyway, glad to have you along for the ride. Just don't touch anything, and if I do anything brilliant I'll let you all know to applaud wildly."

What a hopper could do, and a gripliner could not, was *pass*. Bursts from its cold jets let it leap sideways at the last moment to avoid slower-moving gripliners ahead of it, then return to the cable in front of them. Or now and then, when traffic was heavy for a few hundred kilometers up the line, Kawib would jump a few dozen kilometers in space to a hole in the traffic in a less-busy cable, flashing around yet another gripliner, bouncing off the cable on a burst of the cold jets, seeing the silver flash of the traffic in the sunlight four or five kilometers away, then rolling 180 degrees and firing the cold jets again to match up with the cable.

Kawib was only flying the humanly-possible parts; he could no more have truly hand-flown at those speeds than he could have steered a bullet. (In fact a bullet moved much more slowly.) Computers had to do the linducer grapple-and-ungrapple processes, and even the last kilometer of the approaches. But Jak still noted that their bounces and excursions off the cables and between them were executed gracefully and cleanly, and he liked the air of quiet satisfaction with which Kawib carried out the maneuvers. Perhaps no one had been a "real" pilot since the days of biplanes, jet fighters, or the early shuttles—Jak wasn't sure when computers and high speeds had eliminated them—but if Kawib's piloting wasn't quite real, his panache more than made up for it.

"Weehu, fun one," Kawib said. The cold jets hit with all they had and the hopper zoomed away from the cable; before them, a swath of green and yellow grain fields surrounding little red-roofed villages had been swelling across their forward view. Now they shot across it as they approached, and Jak could see occasional glints from the transparent upper surface. As they drew nearer still, getting close to the edge, Jak caught a glimpse of wide rocky beach and stormy deep-blue water. Then beneath the clear upper surface there was nothing but heavy, dark clouds, rushing up at them.

The black starry sky of space opened beyond the edge, and in an instant the white clouds, the dark air and water, and the black underside of the habitat flashed by, and they were moving back into Arm Eight.

They went on, leaping from cable to cable, springing over slow-moving gripliners, twice more swinging out to pass around the edge of a habitat, and the broad circular lands flashed by in front of them, beginning as disks covering much of the sky and briefly becoming the ground into which they were always about to plunge, just before emerging into a new sky with another bright disk of a world ahead. Kawib worked the controls like a compulsive gambler playing a hundred screens at once, acceleration going from almost two g to zero to minus two g in an endless bounce-and-dance.

Finally, they whipped around the dark edge of a habitat that a moment before had been a broad plain that they were bare seconds from cratering, and Kawib said, "Well, we're here. Make sure those belts are fastened." They moved sideways in a single great swoop and clamped onto the cable; the linducer braked hard, and they hung on their belts for a long few seconds until they were down to arrival speed. This time, instead of flashing by at the last moment, the habitat became more and more solidly land, until finally they passed through the swirling gray fog of the cold lock and emerged into the air-filled space beneath the glass dome of the roof. With what seemed like the painful slowness of an elevator, they descended the last kilometer onto the platform at the station.

Kawib popped the canopy, and it dilated back into the fuselage. "End of the line. Welcome to Greenworld."

"Did you beat your time?" Dujuv asked.

"I missed by over two minutes. I didn't find a hole in the traffic within reach, all the way from Disney to Utopia. And I did a pretty shabby job rounding Kamakura—swung at least ten kilometers too wide and had to use a lot of cold jet to get back to a cable. But there's always another run, masen? Now, if you'll follow me, we'll get you to Colonel

Mattanga, in the Royal Palace, and after that you're *her* problem."

"*Colonel* Mattanga?" Myxenna asked.

"Princess Shyf's personal chief for security and intelligence?"

"Yeah," Jak said. "We just hadn't specked who she was. It just feels funny."

"You mean it feels funny to discover you've been talking with someone who could decide to have you killed, or completely change your life for their convenience? Yeah, I know something about that." Kawib fell silent.

Greenworld was a habitat as rich and beautiful as anyone had ever imagined. Houses were shaped from living rock or grew up out of tangles of trees. Greenswards, tough enough for treaded tractors yet soft enough to sleep on, lay everywhere between the tall straight trees. The trees themselves formed a high canopy from which green tubes of light sluiced down into the clearings, where artfully random trails wandered between shops and houses. Hardly anything required any attention, yet a ripe piece of fruit, a trickle of pure water, or a comfortable place to sit always appeared where and when you wanted it. Furthermore, the slowly varying local gravity was about one-third g, the most pleasant grav for human walking—just adequate for traction and keeping the center gliding level, yet requiring little energy.

The walls of the Royal Palace had been grown directly from the stone base that had itself been made from the slagged materials of the original Greenworld. Checkpoints and guard stations greeted Kawib with flurries of salutes, and they passed through the series of arches and gates into the Royal Palace.

It was a regular hexagon a kilometer on a side, two kilometers from corner to corner—large because the first few Karrinynyas in the Aerie had needed it as a fortress and rally point. The slagging of the old habitat, and in particular the systematic destruction of every site and monument connected with the old Republic, had proven to be unpopular for some generations afterward.

But as the prosperity of the Wager-era reconstruction of human space had continued, wearing on into an economic boom that lasted for centuries, people had ceased to care, and the Royal Palace had become valuable real estate. The inner citadel, a clever circular maze on a gently rising hill at the center of the grounds, had been kept for residences, ceremonies, and administration, and the rest converted to ultra-high-priced residential and retail areas.

When Kawib guided them through the winding green paths of the hedge maze into the inner citadel, late afternoon sun slanted over the hedge-tops into the broader sculpture gardens, where various stone Karrinynyas of the last millennium stood or sat, looking brave or wise or whatever they were supposed to have been. Jak wondered what the statue of Queen Shyf would eventually look like—petulant, or horny?

They came to a crumbling, dark gray, polished stone stairway, constructed to look weathered, with broad steps flanked by unicorns and spread-winged eagles, ascended to a higher lawn, rounded a zigzag hedge, and entered the Royal Administration Building. Kawib led them through a corridor to a door of very old natural wood, carved in an elaborate faux-medieval frieze of soldiers and flags. "Right here," he said. "This is where I leave you. Good luck with everything; it's been a pleasure meeting you."

"And you too," Dujuv said.

"Thanks for taking so much time from a day," Myxenna added.

Kawib smiled. "Before you thank someone for that, you should know what they'd've been doing otherwise. In my case, I really should be thanking you. Good luck." He walked away briskly, seemingly cheerful.

"Do you suppose," Myx muttered, "that he was refraining from telling us that we were going to need it?"

They knocked and Mattanga's voice called out, "Come in."

The office was surprisingly small and spare. Mattanga did not rise; she barely looked up. "Sit down." She gestured at three chairs in front of her desk.

She looked them over; Jak was getting used to gray hair, but the wrinkling and cracking of her skin was more apparent in person. "Well. Now I've had time to digest some history, and I was able to get a few thoughts from the Princess. I hadn't realized you three were part of her rescue in the Uranium affair.

"The message you got was what the communications pokheets call a cowbird. Its front end hid it on our servers here until it detected a message from the Princess to Jak Jinnaka. Then it erased that message and sent itself.

"The message is a top-of-the-line fake—they did it the hard way. They must have had at least twenty million frames of Princess Shyf, from which they then mixmatched at least a trillion frames for their frame alphabet, making light and background consistent across all of them, and the words, gestures, and expressions they sent were homeosemiotized to at least a ninth degree of comparison, which would be nearly as expensive as that frame alphabet. The only reason we could detect the faking was that the Princess told us it was a fake, so that we were looking for how it was done. Without that we'd never have known *that* it was done.

"Now, the kind of facility that can do that is owned either by major media or *very* high end intelligence agencies. If our Intel people had needed something like this, they would have had to hire it out. And we're a well-funded national agency, from a rich nation with a lot of enemies.

"The djeste at the heart of all this is mysterious, and eliminating mysteries concerning the Princess and her security is my job. So what I want to know is who went to all this trouble, for a deception that could only last to this point at most, and what they hoped to gain by it." The Colonel drummed her fingers on the table. "I am forced to admit I'm utterly stymied, or toktru stumped as the Princess might put it. Does any of you have even a possibly relevant thought, or memory, or piece of data?"

"Well," Myxenna said, "this is pretty basic—it's just right out of my text for Deception and Tradecraft class— but if we assume that they intended the deception to work this far and not any further, then either it has already served its purpose or else having us discover it is part of the plan—"

Mattanga made a face. "I don't know whether to hug you or slap you, young lady. I wrote that chapter."

Myxenna started, and Mattanga's eyebrows raised again. "We have many friends in the Hive, you know, and many favors are exchanged. It was an interesting chapter to write, I had the knowledge, a colonel's pay is not much, and it would have been improper for Hive Intelligence to give me a direct assist with expenses. Therefore they happened to find that work for me.

"Well, anyway, whoever the mystery enemy may be, the most they could have planned for, is that you are here and talking to me. To have penetrated far enough into Princess

Shyf's private affairs to be able to carry out this operation, they would have had to know that she had had no contact with Dujuv, only occasionally old-friend notes with Myxenna, and she was tired and bored with Jak and in process of getting rid of him." Colonel Mattanga leaned slightly forward, seeming to probe Jak's face with her gaze. "I do trust that this is not too painful to discuss?"

"Not a problem," Jak said, bleeding internally.

"So the only thing that they could have been certain of accomplishing was *this* meeting. Do any of you see anything that I don't?"

Jak sighed. "Well, weehu, we all kept saying it was too singing-on perfect. So whoever it was didn't just really study Se—Princess Shyf—they dug up plenty about me and my toves, too."

"Mmmph," Mattanga said, obviously not pleased with the thought. "And none of you is easy to research, as I just found out. After all, Jak, you are the nephew of Sibroillo Jinnaka, and he's been wrapping you in nested blankets of disinformation since before you were born. And Hive Intelligence starts concealing information about anyone who might be going into their service well before recruiting them." She nodded at Dujuv and Myxenna. "You would find some interesting things if you were to try to hack into your files."

"I already did, and you're right," Myxenna said.

"So all this cost plenty of time, money, and effort. It must be terribly important to whoever it is. And so far as we know, everything they've tried to do has worked perfectly so far."

Dujuv nodded and said, "So you need to take a spoicke."

The Colonel looked at him with sudden interest. "I don't follow slamball."

"When you have to track all seven balls all the time, a lot of times you can see that the other team is doing something complicated but you don't know what they're trying to do. So if you've got a spare ball at the goal—especially if you're almost at the penalty bell where you *have* to throw it—you just use a privileged-catch call to send two or three of your players into the middle of that. The other team has to change what they're doing, or else take a foul, and cope with a new threat. You don't always know what you did to them, but at least you probably spoiled their play.

"So that's what I'd think about, sitting in your chair. Even just do something real stupid; I sent the ball to my slowest runner, once, with nobody blocking for him, on a spoicke, and they got so mixed up between trying to do their plan and not foul and get his ball away from him and still watch our main offense, that I scored a knockback in the confusion."

For the first time since they'd met her, Mattanga smiled. "You just gave me the first idea I've liked since this thing came up." She sat back, tenting her fingers in front of her face.

An alarm hooted.

The three toves jumped out of their chairs, floating several centimeters upward, then slammed back into them. Mattanga, who was comfortably gripping her chair, was obviously doing her best not to smile. "That sound is the perturb alarm," she said. "Keeping all the habitats on seventeen arms at their contracted gravity is occasionally a little much for even the best software—sometimes it's literally insoluble—and that's when the software turns on engines on all the habitats and gets us tumbling in a different configuration. Gravity usually drops close to zero, bounces up close to full right after, and then settles back to normal. It happens about twice a day.

"If you hear a double hoot instead of a single—those are only a couple of times a year—it's a big perturb, like a slight negative gravity followed by a couple of seconds of one point five g. So always grab something that's bolted down as soon as you hear that sound. Though even that doesn't always help—we had a godawful mess in the public fishing pond a couple of years ago because there were four boatloads of kids out there and we got an unscheduled double hoot. No deaths but some scary moments, and people were finding fish in strange places for months." She smiled. "I did tell Kawib to brief you about life here, but no doubt he was having more fun flying the hopper." From the way she smiled, it was clear that Kawib was in no real trouble.

"All right, my decisions: Myxenna will be a lady in waiting to Princess Shyf. The combination will be unusual—a commoner, not rich, foreign—but not impossibly so. And you two boys are joining the Royal Palace Guard. That's the temporary solution. After that I'm planning to assign each of you to the first unusual duty that comes up, especially duties away from Greenworld. My guess is that they expected you all to be put under house arrest, so that's what we *won't* do. Is that acceptable?"

"It beats house arrest," Jak said.

"Excellent, because that was really the only alternative I had."

"You were planning to offer this all along?" Myxenna asked.

"Oh, of course. Except that I didn't have a rationale for doing it. And trust me, if you're sitting in a seat like mine a couple of decades from now, you're going to find that knowing what you want to do is never enough. You have to be able, in a year or two, to answer that terrible question 'What were you thinking?' Which is why I am so grateful to you, Dujuv, for having supplied me with a very nice answer indeed to that question. Spoicke. I have to remember that term. It's sounds so much more reasonable than 'I didn't know what to do but I knew I had to do something.'"

CHAPTER 6

At the Pleasure of the Princess

From the outside the Royal Palace Guard barracks looked like a bland hotel. The sprite was making the vivid blue-white figure eight, about half a meter tall, on the door, indicating that they had reached their destination. Jak pressed the bell, and the sprite vanished.

The door dilated, and they stepped through to find Kawib Presgano behind a desk, looking bemused but smiling. "It appears to be the Colonel's pleasure," he said, "never to rid me of you. Welcome to the Royal Palace Guard, I guess. Congratulations on being lieutenants."

"We're *officers?*" Dujuv asked.

"Oh, we all are. At least. The Royal Palace Guard doesn't actually guard the palace, so we don't need any actual fighters to do any actual fighting."

"What *do* we do, besides being not actual?" Jak asked.

"Why, we serve at the pleasure of the Princess." Was there a bitter undertone to Kawib's voice? Jak couldn't tell. "You'll be assigned regular patrol duties in which you follow a sprite around the palace grounds—that includes the residential and commercial areas inside the walls—and there will be ceremonial duties of various kinds at court functions. Should you actually encounter any violent law-breaking, you are welcome to try to stop it if you like but most of us just call the pokheets.

"We also have a mandatory schedule of workouts for everyone on active duty, which, since both of you are reasonably athletic, you'll probably enjoy, though being from the Hive, where people are prudish, you might be uncomfortable about working out in just a thong and shoes, in front of a viewer gallery."

"I'm about as immodest as a wasp ever gets," Jak said.

"And I have nothing to be ashamed of," Dujuv added.

Kawib smiled slightly, looking over the panth's compact mass of muscle and his handsome regular features, and said, "I predict a slight increase in attendance at workouts for a while—they're generally popular with ladies in waiting. Remember that any hearts you capture are supposed to be given back."

"Don't forget to warn them about Seubla," a tall, graceful young man said, coming in to sit on Kawib's desk.

"I don't need to warn gentlemen, such as these, about such matters," Kawib said, grinning. "They are not the sort of heets that go chasing after a pizo's demmy. Very much unlike certain members of my guard who we may need to neuter, if we are ever to stop them from humping the legs of the young ladies at diplomatic receptions.

"But I suppose I should explain. Seubla and I have been mekko and demmy since the third year of gen school. The minute I'm discharged from the Royal Palace Guard, she will resign as a lady in waiting, we will get married, and I will drop by the barracks to wang the living shit out of anyone who has ever looked at her with even slightly more lust than he harbors for his grandmother. Is that clear, Xabo?"

"Yessir. But may your lowly XO point out that your demmy *does* attend many of our workouts?"

"Entirely to enjoy the sight of me stripped to the waist, and the sneer of cold command with which I put the rest of you through your paces. Or would you care to discuss it while Disciplines sparring?"

"Having sparred with you, sir, I'd rather just have you beat me with a plank and trust to your sense of restraint." Xabo stepped forward and extended his hand to Dujuv. "You must be the new recruits. I'm Xabo Srijesen, second in command around here, and the skipper's toktru tove and all around factotum."

"Dujuv Gonzawara."

"Jak Jinnaka. And—pardon me, sir, but you're the commander?"

Kawib nodded. "Yes. And I run errands like picking up stray guests. I told you we're a ceremonial outfit. The greatest privilege I have is that when there's any real work to do—which is nearly never—I am able to grab it for myself. My official title here is brigadier general, but when I finally get out of here and get my long-delayed commission in the regular Army, I will be entering it as a captain."

"Royal Palace Guards can't resign?" Dujuv asked.

"Oh, I suppose your embassy would say something if you were held here against your will. It must be nice to have an embassy to talk to, masen? Let's swear you in and get you into uniform. And fitted with your thong. Workout starts in less than two hours, and when they get fresh meat, they want it on the table as soon as possible."

Jak and Dujuv deposited their bags into small, comfortable rooms in the dormitory. They worked out on resistance machines with about twenty other young heets, all of them in just thong and shoes, and a small crowd of fashionably dressed young women watched them. Myxenna wasn't among them, which surprised Jak slightly and also pleased him since it was one less thing to precess Dujuv.

There was no mess but there was a generous meal allowance to draw on; Jak and Dujuv ate in a small Lunar Greek restaurant within the Palace that Xabo suggested. They were to report back immediately after dinner for night assignments.

"I ought to message Uncle Sib and tell him what's going on, except I don't actually know myself," Jak said to Dujuv.

They came around the corner into the office. Kawib returned their salutes in his oddly sardonic manner; he never did anything wrong yet everything he did implied that he knew he was only playing soldier.

"Well," he said, "night patrol tonight. Wear these monocles so you can see the infrared sprite. Follow it. If you encounter anything that looks like it should not be happening, either suppress it yourself or call for help. Every time the sprite flickers into the visible light range and starts running through all the colors of the spectrum, call in to report that everything is okay. If your sprite suddenly glows red and moves quickly, follow it because it's taking you to where someone needs backup. In my two years here, that has never happened. All you'll see is lost, drunken, noisy kids, fresh from a party somewhere. The Princess prefers that we be officious with them and make them afraid, and urges you to feel free to hit them. I am required to tell you that it is an official privilege of your job to be, and I quote, 'moderately abusive for your own pleasure.' (Unofficially I'm adding that if I catch you hurting people for fun, you and I have a sparring date, and I'm a local champion.) I'm sure we'll all see each other before the night is out. The sprites tend to go to the same places."

Darkness was just falling, the lights dimming on the bottom of New Bethlehem five hundred kilometers above as the glass a kilometer overhead changed to opaque, when Jak set out. For the first hour, he followed the sprite, a hand-sized pale gray cross, as it danced along the hedge walls of the central maze.

Jak's stiff, thick coat, tight knee breeches, and high black boots were out of a comic opera. The jingle of all the little medallions and metal decorations precessed him too. When he tried standing still and listening intently, he heard only the faint jingles of other RPGs.

Standing there in the quiet, Jak glanced up. The dome was de-opaquing. When possible, Greenworld used "natural" rather than "room-style" darkness for night. A shiny black circle, as wide as your hand at arm's length, covered the zenith, where New Bethlehem hung above them, absorbing all the sunlight falling on it. Columns of crescents descended around the black circle—habitats on other arms, a few lit brightly and a few dark with just a few lights on.

Around the crescents the stars blazed brilliantly, barely dimmed by a mere kilometer of air. Off to his right, low on the horizon, he could see the bright double "star" of the Earth and Moon, and to the right of that pair, the dimmer, much more distant Hive. He stood on one of the broad lawns, surrounded by statues of Earth animals—his purse said they were trophies of the conquest, and had once stood around the doors of the Republic Hall. The shapes of the horns and the graceful fins on the stone creatures cut into the sky full of stars and crescents, both peaceful and violent, like silhouetted twisted wreckage on the walls of a fortification, many long years after a battle, rusting in the shapes into which it had burned.

The gray cross waited patiently; with no reason for Jak to be here, the AI that steered the sprite could afford patience.

Then the cross zipped toward one entry into the hedge maze, and veered back and forth, like a crazed puppy, urging him to hurry. Jak followed, the silly jewelry on his chest tinkling madly. The sprite led him up a winding pathway onto a low stone platform and turned right.

Jak was on the big stone stairs of the Heir's Palace, facing up the hillside toward the complex neobaroque fractal profusion of doorways and windows in the cascading stone fountain of high arches and vaults. The Heir's Palace seemed poised to fly, either to sail up into the stars, or to plunge down the stairway like an owl on a mouse.

The overhead dome re-opaqued for another pass through daylight, and the bright sky faded as if someone had turned down a dimmer. At the top, the sprite led him to a wall where a hidden door dilated silently.

Down a hall, through another door, Sesh was waiting by candlelight. Nearly Jak's height but less than half his mass, her body was shaped by the admixture of gracile that the Karrinynya line had acquired from the three-century-long Permanent Regency, when the bored captive kings and princes had ennobled showgirls, courtesans, and models as their consorts.

The candlelight, scattered by bozze, sconces, chandelier, and fiber-trees, made her thick, almost waist-length red hair and ocean-storm blue eyes blaze. Her coffee-colored skin was covered with a fine-lined geometric tan pattern, now, different from the tiger stripe she had worn as his demmy.

She wore a scarf tied low on her hips, just enough to cover, and her hair poured over her breasts in a wave of crimson highlight and black shadow. "Jak Jinnaka," she said. "It's been a long time. I've had lovers, but I haven't had anyone touch me gently, or like an equal, or just for love. I . . . would you like . . . ?" She let the question trail off, sighed, stretched, and brushed her hair back over her shoulders; her hands continued in a single motion to release the scarf like slippery smoke. Her soft lips felt his as if try-ing to memorize him, and when he gently pressed his tongue forward her mouth opened wide and soft.

She giggled at the awkwardness of removing his heavy uniform.

The black leather chaise among candlelit mirrors was exquisitely smooth and soft, just firm enough to let him take his weight on his hands. She pulled him into her, and they thrust together, fast and hard, more and more, until she arched her back and his hard thrusts ululated her cat-shriek into a siren.

Jak sat back, spent, panting, heart and mind empty, his eyes wandering in awe across the perfect planes and curves of her body, from her high-cheekboned face to her wide-flung thighs. The sweat on his chest and shoulders would cool in a moment—

The lights came full on, bright and blinding.

"See," Sesh said, in a tone better suited to a lecture than to a bedroom, "that was what I was talking about." She flipped off the chaise in a beautiful back somersault and landed on her feet, turning in a mocking dancer's bow to the candled mirrors.

The mirrored wall flew up into the ceiling, revealing an array of theater seats, occupied by Kawib, Dujuv, Myxenna, and three other young women.

With a cry, Jak rolled and covered, feeling more naked than he had ever felt in his life.

Sesh laughed uproariously. Two of the three girls that Jak didn't know joined her, seeming to compete to see who could laugh hardest. The very pale blonde girl, who sat apart from them, sat perfectly still, as if watching a poisonous snake crawl toward her. Everyone in the seats was naked.

"Well, you all saw," Sesh said. "In fact having you all see is probably what's bothering Jak."

The two girls laughed again. Myxenna and Dujuv were staring into space; between them, and a row farther down, Kawib was glaring, all but hyperventilating.

"Now," Sesh went on, "Dujuv can attest that neither he nor Jak had any conditioning. That was Jak's real, natural response to me. And if you were all watching closely, you saw that I had a lovely time. Bland, of course, but lovely." She spoke directly to the still, pale blonde woman. "So, you see, Seubla, I do know what you mean when you prattle on about gentleness and sweetness and tender love and all those pretty words, all those things you were saying I didn't understand—in fact, that's what *my* first experiences were, too, very much like yours. So I don't just understand, I really *know*, firsthand, that all this kind of tender-cuddles mush causes very strong bonds! Which is exactly why you and Kawib are not going to resign and marry."

Seubla said, "I never doubted you could enjoy any form of sex, Your Utmost Grace."

"You're a tough little bitch, and very stubborn, and you never give up, do you?" Sesh said, with an amused smile that seemed strangely affectionate. "You're going to say that it's different if your heart is in it. And I'm sure you're right, because I know my heart wasn't in it this time, but it has been in the past, and it was different. I really do think that, back on the Hive, when I was Jak's demmy, my heart *was* in it, quite often, very sincerely. At least I have no memory of having any contradictory thoughts. I was actually very much in despair once (for almost a week!) about the certainty that I would have to leave the Hive and that Jak could never be more than my consort, not my husband.

Of course I was sixteen and one has many stupid thoughts at that age, doesn't one?

"Anyway, I toktru could not let you get away with what you said at dinner the other day, Seubla. Nor with your agreeing with her, Kawib, however laudable your loyalty to a demmy might otherwise be. I *do* know what gentleness and tenderness in bed is, and I know what it is like to have sex with someone who has not been conditioned to my tastes, and I *have* enjoyed it. Jak, thank you. Don't dress. Take that seat over there. Sit with your legs apart, that's what we always do in this room. Or rather what all of you always do in this room. I always do what I want."

His feet seemed to lift him from the chaise and carry him to his designated seat. Everyone else's nakedness did not make him any more comfortable.

"Now." Her tone reminded Jak that he was supposed to call her "Princess Shyf." "Come here, Kawib, and we'll demonstrate something for our guests."

As if being marched to the gallows, Kawib got up and walked stiffly to her; Jak looked down, not wanting to see whatever came next.

"Please," Seubla whispered, beside him. Now that he was closer, he could see that she was small, plump, not terribly pretty, nose a little too large and eyes a little too close together. "Please, she punishes everyone if anyone doesn't watch."

"I don't *punish*," the Princess said, "you are to watch and learn because that is what your job is. But thank you for clarifying things for my old friends, Seubla, they *are* new here." She turned Kawib outward to face them, and again her voice fell into the cadence of lecture. "Jak, Dujuv, tomorrow, you will report for conditioning. The first time takes a few hours. After that, once or twice a week we refresh the hypnosis, resensitize to my pheromone mix, and review some special viv, so that eventually—" She smiled, looked at the commander of her guard, and said "Hard!"

His face showed nothing but loathing, but he was instantly erect. She stretched out on the couch and said, "Now, I expect everyone's full attention."

She smiled at Kawib. Jak had seen Bex Riveroma contemplating removing his liver, and this smile was worse.

"Kawib." The man got on her as if he were being strapped face down on a bed of nails, did what he was supposed to with an expression of fury, and kept doing it until she said, "Release." He convulsed briefly, pushed back, and stood at the end of the chaise.

"Good boy," the Princess said. "You may give your *sow* a little peck on the cheek. Report for two hours' refresher conditioning tomorrow. You're not as reflexive as you should be."

Kawib stood and walked slowly back to the seats. Tears were streaking his face. He bent and brushed Seubla's cheek with his lips; the two of them smiled at each other, clinging to each other's hands.

"He lives for this," Sesh said, and she, and her two other ladies in waiting, laughed loudly, a harsh sound, like a clique of children on the playground who have just decided who will be the goat. Myx, Duj, and Jak sat still. Kawib and Seubla remained entranced by each other's eyes. After a while, Princess Shyf lost patience and shouted, "That's enough."

When Xabo dropped into the gym early the next morning, Jak and Dujuv were going through the formal part of the Disciplines, having just moved into slug-throwers. Xabo coughed and pushed the override; the vivid illusion of a black-clad attacker with a pistol disappeared, and Jak found he was holding the virtual, a little cylinder that simulated all the different weapons in the Disciplines, matching its apparent weight, feel, and appearance to each part of the process. Jak was almost relieved—his arm had been glowing dim turquoise, off and on, through all the katas, indicating that he had been fractionally slow and pulled too far low and left. Uncle Sib had often said that it was better not to practice on a day when you were only able to do the Disciplines badly.

Xabo stood still for a long moment. "Report for conditioning at the infirmary."

Jak had been hypnotized before—it was standard practice to teach every small child to "go under" easily. So the machine flashed the light and played the tones, and sent him under, and when he awoke two hours later, his arm felt funny from multiple pressure injections, and he had had an experience that felt very much like (when he was much younger) falling asleep in the middle of a pornographic viv, to awaken with his head a confused whirl of erotic images. It wasn't terrible, but he didn't like it.

Xabo was waiting for them when they had finished the conditioning; he handed them each a large cup of orange juice, and as they drank greedily, he said, "Someone messed up and we have a note that says bags belonging to you two are still sitting at the docking body, and they insist that you come and claim them personally. There's just time to claim them before Jak is due to start his night watch. Please come with me."

Jak was about to say that he had had only one bag, and it had come through just fine, but he glanced sideways at Dujuv; the panth nodded at him, and his left hand flashed *Play along* at Jak.

In their private compartment on the express gripliner,

Xabo pulled out a sensor, scanned all three of them, sighed, and said, "All right, now we can speak freely. Well, now you know what the Royal Palace Guards are for."

"You're all her harem?" Jak asked.

"Her rivals," Dujuv corrected.

Xabo nodded. "Singing-on. We're all the heirs to the patrician families of the Republic, or descendants of any of three lines of pretenders, or of the last Regent General.

"Kawib and Seubla are a special case. He's the son of two of the great houses and she's the great-great-granddaughter of the last pretender on one side and a lineal descendant of the Regent General on the other. The only reason they weren't aborted was because King Scaboron is pretty liberal and open-minded. Shyf is not. What she's doing is brutal but effective, and it will work until the issue goes away."

"Goes away?" Dujuv asked.

Xabo sighed. "Seubla's family are Old Faith. They belong to the traditional Greenworld religion and don't adhere to the Wager. They won't accept genetic remodification after birth, which means no longevity treatments after the third one. Seubla will enter menopause at around age sixty, looking like most people do at two hundred, and Kawib won't look terribly different from what he does today. Have I said 'brutal but effective' yet? I think I did."

"And you?" Dujuv asked.

"Eldest male in a great family of the Republic. I'll be out of the RPG pretty soon, I think. After exhaustive testing, they've determined I'm telling the truth—I'm gay, and I've had myself sterilized, with an intrinsic spermaticide; I can produce clones and in vitro babies, but all the evidence is that I don't want kids. Which happens to be true. I'm not going to bring anybody into this kind of situation if I can help it. But Seubla's religion thinks reproduction is sacred; there's all kinds of things she isn't allowed to do, including marry a sterilized heet."

"So—uh, with everyone in the Royal Palace Guard, does the Princess, er—" Jack asked.

"Yeah. She even makes *me* 'er' with her every so often. Once you're conditioned, all it takes is one rude demand from the Princess and you're painfully capable till she says, 'Release.' Mind you, conditioning takes a lot of maintenance—if Seubla and Kawib fled to asylum somewhere, with decent psychiatric treatment, in a year, or at most two, they'd be able to manage with each other."

"Why don't they?" Dujuv said.

Xabo shrugged. "I'm not sure, really. Possibly Colonel Mattanga serves as a hostage. She's Seubla's mother. That's part of the general Karrinynya strategy for holding on to power; make every family that might pose a threat complicit, watch them like hawks, and execute traitors frequently. It's a lot harder to plot against the government when you're a closely watched security chief than it is as an ordinary worker out in the city. Anyone who's a threat to the dynasty, if they're young, is part of Princess Shyf's sex circus, and if they're older, is working in her father's pokhccts."

Jak looked out the window as they rose toward the little, yellow-lighted hole in the wide black circle overhead; the circle spread out to cover the sky, and the hole became vast, and they shot up past broad terraced gardens and oddly unrectangular ziggurats, and past the sheen of the glass dome, back into the space between the worlds, in less time than it took for one long breath.

He wondered if Sesh would call him to her bedroom tonight. He hated himself for wondering.

Beside him, Dujuv had uncurled into complete relaxation, and was applying what the Solar System Ethnography text said was the unofficial motto of panths everywhere: "When action is impossible, take a nap."

At the docking body, Xabo said, "Oh, well. Weehu. Looks like you have no baggage here. I've got two casinos to visit; there are slec clubs, dueling parlors, and some other ways to amuse yourselves around here. See you back here, Station Eight, in two hours." He airswam away.

They airswam past countless shops selling things they didn't want to buy before they finally settled into a booth in a centrifuged autocafe. The waitron brought coffee and trays of snacks; Jak watched Dujuv eat. It was about as familiar as any activity in a long time.

After a while, Dujuv said, "Jak, this is bad."

Jak nodded and said, "At least, I dak your, uh, Myx-problem better than I ever have. I keep wondering where *Sesh* went. I wonder if I was just so naive that I didn't see what kind of person she is when we were together—"

Dujuv was shaking his head. "Pizo, you're getting the full experience, toktru. Do you know how often I wonder where Myx went? And have to remind myself that she was never the girl I thought she was, that I just made her up?"

"You made her up?"

"Jak, this is the first time I can tell you this because it's the first time I'm sure you won't laugh at me. Because I can see in your eyes what you're feeling about Sesh now. You're imprinted, as much as any panth ever was. I know people say that it's borrowed genes from animals, but it's not—it's something that can happen to most people, it's just that it rarely happens naturally in unmodifieds. Let me just show you. True or false—when you were mekko and demmy, Sesh used to forget your birthday."

"Fal—well, it's true but so what? I mean, she's a princess, she had more important things—"

"True or false, it hurt your feelings—"

"Fal—true. That's true, Duj, but it doesn't feel true anymore. It feels like the whole memory should be false."

"Unh-hunh. True or false, you and Sesh often talked about your hopes and dreams, and her hopes and dreams, and what was important to both of you."

"Oh, now that's true. I know that's true. We did that thousands of times."

"Right. Tell me what the two of you said in any one conversation you definitely remember."

Jak stared into space; beside him, the unclosed viewport in the side of the centrifuge showed the coffee shop whirling by four times before he spoke. "I must have amnesia or something."

"No, you remember it happening because it's what you'd expect for two people in love. And you can't remember any specific time because it never actually happened, old tove." Dujuv stretched and yawned. "You going to finish your food?"

"Have it all, I'm toktru not hungry at all."

"See?" Dujuv asked, between bites of another pastry. "See?"

"Maybe. Explain it to me, please."

"Well, there's part of me that still believes that Myxenna was devoted to me, loyal and faithful as if she were a panth herself, and that remembers all the different ways that she was loyal and how completely I could trust her—don't laugh. I'm only telling you this now because I thought, with what's happening to you, you wouldn't laugh."

Jak tried to hold down his smile. "I see what you mean about you making Myx up."

"Yeah, and the funny thing is, I can know that the truth is more complicated—but I can't forget the parts I made up. Well, what did you and Sesh do for all that time in gen school? Stop grinning, I mean besides that. You hung around and were popular, wore nice clothes, went to expensive places because you were both rich kids, masen? Most of your conversations were probably about how much you liked each other. So you didn't know each other, did you? And you're as surprised to find out that she's cruel as I was to find out Myx is slutty."

"Sesh is not cruel."

Dujuv said nothing; he crushed a whole pastry into his mouth and swallowed it in one gulp, then took another sip of coffee.

Jak repeated, "Sesh is not cruel."

"And Myx is a nun."

"Shut up." Jak couldn't believe the anger surging through him. "People really don't understand her at all. Okay, so I don't remember every little detail of our relationship on the Hive, but I remember that she's sweet and funny and gentle—"

"—and even back then she liked to see the expressions on people whose feelings she had hurt, and she thought it was very funny to cut down people who weren't as popular as she was—"

"She did not. And besides she was young and that was just having fun—"

"Same age as we were, old tove, and who was it fun for?"

Jak groaned. "I've got to help her," he said. "Something is terribly wrong with her, now, she's changed, something must have happened—"

"Jak, they just conditioned me. I'm panth-bonded to her

too. But I have a little more practice at dealing with this than you do. Now pull back and try to think about what's happening to you. And to lots of people around Princess Shyf. You're worrying about *her?* Think about what she's doing to Kawib and Seubla. Weehu, it tears my heart out!" Dujuv stared at Jak for a long breath, as if willing his friend to see.

Jak felt his gaze drop from his friend's. "It's kind of ugly, masen?"

"And water's kind of wet. And the Hive wants us to work for *her.* I mean, aren't we supposed to be the good guys?"

"We're supposed to 'render all possible support to a friendly monarch' and we're especially supposed to 'assist the ruling dynasty of one of the Hive's oldest allies.' I don't remember that 'be the good guys' was even on the list."

Dujuv sighed, raised his purse to his face, and ordered a plate of squab gyoza "to help settle dessert," as he explained. For the rest of the time, they talked about slamball.

That night, when Jak had been walking his beat for about two hours, and the gray-white cross suddenly raced ahead and back, his gut clenched and he felt a cold sweat break out; he was excited, madly joyful, and unable to believe his good luck. The responses made no sense to his conscious mind, but they were indisputably his. He hurried after the sprite, toward the Heir's Palace. Though the greensward was as smooth and gripped the feet as comfortably as a deep rug, and Jak was a trained and disciplined athlete, he stumbled and slipped and almost fell.

The sprite led him in through Sesh's window. She was waiting for him, dim warm lighting already set, the bed a vast soft comfortable sprawl of soft white covers, her face eager, alert, and curiously more innocent than he had seen it since she had been a virgin, years ago. "Undress," she said, smiling sweetly. "Tonight we have all night. And no audience. We have so much to say to each other. But let's make love first, masen?"

She was as tender, eager, and affectionate as ever. And it wasn't as if Jak really had a choice; at every moment of resistance, she whispered a command, and his desire surged up like a fire with the damper opened.

Afterward, there was a buffet of cold meats, cheeses, vegetables, and heavy breads, all sliced and ready to eat, along with chilled white wine. They made large sandwiches and sat on a thick rug in front of the fireplace, eating, feeding each other, getting deliriously drunk. The depths of her eyes were blue as the metal in a fine pistol.

Sesh's sudden brief pout delighted him so much that at first he didn't speck she'd asked him a question, so she repeated it (she was so patient with him!). "Don't you approve of what you've learned about life here?"

"I approve of you," Jak temporized, feeling *that* with all his heart. The wine chilled his teeth. The room became slightly too clear and cold. "It's hard for me to see someone I love so much doing things that seem so cruel."

"Cruel is kind of a matter of where you stand, isn't it?"

He made himself imagine that Dujuv was there at his shoulder telling him what to say, and said, "Not for the person you're being cruel to."

Sesh smiled at him, teasing him, and said, "Now, haven't we both always noticed how stupid most people are? We used to talk about that all the time back in gen school, when we'd sleep over with each other. Most people need to be governed. And you govern by love and fear, masen? How are they going to feel fear if we aristos are not 'cruel,' as you put it? No more than they could feel love if we weren't beautiful. And to rule effectively, we must be both, at the same time."

Jak remembered her smile from their little teasing lovers' arguments, and wanted to hug Sesh. Instead he said, "Why do you torment Kawib and Seubla like that?"

Her eyes flashed in the firelight. "A leader I admire, in a similar situation, once said that little snakes are dangerous, too. I'm sure someone has told you who they are, what families they are from. I can't imagine why my father was so careless as to let them live this long, and now that they have, the death of either of them would be laid at my door unless there were an ironclad alibi. So since I can't poison either of them, I'm poisoning their relationship, masen? This way, if she does manage to breed despite all my precautions, their pup will be raised by such damaged parents that it will probably spend its silly, pathetic life in psychotherapy. More likely she won't whelp at all. Without their child, no civil wars, fewer attempted assassinations, no weird whispers in corners that turn into public massacres of the best people. The only cost is that one fat little religious weird-girl grows old and dies without laying any viper's eggs—or laying Kawib, which is another part of the fun; they won't do it with each other until they're sure they've been used for the last time at the Palace. Trying to keep it pure for each other, you see? And of course, when they finally do—well, wouldn't it be just delicious *fun* to watch them both *try* to make love?" There was something about the way that Sesh said "make love" that was far more obscene than "fuck" could ever be.

"Why are you telling me this?" Jak demanded, almost a cry. His heart ripped between the claws of his furious disgust and his conditioned adoration.

She giggled, a sweet, high sound that he remembered so well, the sort of thing she usually did when correcting a faux pas or explaining to him why he needed to remember any of the dozens of anniversaries on which she expected presents. "My delightful ex-mekko, all that tenderness and gentleness you are so good at giving really does make me happy; but don't we all like to be loved for who we really are? So I let you see who I am . . . and then you give me the tender love . . . and it just feels so good!" She kissed his shoulders, tasting and rubbing them with her lips, and her hands slid down his taut belly. She kissed him lightly on the lips and said, "You see, I want you to be like this, and I want you to let me hold you this way—wanting me and afraid of me. Love and fear. The elements of being ruled, masen?"

"What kind of love do you think you'll get if everyone is afraid of you?" he whispered.

She giggled like a twelve-year-old hearing a dirty joke that she doesn't quite get; in the firelight her face glowed with life and pleasure. Her hand closed on him gently. "Kiss me, silly."

He did; she returned the kiss passionately, but as he warmed to it, she suddenly squeezed hard. With a clenched shriek of pain he pushed her away.

She laughed. "Hard."

He was, suddenly, and she pushed him against the wall and all but yanked him into her; for a moment her eyes were flat and cold. Then she dissolved into giggles. "See?" She leaned forward and kissed him tenderly. "My sweet boy. What's the difference?"

"It makes a difference to me," he said. "And you had me conditioned."

"I told you why. Don't be a slow learner. You'll make me

feel like I'm with Dujuv." She tenderly licked at his throat, murmuring, "Now, *hard*."

Afterward, as she lay with her head on his chest, Jak said, "I would have been tender and affectionate to you—I would have loved you—without any conditioning, you know."

"Well, then it doesn't matter at all, masen?" The fire glinted off her hair; she was utterly beautiful. "Anyway, enough of all this, I'm bored. Go home."

CHAPTER 7

"Are You Sane?" "I'm Trying."

He dressed quickly and went out through the dilating door, into the dark palace, without speaking again. The corridor was dark, and Jak had no sprite, nor had he quite known how to ask Sesh for one, so he kept repeating directions to himself mentally—right at the first turn, left at the second, out through the big French doors—as he crept through blackness, hoping not to bump into anything noisy.

A hand took his, gently but firmly. Jak froze. "Psst." The unseen person seemed to wait a moment for him to react, and then made another "psst."

"What?" Jak breathed.

"This way." The hand guided him gently; he had a sense of a door dilating around him in the darkness, then irising closed behind him. Dim light from the outside edges of a black rectangle told him there was an uncurtained window behind a screen; he could make out the shape of the person guiding him, barely, and realized it was a woman, much shorter than himself.

Who reached up, put a hand on the back of his head, pulled his face down to hers, kissed him passionately, and guided his hands to her full breasts. The small woman led him to a thick sleeping pad on the floor.

Sometime later, when he was thinking in words again, Jak whispered, "Myx?"

The girl riding on top of him with a wild, bucking motion whipped her forearm into her own mouth, making a strangled whooping sound as if she were trying to eat it. She didn't lose rhythm at all, though her lungs convulsed with the force of her laugh. At that moment, the perturb alarm hooted, but neither of them had anything to grab; they floated a few inches upward, pushed by Myx's bucking. She grabbed his shoulders to keep them together.

Sudden weightlessness felt like a plummet through the floor. Surprise added just enough excitement to end the event in progress sooner than expected, just as gravity returned with more than usual force, dumping them both back onto the padding. They fell face to face and chest to chest with a heavy "Oof."

As they disentangled, she whispered in his ear, "So did you think it was Dujuv in drag?"

By then Jak was laughing too. "All right, who thinks at a time like that, masen?"

"That's kind of the issue. How are you feeling?"

"Uh, tired, sore, wind knocked out of me—"

"Sorry. I mean, how do you feel about me?" She rolled off the bed and knelt, her face close to his. The beginnings of the daylight, just being brought up, reflected from the domed ceiling and caught her face.

Jak was astonished. He had never before noticed how beautiful Myx was, or how deeply he cared for her. "I—um. Weehu, I'm glad we did this, Myx. I—you're the most beautiful woman I've ever—"

She slapped him, across the face, not hard, but enough to hurt. "Unh-hunh. Unh-hunh. Unh-hunh. This is just what the other girls told me about. The conditioning doesn't fully take until you've actually consummated it with someone.

Half an hour ago you wanted the Princess more than anyone you'd ever met. Masen?"

"Toktru." He felt cold in his belly.

"While the drugs are still in your bloodstream and
you're still recovering from the subsonics and the rhythm
patterning, you can be imprinted by anyone. Not that I'd
suggest it, but Dujuv in drag would have worked, too. I imprinted you so that you wouldn't be controlled exclusively
by Sesh."

Jak shuddered, grabbed his trousers from the heap beside the bed, and draped them over his crotch.

"You see?" Myx whispered. "The question is, why
would Sesh want to imprint *you?*"

He had never noticed before what beautiful hair Myx
had, or how lovely the curves of her body were.

She slapped him again, impatiently. "Come on, get over
it, my hand will get sore—I need you thinking, not making
cow eyes at me."

"It's really not easy," Jak said. His stomach was turning
flip-flops as he considered the utter impossibility of having
to choose between Myx and Sesh.

"I know," she said. "Your expression looks way too
much like Dujy. Nakasen could only guess what's happening inside him emotionally—I saw him being led by his
sprite to her window, just before I heard you in the corridor."

Jak gritted his teeth.

"What's wrong?"

He wanted to grunt *Nothing* but made himself explain.
"Jealousy. Haven't had it like this since puberty," Jak said.

"Are you sane?"

"I'm trying."

"All right, look, try to think. Why is Sesh conditioning

you, if she didn't want you here? Why, with a mystery as big as that faked message, are we all walking around instead of being completely, thoroughly interrogated, or even brain-read? Mattanga is acting like she's not even worried. Either Mattanga has some way of knowing that the question doesn't matter—or she already knows the answer. Masen?"

She was absolutely beautiful in the early morning light, and Jak was having a hard time understanding the words. He opened his mouth to speak, couldn't think of anything to say, barely restrained the urge to reach out and touch the dark thick hair.

The whole window frame crashed in.

Jak rolled and jumped to face the attack.

Dujuv flung the big multipaneled screen halfway to the ceiling, as if it were a sheet of cardboard, and rushed under it, straight for Jak's throat.

Myx screamed, "No!" She might as well have screamed it at a volcano. The two utterly mad rivals slapped, chopped, and jabbed furiously at each other, centers bobbing and faking. Dujuv found an opening—Jak could never have seen it—and walloped Jak in the solar plexus. He crashed backward across a table and tipped over a bookcase. Dujuv sidestepped and closed in.

Something stung Jak savagely, all over his body, and he collapsed; on the other side of the room, he saw Dujuv hit the floor. Jak tried to crawl forward, longing to break that ugly half-animal mongrel's neck, but he couldn't move.

There was another all-over shock, stronger, more a burn than a tingle.

"Hold it, right now, stay where you are, that's an order," Kawib said, climbing in through the hole where the window frame had been smashed down. "Don't move, Dujuv, or I'll keep zapping till you can't. Are you both going to hold still?"

"I am," Jak said.

"Me too, I guess," Dujuv said.

With a soft click and sigh, the door to the corridor dilated. Xabo moved in, stunner leveled and ready.

"Trust you to show up late," Kawib said.

"You assigned me to come to this door! I came as fast as I could!"

"I was teasing—I shouldn't have done that when everyone is under so much stress. Myxenna, sorry about having to be so rough with your friends."

"It's all right, I wasn't going to use either of them for anything else tonight," she said. "Are they going to be all right?"

"As much as any of us," Xabo assured her. "Right now they're regaining control. Then we'll all go back to the barracks for sleepy drugs and happy drugs, and be the best of toves again when we wake up. Kawib, you have them covered?"

"I do. Pizos, this is for your own good—we need to check that you can control your rages. Xabo is going to say something that will trigger another rage. If you control the rage, fine, we know you're sane enough to work with. If you don't I stun you and we try again in a few minutes. Clear?"

"Toktru," Dujuv agreed. "But it's not the conditioning; it's panth imprinting. I'm better now. I can feel that I've got control."

"Oh, good, then I'll fuck Myx," Kawib said, conversationally, "it's high time she had a *human* boyfriend."

Dujuv froze, then relaxed and sighed. "All right."

"Jak, you know that Princess Shyf is all mine and you

can't have her and I'm a better fuck than you are, and don't get any ideas about Myxenna because I'm taking her too."

Jak was about to laugh when his field of vision became a narrow red tube, the blood thundered in his ears, and the world seemed to slow down. He had never felt so ready for a fight before.

He stayed down on the floor anyway, drew three long breaths, and said, "Close, but I think I'm okay."

" 'Close' is all the better any of us ever do," Xabo said. "The people who do the conditioning dak their business, singing-on. All right, get up slowly, keep your hands where we can see them, and let's all walk out of here just as if we were four good old toktru toves and nothing in the world could ever be wrong."

Myxenna said, "One suggestion?"

Kawib nodded. "Of course."

"Have Jak put his clothes back on. He'll be less conspicuous."

It wasn't the friendliest or most comfortable time they had ever spent together, but Jak and Dujuv made a point of having breakfast together, when they finally got up, around lunch time. The schedule said they were excused from workout but that there would be guard duty for a reception. At least they would have the afternoon to recover.

They had gone to a twenty-four-hour breakfast buffet, which meant they could further avoid each other by taking turns going to the serving area. Even when they sat across from each other, sharing the sweet bread, rice, olives, omelet, and miso, they didn't speak much. Jak didn't know how things felt to Dujuv, but for him, the world seemed cold and gray and vaguely threatening, with no prospect that anything really good would ever happen again. Away from Sesh, and partially deconditioned, he loathed himself for the way he had felt the night before, but at the same time, it seemed as if those had been the only hours of his life worth living. Apart from that longing, all he seemed to be capable of feeling was irritation, like a bad hangover.

"I know we're excused, but do you want to make work-out anyway?" Jak said. "I know they were trying to give us more rest before this reception, but I think I'd feel better for the exercise."

"Toktru, I was already planning to."

Neither Kawib nor Xabo seemed surprised to see them, and the pleasant no-mind state of just working the resistance handles over and over soothed Jak like two big glasses of fruit juice after a hangover. He was almost cheerful in the big communal shower with the other Royal Palace Guards, only glancing occasionally at the viewing windows under each shower head.

As they were dressing, Kawib and Xabo approached and said, "How about having dinner over in New Bethlehem this evening? We need to eat early because of the guard duty. It'll be just lunchtime over there and they do a great lunch." Almost all habitats maintained twenty-four-hour days—that was what people found most comfortable—but the timing of midnight, and the length of dark and light, were purely local options.

Xabo, Jak, Kawib, and Dujuv emerged from the gripliner station into bright sunlight. Fields of grain stretched down to a lake. A heet in a tall hat, wearing heavy, awkward clothes, rode by on horseback, looking bored. "It's this way," Xabo said.

They walked by the side of a dirt road that seemed remarkably realistic to Jak; except for the black sky beyond the transparent dome overhead, and the bright ellipses of other habitats in the sky, and the two occasions when an alarm sounded and they had to squat down and wait out changes in the gravity, it might have been "farm country in Africa," Jak said to Dujuv.

"Toktru, I was thinking that."

The inn was a copy of a clapboarded farmhouse on the outside, but it was comfortably clean and modern on the inside.

At first they just ordered, and ate, and made small talk. Then Dujuv said, "I don't really want to talk about any of the things we ought to talk about."

Kawib said, "Toktru. Nobody likes to. Talk anyway. It's how we get through it."

Dujuv nodded. "I was telling Jak that at least, thanks to his being conditioned, he gets an idea of what panth loyalty feels like." He ate a last bite of pancake, and held his plate out to the side. The waitron put his third stack onto it. "I mean, if I dak it all toktru, you're all feeling, about the Princess, what I've felt about Myxenna for years. So believe it or not I sympathize. Even though, now that I also feel the same bond toward Princess Shyf, I want to kill you all. At least I dak why it seems like everyone in the Royal Palace Guard is crazy, and—forgive me for saying this— Kawib, why you're eating your heart out." He finished smearing jam on his pancakes and began methodically folding and swallowing them.

Kawib looked across his long-abandoned plate and said, "Dujuv, you don't even speck me. At all. Your bonding to Myxenna, and now to Shyf, just makes you miserable, masen?"

"Gnokgnu," Dujuv agreed, nodding and chewing.

"Well," Kawib said, "the feelings I have for Seubla are the only good reason I've got for continuing to exist. Our

gen school years together were not only the best of my life,
they were my life. The hope of being able to continue it—
even when she's dying of old age—gets me through every
day."

"How long since you've been able to just sit and talk
with her?" Jak asked.

"Two years. Since Shyf returned. King Scaboron had
been tolerant; some people say he's republican at heart.
Then the Princess came back and refounded the Royal
Palace Guard and the ladies-in-waiting program. She
grabbed Seubla and me in the first week she was back."

While Sesh had been doing that, she had been sending
Jak very long, passionate, I-love-you-I-miss-you-I-want-
you-forever messages, two and three times a day. He imagined her compelling Seubla and Kawib to do those
things . . . and then getting into a warm bath to tell Jak how
much she loved him and missed him. His conditioned mind
worked hard to find a way to love her for it.

"What will happen to you?" Dujuv asked.

Kawib looked at the wall. "Well, I don't know, really,
what Seubla thinks or feels anymore; how would I? I suppose she doesn't know any more about me. Our time together now seems like just an old story. I suppose if we'd
been left undisturbed it might have all been over by now,
anyway. But, still, anyway, Dujuv, though I feel sorry—"

A tiny, elegant woman, very petite but built like a lanky
model, strode in, her hair in the traditional journalist's plat-
inum blonde helmet cut, her olive skin tanpatterned in fine-
grained Fractal Leopard. Her clothing was singing-on this
week's clash-splash-and-smash: a pseudoskirt with ultra-
brief flaps emphasizing her several pairs of hip-hugging
gozzies, with a smooth, clinging, self-lighting top. A swarm

of drone cameras zipped and hovered around her like voyeuristic hummingbirds.

She sat down on their table, braced a hand between Jak and his plate, leaned back, and twisted to prop one long leg into the view of the active, green-lighted drone. "Hi, I'm Mreek Sinda and I'm here with Jak Jinnaka, whom you'll recall from my award-winning series 'Kidnapped by the Duke of Uranium' as the brave young rescuer of Princess Shyf Karrinynya. Also his faithful panth sidekick and tok-tru tove, Dujuv Gonzawara—"

A drone buzzed in for a close-up of Duj. Without looking up from his pancakes, he snatched the drone out of the air by its lens barrel and hammered it against the table, shattering it in three quick whacks.

Mreek Sinda observed him with the mild interest usually given to ten-year-olds who have stuffed straws up their noses and are making strange noises. "So what we have here is—"

"A private conversation," Jak said, "and I haven't consented to an interview, and anyway—"

"You're in a nation that absolutely gives all media their feets," Sinda informed him, putting on what he specked as the "coolly elegant face of steely resolve" mentioned in her service's ads. "I have a right to an interview if you're in a public place and not on duty, and since you are technically armed forces of another nation, you can't be on duty while you're here."

"Dujuv, if you're done with the pancakes, we should probably go," Jak said.

"Let me finish this plate, just a second or two." Another drone crept close. This time Dujuv caught it by the tail and decapitated it with a hard rap against the table edge.

Mreek Sinda turned back toward Jak; her self-lighting

top took out shadows on her neck and enhanced them under her bust. She wet her lips. "I'm going to try to find out if Jak is on some secret mission on behalf of his beloved Princess Shyf. Jak, what can you tell me about your reasons for coming to Greenworld?"

"Rogga bogga erf ganoo," Jak said firmly. "How are the pancakes coming, Duj? I hate to rush your eating, but—"

Duj swallowed hard, taking in all the remainder. "Understood, old tove."

"Then you'll neither confirm nor deny that this may involve matters at the highest level for Greenworld's ruling dynasty, as well as your own connection to Bex Riveroma, possibly the most wanted criminal in the solar system?"

"Ergle argle farf, skweedong pretzels," Jak said. "Wanna race back to the hopper?"

"Sure," Dujuv said, and all four guards charged out the door and back up the dirt road.

Camera drones are built for stability, not speed, and Sinda was wearing extremely tall heels. They were boarding the gripliner by the time the first drones flew into the station, and Sinda was nowhere in sight.

"She produced a really long silly documentary about my 'daring rescue' of the Princess," Jak explained, as the gripliner pulled out of the station. "I guess it was popular in the Hive."

"Here too," Xabo said, "but I didn't follow the series because I was busy being drafted into the RPG. To tell you the truth I only just now connected you with Princess Shyf's rescue."

Jak nodded. "Well, anyway, it was Sinda's big moment. Her only really popular work in any medium. Every few months she turns up, as if she's hoping I'll do something interesting in front of her again. The fact is, she was a minor fashion reporter who got lucky enough to be the only one with a camera when the Princess was kidnapped. That got her the assignment. Then she slapped together a show that people bought because of who was involved, not because of her work. It was all lies anyway."

Xabo said, "I don't know about that, but I did hear that the rescue was pretty impressive."

Jak made a rude noise. "I was practically set up with a script and more or less followed directions, and more people were on my side—"

"It was still impressive," Dujuv said. "You always underrate yourself. Your uncle thinks you did well, and we got into the PSA based on how well we did, and the Duke of Uranium practically buried us in medals."

"You know him?" Kawib asked.

"We met during that adventure. I did him some favors. Entirely by accident, but he didn't seem to quibble about that."

"Well, you'll see him again," Xabo said. "The reception we'll be pretending to guard tonight is for him."

"Psim Cofinalez is coming here? But he only just made duke, three months ago, when his father died," Jak said.

"Well," Xabo said, "the official story is that he's doing the Big Circuit for the next two years, to celebrate his having succeeded to the duchy, I guess, and probably also so that he's conveniently out of reach of suspicion when various long-term enemies happen to suffer dreadful accidents or to commit suicide. Plus some officials will have done things that were necessary but unpopular, and he will come back and fire them (into some cushy retirement), thus becoming very popular."

"But is it smart to be away from Fermi right now? He

has an older brother with a claim to the title and a nasty, treacherous disposition," Jak pointed out.

"Not anymore. Two days after Duke Psim Cofinalez started the Big Circuit, Pukh Cofinalez, who was living in the penthouse of his brother's palace, was assaulted by persons unknown who somehow penetrated three layers of defenses to reach him in the roof garden. He heroically resisted them but was driven back until, already mortally wounded, he fell over the parapet, dropped twenty meters or so, landed on his head (four times), and was run over by the arriving ambulance."

"And the killers?" Dujuv asked.

"Escaped completely. Psim has pledged to find them no matter how long it may take. Anyway, the Aerie is the second stop on the Duke's Big Circuit, and he'll be here tonight. I'm assuming he'd be glad to see the two of you?"

"I think so. We'd like to see him," Jak said.

"Then I'll station you both inside the ballroom. That means you can't have any projectile or beam weapon of any kind, but if armed commandos crash through Palace security, building security, wing defenses, and room defenses, killing all the real guards on the way—with the three or four hovertanks it would take—then you are allowed to stop them with your bare hands."

"Just so it's a fair fight," Dujuv said.

CHAPTER 8

You Saw Too Much and
Know Too Much

Your basic job," Kawib said, his sardonic half-smile firmly back on, "is to be attractive. Try not to spend too much time around the canapés, make pleasant conversation with wallflowers—*not* concentrating on wallflowers your own age and of your preferred gender. If anyone wants to invite you for something in a private room, you can accept but only for when you're off duty. Unless, of course, it's the Princess. Don't consume alcohol or anything else that might alter your judgment. Don't duck out and catch a nap. And toktru, you'll be tempted." The more experienced guards in the room chuckled. "All right, Xabo has overall command inside the ballroom. Call me if the rich people riot, masen?

"I'm feeling good about Vifu, Yib, Coxiz, and Pelorni, at the moment, so you lucky devils get to stand ceremonial guard at exterior doors with me. You'll be farther from the food and the ladies in waiting but also there's less danger of having to make small talk with some bored aristo. Kewoi, Pusaf, you have the outer-doors receiving area. Jak, Dujuv, walking post around the central staircase, which is between the kitchen and the dance floor. If anyone suddenly goes berserk while dancing, it's your duty keep them from getting their hands on a pastry cutter. I regret to say, toves, it's about time, so make sure that your uniforms look presentable, take five to visit the little room, and we'll all walk over to the King's Palace together."

Forty minutes later, Jak and Dujuv were standing with their backs to a pillar, trying to avoid leaning or moving, when a whistling voice behind them said, "Jak Jinnaka, and his tove Dujuv Gonzawara, I am astonished to find you here! Clearly my gods are pleased with me!"

"Shadow!" Jak embraced his Rubahy oath-friend. "I had wondered if the Duke would bring you along."

Before he had gotten to know Shadow, Jak would have sworn that all Rubahy looked alike: a tyrannosaur wearing a gorilla's arms, a Yorkshire terrier's head, and a rabbit's tail, covered all over with chicken feathers. Now he could have picked Shadow out anywhere—his friend's long slicing teeth were slightly, distinctively crooked to the left; a small extra curved lobe extended down the arm from the big black patch on his right shoulder that indicated he was of warrior ancestry; Shadow's squarish head was squarer than most; and he was slightly short for a Rubahy, taller than most tall men. Because his scent organs (two flaps of flesh covered with thicker feathers, on the top of his head) were longer and narrower than average, about the size and shape of short bananas, some of the Duke's Rubahy guards had nicknamed him "Bunny" (he detested that; he had explained in a message to Jak that rabbits were the most common Rubahy pet back on Pluto, so it was like nicknaming a human being "Doggie" or "Woofums").

At the moment Shadow on the Frost wore a heavy, short leather skirt with many pockets, serving as holster and bag, and of course his purse on his left hand. Rubahy have no facial muscles, and their eyes have no whites, so he had no expression, but his scent organs stood up straight, catching and treasuring the welcome scent of his friends. "You have kept your sense of humor? You have learned things that mattered to you?"

Jak had only accidentally befriended Shadow. At one strange moment during the wild adventure of rescuing Sesh, Jak had happened to say exactly the words that, translated from Standard to the Rubahy language, constituted a binding honor-oath, which had made Shadow his devoted friend for life.

"My humor is intact and my knowledge is greater," Jak said. He asked the ritual question for a warrior in service: "Do you gain honor by your service to the Duke?"

Shadow on the Frost said, "Well, for tonight, we have very similar duties—I will do for the Duke what you do for the Princess."

Jak glanced sideways at Dujuv. His tove was compressing his lips and trying very hard not to laugh out loud.

"Same old Shadow, I can tell," Jak said, and the Rubahy made noises like big slow bubbles in a metal bucket (the equivalent of laughter). One of Shadow's favorite jokes was to pretend to misunderstand Standard, or human culture, say exactly the most inappropriate possible thing, and watch humans struggle to decide whether or not to explain.

"It is good to be with humans who dak jokes, again," Shadow said. "The Duke of Uranium is a fine person, but he lacks your gift for laughter. I have been promoted to his personal guard. No merit involved, I assure you—it was just essential for me to have some post other than common soldier in his Rubahy mercenary battalion."

"Essential?" Dujuv made the mistake of asking.

"A simple matter, really. My uncle-group-for-shared-honor was at odds with my uncle-group-for-bloodline-distinction, over the behavior of a few distant cousins, and everything else got pulled into the dispute—you know how these family things can be. Anyway, all of my uncle-groups at least agreed that my service to the Duke gained honor for both me and my family, which meant of course that my sister-side cousin-friends therefore felt I was gaining too much of the sort of personal honor that could upset the political balance in the family, and they threatened to have me recalled, which might actually have been merely a ploy by some of our noble houses to get me where it would be socially acceptable to assassinate me. You can imagine I was not in favor of *that*. So a friendly aunt, married into my circle of mutual and interlocked oath-friends, happened to be the cousin-sex-partner of my commanding officer, who, I am happy to boast, did not want to lose me. He promoted me to a higher rank at which point I could no longer serve under him but would accrue less honor for each act, which perfectly qualified me to be a bodyguard, and then recommended me to the Duke, who graciously accepted."

"I'm glad things worked out," Dujuv said.

"And your schooling, Dujuv, tove of my tove, it goes all right?"

"It goes better than mine," Jak admitted. "Dujuv works harder, plus, toktru, I speck he has more brains."

"I'm a panth," Dujuv said, firmly.

"And that is a chair, and I am a Rubahy," Shadow said, gravely. "It is good to see both of you. I have duties now, but we will be in the Aerie for a month or more, and surely it can happen that we will all have some off-duty together."

"I'd like that a lot," Jak said.

"Well then, a quiet night to us all, and I will call you in the morning." Shadow moved away into the crowd.

After a few more minutes of watching well-dressed people mill around, Jak specked it was "quite possible that the most exciting part of the evening has already happened."

"Toktru, masen? And no naps. I think I'm going to stretch the rules and get into the food; Kawib can always tell the Princess that if you're going to keep a panth, you've got to feed a panth."

"I speck I can hold this job down by myself till you get back," Jak said.

Duj vanished into the crowd, leaving Jak alone with what passed for thoughts.

"Excuse me, er, Jak?"

It was Seubla, Kawib's demmy, in a pale lavender gown that had probably been chosen for her by the Princess, since it seemed deliberately unflattering. With her nearly-white hair pulled back, accentuating her plain proletarian features, she looked like a vacuum-welder's daughter going to a costume party as the fairy queen. *And this is someone Sesh fears so much,* Jak thought, and was glad, not for the first time, that there wasn't a drop of aristo blood in his own veins.

"Yes," Jak said.

"I have a message from the Princess, and excuse the rudeness, but she insists that I tell you that it is absolutely an order. 'You are to talk to Mreek Sinda, who is waiting outside to interview you. You will give her exactly ten minutes of your time, and answer all questions in a way suitable for accesscasting, and not do anything stupid.' All a quote, Jak, I'm sorry, that's not how I'd have said it."

Jak allowed himself a slight smile. "I know that, Seubla. I recognize the style."

The corner of her mouth twitched. "It's nice to be understood." She disappeared into the crowd.

Jak sighed and went out for his interview with Sinda. It

wasn't terrible—none of the ones back when she was making her hit series had been, either. Jak's answers seemed bland even to him, but Sinda didn't seem terribly worried about it one way or another, and she thanked him, nicely enough, at exactly ten minutes. He headed inside. Apparently tonight was going to be a series of switches between dullness and dullness, with dullness in between.

At his station by the main staircase, Jak found Dujuv standing and chatting with an old, good friend—Psim Cofinalez, the Duke of Uranium himself. Psim shook his hand as if he were grasping a lifeline, and his smile was warm with pleasure. "What an odd—but delightful—coincidence that you were here just when we were. It's so good to be able to see someone who was a friend back before they had a reason to be." The Duke was about ten years older than the two toves, and he was muscular, with wide-set shoulders, very dark hair and mustache, and very pale skin. "We'll have to find some time when we can talk without formality—I know that's always impossible but I also know that it's always worth it to try."

"That would be wonderful, sir."

"I'm also delighted to hear from Dujuv that you are continuing to be your usual selves at the PSA." The Duke's eyes twinkled. "Just remember you promised to defect to the Hive, and that I don't want two proficient bureaucrats showing up at my door when you graduate."

"Not a chance."

"Though two corrupt graft-grubbers are always welcome."

Subsonic thunder announced that slec was about to begin. "They're founding the first set," Jak said. "I didn't speck they'd do slec when they have so many older guests."

The Duke grinned, a flash of that common touch that the

media played up so much. "Thanks for not adding 'such as yourself.' This is the Princess's party, even if her father is here. She gets her way. I can't imagine that that's unusual. Anyway, I must go demonstrate that I dak slec; Princess Shyf won't speak to me if I don't."

He bowed and faded into the crowd, working his way toward the dance floor. Jak climbed up a few stairs for a better view. He was curious. He'd only seen slec in a big sphere with gravity low enough to airswim—all three dimensions equivalent. Here, in two-and-a-fraction dimensions, on a dance floor, it seemed tighter, more constricted, apt to fall into repetition.

Dujuv, standing next to Jak, said, "It's not obvious, but the problem is the Princess. See how she's almost always on a screen and how often that screen has the green dot? They're mostly sampling off her, and barely changing the synesthesia. So it's not as much of a conversation as it's supposed to be. Kind of like if she was talking and people kept asking her to talk more about her favorite subjects and retell her favorite jokes—she gets more attention but it encourages her to be less interesting."

Jak nodded. "How did you know that was what I was trying to figure out?"

"The way you kept scanning from screens to floor and back. Sesh used to be so graceful, creative, and clever— slec groups would beg her to attend because they loved sampling off her. Isn't it toktru strange that now that she has control, she makes herself duller?"

Jak's thoughts spiraled off; somehow it seemed to fit with Sesh's slow torment of Kawib and Seubla, and with how friendly and cheerful Psim was after having had his brother thrown to his death just weeks ago, and even with the way—

"Weehu, watch the King," Dujuv said.

King Scaboron was a small, slender man. He might have been a fencer or a gymnast in his youth, 150 years ago. He stood at the edge of the floor, watching his daughter mesh slec with Psim Cofinalez—they meshed well.

The King frowned, advanced onto the floor, and, to Jak's surprise, slowly swayed to the midbeat, the slowest at the moment. Scaboron glanced at a screen; he moved less tentatively, more firmly, he was definitely dancing now, and a green light went on as the low beat and the three high beats all began to sample off the King's motion. Sesh looked enraged for just an instant; Jak thought only he had seen it, until Dujuv whispered, "Well, *that's* precessed her."

"I don't think the King wants his heir interested in a Cofinalez," Jak murmured back. "They went to a lot of trouble—hell, *we* went to a lot of trouble—to prevent any possibility of a match. And she's definitely got the look for Psim."

Scaboron advanced slowly onto the floor, and the crowd parted around him. Behind him, a few of the older ladies followed, copying his moves, creating a kind of impromptu line. He danced seriously, precisely, never reaching beyond what his body could do, displaying his command of a farrago of the steps of the last two hundred years. Responding, the musician-engineers extended the synesthesia and opened its loops, adding dimensions and moving the quadratics into their period doubling and period quadrupling ranges.

The slec became more architectural, less tactile, the harmony more aggressive about its ambiguity. Chords marched through it in ranks of feeling, counterpoint congealing into alert flanking guards of meaning. The line behind King Scaboron formed a long spiral that turned toward the center. The timbre flavored its way through woodwinds and cymbals and then spiraled sideways into horns and bells. It wasn't slec as Jak had ever heard or seen it before, but it was beautiful.

Scaboron raised an arm, extending it toward Sesh. She ignored it, turned her back, and walked off the floor. She hurried, seeming on the edge of running.

In his left peripheral vision, something raced around the end of the curving staircase on which Jak stood.

The tail of a server's coat flickered past the farther newel, as the running man turned under the staircase.

When he had first arrived, Jak had noted without thinking that it was open down there. Before he dakked in words, Jak had jumped over the balustrade, turning to face the space under the stairs.

He misjudged slightly. As his feet planted, the running heet was off to Jak's left. The man whipped a small black globe up behind his ear.

Bomb.

Jak sidestepped left, foot closing to foot, not crossing, and as the ball of his right foot took his weight, the attacker's arm was already whipping forward, the globe moving with swift certainty from its spot by the man's ear toward the moment of release. Not more than five centimeters short of where the bomb would have been released, Jak's roundhouse kick lashed against the throwing arm, catching the assassin's carpal bone with the curl of Jak's big toe, making the throw go wild and the bomb sail all the way over the dance floor into the crowd beyond.

Jak cat-screamed as, on a polished floor in the one-third g of Greenworld, he felt his planted foot lose contact. His angular momentum carried him around. He would fall with his head in reach of his opponent's kick. He braced—

Dujuv landed beside him, slamming three hard blows into the stumbling assassin, shattering his ribcage and skull and breaking his neck. As Jak caught his balance, he heard the slec sound slew into a weird gabble as everyone on the dance floor moved at once and personal bodyguards rushed in from all sides. Then the slec chopped off all at once. One great gasp/shout from the whole crowd started—

The blast was deafening, but it was a smallish concussion bomb. As Jak rolled to his feet he thought, *Probably a diversion*—

A serving chef with a slug-thrower raced toward the dance floor. Jak sprang at him, trying to close the distance. The man turned. The gun came up at Jak.

With a familiar wild full-throated pulsating shriek, like a dinosaur on fire mixed with a monkey shaken to death, a white-and-black smear howled through Jak's vision, throwing the shattered and torn man sideways. Shadow on the Frost was getting into the fight.

Dujuv leapt, knocking a pistol out of another heet's hand. Bewildered, Jak looked around. Four attackers had rushed out of the kitchen just as the bomb burst. Hampered by the crowd, confused by the sudden appearance of a Rubahy and a panth at their rear, they were perhaps two steps slow, and all over the ballroom, personal bodyguards had time to get their principals down and under cover.

The two assassins still standing could not see their targets. Turning back to back, they looked around. Jak took two steps toward them.

Then Dujuv and Shadow, in tandem, bounded onto the two gunmen, arms and legs blurring in a furious assault, shattering faces, chests, and bellies with more than human speed and strength; both assassins were dead before they skidded backward onto the floor.

Most people were only becoming aware that anything had happened now that it was all over, screaming because they had turned to find the person beside them covered with blood, or torn open, or horribly burned.

The world almost came back to normal speed, before Jak heard Dujuv's battle-scream and the hiss of a laser burning flesh, just behind him. Jak rushed toward the sound, against a stampede of girls in long gowns. Dujuv stood in a clearing in the crowd, his hands locked in the kata juji jime grip, holding the dead man up by the neck. The dead man's head bobbled on his broken neck; Dujuv must have grabbed deep and put a lot of left hand pull into it.

"Duj, are you all right?"

His friend looked at him with a stricken, sick expression. "A lot of people were running around over here. I just happened to look when he did it. He must have been trying to use the crowd and the excitement to cover what he was doing. He just pulled out a military laser and shot her." Dujuv finally let go, absentmindedly; the corpse slid to the floor like a doll stuffed with wet sand.

"This is Xil Argenglass," one woman said. "I saw him with the laser too, but why would he do that? He's just a businessman with an import-export franchise. He's at all the parties because he has money, even though he's very dull—I guess that he won't be at any parties anymore—I mean, I don't think I should have said that, isn't there some rule about not saying bad things about dead people?—well, anyway, I don't know why he'd even be carrying a weapon, let alone—"

"Shut up, Ania," the heet beside her said. "I saw it too. We need to leave." They turned and went.

Jak looked up and saw that there was a body on the floor,

perhaps five meters beyond Dujuv, in a pale lavender dress—he ran.

Even with a two-finger-wide charred strip running from ear to ear across the bridge of her nose like a mask, black burned craters where her eyes had burst from the heat, the dead girl was still unmistakably Seubla.

Jak looked up from her, his eyes stinging with tears, hoping he would not have to be the one to tell Kawib, and saw Myx being loaded onto a gurney; when had all these medics come in? There must be twenty or so injured by the bomb and stray shots, and the ballroom was now flooded with medics. Myxenna's gurney bore the tag for a serious injury that had been stabilized; she'd be in the second group to go to the hospital.

Jak walked slowly toward her; Dujuv rushed past.

Myx was conscious. The way the blood-drenched sheet draped over the hash of her left leg indicated that she would be spending the next month in the regeneration tank. She nodded at Jak, then ran her hand over Dujuv's hairless head, tenderly, firmly, and said, "Look me in the eyes, Dujy. Don't look at my leg. Come on, Dujuv, up here, just look at my face. Poor old silly tove, this might be worse for you than it is for me, masen? The pain block is working, I can't feel it at all, toktru. Now, they're going to take *good* care of me, and I'll be *fine,* and you did your best. It's *not your fault.* All right?"

Dujuv's face was streaked with tears. "All right."

"Feel better?"

He nodded, unable to speak.

She touched his cheek, made eye contact, and said, very directly, "I am very pleased with you."

"Thank you." He sobbed, little squeaks as if he were being punched hard and fast in the belly.

Myxenna looked up at Jak. "He's a panth, Jak, he needs to know I'm grateful and pleased with him, otherwise he can get severely depressed or even suicidal. And you've been very good, Dujuv. Very, very good. I trust you and I know I can depend on you." She wiped his eyes with her hand.

Dujuv covered her small, delicate hand with his big square one, and pressed her palm against his cheek. "Thanks. So stupid, masen? I feel like a big dog. And you shouldn't be the one taking care of *me*."

"Not stupid at all, Dujy. It's all right. You saved me and a lot of people. And I *am* taken care of; I'm not in any danger now." She looked up at Jak again. "I saw Seubla fall. Is she—"

"Dead. I saw her die," Dujuv whispered. "I was only a step away from him. I'd seen him pull the weapon but I couldn't get there in time—"

"You did your best," Jak said, "and Dujuv, without you and Shadow, this would have been a massacre."

Robots grabbed Myxenna's gurney and wheeled her out. Dujuv stood there, still weeping and shaking, and Jak said, "Come on, we have to get ready to report. You were great, Duj. Absolutely the best there's ever been." He put his arm around his friend.

Dujuv dragged the back of a huge hand across his face, smearing tears most of the way around his bald head. "I appreciate how hard you're trying, but I'm going to feel like shit for a while, masen? It'll pass."

Shadow on the Frost stopped by. "Until the Duke is secure, I am not free, but I will visit as soon as I can. Dujuv Gonzawara, I earned glory here today merely by having helped you. You are a splendid warrior."

They stayed, not sure what else to do. Kawib came in,

learned it was true, and rushed off to see Seubla's body, and Xabo went with him, without giving them any further orders. Jak and Dujuv guided people to transportation, called ambulances, started a table of lost-and-found objects, made sure that the people who seemed to be in shock had someone to escort them home, and in general helped out like a couple of traffic cops. When almost everyone had gone except the pokheets, who seemed mostly to be standing in a circle asking each other if any of them had any ideas, a uniformed soldier from the Greenworld Army asked the two toves to follow him.

He led them to Colonel Mattanga's office. She sat behind the desk, face blank.

"First of all," Jak said, "we need to say how sorry we are about the loss of your daughter."

"I'm so sorry," Dujuv said. "I tried, but all I could do was avenge her."

The Colonel smiled, her eyes wet. "Thank you," she said, "but we have things to do before someone remembers to fire me. I have no living descendants and my line is barren." For a moment her lower lip trembled; she wiped her eyes and made herself go on. "The Karrinynya have no reason to fear me now, so I'm sure they won't be keeping me. At least it means no more having to do the best possible job to avoid suspicion.

"Now about your situation. We know that Scaboron was the main target, because thanks to your swift action, and that of Shadow on the Frost, we recovered much of the data from your opponents' purses before it could self-destruct. So my successor will be much better able to deliver a stern warning to the heir."

"So you speck Princess Shyf is behind this." Dujuv

didn't sound as if he wanted to argue; just as if he wanted things clear.

"Well, one death was planned and attempted tonight. One was opportunistic. Only one person would have profited by *both* deaths. That person walked out of danger less than ten seconds before the attack began. And, knowing about the major attempt, she might have whispered a hint to someone about a chance for the minor attempt, as well. That would be my thought about how things might have happened." Colonel Mattanga was reasoning just as Uncle Sib had taught Jak to do, the way he had studied at the Academy. His mind wanted to assent.

But his conditioning made him want to scream and slap Mattanga. He wanted to kick Kawib for making him care that Seubla was dead. He wanted to punch Dujuv for agreeing so readily. Most of all he wanted to cry in Sesh's arms because it was an evil world where his beautiful princess had to have blood on her hands. Not trusting himself to say anything, or even to react, he tried to sit perfectly still.

"Dujuv, you and I are in somewhat similar trouble. I still don't know how to thank you adequately, I admire you beyond all words—you did very well indeed—but I have to say that your bravery and coolness under fire is going to cost you dearly. Xil Argenglass, the man who killed my daughter and whom you killed, was an agent of Hive Intelligence."

"What? How could—why would *he*—?"

"Your intelligence service has a principle of 'assistance to a friendly monarch,' with which I'm sure you are familiar," Colonel Mattanga said. "Obviously, as long as they didn't get caught ordering it, Seubla's death was good for the Karrinynya. Now it will be blamed on a 'rogue' Hive agent, as will the assassination attempt, and you two will be heroes—also targets, for though Hive Intelligence will write off one stringer agent, the Princess will not so easily forgive the two of you for having foiled the assassination of Scaboron.

"We need to get you out of here. Myxenna should be safe—she didn't help save the King, just got into the line of fire. But I'm not going to have my job much longer, and Dujuv, you have done powerful people damage, which they must pretend was a favor—I can't imagine a more dangerous situation. Jak, you didn't actually kill a Hive agent but you were vital in foiling the assassination attempt, and you saw too much and know too much.

"So what we must do, before I'm discharged from this job, is get you both far away, giving everyone time and grounds to forgive and forget. I think I have an assignment that will work. Now, we have some private audiences tonight, first with the King, and then with the Duke. Do you have any questions?"

"I don't think so," Jak said. He swallowed hard. "You speck that Sesh—"

"Everyone knows that she's harsher than her father. The republican underground might try to kill *her,* but never him. There's a lot of hereditary enmity between Greenworld and Uranium, so I suppose it's possible that Duke Psim could have been responsible, but why try it on the one occasion on which he *doesn't* have an alibi? Theoretically it might have been one of the zybots, possibly Triangle One, or it might have been one of the other habitats on the Aerie, but that would be very high risk, for very little profit, for any of them.

"But the Princess has made it clear she despises the King. And he doesn't even try to conceal his distaste for her anymore. Had he been killed, she would have benefited greatly, and there would never have been any successful investigation.

"You know, Scaboron took the throne late in life—his older sister died childless—and he will be a short-running king for Greenworld, just twenty-eight years so far. Of my four children, now all killed by the Karrinynya, three died in unprovable murders (but murders nonetheless) during Scaboron's predecessor's reign. I cried when I found I was pregnant with Seubla. None of her siblings had lived to age six. And yet Scaboron somehow never felt it necessary to take Seubla from me. He has made me really, truly loyal to my King, against all others. After decades of intelligence work, I've known a lot about many high ranking aristos, and I know how unusual Scaboron is. I am afraid (for your sakes) that Shyf is a much more conventional princess."

"You continue to impress me," Psim Cofinalez said, "and so there's a small favor . . . I'm not sure whether it's one that I'm doing you, one that you're doing me, or just a set of favors. Shadow has become persona non grata. Again. If I understand correctly, he offended his own people by turning his status loss around so quickly that it became a kind of coup that he was felt not to have deserved. Or then again he may have scratched his butt with his left hand on Tuesday, thus humiliating his brother's cousin. I've known Rubahy all my life and I'll be damned if I can speck them.

"The important thing is that I can't take him with me on the rest of the Big Circuit; everywhere beyond here, he'd be liable to sudden assault by his enemies.

"So Shadow on the Frost is extremely welcome to reenlist in my Rubahy mercenaries, if he wishes, whenever I return to the lower solar system, and I'm sorry to lose him, but not as sorry as I would be if he were killed for some obscure reason.

"Now since Jak and Shadow have again fought together, and their oath-bond is thus fresh and renewed, and since it would be very acceptable—I also verified this with Shadow—for Shadow and Dujuv to also oath-bond with each other—"

"Highly acceptable to me, too," Dujuv said.

"I knew that without asking, but you're right. I should have asked. Time was short. At any rate, I propose to pay Shadow's salary to bodyguard either or both of you—it will be up to him to assess where he's most needed. That means he's employed, you stay alive, and it's less than pocket change to me."

"It sounds like a great idea," Jak and Dujuv said, simultaneously.

"Of course it's always awkward to thank anyone for saving one's life, now isn't it? And yet that does seem to be what I should do. So thank you for saving my life."

King Scaboron looked very much like his daughter would have, if she had been twelve centimeters shorter, her red hair dimming to gray, without tanpatterning, and with a small white goatee. He blathered on a while, particularly thanking Colonel Mattanga, which seemed to really precess Sesh; Jak dakked that Colonel Mattanga had called it singing-on—Sesh had been planning to get rid of Seubla's mother, now—and that the King's warm approval was going to delay matters.

"Well," the Colonel said, when the King had finished blathering, "I have a thought. We shouldn't waste resources like Jak and Dujuv just standing around the palace on guard duty. They have proved to be very effective, and already have experience operating independently, so I thought perhaps we might put them on the Mercury situation."

"By all means! The Mercury situation! The very thing!"

"Of course they may not achieve anything at all while they are there—the odds are against—"

"But you know, Colonel, we are so often reminded of Principle 181: 'Whether you succeed or not is not under your control, but whether you try is.' And I dare say that one reason for your choice might be that these two young men are, in your estimation, likely to succeed at resolving the Mercury situation?"

"I would say their odds are better than many others I could send."

"Well, then, the Mercury situation will be their first assignment. Excellent."

The King bowed, rose, and left, catching them all in midbow; Princess Shyf waited for them to get secure footing, collected a good graceful bow from all of them, and swept out. Jak had to admit that while she might not be the human being her father was—and he still missed the sweet girl he had thought he knew—she was very good at the royal and majestic side of things.

Afterward, Jak, Shadow, and Dujuv gathered with Mattanga at her office. She looked drawn and tired, near collapse. Jak asked, "What's the Mercury situation?"

"I was just about to tell you, and once I do, you'll know much more than the King. Since he actually didn't know anything about it but wasn't about to let anyone see that, suggesting it when I did assured us of his approval. It gets the two of you far away, and may help Greenworld.

"We can never afford even a fraction of the agents we need, and sometimes trouble breaks out in a place where it's been quiet for so long that all we have is a couple of stringers who send in a report every three months. Even a really vital interest like Mercury has to be neglected if you never have any trouble there."

Dujuv scratched his head. "This may sound stupid—"

"There are no stupid questions," she said, "only undiagnosed ninnies."

Dujuv laughed. "Thanks, I think. It's just, when I think of a place like Greenworld—all these parks and clear water and trees and so on—I wonder what you could need from Mercury, which is one big hot nasty slag heap."

"Greenworld's wealth is founded on solar power. Our biggest export, both manufacturing equipment and licensing patents. Solar power depends on weird, scarce metals that are easier to get from Mercury—strange stuff like yttrium and lutetium and actinium. You'd have to ask the engineers why they need all that stuff, or what they cook up from it, but it adds up to a lot of money through here, so when the engineers say they need two tons of terbium—that was an actual situation a couple of years ago—then we will get them two tons of terbium."

"And Mercury's the only place they have it?" Dujuv asked. "Sorry to keep asking questions that are probably turning me into a diagnosed ninny."

"It's the *cheap* source for most lanthanide and actinide metals. First of all it's easy to get at there—impacts and volcanism left the whole planet honeycombed with veins and splattered with drifts of hundreds of different ores, and then the Bombardment put a lot of deep fractures into that thin weak crust, creating even more pathways down to the core. The Rubahy attack probably did as much as four or five centuries of exploratory mining, in fact—we have a more complete map of what metals are where, for Mercury, than we do for any other planet, including Earth."

"Not our intention," Shadow on the Frost said, "but you're welcome to any good you got from it."

"Then it's cheap to extract the metal—there's more solar energy per square meter than on any other planet. *And* it's cheap to haul the metal once you extract it—very low delta v for escape, and all that solar power on the sails. Even if the whole solar system were one big free-trade zone or one big socialist economy, Mercury would still be our mining world."

"So the way the Mercurial miners get screwed is just sort of icing on the cake," Jak observed, remembering some Solar System Ethnography and only mildly horrified to realize it was useful.

" 'Getting screwed' is a little overdone," Mattanga said mildly. "Most of them are convicts or undesirables from around the solar system, so in the first place, they don't deserve much. Mercury has been settled for twelve hundred years out of the solar system's prisons, deadbeat bins, and welfare rolls, so, frankly, who cares? And in the second place, they screw themselves—that anarchist setup they insist on means a corporate free-for-all."

"Um," Jak said, "I don't know if they insist on it."

"Every time someone tries to set up a government on Mercury, the League of Polities pays a handful of mercenaries to organize the Mercurials themselves to overthrow it. That doesn't look like people who really want a government."

Jak was remembering that his test scores hadn't been very good in that area, so he nodded for her to go on. After all, he'd be there soon enough, and then he could have whatever opinions he wanted.

"Anyway," Mattanga said, "in the last few months, prices have gone up, quantities have gone down, a lot of our old suppliers won't talk to us at all, and we hear about sabotage, unsafe conditions, and a severe labor shortage. Some crime syndicate or zybot is organizing Mercury. It's not the workers. People who live in a scary environment like Mercury don't *do* sabotage.

"On the whole planet we've only ever really been able to afford three stringer agents. Just as the trouble started, two of them stopped reporting and became much wealthier—so we assume they were bought and turned. The third one is Kyffimna Eldothaler, of the Eldothaler Quacco, which works Crater Hamner. She's been sending us all sorts of wild tales—no wonder the opposition, whoever that is, left her on our side. She'll be the contact who picks you up but she won't be an asset; your job in part is to find out what the truth is, as opposed to what she's been sending us. Once you find out—act in our interests. It's not at all unlike the assignment Dean Caccitepe gave you." She smiled at their startled expressions. "Oh, yes, we've been in touch. We're old friends. We share a sense of humor, you know."

Jak suddenly saw a resemblance in the smile; he didn't care for it at all. But before he could feel really nervous, Mattanga turned to Dujuv and said, very quietly, "And by the way, for what it's worth—probably nothing—you made a friend tonight that you can never lose."

When they called the hospital, they learned that Myxenna would be unconscious for the next month, while they grew her a new left leg.

CHAPTER 9

Which One of Us Is the Princess Here?

Xabo said that Kawib was on leave for a few days. "He did say to thank you, Jak, for demonstrating that the RPG is not just the Rutty Princess's Gigolos, and as for Dujuv—well, he couldn't quite say, even to me, how much he thanks you."

"I just wish I'd done something effective," Dujuv said.

"You did. If you hadn't done that, Xil Argenglass would have spent the rest of his life collecting rewards. You put some justice into a universe where it's hard to come by. If you don't mind, I'd like to shake your hand."

That night, as Dujuv and Jak sat at dinner in the farmhouse restaurant in New Bethlehem, Dujuv said, "I'm not feeling very proud of being a wasp just now. 'Friendly monarch'—Shyf isn't anybody's friend except maybe her own. 'Assistance'? Murder. And that was a *wasp* that did that to her."

"It was quick," Jak pointed out, mildly.

"I can do all kinds of things quickly," Dujuv said, "leaving you as dead as Seubla. Would it be okay if I did?"

"I was looking for a good side."

"That's like looking for the straightforward side of Dean Caccitepe, or the chaste side of Myx, old tove. You can walk around in circles a long time but you're not finding it."

"Toktru. Sorry."

"Well, you saw what it did to her, and I don't care that it only hurt for an instant; that *had* to hurt, and for her mother and her mekko to see her like that . . . and like I said, that was done by a *wasp* as a favor to get in good *with a hereditary monarch*. Doesn't that seem to you like pretty weird behavior for the biggest republic in the solar system, the 'mother of republics'? The djeste makes me want to puke."

"Duj," Jak said, "you can get into incredible amounts of trouble for saying things like that."

"Is that what you're worrying about, Jak, or is it that you could get into trouble if you listened and didn't object?"

Jak had no reply.

That evening, as he walked his night patrol, Jak's sprite veered toward the Heir's Palace, and despite the beginnings of conditioned physical excitement, his stomach dropped to the ground. He felt as if he were about to attend a Christmas morning hanging, but as he neared the Palace, whether it was the sprite urging him on or his own mounting eagerness, he hurried more and more. When the door dilated in front of him and Sesh said "Come in," he was smiling despite himself. He stepped through.

His face stung and his ear rang with the force of her slap. The door shuttered closed behind him. She hit him again, backhand, her knuckles scraping across his face. She stood naked before him, a magnificently raging slim redheaded elf. "You stupid side of almost-attractive beef, I really ought to have you killed. You fuck competently, but your real talent seems to be with fucking things up."

Sesh grabbed him and gave him a long deep kiss. He had never felt so ill, or so aroused, before.

"See?" she said. "When the conditioning is fresh, you don't have any choice." She pulled his face down and kissed him again; his heart pounded and he felt more excited than ever. Then she pushed him away and slapped him. "You are *supposed* to be a Royal Palace Guard. Look good and do what I like. *You* had to jump in and be a hero and everything, and with your silly Disciplines, and your big stupid friend leaped right in and killed the only person in the room who was doing his job. And it might be a decade before I can try again."

Jak didn't know what to say, so he blurted out the only thought in his mind. "But he's your father. And he seems like a kind person . . ." He barely avoided voicing *kinder than you*.

" 'Kind!' That's all I hear about him. Kind, kind, kind. He acts like he wants to end up in the official history as Scaboron the Kind! Let me tell you that I feel a lot more for my old nurses and bodyguards than I'm ever going to feel for that silly stupid old sentimental gwont. He actually believes in all that 'Make sure you appear to deserve your privileges' crap."

In the middle of it all, Jak felt a remote shock because "Make sure you appear to deserve your privileges" was Principle 133, and although he himself never felt much about the Principles, he felt vulnerable and frightened about people who could mock them or repudiate them. Perhaps it was what Nakasen had said in Principle 163, "If you are a thief, always make sure you have good locks, because being robbed will really upset you."

She must have mistaken hesitation for judgment. She added, "Grow up, Jak. This is how the aristos live and die, and it's how it has to be. When I think about what that old fool has done to Greenworld—we have peacekeeping forces in fifteen nations, and relief and reconstruction workers everywhere, and useless people on science scholarships at a dozen useless institutions, and at the same time the Royal Palace is turning into a fuddy old *ruin,* and Greenworld hasn't been on any media or party circuit for so long that no one even remembers when it last was, and there's no style and no sense of place and *nothing* happening here. And all that stuff he does just encourages the republicans, which costs us a fortune in secret police. When I take over, things in the Palace will be *gorgeous,* media will *swarm,* every hot artist will *die* to be here, and there's going to be such a thing as Greenworld *style!* And it will be so easy to do!

"I just feel myself so bursting with pride and energy and *life.* And that ... old ... tired ... *kind* gwont just sits around *being* loved while all my energy is waiting to *do* things! If aristos aren't fierce and wild and terrible, what's the point of being us? We don't live like ordinary people, we take what we want when we want it, and you know we don't fuck likc ordinary people, and if the major thing we die of is predation on each other, well, that's just part of it." She breathed on him and said, "Here, I've had a fresh squirt of the pheromone maker. Feel my breath on your face ... smell me ... deep breath, deep breath ... take off your clothes."

He had never felt his heart melt like this before. They stood together, naked but for their purses. The lightest touch of her index finger relaxed his jaw. He was aware that in the deep kiss she was breathing pheromones into him; he was also aware that gravity keeps the planets in place, and that he didn't much like asparagus, and all those facts were equally irrelevant.

When she finished the kiss, he was warm, tingling, crazy

in love. Tears ran down his face. She was so beautiful and he was so unworthy. "Now," she said, "I'm a tender little scared virgin. Teach me gently and make it good."

An hour later, when she had finally had enough, she rolled over and said, "All right, no more hard, stop being interested."

He could not have felt more cold and sick if he had awakened in the middle of sex with a corpse.

"Calm love." She hadn't used that command before. An entirely convincing peace settled over him. "Lie on your back. I want to use your shoulder for a pillow, and I want to talk. Listen to me and comfort me."

His arm knew how to hold Sesh, but his heart did not know how to see her. She sighed, snuggled, and said, "My stupid worthless father insisted on making me go to school with the 'real' kids. Like I was virtual or something. Like being real would rub off on me. Like I would want to be 'real' if I could."

She turned further into Jak's shoulder; her hand lightly stroked his chest. "Everything was a fake, of course. My father is stupid and gets brainlocked on weird ideas but he isn't so stupid that he trusts to reality or to chance. So of course he had it faked up to make it come out right, and I have to say he did a good job. He hired Circle Four, your uncle and his people, to not only watch over me and guard me, but to arrange for experiences for me. They picked Myxenna as my best friend, and set it up for me to run into you and lose my virginity to a tender, awkward, good-looking goof, good-hearted and smart but not too smart, so I could do all the nicey-nicey romance stuff."

Jak tried to say, *Even if they did bring us together, I still loved you for real.* He could think it just fine, but apparently her last command wasn't going to let him talk. He knew he felt differently, but all he could do was lie there and gently stroke her back and listen.

"They really picked you well, too. Pretty much the way they pick out a plush toy for babies—*do his button eyes pop off?, does he have any toxic paint?, is he a possible reservoir of streptococcus?* You never gave me one moment of teenage heartache, and I got to do all that adolescent lovey-stuff really sincerely—I fell for it myself from time to time—and I learned how to get a heet to love me. Half the RPGs don't really need conditioning anymore, because they've had enough of the big sincere eyes and the sweet trembly lip and the little wrinkles in my nose when I smile, all the things I've learned to do that are sort of the relationship-equivalent of sucking in your gut and sticking out your tits, and they're toktru never going to love anyone else. And it worked on me too, you know, unlike other aristos, I really enjoy this kind of super-soft romantic sex—it does so much with such a limited range."

Jak tried to speak again, and this time—apparently because he wasn't contradicting her—it was possible.

"Doesn't it get lonely?"

"Yes and no. Poor pathetic stupid Seubla depended on that, you know; she kept working really hard at being my best friend, partly to save her own life and partly because she thought that since I was cruel I must be lonely, so if she fixed the loneliness maybe I'd be less cruel. And I have to admit, she was a good listener and very nice to me when I didn't deserve it. I really did get in the habit of turning to her for comfort, and I'll be much lonelier now that she's dead." She rolled even closer, brushing her lips on Jak's chest muscles, and whispered, "You feel so sorry for me having lost my friend."

To his horror and disgust, Jak did. But he couldn't move

away. He went on stroking Sesh's hair and holding her while she told him two or three stories about Seubla's kindness and generosity, and even left a little tear on his chest about the dead girl.

"You see," she said, finally, "I can get all the tenderness and kindness and gentle love I want. And I can enjoy it. This has been just lovely, and now I shall have a pleasant, deep night's sleep, and be all ready to get on with my busy life. My father was almost right about this 'real love' stuff, you know. It *is* better for me. It's sort of like fresh-squeezed pure cold orange juice after a day of nothing but screwdrivers." She snuggled, rubbed her face on him. "You smell good; it's all that staying in shape. Aristocratic boys never do. I can feel you wanting to ask something."

He felt the little mental release and said, "*Almost right* about love? What was your father wrong about?"

"Well," Sesh said, "sometimes it hurts a little bit, and you feel a little sorry, and that's inconvenient. But as long as I can get as much real love as I want, it's only a little inconvenient. I can just call someone in and get real love from him, and no matter what the matter was, soon I'm all better." She pushed herself up with her hand. "I just bet you're resenting every moment of my telling you all this."

"Uh, yeah."

"See, I know you perfectly. Just like being your demmy again." Sesh snuggled closer.

"But it's not the same for me."

She laughed. "It's not the same for *you*."

"That's what I said."

She laughed again. "And which one of us is the princess, here? All right, I want a long comfy sleep now. *Numb. Dress. Back to the barracks.*"

Numbly, Jak reached for his tunic.

*   *   *

When Jak walked into the main office at the barracks to check out, he was tired, sore, loathing himself, and looking forward to a hot shower. He planned to scour till his skin came off, and scream a few times with the roaring water to mask it.

In the office, Xabo and Dujuv were huddled in an intense conversation. They both looked up, startled, and Xabo said "Oh, well, we can settle it now, I guess," in that flip tone of voice that he used to tell the world that something didn't concern him—especially when it was ripping his heart into gory shreds.

"Something important?" Jak asked.

"Xabo's trying to convince me that it's nothing, and I'd like to convince myself. Does Mreek Sinda mean anything to you, is there anything special about her to you?" Dujuv asked the question very seriously.

"Well, she did that embarrassing documentary about me after that time we rescued the Princess, so I had three interviews with her then. There's that. She came in and asked a bunch of rude questions at the restaurant, that time you were there. And Princess Shyf made me do a blah, nothing interview with her early on at the ball, last night. That's all I can think of. Why?"

Dujuv nodded and said, "Can we dismiss early? I'd rather talk with Jak about this privately."

"You're clear." Xabo looked up and said, "And Dujuv, try to remember that Jak hasn't been talking about this for the last couple of hours. He's a little behind you, masen?"

"Thanks, tove. You're right."

Out in the corridor, Jak wanted to ask *What?* but he could tell that Dujuv would not talk until they had privacy. So he followed his panth friend as they hurried down the hallway; Dujuv, too antsy to hold still, leapt up and down, constantly, turning big somersaults in the air, rising high enough to plant his feet on the ceiling with each one. Jak wished he could tease Dujuv about that.

In the dorm room, Dujuv lifted his left hand and spoke to his purse. "Selection specified, play it for Jak, on the room projectors."

The lights dimmed and the image of Mreek Sinda appeared on the wall, sitting at the traditional anchor-desk with the traditional smile. Her clothing wasn't quite so traditional—it looked like she was planning to go out to a sex club after the broadcast—but it certainly worked for her.

Words swam into focus in the corner to the left of her head. "The Perils of the Princess."

"Oh, no," Jak said, and sat on Dujuv's bed, putting his head down between his hands. "Oh no, oh no, oh no."

"Listen to it all," Dujuv said, flatly, anger leaking around the edges of his voice. "Start again at the beginning," he added to his purse. "Jak, you have to look up at this one and listen, because whether you like it or not you're going to hear a lot about it for a while."

"Okay, but please, Duj, please—" His tove's expression was implacable. "Oh, all right, roll it."

Sinda's piece told the story of how Princess Shyf of Greenworld had summoned her knight/protector, the boy who loved her when she was just an ordinary girl, to deal with a mystery menace. That was bad enough, but when the story reached the subject of the assassination attempt at the ball, the last tenuous touch with reality parted like overcooked spaghetti used as parachute lines. According to her account, Jak's brilliant detective work, superb Disciplines skills, and sheer courage had foiled the assassination attempt single-handedly.

Then there were three one-minute spots in which Jak bragged about it all and sounded like the most arrogant gweetz ever to pull on pants.

Jak was all but screaming with rage. "I never! I never said—she interviewed me before, not after! This isn't me!"

Dujuv said, neutrally, "Well, Jak, we both know it's possible for things like this to be faked. The one with Sesh inviting us was faked—"

"And this is much shorter than Sesh's message! Of *course* it was faked, Dujuv, I wouldn't *do* that to a friend—let alone be so stupid—there must be a thousand witnesses!"

"That's what Xabo was trying to tell me." Dujuv didn't look up, watching his hands squeeze each other in his lap.

Jak took a deep breath and looked at his friend. "That must not have settled it."

"No, it didn't. Jak, all I see is that everything always turns out so well for you, and I always seem to be the passenger in the process. If not the servant." Dujuv pressed the button to dilate the door, and wordlessly gestured for Jak to leave.

The next time Jak and Dujuv saw each other was two days later, when they were summoned to Mattanga's office. Colonel Mattanga seemed to know something; she had set their chairs with a tea service between. When she had poured, she began without preamble, "We've gotten passage for you two, and for Shadow on the Frost, on a sunclipper downbound to Mercury. Closest approach will be in twenty-two hours, so you need to get packed and ready. It's a sunclipper that Jak, at least, should be familiar with, since he once shipped on it—the *Spirit of Singing Port*."

"Yeah!" Dujuv said. "Oh, yeah." He bounced up and

turned a quick backflip, as he often did when he was excited.

"Oh, you know the ship, too?"

Jak was grinning at least as broadly. "We both have a lot of friends on the *Spirit*. It's a fine ship. Any chance of getting CUPV berths for the trip?"

"Of course." Mattanga smiled. "I signed both of you and Shadow on the Frost as CUPVs. I knew it was what you all preferred."

"This is great," Jak said, "the first good news in a long time."

"Fine. Here are the details—" A cover story had been established for them as the kind of seditionists the Hive preferred to ship into exile.

They dropped by Xabo's office to muster out. "All right, you're off the duty roster, officially inactive, and on your way. Best of luck. I wish we'd met when we could have been better toves."

Duj nodded and said, "We could have met at a better time, but you couldn't have been a better tove."

"Aw, quit the sentiment, you'll make me cry," Xabo said, trying for sarcasm and toktru not succeeding.

A whirling belt of superconductor, forming a loop hundreds of kilometers wide and moving at ten kilometers per second, would have made a tremendous gyroscope which would have fought against the Aerie's necessary constant precession, so a loop would have cost a fortune in energy. Instead the Aerie had a twenty thousand kilometer strip of superconducting loop material, about five centimeters across, with one end at the docking body and the other pulled constantly outward by a small stabilization-and-propulsion module. It was purely a launch device; arriving

craft came through the big doors on the docking body to
land on linducer tracks, as *Up Yours* had.

Boarding the ferry, however, was exactly like boarding
every other ferry in the solar system. "Attention all passengers. Boarding for the ferry to the *Spirit of Singing Port*
commences immediately. Repeat, boarding for the ferry to
the *Spirit of Singing Port* commences immediately. Launch
in seven minutes forty seconds. Please advance through the
boarding doors at once."

Shadow, Jak, and Dujuv airswam through the dilating
door in the side of the little ferry, only about five times the
size of the hopper, just a metal can with windows and cameras, linducer, fuel tanks, a hot jet cluster on one end and
cold jet nozzles all over. They strapped in, and the door
closed, but it redilated just an instant later.

The late passenger who airswam in was Mreek Sinda,
towing two extra cargo bags and two jumpies. She hurried
to secure baggage and strap in before launch. Just as she
strapped in, the tractor platform carried them into the big
airlock.

The inner door closed behind them. With a strange shim-
mer, air left the surrounding chamber. A mechanical voice
said, "Vacuum tight, power systems good, all systems go."
The outer doors dilated. The tractor platform slid forward
again. The craft rolled 180 degrees as it matched up the linducer grapple with the tube.

They were launching away from the sun, and from Jak's
viewport, three of the arms of the Aerie were visible, each
a long string of habitats reaching far out into the starry sky.
In the forward camera, the *Spirit of Singing Port* was now
fully in view, and with her vast shining sails, a mere few
hundred molecules thick but with as much surface area as
Earth, Venus, and Mars put together, now only about half a

million kilometers away, she covered much of the sky with graceful bright arcs and curves.

They accelerated through twenty thousand kilometers (two-thirds again the diameter of the Earth) at about a half g, going from the docking body to the end of the line in barely over forty-five minutes. The effect of continuous acceleration was that they seemed to creep along at first as the early habitats went by; it took them eight minutes to get as far out as the innermost habitats, but they flashed past the last ones at the thirty-sixth minute, moving at many times the speed of a bullet. After a five last minutes in which they traveled the diameter of Mars, the hot jets flared, the linducer grapple released, and they shot into space.

The hot jets fired three bursts of a few seconds each, putting the ferry on trajectory to intercept the sunclipper, and cut out. All onboard gravity ceased. The mechanical voice announced that about ten hours of free fall could be expected, a very short ferry flight. The upbound ferry and the downbound ship were in virtually head-on courses, and the distance—only about twice that from the Earth to the Moon—would close very quickly.

On the other hand, ten hours might be a short ferry flight, but it was a very long time to be trapped in a metal box with Mreek Sinda, especially when there were far more interesting things in every screen and window. From the sunward side the *Spirit of Singing Port* was almost too bright to look at; drag-tacking, as she was doing right now to drop into Mercury's much lower orbit, the ship had dozens of Asia-or-bigger-sized mainsails spread with hundreds of droguettes, prabs, funnels, and tripos in wild profusion; the smallest prab merely about the area of Greenland, the largest mainsail bigger than the Pacific Ocean, all woven of stuff that was bright as a mirror, less than one-ten-thousandth the thickness of sandwich wrap, and stronger than steel plate. Reflections of the sun danced off all the sails, bright as the original, and in the gentle ripples and waves that ceaselessly played across the sails, sunlight and starlight in sudden, bright, moving curves that briefly formed recurving circles, s-shapes, and bows. Now and again the Aerie itself reflected in the sails.

After about an hour, Mreek Sinda cleared her throat. "I think I'd be remiss in my duty if I didn't at least try to interview the three of you while we're all trapped here." They were in free fall, now, all drifting around the small ferry cabin. Camera drones circled Jak and Sinda.

" 'Trapped' is the word," Jak agreed. "First of all I have a question for you. Why did you make me look like the biggest gweetz in the solar system? Especially when there are literally hundreds of witnesses to contradict that silly story you had coming out of my mouth? You made me look like a liar and a braggart and a complete idiot! *Why?!*"

"The camera sees what the camera sees," Sinda said. She had smiled as if dealing with a four-year-old throwing a tantrum.

Jak gaped at her, his outrage an aphasic spike pinning his jaws closed; he glanced at Dujuv, who was pretending to be fascinated by something out the window.

"I did not say any of those things," Jak finally managed to sputter, and somehow he sounded like a liar even to himself, even knowing that it was perfectly true. "I didn't say any of them. You or your accesscaster or somebody made all of that up, and created an interview where there wasn't one, and I want to know why. Why did you do that to me? You've made me out to be a bragging lying fool and cost me the trust of many friends and I want to know why. That's what the question is."

Sinda shrugged. "If you didn't want me to put it out on the nets, why did you talk to me? With that poor girl hardly cold yet—and away from your duty station—you were right outside the hall telling me everything. Check the background of the shots and you'll be able to see that it must have been less than ten minutes after the assassination attempt. In fact—"

She touched her purse and said, "Cue up the lead in from the ball for the Duke of Uranium, post major event, outside the Great Hall doors, Royal Palace, Greenworld. Project on inboard system if they'll give you access—"

"Got the clip, got access," her purse said. It had a very resonant baritone, like the second lead in a romantic-adventure viv. "Here it is—projecting."

The screen formed on a blank wall; the image was sharp and clear, as might be expected with top-of-the-line media gear, showing the crush of celeb-watchers, people who collected sightings of the famous, just outside the main doors. The muffled thud of the bomb, the pistol shots, and the weird veering of the slec only took half a minute before the shrieks and screaming started. (It had seemed like forever while it was happening.) The crowd of celeb-watchers swarmed toward the doors like vampires around a hemophiliac. Royal Palace Guards at the door were reinforced by regular troops as the concealed doors and vomitoria dilated all over the front of the building.

A side door, barely in the frame, opened a crack, and Jak saw himself emerge, look around, look toward the camera, fix his gaze, and run forward, waving a hand. "Mreek Sinda! Mreek Sinda! I need you to interview me right away!"

"Now, are you going to say that that didn't happen?" Sinda demanded.

"I did not do that! I was right in there in the hall with Dujuv and Shadow and several hundred witnesses, and I didn't leave till hours later when Xabo officially released us. I don't think I was ever out of sight of either of my toves here, and I know plenty of people saw me."

"Do you have any idea how unreliable an eyewitness is?"

"Ahem," Shadow said. "I—er, Jak, I wish I could completely confirm your whereabouts, but as you know I was engaged in ending threats to the Duke, and that was where all my focus was. And I rather suspect that Dujuv was in a similar situation."

"I was," Dujuv said.

"I couldn't possibly have had time to slip out during the fight," Jak said. "Remember, I tripped up the one with the bomb, and then I was in it until you two took out the gunmen. I was never more than ten steps away from either of you. Dujuv, I could not have run outside and done an interview, not and been right back at your side when we were dealing with poor Seubla."

"I still don't see why you gave an interview if you didn't want it accesscast," Sinda said. "But since you're acting irrationally, I'm going to invoke my media privileges under the safe-conduct treaties, because I don't want to be harassed while I'm doing my job. If you try to approach me or speak to me I'll swear out a formal complaint. When I want another interview, I'll talk to you. Till then, don't approach."

Jak wanted to say something, but he felt his tove's hand over his mouth. "I don't know who's telling the truth," Dujuv said, "but even if you are a liar—and you might be (I guess)—then I'd rather not have my pizo go to jail."

The rest of the trip was uneventful; conversation was

only about the occasional glimpses of interesting things in the sky, backward glances at the Aerie, a moment when the Hive and Earth passed in near conjunction, and the distant view of the outward bound *Serendipity of Alpha Draconis,* a Rubahy sunclipper making the long run from Mercury and Venus back to Pluto. "I have cousins aboard her," Shadow said, "but then there are so few of us, and we have been isolated for so long, that it is hardly possible for ten Rubahy to gather without there being cousins present." He stared at the bright curves and bows in the viewport, very quietly, for a long time.

Dujuv asked, "Do you wish you were on it?"

"At least four of the crew would gain great honor by assassinating me," Shadow on the Frost said, "but if you mean, do I long for home? Well, I long for many of the people there. Eventually these problems of honor and precedence and so on will work out, but just now, it seems so very long until I can be out working the lines, every day for three years, upward into the dark, feeling that every time I turn a wrench, set a dial, or read a needle, we sail a little closer to home. There is a poet of ours who speaks of the three-year homeward journey of a Rubahy sunclipper from Mercury to Pluto." He whistled a short passage; it was melodic and sad, with an odd, perky lilt in the last few notes. "Translated into your words, it would be:

> *A year. Sol gutters to a bright star.*
> *A year. Empty dark between steel stars.*
> *A year. Dim snowy globe. Oaths kept. Home.*

"But I am told that our poetry says nothing to you, so enough of this. I shall talk myself into depression, which is bad for reflexes and alertness, and that in turn is bad for survival."

"I do hope you find your way home, old tove," Dujuv said.

As they approached the *Spirit of Singing Port,* the vast sunclipper filled almost 180 degrees of their vision. Sails, lines, and all spread for tacking, the ship was over sixteen thousand kilometers wide at its widest point, and almost ten thousand kilometers long from its outermost tripo to the tip of the trailing heat exchanger.

In all of that, it was hard to see the little glittering star of the one-kilometer-wide metal sphere where several thousand crewies, men, women, and children, lived their whole lives. Solar sails are fast but not powerful, and all that vast microns-thick spread of sail was only to drive that little ball, barely a kilometer across. The sky was filled with the sails, but the home of twenty-five hundred crew would barely be visible until they were nearly there.

Presently the mechanical voice asked them to strap in, and they did. After some minutes the little ferry jumped sideways, then up toward their heads, then back, a kickboxer's footwork. The accelerations were brief and small, not more than ten seconds or a quarter g.

The ship proper was now a dark circle about the diameter of a pencil at arm's length. Neither Jak's viewport nor any of the screens showed the ribbon of the sunclipper's loop until they aligned. Half a minute before coupling, their seats began to rotate and extend under them so that they could take the coming acceleration fully supported, lying on their backs.

One view camera switched to a close-up and Jak saw the linducer grapple grab the loop. The instant it closed, four g slammed him down against the padding of his seat. He could have raised an arm only with difficulty, and breathing was a struggle. He relaxed and let his breath woof out, knowing it wouldn't be long.

The linducer grapple pulled mightily against the loop, which whirled halfway round the thirty-kilometer circle in less than a minute, bringing their velocity to zero relative to the ship. The grapple let go, the acceleration stopped as if turned off by a switch, and they floated weightlessly into the *Spirit*'s receiving dock. "Everyone on board will deboard *now*," the automatic voice said. "Relaunch is in six minutes twenty-nine seconds, repeat six minutes twenty-nine, from *now*. Everyone off *now*."

Jak slung his jumpie on and airswam forward through the hatch into the flextunnel to the ship's receiving bay. In the big airlock, a DNA reader scraped the inside of his arm and turned green when it confirmed his identity.

He airswam through the inner hatch and was wrapped in a twining human body, tumbling in midair. A hot face pressed against his and then a warm tongue was in his mouth, thrusting deep, and the girl's mouth against his softened and opened further as he responded. The kiss might have gone even longer if in their tumbling Jak's back hadn't finally bumped against the wall, jarring them from each other. As they came up for air, Jak looked into the familiar big dark eyes with a slight epicanthic fold, and the delicate features in soft cocoa skin framed by short coppery hair. "Well, hi, there, Phrysaba."

" 'Well, hi, there.' What do I have to do to get some enthusiasm? Eat your head?" Her eyes were twinkling with pleasure. She still had a smile that could grab Jak by the heart and squeeze till he thought it might pop.

Jak became aware that something was buzzing around him in a cloud—Mreek Sinda's drones were swirling around them. One was shooting a close-up of Phrysaba's breast, three of her buttocks. Beyond the tiny flying cameras, he saw Dujuv laughing madly and hanging on to Shadow, who was making the resonant bloop-and-tang noise that was Rubahy laughter.

He looked a little to the side, where something else was moving; it was Phrysaba's brother, Piaro, Jak's oldest tove on the ship, and beside him, Pabrino Prudent-Reckoner, a brilliant younger heet of whom Jak was very fond, and who seemed to have grown about a head in height since Jak had seen him last. Piaro was grinning broadly and said, "I hope you won't expect everyone to welcome you the way my sister does." Pabrino smiled at that, but seemed quiet and thoughtful.

Then Mreek Sinda loudly said, "So how does this affect your relationship with Her Utmost Grace Shyf?"

Jak looked very, very seriously at the camera nearest him and said, with undisguised deep passion,

> *Mary had a little duck,*
> *She kept it in her bed,*
> *And everyone—*

Sinda made an annoyed noise; the drones flitted back into her bag as she demanded that someone show her the way to her stateroom.

"Nobody appreciates art anymore," Jak said, and Dujuv smiled at that and said, "Toktru." Jak was happy just to be where he was, for the first time in a long time.

CHAPTER 10

About Fourth-Level Famous, for Free

Jak, Shadow, and Dujuv had all CUPVed on a sunclipper before, Shadow most of all. Dujuv started off replacing panels in the auxiliary propulsion tubes, grumbling amiably that it was just like being back in the Spatial, but after three days he was rotated to the reactor room to broaden his experience. Jak started outside in the rigging, doing the never-ending untangling, separating, and mending of lines; it was challenging work, moderately dangerous because monosil cables were so fine that they could sever a limb with very little force. Shadow, with much more experience—he was a proficient astrogator, and he always traveled as a CUPV on his many voyages—worked in the worryball.

In between CUPV duties, there were the endless amusements of shipboard social life: games and sports plus all the passionate little clubs that followed opera, or flatscreen film, or poetry, or anything that could be something to talk about. Dujuv, with few people around who could really give him a workout at any sport, was in danger of boredom for a day or two until Phrysaba invited him into the Ancient Languages Club, which was just starting a project of reading Late Medieval and early space-era Mexican poetry;

soon he was constantly practicing his Spanish, murmuring back and forth to his purse.

Shadow was fond of chess, poker, and go. The Rubahy approach was different from the human, which made it more interesting to play each other, the Rubahy trying to grasp why humans disliked purely ground-taking go, or emphasized bluffing, the humans trying to dak why the Rubahy so valued knights, and what they meant by the "rhythmic backflow" of a hand.

When he wasn't with Phrysaba, who seemed to want to spend all of their time together just chatting and making love, Jak spent as much time as he could at Disciplines katas, performed while interacting with viv. The Disciplines were the climax of a story at least two thousand years long, the story of how humans became fighters, through a progress from necessity to raw sport to refined art to interactive game and finally to a True Way (in the sense of Principle 158: "Respect every True Way, but not because it is a True Way; distrust every True Way but keep in mind that it may be a True Way"). They were endlessly time-consuming and fascinating, and Jak had been introduced to them young enough to have no memory of having resisted them.

Each blow, stroke, shot, throw, block, or burn was executed seven times on each side; for each, your fist, foot, blade, elbow, knee, forehead, pistol, or other weapon must be exactly on trajectory, or in your viv goggles the out-of-place, off-target parts of your body would glow, in colors for which direction you were off spatially, the brightness indicating the error in timing. About half of the time, now, Jak could get all the way through the Disciplines, 1,918 attacks beginning with a left jab at the larynx and finishing with a right backhand diagonal eye-to-ankle burn, covering unarmed, short blade, long blade, slug thrower, and beam combat, in about an hour, attacking slightly slower than once every two seconds, with his virtual body black the whole way.

Of course his only serious, trained opponent—Bex Riveroma—in his only real fight, ever, had wanged the living shit out of Jak. And no matter how many times Jak dove into the Disciplines, or how attentively he tried to work the katas, or how passionately he pursued them, he could not seem to defeat that horrible Sesh-craving. His ache for the Princess was a screaming monkey that sat by his side when he meditated, chattered in his ear while he warmed up, shrieked at him all through the katas, and seized his attention again, undiminished, the moment that he dragged his exhausted body out of the centrifuge and to the showers; compared to the challenge of shutting that out, Bex Riveroma had been a teddy bear.

On his first day off, as Jak was just stuffing his fighting suit into his bag to head for the gym, Pabrino dropped by. Pabrino was eighteen, a skinny young heet who would be handsome as soon as he filled out and added some grace to his height—a potential Great Master, or even higher, at Maniples. A couple of years ago when Jak had played him, it had been grotesquely unequal; within a year, before he turned seventeen, Pabrino had been declared a full Master, and there was talk of his being a Great Master within the next year.

Jak had assumed Pabrino would not want to play with him for the same reason that Jak didn't want to play Scrabble against a hamster. But Pabrino arrived with viv sets ready to go, and a room already rented, and said, "I know this is short notice but I just got dismissed from a shift early, and I was thinking maybe we could play."

"Sure, if you don't mind my being totally inept."

"You're epter than anybody else on the ship right now is ept, pizo, except Shadow, and I need a tune-up against someone human. We'll be in Mercury orbit for six weeks, and I'm playing a dozen Masters, two of them Great Masters, with maybe even an exhibition match against a retired Greater Master. And I was looking at your numbers from your last season for PSA. Your game is a lot better than it was when we played before. Now, do I get a friendly match with an old pizo?"

"Absolutely of course, toktru."

Every few hundred years human culture seemed to spontaneously generate a game with no known author, limitless challenges, and an odd combination of extreme simplicity in concept with a complexity in execution that would baffle any but the finest minds. Chess, bridge, go, and belludi had each been such; Maniples was the latest, if you could call a six-hundred-year history "latest." It was nominally a battle between two equal sides over a Mars-sized planet with a randomly chosen configuration of exactly equal land and water, using the forces a minor military power might have on hand. Of course there were no known actual empty planets like the one fought over, any more than there were perfectly level battlefields without cover as there were in chess and go, or perfectly competitive markets as in belludi.

In Maniples, when combat occurred between pieces, the circumstances of the combat were determined by the play up to that moment, but the combat itself was fought as a duel in viv. A player with combat skills might, on occasion, fight off an ambush, or make a less than sterling set of moves come out right, against a weaker combatant.

The match puzzled Jak. He won the coin flip and started, as Green, with Pabrino playing Black. Pabrino's opening game was clearly not about winning; his adroit fakes and sudden reversals were built around very unfavorable sacrifice ratios, so that he stripped Jak of all his major pieces (except the battlestation, which was the equivalent of the king in chess), but left Jak with large advantages in B&Es and submersible aircraft, plus one warshuttle (of the nine he began with) still remaining.

Clearly Pabrino was so far ahead of Jak that he was just playing with him, but there had to be some point to the play; the younger man was not the sort of egomaniac who would be doing all this just to show that he could. Jak was supposed to do something; the standard thing to do at this point would be to resign, but they were only twenty minutes into the game.

Well, the first rule of any competition is that you work with what you have; no point wishing to be a genius at Maniples, any more than to wish for longer arms to box with or bigger lungs to run with. Unable to concentrate on a few big pieces that would take the lead for and in turn be supported by the small ones, Jak fragmented his forces further and approached things in the spirit of Principle 22: "In conflict, if you are the flea, do what harm you can; if you are the dog, scratch no harder than necessary."

Jak's Green B&Es strapped on their missiles or bombs, got on their little transport craft, and began trying to filter across the planet's surface into Black territory. His aircraft popped low when they flew, just enough to scout, staying submerged most of the time. Quietly, as his scouts developed a picture of a major attack shaping up in the northeastern quadrisphere, Jak moved his battlestation, so that the attack would be exposed about ten minutes before it expected to be, and prepared his warshuttle to pop over the horizon 180 degrees away. It was always possible that one of his smaller units might get a chance to lock a missile on to the Black battlestation, the move that ended the game.

His forward B&Es moved farther into the northeastern quadrisphere, and at a cost of three beanies sent in on suicide LRPs, found the main concentration of Pabrino's forces, right where Jak had guessed they might be, starting to move. He sent every other beanie within reach forward, tasking each of them to do as much harm as possible. Almost immediately one of them nailed a low-passing Black orbicruiser with a surprise missile hit.

Meanwhile Jak's battlestation descended ever lower, well below synchronous orbit, heading northeast. Then Jak was tied up in viv combat for a while; he and Pabrino fought a dozen small combats as Jak's B&Es and submersible aircraft covered Pabrino's forces with pinprick attacks.

Since Jak was always attacking with low-value forces, the exchange was almost always in his favor on paper— each attacking beanie or submersible aircraft cost Pabrino far more than their nominal worth, just as if Jak had been playing chess with nothing but pawns and Pabrino had had nothing but rooks. But since every attack amounted to a suicide attack, and low-valued forces were all Jak had, this couldn't go on long. Still, Pabrino's forces were in very satisfactory disarray when Jak's battlestation cleared the horizon, and, a whole planet away, Jak also launched his warshuttle.

The battlestation put a gratifying amount of fire all over Pabrino's scattered forces, and his matériel losses were huge. But then Jak's sneak attack warshuttle was pounced on by a waiting Black orbicruiser, and three man-carried missiles, sitting quietly in concealed forward positions, locked on his battlestation. The game was over, with another win for Pabrino.

As they pulled off their viv helmets, Jak saw that his tove was panting, sweaty, and pale. "Are you all right?"

"You nearly had me. That was magnificent, Jak. Just what I needed. You're pretty amazing—I knew I could count on you but I didn't know how much."

"Count on me for what?"

"To improvise well." Pabrino bent over and rested his hands on his knees, sucking in more cool air. "Maniples has gotten stale, pizo. I know that, even if most of the Masters don't. Look at games from a hundred years ago, when most of today's Masters were apprentices, and they're no different from today. Nobody at the top rank has had to play under extreme conditions or any way other than by the book for decades. So nobody knows anything about it, except the stuff they learned back when they were beginners—and what they mostly learned then was not to get into those situations. Maniples is getting to be a game of mastering the book and being good at viv."

"You think you're good enough to change that?"

"I'm good—good enough to find almost all of the last century of recorded games boring—and I want to."

"Weehu. Well, I would have to say that even knowing I was losing, that was the most interesting game I've played in years." Jak was stripping out of his viv suit, and he reached for a cold glass of juice. "Public baths after this?"

"Toktru. Speck we can get in a couple more matches before Mercury?"

"As many as you like," Jak said. The young genius had shown him twenty things in that game that he'd never known about Maniples before. Next season PSA might do better than anyone expected.

*   *   *

One night, when his tove had a work shift, Jak and Phrysaba were lying in the cabin he shared with Dujuv, cuddled after lovemaking. "Jak, I feel funny about some things. Will you ever get over this obsession with the Princess? I mean, I know she had you conditioned and you had no choice—"

"Uh, they say it wears off but never completely."

She sat up in bed, leaned forward, kissed his cheek, and breathed in his ear, "Do you love me?"

"You're important to me and I like you a lot. I like sex with you."

"And since you didn't just start off with yes, that means you don't."

"That's right."

"Can you?"

"I don't know."

"That witch!" Phrysaba squeezed Jak as if trying to mash Sesh out of him. "She was so *evil* while she was on the ship—ordering people around and objecting to everything that was just normal shipboard procedure and . . . she particularly hated *me* . . ."

Jak felt the rage boiling up. He kept his voice very level and said, "Remember my conditioning. I'm getting furious with you for saying such things."

She made a soft little fist and lightly pounded on his chest. "You're not open and free and friendly the way you were before, and she's just using you—she'll never be yours, she's a princess, and even if you can overlook that, she sure can't—and so here you are, hurting inside, I can tell, and because she had you conditioned, right now you can't even listen to me call her a nasty exploitive bitch, which isn't half of what she is."

Jak felt all his muscles tense and rage rising along his

spine; he raised his hand in warning. Phrysaba grabbed it, pulled it to her mouth, and kissed the mound below his thumb, firmly, tenderly, and very slowly, pressing it between her lips and warming it with her breath. Jak's hand turned and stroked her cheek. She pressed back against it and whispered, "Now roll over and let me rub the knots out of your back."

Her soothing, warming fingers paused below his left shoulder blade. "What's this scar?"

"It's where they put in the sliver that contains a list of locations for all the evidence of five of Bex Riveroma's major crimes. It's in my liver, someplace hard to find. I guess that was the easiest direction to put it in from—easiest on the surgeon, not necessarily easiest on me."

She pressed her fingers in deep around the back of his neck. "So how would they get it out?"

"Well, doing it singing-on, Riveroma has directions for a surgeon to follow, because we got as far as exchanging some information. Doing it crudely, they'd just cut my liver out and gently puree it to find the sliver. Either would work."

"Scares you to think about it?"

"Unh-hunh. Ever since that fight at the Palace, seeing people killed and mutilated up close, I'm feeling a certain amount of kinship with everything that's made out of meat."

"Even Rubahy?"

He rolled over to face her. "Maybe especially Rubahy. I really was a bigot a couple of years back, wasn't I?"

"Yeah, too much of a bigot even to speck that I was criticizing you." Her hand traced over his upper belly. "So where would that sliver be, here?"

"No idea. I don't actually know enough about the human

body to be able to picture it at all, to tell you the truth." He turned toward her and for the first time since boarding the ship, more than a week ago, relaxed all the way. He held her as if he had suddenly, like a trusting child, decided to be comforted.

"And it's where the evidence of five crimes is?"

"It's a list of all the locations where all the evidence can be found. Places like safe-deposit boxes and archives and police inactive-file cases, and for all I know shallow graves and hollow trees. I gather there's a lot of evidence and it's stored in a lot of places, and from what I know about the five crimes, that makes sense."

"What are the five crimes?"

"Well, in the words of the message that I was supposed to recite to Riveroma the first time I met him (I did, and it got me a hell of a beating): 'The information concerns the location of all the extant, court-admissible evidence regarding the Fat Man, the Dagger and Daisy, the business about the burning armchair, the disappearance of *Titan's Dancer*, and KX-126, including all such evidence regarding your involvement.' You know, when I was first carrying that message, I didn't know what any of them were, which gives you an idea how much I followed the news or anything else, since two of them are famous. Now I know all of them except the burning armchair.

"The one I'd really like to know about is *Titan's Dancer*. How could anyone have *had* anything to do with that? A ship is missing for two hundred years after, to all appearances, going dead on a routine cargo voyage and floating out of the solar system because there was nothing nearby to salvage it. Then it comes back at the highest velocity ever recorded from a crewed vehicle—this from a sunclipper that can maybe get up to a fifteenth of a g—hails us from outside Pluto's orbit, comes in to Earth without making any further communications despite all the requests, furls sails, comes all the way into the docks at Singing Port, there's even vid of people waving from the windows, and it vanishes—just totally disappears in an interval too short to register on any instrument—just before it was supposed to dock. What technology is there that could do such a thing, and how would a petty hood like Riveroma have access to it?"

She shrugged. "Well, I can at least fill in one part of the mystery, it's a pretty open secret among the spaceborn. *Titan's Dancer* faked the original accident. There was an experimental star drive, not faster than light or any such miracle, but enough to get you up to some nines of lightspeed so that time would almost stop and you could go anywhere about as fast as a radio wave could, slow down there, visit, crank it back up to speed, and come back. Of course you'd return a long, long way into the future, but thanks to time dilation, you could make the voyage, and return without having aged much.

"The Council of Captains meets every now and then in a secret electronic conference, and what they decided to use the drive for was to send *Titan's Dancer* out to scout a star system as a candidate for Canaan. Which they found, and returned on schedule, and gave us a report on encrypted tightbeam as they came into the solar system. That's how we know that Canaan is out there."

Jak sank into his bed as she worked harder on his back, and let his mind drift. When he had first heard of Canaan, it had been an interesting bit of legend; now he knew from his Solar System Ethnography class that "Canaan myths" were supposed to be "a major sociosemiotic problem for Hive policy," though all the textbooks were silent as to why, and his tutor had only replied to Jak's inquiring message with, "Restricted by Hive Intel, need-to-know basis."

Out here, though, Canaan seemed to be no myth at all, but about as real as any other place Jak hadn't visited yet. No one knew when or how the Galactic Court now sitting in the Hive would arrive at its verdict on the war crimes trials arising from the First Rubahy War—the age of the Bombardment and the grand invasion, three hundred years before Nakasen's time—but both humans and Rubahy had committed acts which might be counted as major offenses against the Galactic State, and not having known that there even was a Galactic State was in no way an excuse or even a mitigating factor.

Human and Rubahy analysts alike believed that probably in a few centuries the court would issue an Extermination Order—a death sentence for both species. The two species would be each other's only allies in trying to fight off the exterminators, whose power and numbers were unknowable.

But if that day came, because the merchant sunclippers were utterly unsuited to war, all of them planned to furl sails, run black, drift out of the solar system, and set sail for Canaan, a marginally habitable world rumored to be more or less forty light-years or so from Earth. Presumably the humans and the Rubahy would find a way to share that world peaceably. "What was *Titan's Dancer* going to do when they got to Singing Port?"

"Publish the details of the fast star drive, for one thing. It was a cheap gadget; the solar system is full of dissidents and rebels of all kinds, and with a cheap enough drive, a lot of them would have been leaving. Human and Rubahy could have scattered all over this arm of the galaxy, and then see if the Galactic State could wipe us out. Also, scout-ships could have gone out and found out how big the Galactic State really is, whether it has any other enemies, things that might make a big difference if the day ever comes."

"But surely the only copy of the directions for making the fast star drive wasn't on *Titan's Dancer*."

"*Titan's Dancer* was the one that disappeared with a lot of publicity, but the other copies disappeared too, some of them in pretty nasty ways. But every adult crewie knows what it was—it was a way to make a Casimir volume laser directly, so that instead of having to capture heat and run a generator, you could use the whole output as propulsion photons. But the reason we know what it was, was that a warning came back to the Council of Captains. And if you check, you will discover that all research on lasable Casimir volumes ceased a few decades ago, and the older papers are all missing. Most people think the Galactic State caught the project and quietly put an end to it. But that makes it all the more puzzling what Bex Riveroma had to do with it. If he was some kind of operative for the Galactic State, and a traitor to our species, why bother to keep that secret? Wouldn't they be able to protect him?"

"Not if he wanted to live among his own kind," Jak pointed out, "to have someone to talk to, or for sex, or just to have someone sleep next to him. It's a pretty basic impulse, you know."

She snuggled against him. "Never heard of it."

Jak had only fifteen minutes left in his shift when, through a moment's inattention, he let a couple of lines fuse on one mainsail. Forty-five minutes to repair it, at least—no one would blame him if he left it for the next shift—but it was his fault. He rigged up the line car and let it take him sixty kilometers up the cable.

From the open car, vaults and curves of the sails covered the sky, as if he were approaching the surface of a planet covered with clean metallic laundry, with a distinct horizon far out in space. A dozen or more reflected suns shone from the sails, and of course the big real one lay behind. The *Spirit*'s habitat behind him alternately eclipsed and revealed the sun; its shadow lay on the sails in front of him. At each eclipse, the stars appeared, as if turned on by a switch. Presently he could see his own car's shadow dancing back and forth on the sails, sometimes ducking into the shadow of the habitat.

Near the point where the fusion had started, Jak used the manipulator arms to weld a new piece of monosil onto the cable that lay outside his car, just a kilometer short of the fusion point. Monosil rolled out from the spool as he gingerly advanced toward the fusion. If he went too far too fast, the nearby cable could slice into the car, or into Jak.

As he drew near to the point where the cables would converge, he cut the outside cable, and the mechanical arm flung it out to the side; the free end would be sucked through the car's central column backward and fuse onto the already fused monosil there.

Then Jak let the little car, resembling a metal garden gazebo, climb four kilometers of fused monosil, until it was just below the Y where the fused cable again bifurcated. The sails seemed close enough to touch, but it was an illusion; in fact they would have been many days' walk away, if anyone could have rope-walked the lines. Now Jak used the mechanical arm to pick up the spool and hold it far away from the car, up beyond the gazebo-roof; he welded the new length onto the free cable, and then snipped it free of the spool. At once, the monosil line moved away from the other line that had trapped it, and swung back out to-

ward its proper place, four hundred meters away. Jak rode
up his line to finish fusing the old surplus on, and it was
done.

He looked back toward the ship, which was about as big
as Earth seen from the Moon, a big dark metal ball, and it
seemed very welcoming; back there, a whole small town of
people were born, lived, and died, and got up every morning with something to do. Jak considered the possibility of
turning crewie permanently, as he often did when life was
difficult, and as always, he had no real objections, just the
feeling that his destiny was elsewhere.

He set the car to return to the tending platform on automatic. The ship grew from a ball in the sky to a world, the
platform braked, vacuum-silent, to the deck, and Jak
grabbed the pull-rail and went inside.

He had had a late shift that day; after his post-shift
shower, it was too late for the Bachelor's Mess, and it was
too late to com Phrysaba and see if she wanted to eat in one
of the cafes—she'd be at mess, probably, with her astrogation class. For the first time, ever, Jak was going to have to
dine at Passenger's Mess.

The food was the same, but the noise level was a small
fraction of what he was used to. In Passenger's Mess the tables were small and isolated, and people huddled murmuring over them, except for the table where a large, loud heet
with a Hive accent (fast, flat, and slurred) was explaining
everything about Venus to three bored women. The conversation, or lecture, really, was interrupted now and then by
laughter, giggles, and squeals as they all revealed that although they had been on the sunclipper for at least three
months, they hadn't really mastered eating in low grav yet.
Jak sat at a table by himself, as far as possible from them.

He had no more than touched his meal when Mreek

Sinda slid into the seat opposite him. "Hello, I thought I'd see you before now, I suppose CUPVs usually eat with the crewies, can't imagine why they do that, they're visiting people who never visit anyone, that can't be lively, but that seems to be what all the CUPVs do, or at least what you and Dujuv Gonzawara and Shadow on the Frost do. Anyway, this won't take long but I do have some further questions."

Jak took a very large bite of his suddenly flavorless meat loaf and bolted it; he had consumed about half the piece before she tried speaking to him again.

"Well," she said, "I can understand that you have a lot to think about. You know, there are some people who might say that what you really need to do is to give up this obsession with Princess Shyf, who after all is so far above you socially, and I was wondering if you might have a comment on that."

A drone buzzed between Jak's plate and his face; he got a blob of smashed potatoes on it by flipping his fork hard. It moved to a more respectful distance.

"Well, then," Sinda added, "what about the rumors that Bex Riveroma has put a price on your head, or rather on your liver, and that anyone who brings it in gets a megautil of untraceable credit?"

"Liver? I don't *like* liver. I'm having meat loaf," Jak said, "and he could have my meat loaf for fifty utils, no problem. Or I'd trade him liver for two apples and a snack cake."

"I suppose you think that's funny. You've consistently tried to make my interviews with you impossible. Why is that?" She tossed her head; it overstepped the intended "magnificent rage" and ventured into "mild spasm."

"You have publicly humiliated me, and forged all kinds of things I never said or did, and damaged many of my friendships," Jak said. "And no matter what I do, you're going to compose an animation of me saying and doing whatever you want, and nobody will be able to tell the difference without tearing the signal apart on a good-sized computer. So since you can just script what you need, why do you need me to play along? You can have me saying whatever you want for decades to come. So what is all this about?"

"You're important to me," she said, and it was the first time he'd ever heard her voice not in broadcast mode. She had a slight lisp that suggested one of the big Martian cities, or perhaps Ceres. "You're very important to me. A few years ago I was nobody, I was covering dance trends, not even fashionable ones, I was doing the story on slec so that the old gwonts who didn't follow anything current at all would finally know what slec was because it was about to be over, masen? Then I got good shots of a brawl and followed up and found the most amazing story about a young man going off to rescue a princess—"

"You made most of it up."

"Of course." She said it as if he had asked her whether she could fasten a zipper. "I had to, nobody would talk to me. But anyway, it was a fabulous story. But you know what they say, you're only as good as your last, and here it is two years later and I haven't developed even one viv series that was faintly comparable. It's like I'm not even in my own league. And they're starting to mutter about my allocations of space on the agenda and processing time and everything else, and that's when you know the vultures are sharpening their knives—"

"Circling," Jak said.

"What?"

"Ever been to Earth? Vultures circle. I didn't know what

they were the first time I saw it, but vultures circle. People sharpen knives, especially butchers. Vultures don't have any hands. They wouldn't sharpen knives, because they don't use them."

"Where do you learn all this stuff? If I worried about things like that I'd never get an accesscast done, and nobody would ever know anything." She shook her head; the traditional blonde helmet never moved. "My career really needs a restart, and here you are—the one who started it in the first place, by going on a secret mission on behalf of Princess Shyf—and you are on *another* secret mission for Princess Shyf. Well, it worked for me once, it could work for me again. Not to mention that it made you temporarily about fourth-level famous, for free. Some people pay a megautil to a publicist every year for that."

"I didn't want it." Jak got up and looked around to empty his tray before he remembered that in the passenger areas, servant robots did things like that. He set his tray back down and airswam out.

"So any comments on your growing rift with your toktru tove Dujuv Gonzawara?" she said, swimming after.

He turned in midair, caught a drone, and pounded it against the wall. "This is how Duj deals with these, and I think he's singing-on right. Any problems I'm having with Dujuv are problems you created, by falsifying interviews and accesscasting things I never said." He spun away, repulsed and angry.

Jak would just make it an evening of studying in the stateroom he shared with Dujuv. He was getting close to finishing his second time through Solar System Ethnography since the Dean had set him the task. (One drawback of a correspondence course was that you were done sooner). It would be nice not to have to worry about it while he was on his mission on Mercury.

He did his best to ignore Mreek Sinda airswimming after him, trying to narrate the situation as if she were pursuing a criminal. He opened the door as she was shouting, "Is there any chance—would you care to speculate—the Duke of Uranium's loaning you his personal bodyguard, Shadow on the Frost, and your joint investigation of a possible organized crime operation on Mercury, may indicate some interest in a personal alliance between the new Duke and the heir to Greenworld?"

Jak was starting to close the door in her face when he saw Dujuv and Phrysaba, sitting on Dujuv's bed, cross-legged, facing each other. Though he couldn't have said why, there was a feeling of interrupting something—

Sinda barged in and said, "And here's my opportunity to talk to both of you and settle discrepancies in some of your versions of what actually happened—"

"I'm calling security," Jak said. "Sorry, toves, she was following me and I was trying to get away. Didn't get the door closed fast enough."

"Dujuv Gonzawara, do you feel that your friend's deliberate attempt to steal credit which we have established clearly belonged to you—"

Dujuv sprang out of the cross-legged position like a missile, and ricocheted off three walls in the crowded little room. When he had finished his sudden flight—while not touching anyone but making the other three jump back, all shouting in surprise—he had two drones in each of his two big fists. Smiling, he beat them all to pieces against each other.

Jak gave Sinda a hard shove on the forehead and she fell in a backward somersault out the door, which he slammed.

"That'll probably be a hundred credit fine," he said, "but it was worth it. Sorry, pizos, I just didn't stop her before she was in here."

Duj had a slightly smug look. " 'Sokay. The exercise was good for me."

"Did you want to say hi or anything tonight, Phrysaba?" Jak asked awkwardly. "A fusion happened late in my shift and by the time I got back it was too late to call you and suggest dinner."

"That's all right," Phrysaba said, eyes sparkling. "I called Dujuv. I've just been hearing the story of his life."

"A lot of meals and a lot of beating people up?" Jak asked.

Phrysaba looked slightly outraged. "Your friend is a sensitive, intelligent young man and there's a lot to him."

Dujuv turned an odd shade; his skin was dark enough so that it wasn't easy to tell, but Jak sort of assumed that a major blush was happening—either that or a cerebral hemorrhage. "Weehu, I dak *that*, Phrysaba. Always have. I just don't mention it because it always makes Dujuv toktru tongue-tied."

Dujuv emitted a squeak of agreement.

"Then were you kind to point it out and make it worse?" she demanded.

"No, I wasn't. Sorry, Duj."

"Eek hoo kay," Dujuv managed, sounding as if his neck were being squeezed.

Phrysaba said, "Well, what's really sad is, I have a short swing sleep tonight, they're moving my shift a little earlier to give me more lab time for school, so I hate to do this, but I'm officially breaking up the party. I can find my own way home—I kind of remember how the ship's laid out—" she said, smirking, as she saw both of them about to offer to escort her back to her cabin. "Duj, it's been fascinating, re-ally, and I want to hear more, and I mean that, masen? Jak, I really do have to just sleep tonight."

After she was gone, Dujuv said, "She's a nice girl."

"She is. She's one of the best arguments I know for get-ting over the conditioning that Shyf gave me."

"Shyf?"

"Princess Shyf. You know, red hair, nice body, psycho-slut maniac, tyrant-in-training? I'm sure I introduced you."

Dujuv laughed. "You didn't call her Sesh."

"I don't think there's very much of Sesh left. Which is another reason why . . . well, Phrysaba's just one of many reasons."

"Reasons like Fnina?"

"Oh, Nakasen's bulging bag! Not her. She's probably al-ready been through two boyfriends since she last wrote, and she'll have another six before I get home, Duj. Though if Sinda keeps putting those animations of me on the viv, I'm afraid Fnina will be right back when I get home."

"What was that Sinda bitch after this time?"

"I speck footage she could chop up and use to create an-imations that have me lying and bragging like a toktru gweetz. Hey—I just had a thought."

"Did it hurt?"

"It was just a little one. She said something about dis-crepancies in our versions of what happened. Did she inter-view you and Shadow?"

"Uh, yeah. Maybe it was a big mistake, but . . . well, I wanted to know she'd actually heard someone tell her what had really happened."

"I did."

"But I wasn't there to hear you—and you have to speck that if she cooked up your version, it was awfully convinc-

ing, pizo, masen? So now I know that she had the truth, at
least once. And that makes me feel better."

"Well, then it's good that you talked to her."

After some uncomfortable silence, Jak pulled out his
reader, to review the cultural ethnography of Mercury, and
Dujuv rolled over and went to sleep with his clothes on.

CHAPTER 11

Start Chopping the Parsley

While they waited for the longshore capsules to come around to the cargo bay, Jak had his purse review his Solar System Ethnography notes; he was finding it harder and harder to pretend that this stuff was useless. Probably Uncle Sib was right, and the conspiracy of the entire rest of the universe was winning.

Mercury is the densest planet in the solar system, and the density is caused by its very high percentage of metal; it resembles the stripped core of a big planet, with just a thin crust and mantle. Its atmosphere is thinner than any vacuum you can make in a laboratory and it races through its short orbit, down close to the sun, faster than any other planet. That much was physics.

Physics dictates economics. Mercury had more metal and power to smelt it, more powerful sunlight for solar sails, better conditions for gravity assists, and more windows for them per unit time, than any other planet, by far. Quick to get to, quick to come from, available more often, and made out of valuable cargo, Mercury was the merchanters' best friend. The saying was that there was always gold in Mercury.

Economics, in turn, dictates politics. Jak, Dujuv, and Shadow were going to Mercury's second-largest city, but it was doubtful that anyone other than a Mercurial would call it a city rather than a shantytown, or perhaps just a warren. There was gold in Mercury but not for Mercurials.

Mercury was to the solar system what the Netherlands, Persian Gulf, or geosynchronous orbit had been to medieval Earth: a place so valuable that no one could be allowed to control it. A League of Polities treaty disallowed permanent claims and pledged the big powers to prevent anyone's gaining permanent control over Mercury. Custom interpreted this to include any local government, which was fiercely choked back by treaty officials. Bigpile, a city of millions, had a police and emergency force of about two hundred and a municipal bureaucracy of three dozen. Law enforcement extended only as far as the line of sight of the nearest pokheet, if that. Officially it was believed that Bigpile collected one percent of taxes due; unofficially no official believed the number was that high. About two hundred corporations headquartered there, with perhaps a thousand branch offices of offworld corporations, and in every office bodyguards were about as numerous as workers, and it was a treasured employee benefit to be given sleeping space inside the corporate keep.

Nothing dictates culture but everything shapes it. The fierce conditions, unfavorable economics, prohibition against an effective state, sanctioned lawlessness, absentee ownership—and Mercury's role as de facto dustbin for the prison-sweepings of the whole solar system—had created fierce loyalties to the quaccos, which were in various ways like a clan, an employee-owned company, an extended family with many adoptees, and an infantry company, but mostly were just like a quacco. The text had spent a long time on that; the one thing that Jak gathered, most clearly, was that bitter experience had taught treaty administrators that anything that forced any substantial number of quaccos to leave their home kriljs, either to migrate or to break up, would mean instant revolution. You could call a Mercurial a son of a whore with a fair chance of being right, and he'd shrug and say, "You should've seen what *Dad* used to do," but suggest that his quacco was in any way not the very best one on Mercury, and you'd be in a fight to the death (and if you won, between forty and a hundred quacco-mates would be looking for their turn at you).

The *Spirit* would be going into orbit around Mercury for six weeks or so; after her shakedown to Jupiter during the past two years, it was time to do a real tune-and-fit now that they knew the peculiarities of the new rigging, Duke Psim's gift to them for services rendered on Jak's last great adventure. They had excellent reason to choose this world for refitting. Mercury's quaccos of fitters and riggers were legendary for their precision and craft, and intended to keep things that way. Furthermore, Mercury was the fastest and cheapest planet to get away from; after setting sail from stations around Earth or Venus, it would take a full month to reach escape velocity and get out into solar orbit, but from Mercury it would take less than ten days.

With so many weeks in orbit, they didn't need to do a rushed cargo switch. Jak, Dujuv, and Shadow had volunteered to fly longshore capsules down onto the Bigpile loop; it spared the expense of a ferry, and three crewies would not have to touch the hated dirt.

They tossed their jumpies into the cabs of the longshore capsules, closed suits for takeoff, and let the linducers move them gently out through the cargo airlocks and onto the outer surface of the ship, then up the track to the loop. Longshore capsules didn't have to be piloted in less-crowded parts of space, but Mercury saw at least one sun-clipper a week, and about twenty short-haul merchanters,

most of them doing fast flybys, and so the little planet lived
in a near-swarm of longshore capsules and ferries. Supposedly a human pilot added judgment; Jak specked it was
more like requiring a mindful hostage with every cargo.

They lined up and whipped around the *Spirit*'s loop,
flung in an elliptical orbit down to the Bigpile loop. Bigpile
was a Maltese-cross-shaped city, a wadded tangle, mostly
underground, of tunnels and chambers where no one held a
single clear title to any of the land and the laws amounted
to, *Don't precess any private security guards enough to
make them shoot you.* Above the tunnels, its surface was
covered with the brightly glowing observation domes of the
big hotels, pricey condos, and corporate keeps. It lay just
northeast of the Caloris Basin (the vast crater in Mercury's
northern hemisphere that was almost a tenth of the planet's
own diameter), between the inner and outer scarps, in very
heavily broken, pitted, cratered, and domed highlands.

As the three longshore capsules descended, Jak was flying rear; Shadow's longshore capsule, twenty kilometers
ahead, was a little glinting cylinder, about the size of Jak's
thumbnail at arm's length; Dujuv's capsule, half as far
away, appeared twice as big. Mercury swelled into a world
beneath them, and as they passed from night across the
morning terminator, the land below changed from strands
and sprays of lights to the face of hell: dust and rock, in
craters and peaks and smeared plains, fractured and cracked
all over. Thirteen hundred years of mining had changed
everything and left it the same.

Short bursts from the hot jets sent them out of a high
equatorial orbit and into a lower one angled to catch the
Bigpile loop, far north of the equator; the cold jets rotated
the little vessels and the hot jets fired once again, dropping
them into a lower, faster orbit, and then the cold jets fired

once more to reorient them. They approached the loop flying forward, with their heads pointed toward the planet (not
"down" yet, for they were still in free fall).

Jak watched the loop approach at about three kilometers
per second. Ahead of him, Shadow's longshore capsule
grabbed and whirled down toward the surface. Three seconds later, Dujuv followed. Now the two sides of the wicket
seemed to drift together to form a single white line in the
window, reaching toward Jak from the lighted cross of Bigpile. At such speeds, human steering and judgment are useless. Jak saw that everything was green, and with a second
to go, pushed the "okay to land." A moment later, the cold
jets fired a series of highly calibrated bursts, which sounded
like clearing a clogged sinus. The longshore capsule
bounced around for a moment, and then the linducer grapple grabbed the loop.

Gravity appeared instantly in the "wrong" direction,
away from Mercury, so that the planet seemed to be overhead. Two g's pushed Jak down into his seat cushion. In the
space of a minute and a half, Mercury seemed to roll from
overhead to directly in front of him to underneath him,
drawing closer all the time, and as the centripetal forces
from the loop aligned more and more with the planet's
gravity, he seemed to become steadily heavier, then lighter
as the velocity slowed to a few meters per second. The
longshore capsule coasted down to Bigpile Station.

As gravity became comfortable, steady, and footward,
and the land below rose up toward him, Jak closed his faceplate and pressure-checked for arrival. The longshore capsule's upper inducers released it from the loop, its lower
ones grabbed a track, and Jak was moving slowly over the
melted-and-shattered short-horizoned landscape, between
the silvery domes, dishes, boxes, pipes, spheres, and wires,

as if in a Pertrans car. They passed through an airlock into the main receiving area. The pressure safety sign came on, and he unsealed.

His longshore capsule came to a stop between Shadow's and Dujuv's, in a docking bay. Jak slung up his jumpie, popped the door, and got out to join Shadow and Dujuv.

"Hey! Hey! Are you all Jak Jinnaka, Shadow on the Frost, and Dujuv Gonzawara?"

They turned to see a tall, heavy blonde woman in a pressure suit, her helmet slung to one shoulder strap and heavy gauntlets and boots slung to the other, hurrying down the quay toward them. "I'm Kyffimna Eldothaler," she said. "I was afraid I was late."

"We just got here, ourselves," Dujuv said.

She had a toothy grin, *Like the ogre's wife in a fairy tale,* Jak thought. In an age of cheap plastic surgery and metabolic adjustments, when it was well-known that a little tinkering with the body when a child was young saved all kinds of body-image problems and psychological damage later, she was not only the ugliest girl Jak had ever seen, she was the first ugly girl Jak had ever seen. Her face was blotchy and oily. Her jaw was big and square. Her pulpy lips did not quite cover her horsey teeth. Her crooked nose was large, and her blonde hair thin and stringy. Even in a pressure suit he could tell that her body was bulky with muscle, no stronger than the lean dancer-bodies he was used to, but far less pleasing.

"We're glad to see you," Jak said. "I'm Jak Jinnaka, this is Dujuv Gonzawara, and Shadow on the Frost."

She shook hands with all of them, starting at Shadow's double-thumbed hand. "I've been begging Mattanga for some help for most of a year, now, and all I've gotten is vague notes. Where do we go to pick up the rest of your unit?"

"Our unit?" Dujuv asked.

"Or does each of you have a unit? Mattanga's information didn't come through the decrypt real clear."

They all glanced at each other. "Perhaps it is because I am an alien," Shadow said, "but I have no unit."

"Well, then I hope each of you has a large unit," Kyffimna said to Jak and Dujuv, "because I don't speck anything small will be enough. If it's big enough there might actually be an intimidation or fear factor, which would help; I can't tell you how many nights I've laid awake thinking that the right heet with a big enough unit could make everything better overnight."

"Umm," Jak said, desperately trying to clear the horrible images dancing through his mind, "exactly what are you expecting us to be able to do for you?"

She stared at him. "Oh, no. Did anyone tell you anything about MLB?"

The three friends looked at each other. "No," Dujuv said, "I have no idea what that is."

Kyffimna seemed almost to sway, as if for an instant she felt faint. "MLB is the organization that I asked Colonel Mattanga for at least a battalion of B&Es to attack and put out of action. When I saw that there were three people coming, and I was supposed to meet you, I thought you three would be the company commanders, or else the commander, second, and senior techny."

There was a very long, awkward silence.

"Why is it," Dujuv said, "that no matter how far down the river we get sold, there is always more river to sell us down?"

Shadow emitted a single bubble sound. "If it were happening to anyone else, Dujuv Gonzawara, I would find what you just said hilarious."

"Well," Kyffimna said, visibly trying to brighten, "what are you officially here to do?"

Jak sighed. "Investigate. Whatever that may mean. Mattanga told us that she had no idea what was going on here."

"But I've sent reports every week for the past year!"

"I don't know whether anyone ever read them, Kyffimna. In fact I speck our real job is just to not be on the Aerie anymore, because politically we were a problem. If we happen to solve your problem, Greenworld will be happy with us, of course, but mostly we're doing our real job just by not being in Greenworld. So first of all, what's MLB?"

"Safer to discuss that once we're moving," Kyffimna said. "Listen, when we get back to the krilj, most people are going to be pretty disappointed at the fact that you are not arriving with a battalion of troops, which is what we really need. Masen?"

"Toktru. Thanks for the warning."

"You got anything besides those jumpies to bring along?"

They didn't, so she just shrugged, gestured toward one of the tunnels, and said, "All right, then, this way. We're cutting a corner off Bigpile to the rocket port, then flying out to the Crater Hamner krilj, just a couple of kilometers but it's tangley going through town here."

They blundered and stumbled after her through uncountable corridors, none level, straight, or at right angles, all lined with shops, shacks, and shanties. In the perpetual room temperature of the sealed city, walls were only for security against theft, surfaces to hang things from, and modesty.

Kyffimna explained that the older spaces in the city were played out mining tunnels; as Bigpile's population grew, it gained density as developers drilled and sold off private tunnels between tenanted spaces. As each new tunnel filled up and became less fashionable, successively poorer waves of new immigrants took advantage of falling prices to put in successively more appalling shacks. When there was no more legal room left, the poor waited till no one was paying attention, and filled in the rest of the space one way or another. The center stayed clear only as long as affluent neighbors were willing to pay the pokheets to knock apart any building that blocked a traffic path.

"Why are the tunnel walls so many different colors and textures?" Dujuv asked.

"Because slag is always being remelted and repoured," Kyffimna said. "Say in one year titanium is high priced. We get a bunch of titanium-bearing rock together, melt it, run it through a separator; along the way maybe we take out the nickel or the silver, if prices are good on those, as lagniappe. Any oxygen, nitrogen, or valuable bio-stuff like that, we claim for our own use. Then we have this big load of waste magma—liquid rock, mostly metals, nothing of value in it, white-hot and dangerous. It gets used for fill in old tunnels, or for paving, or as the heavy stuff in substitution pumping."

"So how did that turn all the walls all these different colors?" Dujuv asked.

"You *are* a panth, aren't you?" As if she were explaining things to a not very bright child, she said, "In all those centuries of mining, a lot of waste magma, with a lot of different composition, goes down a lot of holes, masen? There's veins of stuff that's been melted, pumped, processed, and dumped ten and fifteen times, all over Mercury, depending on what was needed and where there was stuff. If a field is rich and has a lot of different ores of different grades, there will be a lot of hole-making and a lot of hole-filling over a few centuries. Then if a city—like Bigpile—grows there, all the tunnels you drill are going to be punching through all those old deposits of six-times-cooked rock, which will have all kinds of stuff in it, which will make it all different colors. Masen?"

"I did not speck your point at first, either," Shadow on the Frost said, "so I do not think that the problem was that my oath-bound tove Dujuv Gonzawara was a panth. I speck it was that the explanation was needlessly obscure, with too much assumed."

Kyffimna stopped walking and stood still. "I think you are trying to tell me that I was rude to your friend."

"Singing-on," Shadow said gravely. "Do you need any further explanation?"

She winced. "Dujuv, did I offend you?"

"Somewhat. When you're a panth you get used to being treated like an idiot."

"Then I'm very sorry," Kyffimna said. She extended her hand, and Dujuv shook it.

"Now," Kyffimna said, "we're far enough out of our way, so maybe nobody's listening. The malphs are MLB, the Mercury Labor Brigade, which is set up as a vested corporation but is actually a protection mob moving in on about a dozen mining sites, and taking control of maybe sixty quaccos, so far. MLB has juice everywhere. Corporations won't try to do anything about them, the union tells us to cooperate with them, we contacted a couple of zybots and they wouldn't talk to us. Even stringers for spy agencies say that their home offices aren't interested.

"So whoever MLB are, they're richer than God and with

more guns. Their headquarters is in Crater Hamner, which my quacco has been working for a generation—and they just showed up, started drilling in the central pinnacle, we went out to talk to them, and they shot two of the quacco dead, beat the shit out of our leader, and told us from now on they were our sole customer and that they would take care of supplying all our old ones. They're recruiting young dumb muscle right now, taking over more sites and more quaccos, building up strength—at the rate they're going, they'll own Bigpile in a month, and Mercury in a year.

"That would be fine if all they were doing was taking over. Every Mercurial knows what this place needs is a good strong tyrant to organize things and make the off-planet companies stop the competitive plundering, pay for some public works—you know there's not a public school or waterworks, or one kilometer of nonprivate pipe or wire, on this planet?—and put down the cutthroat way we all steal each other's business. If these heets were just vicious tyrants, half of us would be on their side, just to get out from under the Invisible Thumb."

"The Invisible Thumb? Is that what their organization is called, like the Black Hand?"

She snorted derisively. "It's a nasty joke. Like everything on Mercury. The only free education available on this planet is the accesscast stuff with all the advertising, and to get your certificate from that, you have to learn a lot of free-market economics. The first-year class, for seven-year-olds, introduces Uncle Adam Smith, this weird-looking heet in knee britches that I guess was the pope or the president or something back on Earth a long time ago, and he teaches the first economics class, which is called 'The Wonderful Invisible Hand.' When a miner discovers that the price of something changed between taking out the loan and getting it out of the ground, and the buyer can walk away from the contract but the bank can seize the miner's gear, and the explanation is 'the free market'—the miner feels that Invisible Thumb going in deep.

"A lot of us would throw in with anybody who promised to take over and give us some order, just to get a gentler, more predictable Invisible Thumb, but these MLB heets are actually worse than what we had before. They set prices too low to live on, force us to take out loans, and take advantage of the fact that the Freedom for Mercury Treaty authorizes peonage."

"Peeing on what?" Dujuv asked.

"Peonage," Shadow on the Frost said. "Hereditary and heritable, no doubt."

"That's right."

Jak looked at Kyffimna and didn't want her to jump on Dujuv for not knowing again, so he said, "All right, obviously Shadow knows what peonage is, but I don't."

"Debt slavery. Get behind enough payments and the bank owns you—and your kids—till you work it off."

"Nakasen's bulging bag," Dujuv said, "you're talking about bank banks. Real banks. I didn't even know those still existed."

"They do here," Kyffimna said. "Mercury really is the place where everything is for sale, and where the buyers are the kings. Want to set up a bank? They're legal, because everything is legal here. Want to sell *xleeth,* and start all your customers down the road to being severely retarded but with the biggest, happiest smiles you've ever seen? Nobody would stop you from setting up your booth on a playground, unless you weren't giving the owner a cut. Want to cook and eat a kid? If you can find a seller for a five-year-old peon, and cover all the liens, hey, you can start chopping the parsley and preheat the oven. And no pokheet will come around to bother you. We have our feets here; the vid is always reminding us how we're completely free."

Jak shuddered. "You know, there are people who say they could never bear the regimented society of the Hive, and that the idea of being a wasp makes them ill, but I don't think I've ever been so homesick."

"Just remember that at least half the metal the Hive is made out of came from here. And now you know how they get it. I'm glad you all live better there—really I am—it wouldn't help us for you to be poor. But don't think this place has nothing to do with you."

Dujuv was staring blankly, as if looking for something to say, and finally he just choked up and let tears run down his face. Kyffimna looked at him in amazement.

"Since you had heard that panths were supposed to be dumb," Jak said, sarcastically, throwing an arm protectively around his old tove, "didn't you hear that they're also supposed to be unnaturally sensitive? It goes with their big hearts and deep loyalty." He turned to comfort his friend, putting Dujuv's face against his neck, as he had learned to do when they were young teenagers and a viv or a movie got to his friend.

"I'd never heard that," Kyffimna said, "but . . . well, there are lots of panths here. You'll see plenty. And because they're valuable for the kind of work we do, the banks have a real tradition of pushing them into peonage if at all possible. It's the same with simis and kobolds and just about any other breed that does well here. A lot of women get out of peonage by agreeing to carry three or four fertilized panth ova to term; since they're born while their mother is a peon, they are automatically peons too; she goes free and they're peons till middle age or so. But . . . no, nobody ever told me panths were sensitive. Toktru, mostly people just tell them what to do."

Jak felt Dujuv's hot tears dribbling into his collar, and held his sobbing friend's shoulders. The vault where they were standing was mostly empty except for some tents made up of old wrapping plastic. It was lit by a dozen wavering fuel-cell lamps that were clearly at the end of their lifetimes and had just been left here, on top of piles of similar dead lights. A group of kobolds ran through the vault, carrying boxes, and the one unmodified human woman with them was the only one wearing a purse; Jak specked what that must mean. "You know, I really think they've sent us to hell."

"That's right," Kyffimna said. "To meet the newest, meanest devil here."

On airless Mercury, a rocket is just a nozzle, below a spherical thermos tank full of very high-pressure liquid sodium, below a wide disk-shaped cab, all held together with a minimum of struts and girders. Vented to vacuum, hot high-pressure sodium makes a fine propellant, and since sodium is so common and abundant in the surface regolith of Mercury, and apt to clog and contaminate separator plates, it is given away free just to get rid of it. The rocket stays plugged into the electrical mains to keep the sodium hot until the moment of launch; it takes off in one burst of sodium and lands tail-down in another. The sodium in the tank stays more than hot enough, for a ballistic flight to the antipodes takes only fourteen minutes.

In this case, the flight was less than two hundred kilometers, and the time was less than a minute; the little ship kicked hard once, they were weightless for a short period, and then it kicked hard again and they touched down. The landing area was just a broad, flat space within Hamner, a ten-kilometer-across crater where the main krilj of the El-dothaler Quacco had been for seventy years.

A strange-looking tractor rolled up to the rocket, towing a sodium hose and a power lead. On top of it was a small passenger cab in the middle of a large, bare gridded plat-form, about three meters off the ground. Underneath, five trusses formed a pentacle of long arms, each ending in two big wheels of open steel mesh. "Pop brought the ten-wheeler," Kyffimna said. "We can all ride inside."

The little rocket didn't have an airlock or an elevator, just an air capture to depressurize the cabin, a door that opened, and a permanently mounted ladder and fireman's pole; Jak and Shadow opted for the ladder, Kyffimna and Dujuv for the pole, and they dropped the fifteen meters onto the mirror-bright smear of freshly frozen sodium. Kyffimna trotted up to the ten-wheeler, and they followed. The big woman reached over her head to grip one of the big steel mesh tires, and climbed up it to the truss, then on top of the upper member of the truss and across the platform to wait by the cabin.

Around them, the crater walls loomed high and steep. Frozen falls, curtains, and spouts showed where waste magma had been dumped.

The tops of the crater walls formed a jagged rip in the black sky; with sun glinting from his helmet, Jak could not see the stars, but presumably at night, or from deep shadow, they would be as numerous as they were from the dark side of a spaceship. Long low dust piles lay at the feet of the crater walls.

Kyffimna's father dragged the sodium hose over to the rocket and plugged it in, then hooked in the power lead.

In less than a minute the light over the rocket's sodium

connection glowed green. He unhooked the sodium hose and dropped it; it went dragging back toward its unseen origin, bouncing and slapping over the dusty, pitted surface. He left the power lead connected and tucked the cable so that it ran under the nozzle; whenever the rocket got a passenger or a call and took off again, it would signal the station to shut off the power, then burn away the cable as it took off.

Then he climbed up the wheel and the long arm of the ten-wheeler and joined the group, gesturing for them to follow him into the cabin; the door irised closed behind them, and a moment later the green pressure-okay came on. He removed his helmet and clipped it to his shoulder strap; everyone else followed suit.

Jak thought the man must be close to three hundred. His hair had probably once been whitish-blonde like Kyf-fimna's, but now it was a messy mix of yellow, white, and gray; his watery eyes were ice-in-gin blue, his skin streaked with red patches and little exploded veins, and the imperfect symmetry of his strong-featured face suggested that he had been the practice partner for either a not-quite-proficient plastic surgeon or an all-too-proficient boxer.

"My name is Durol Eldothaler, and if you don't mind, our order of precedence is such that I call everyone else by first name, which means you are Shadow, and one of you is Jak—"

"That's me."

"So you are Dujuv."

"Right, or Duj, informally and with friends."

Durol Eldothaler nodded. "You can call me Chief, Boss, or Eldothaler-san. Clear?"

They all nodded.

"I noticed you looking at MLB's main base, there." He

nodded toward the central pinnacle. It looked like the tower of the evil enchanter in a mediocre fantasy viv. Impact craters form with a splash, more like a pebble thrown into a bathtub than a rock against a wall, for at the speeds and energies involved, the distinction between liquid and solid is shadowy. As the spherical spreading wave in the ground encounters resistance, either at its outer edges or far below, a portion of the energy is reflected back, where it sometimes erupts onto the surface, hurling rock and soil upward in a heap. Just as a crater wall is a frozen wave in the surface, so a central pinnacle is a frozen backsplash. Old Eldothaler said, "It's not much of a pinnacle—a crater this small hardly ever even has one—but enough to make a fortress, or a prison watchtower, eh? Anyway, that's the problem to be coped with."

"Pop," Kyffimna said, "I guess I better tell you before we have to tell all the others. These three are all that's coming. Either all my messages never got through (which I don't believe for one second) or more likely what's going on is that Greenworld Intelligence is not really intending to help, but they sent us three agents that they'd just as soon be rid of—no fault of the agents, nothing wrong with them, I don't think."

"Thank you," Shadow said, with immense dignity.

"So we have to break the news to the others," Durol said, rubbing his face with his hand. "Well, this is a blow. I don't suppose any of you is a military genius, a trained saboteur, or a commando?"

"Well," Jak said, "Dujuv and I are agents in training, and Shadow is a warrior, so we're not helpless. But no, we aren't like the teams-of-heroes they send into the situation in the intrigue-and-adventure stories. For your sake, I wish we were."

"So do I. But you're who we have, so we'll have to make the best of you, and ideally find a way to like you while we're doing it. I don't imagine that will be too hard, really."

The ten-wheeler jounced along in the low gravity. Kyf-fimna brought them up to big steel doors set in the side of a steep cliff in the inside of the crater wall. They passed into the dark shadow and Jak had just an instant's vision of stars overhead before the big doors dilated in front of them, and they rolled through into the krilj's airlock. Bright lights came on overhead, the pressure light turned green, and a small mob of Mercurials—old and young, kobolds and simis among them—rushed toward the ten-wheeler, all chattering excitedly. "This is not going to be my favorite speech of all the ones I ever give, I just know it's not," Durol muttered, as the cabin door dilated.

CHAPTER 12

Radzundslag

That went better than I was dreading," Jak said, quietly, to Dujuv, as they scrubbed for dinner, sharing the sink in the little chamber they had been assigned with Shadow. Kyf-fimna had explained to them that all bathrooms here were arranged to pressurize instantly as needed, but in any other room they would be expected to wear their pressure suits at all times with the helmet always to hand, "especially when you sleep."

"I don't know, Jak, yeah, they accepted it coming from him, thank Nakasen and every Principle that he had that much authority and respect, but I don't think they're happy at all. And you're singing-on right, this place is hell. How come in gen school all they ever did was show us pictures of miners standing around machinery, and at the PSA all they do is talk about making sure that Mercury never ends up controlled by any nation unless of course someday the Hive is in a position to grab it?"

Jak shrugged. "That's what it's convenient for us to know. Same reason anybody lies or shades the truth, I guess."

"Yeah, but . . . well, how come I never knew there was a place like this? Did you hear what that little kid asked his mother when we passed in the hall?"

"Yeah, I did."

A small boy, maybe seven or so, had audibly asked his mother if Dujuv was Jak's peon.

"You *dak* that? Most panths they've ever seen are peons. And these people *despise* peons. No matter how somebody ends up as a peon, they assume it's a character flaw or something. It's like something out of the industrial half of the Middle Ages, back when they thought that regional skin color variations meant things. I'm starting to realize something—it's not all that different with breeds."

Jak could think of nothing else to say, so he changed the subject. "I'm about as clean as I'm getting without a shower. How are you doing?"

"I'm there. Let's dress."

In the dining room, all of the children, from about the age of fourteen down, were piled on Shadow, sitting on his lap, staring a few inches from his face, and spraying questions at him. Under the pile of children, Shadow seemed to be enjoying it.

They asked amazingly rude questions, ones that Jak would normally have expected to see make a Rubahy's rage spines spring out, but Shadow on the Frost mostly made the bubbling noise, explained that that was a laugh, and answered. Yes, he could feel it if they pulled a feather, so please not to do that. No, he didn't really look much like a terrier dog and he didn't know why people called Rubahy that. Yes, he had a very large family, and he didn't always get along with all of them, but some of them were very nice and they were all family. (He glanced up at Jak and Dujuv and bubbled after that one.) No, his teeth were very sharp and scary, but he had never used them to bite a human, and he had no idea what we tasted like.

"I hope you will *never* see my rage spines," he said to one little girl. "I know what they show in the movies, but we don't have them permanently sticking out of our backs—how would we ever sit in a chair, eh? And we don't really control them. When we're angry and need to fight, they just pop out. And I don't like being angry or frightened, any more than you do."

"You never smile."

"There are no muscles in my face; I can't move it."

"And you whistle when you talk."

"That's because my voice box is shaped like one of your old-fashioned slot-flutes. Yours is shaped more like the noisemaker in one of your whoopee cushions, which is why it buzzes."

One of the older boys laughed and said, "When we talk, do we sound like we're farting, to you?"

Shadow made the bubbling noise so hard and loud that it sounded like the metallic bucket might shatter, a weird burst of blooping and clanking that seemed to delight the children.

"And are Rubahy ticklish?" one little boy asked.

It turned out they were. After a while, Jak and Dujuv rescued Shadow, gently reminding the kids that though fun, their tove was not a toy.

"I'd have thought, with the way your people emphasize courtesy," Jak said, "that our kids would make you miserable or furious, since it takes us a long time to learn manners."

After catching his breath, Shadow said, "Oh, if they were adults I'd have eviscerated a dozen of them, but they're *children,* Jak. Bright, funny, brave, and harmless— like kittens."

Dinner was served, and just as Jak's SSE text had warned was customary, they all got bowls from a common pot rather than individual orders. It was a pleasant gooey mess of chunks of beefrat and vegetables in thick broth; Jak specked it to be "stew," the stuff they were always eating in fantasy vivs. Those elves knew what they were doing.

"Shadow," Dujuv said, "you mentioned that you thought the kids were nice, uh, the way kittens are nice, masen?"

"Yes, Dujuv."

"Well, this is a stupid question—I know the Rubahy keep some Earth animals as pets, rabbits, cats, ferrets, and pigs I've heard of . . . does your species have pets of your own?"

Shadow whistled a low resonant blat, equivalent to a deep sigh. "We did have pets. But the invasion fleet did not bring pets, and when the human secret weapon sent Alpha Draconis nova, everything back there burned. We might have salvaged DNA, but as you know, the Beyobathu sued for our homeworld as a salvage-of-war planet, and they pull much influence with the Galactic State. They got court permission and had already sterilized our homeworld, to improve their case that it was available for salvage, before we even found out that there was a court. So we have a few meat animals, cloned from frozen samples in the invasion's food lockers. Nothing we kept as pets."

Jak had seen pictures of Beyobathu; they were sort of two-headed plesiosaurs, supposedly sole proprietors of one whole globular cluster, with almost a billion years of recorded history. "Isn't one of the judges on the Galactic Court a Beyobathu?"

"Yes. He has promised to be fair." Jak was always amazed at how much irony a being with no facial expressions could communicate. "Anyway, yes, we had pets. Especially the elawathil, which I suppose you would say looked like a half-sized, short-necked ostrich. They had some of the loyalty and playfulness of your dogs, but could talk a little, like your parrots, and were about as bright as your dolphins. They co-evolved with us—one of our great poets says that 'elawathil and Rubahy were together before we were ourselves.' In a thousand of your years, we have not ceased to miss to them."

The table fell quiet. Then Shadow on the Frost said, "But I am spoiling the gathering! Someone start some fun, please!"

As if on cue, Tlokro, one of the kobolds, came in with a gigantic bowl of chocolate pudding, announcing that there was plenty. Jak had filled up on stew, so he had only one bowl of the pudding, but everyone else seemed to put away at least three or four bowls. "Wonder what their calorie demand is like around here," Jak murmured to Dujuv.

"Something like mine, I bet. Toktru, Jak, it may be hell, but the food is wonderful. And I haven't seen a fat Mercurial yet, either—the big-boned people really *are* just big-boned. They must exercise."

Kyffimna, who had been sitting next to Dujuv quietly for the whole meeting, made a strange sputtering noise that sounded exactly like a woman trying to suppress a giggle so that she won't spew chocolate pudding through her nose. "Oh, yes, Dujuv. Plenty of that." She rested a hand lightly on his arm. Dujuv sat up as if shocked. It was Jak's turn to work on controlling his pudding. Obviously it was tricky stuff.

After dessert they passed big jugs of a heavy-bodied, thick red wine, laced with soporifics, painkillers, and euphorics; it didn't taste like much but the effect made up for it. Everyone older than toddlers got roaring drunk, musical instruments came out, and the chamber rang with laughter and singing in harmony in the echoing vaulted main chamber of the krilj.

These people definitely deserved a better break, Jak thought, *and I have no idea how to get it for them.*

Soon wine and comfort took their toll. After smaller children and older adults had drifted off to their chambers, and the stories—mostly about accidents in which people had been killed, as far as Jak could tell, with a leavening of tales of people caught having sex in odd circumstances— began to ramble and repeat, Durol said, "Well, before we tire them out any further, I guess there's a little conversation that I ought to have privately with Jak, Dujuv, and Shadow. Kyffimna, I need you in it too, since you're my second in command, and then I guess I want Bref in case we need to look at some computer stuff."

An older boy or younger man (his face was young and blotchy but he was tall, the neck that stuck out of his pressure suit collar was long and skinny but the shoulders were wide), said, "And me too, please? I should know too."

Durol resisted a smile. "Narav, if I tried to exclude you, you'd just listen at the door. And besides, you're right, as a family thing, you should get used to going where your sister and brother go, and seeing what they're responsible for. Say Kyffimna and I get drunk one night and knife each other, you might be second in command."

Narav looked like he wanted to complain about the teasing, but he just said, "Thanks," perhaps because he was grateful to be included.

They gathered around the screen in the little domed chamber that was Durol's office, lounging on the mats on the floor, and Durol said, "All right, so we aren't going to solve this with a battalion of B&Es, which would work. So we're back to using what we have at hand, plus whatever advantages we can get from two apprentice spies and an ex-

perienced mercenary that the other side probably doesn't
know we have yet."

"It might help our guests to have some idea how all this
happened," Bref said, "and some of what we already
know." He was about seventeen or eighteen, Jak guessed,
filled in more than his rawboned brother, with a quieter,
more serious affect.

"Give it to them. I'm going to go get us all some cocoa.
Just realized this little meeting might go an hour. Would've
started sooner if I'd thought of it." Durol lurched up and
through the door, muttering about getting old.

"Pay no attention to the old gwont," Bref said, "he'll
make it to a hundred and twenty. He's too tough and mean
to go sooner."

Dujuv glanced at Jak as if he'd been stung; Jak nodded.
To a hundred and twenty? That was middle-aged . . . or it
was everywhere they had ever been. Jak saw that Kyffimna
had noted the look that passed between them and didn't
look happy about it.

"Anyway," Bref said, "it's easy enough to tell. Just over
a year ago—Earth year, of course, not our little bitty Mercury years—we were getting a little broke because prices
had been kind of low, and we'd had a magma accident
where one of our fifteen-wheelers ended up slagged—"

"I'm still real sorry about that," Narav said, "but it was
a perfectly understandable accident, and—"

"Brother, I wasn't going to mention you at all, till you
brought it up." He glanced sideways at Jak. "And Narav's
right, could've happened to anybody, ain't his fault, ain't
anyone's. You want to fault anyone, you fault that Safe-
world Mercurial Insurance, because they decided it was
twenty percent negligence so what they did was, they gave
us thirty percent of the payout as a loan instead of cash

money, and that put us over the line so that other creditors started jacking rates and payments and all on the variable loans.

"Anyway, we were in some trouble, not bigger than trouble we'd had before, but trouble, so we leased the other side of the crater, a hundred-and-twenty-degree slice of just the rim wall, to MLB, which at the time just looked like a new startup labor company. After two generations in this crater we knew there wasn't much over there, and we told 'em, but they wanted it anyway. Well, less than a hundred hours after they got here, they were doing all kinds of things in the central pinnacle, which they hadn't rented at all, so Pop went over to tell them that he didn't like squatting, and they shot the two heets he took with him, and gave him a beating. Which is actually why he walks that way, not because he's getting old.

"Then they showed him that they'd bought up about three-quarters of our debt—I guess they just shot Prano and Bleron, and gave him the beating first, for fun, because they already knew they had his nutsack in their visegrips—but being our friends and all, they were prepared to offer us a way out. They made us their subsidiary, took a hundred percent control, and we get out just as soon as we pay off all the loans, which at current rates ought to be about seventy-five years. We stopped discussing the central pinnacle, and since then they've built that into a regular fortress. And nobody from here, even though theoretically we're their landlord, has been allowed to have a look at what they're doing on their side of the crater wall, but I can tell you anyway."

He raised his left hand, pulled off his suit glove, faced his purse toward him, and probed and spoke to it.

"We got you one of those over-the-suit-glove ones," Narav pointed out.

"*Radzundslag* got it. Gets everything, sooner or later, masen? Now quiet for a second, so I can get this display up."

The screen lit up and a set of columns appeared; on one side, there was a list of family names—or rather quacco names, Jak realized—including "Eldothaler," this quacco. Then there was a list of metals, with masses and prices listed; and then a column of zeros. To the right was a list of "Metals sold, MLB" which listed about the same masses and much higher prices.

"It's like this," Bref said. "One of the few Treaty Laws we have here that's any good is that the quacco that extracts the metal has to get eighty-five percent of the price of that metal when it's sold offplanet—which is defined as actually received and paid for at the other end, up at the Hive or the Aerie or Ceres or wherever. Or another way to look at it is that all the middlemen combined aren't legally allowed to get more than fifteen percent. It tends to encourage direct buying between industry out there and mining back here, which is good for both—lowers their prices and raises ours.

"Now, on the books, it looks like we've sold everything to MLB for the past few months, at way below market prices, and they should only be able to go up fifteen percent on what they've paid us. But supposedly none of that cheap metal we were forced to sell them has been resold. Just suspiciously similar quantities have been sold—at much higher prices—by MLB.

"Now, the way the enforcement works is, there's a trace isotope mix, registered and recorded, that every quacco puts into each metal lot before we deliver. The central office assigns each mix, so that every metal lot ever shipped is unique, and theoretically even if it's melted down, the stuff stays labeled."

Jak asked, "What if someone melts metal from a bunch of different batches, mixes it, and sells that?"

Narav laughed. "My brother can give you a very patronizing lecture on that subject, like he did me. 'Because, Slag-in-Your-Skull, you can't sell it legally unless it matches one of your assigned tracer mixes, and metal from mixed lots will always have a bunch of tracers in it that you weren't assigned, so the only way to resell stolen metal is to put it all through isotope separation, clean it completely, and then put your tracer in it.' Which is why Bref thinks they're probably not even mining over on the other side of the crater."

"My guess is," Bref said, "that what they wanted there wasn't rocks, but empty space—there are a bunch of very big chambers we never filled in over there, places where we did a lot of extracting the last time tin was high-priced, and instead of refilling we dumped waste magma onto the crater floor. Huge spaces that would be perfect as a place to hide their isotope separators for three reasons: plenty of flat crater floor nearby to spread the solar collectors on, great big enclosed spaces to hide the machines in, and since isotope separation is a slow process no matter what, lots of room to store the metal ingots until you can get them converted. If you look at the dates in that table closely, it looks like they started out with about a three-month lag between acquiring metal and selling it, and now it's more like five months; I would bet they're adding laser-centrifuge and plasma spectrometer setups over there as fast as they can, but it's not enough to process all the metal they're grabbing from sixty quaccos."

"Isn't that expensive?" Dujuv asked.

"Very, but they seem to have deep pockets, and meanwhile the shortage it's creating is raising prices in the upper solar system. In the long run it's more revenue for them—what's it worth to have a near-monopoly on practically all the industrial metals?"

Durol returned with a pitcher of cocoa that tasted as if it were an experiment to determine how much chocolate would saturate a solution in heavy cream. "Well, so you heets all have the basics on it, then?"

"I think so," Dujuv said. "How many people does MLB have?"

"Only around a hundred, but they're dug in. None of 'em miners of any kind," Kyffimna supplied, edging a little closer to Dujuv. "Meet 'em in Bigpile and you know right away—these are pure thugs. Not tough or disciplined or smart enough to be in a military outfit, but able to scare the hell out of miners."

"We're tough but not fighters," Durol said. "We never really had much of a chance to learn. An injury that takes you off the job is so expensive to your quacco that your pizos won't lct you fight. I don't suppose you three trained fighters could make much of a difference?"

"One-on-one, sure," Jak said.

Dujuv nodded emphatically. "Any of us could tackle any onc of them, but against ten not-too-trained goons, the three of us might have a fifty-fifty chance, and that's not—"

The two boys were snickering. "Now that's a panth," Narav said. "Last week, the two panths in our quacco were in a bar in Bigpile, and they got to talking and decided to try going up against three MLBers, so they called 'em out right there in the bar. And our panths got their butts handed to them. They're both in the Uninsured Charity Hospital, right now. Nothing against panths or anything, I mean I've grown up in the same krilj with 'em and all, but figuring odds, or any kind of figuring, isn't exactly their strong suit."

"I am sitting in front of you," Dujuv said, very quietly, "and I would rather you didn't talk about panths in general as if I were not here."

Shadow made a strange, throat-clearing noise, and said, "Dujuv's figuring is singing-on. Your two panths had no combat training, and didn't attempt surprise. If the three of us were to try to attack an MLB party of ten, we would hit from behind without warning, each taking out one before the rest were fighting back. That's down to seven. As you may have heard, my species is faster and stronger, individually, than yours, and I am also proficient and brutal. I could probably eliminate at least three more of them from the fight. That leaves four. Though he is only an unmodified human, Jak is skilled and practiced. He would almost certainly eliminate his first opponent, and might get a start on his second. Dujuv is as skilled as Jak, and a panth; he would take out one opponent quickly and entangle the other two in the losing game of trying to stop him. When Jak and I finished our opponents, there would be only two of them, and three of us, and we'd overwhelm the last two easily. If their numbers were much above ten, though, they would hold the advantage.

"I cannot say whether or not Dujuv calculated as I did, but in my view, he came up with the correct answer."

"He's talking about you like you're not here, too," Narav said.

"Shut up," his brother explained. "You're right, Shadow on the Frost. Narav, we both owe Dujuv an apology. I'm sorry."

Narav glanced at his father and sister, and apparently

didn't like what he saw. "I'm sorry," he said. "Obviously you know your business better than I do."

"Accepted, of course," Dujuv grumbled. "And it's all irrelevant anyway since there are a hundred of them."

Jak said, "Here's half a thought. My Uncle Sib has been a mercenary and a spymaster for a lot of his life. He might have ideas. I'll back-channel something to him and see what he thinks. While I'm at it, I want to see what Colonel Mattanga has to say for herself."

"At least you'll give her someone new to ignore," Dujuv said. "I just wish we had some ideas of our own."

Shadow added, "I shall send the Duke of Uranium a short report, also back-channeled. He is ruthless where his monopoly is concerned. MLB is a threat to some of the best uranium and thorium mines in the solar system. That will surely get his attention."

"Anything that you think might help," Durol said, with a sigh. "Well, I guess you were supposed to infiltrate, so tomorrow we'll infiltrate you into our quacco. Which is a real simple way of saying, congratulations, pizos, to go with your bed and board here in the krilj, you've got jobs. Meeting's adjourned."

Dujuv stayed behind to talk with Kyffimna. Back at their shared sleeping chamber, Jak sent his messages to Colonel Mattanga and to Uncle Sib, and had just finished figuring out how he was supposed to sling the pressure suit hammock when Dujuv came in.

He didn't move like a panth in moderate gravity. He sat down on the room's one low bench and said, "Jak, Shadow, I don't know how this can get any worse."

Shadow on the Frost looked up from his reader. Rubahy do not sleep, and he had been planning to spend the night trying to solve some minor mysteries in the history of his family. "Dujuv Gonzawara, my tove and pizo, it can always get worse. We can be badly wounded or dishonored, or misfortunes that merely seemed inevitable can manifest in the present. What has so discouraged you?"

"Well." Dujuv sat there, staring at the floor. "*Radzundslag,* first of all."

"The heet who stole Bref's outside purse?" Jak asked.

"It's what got Bref's outside purse, but it's not a heet. And it's the reason why they think a hundred and twenty is a ripe old age. And a lot of things. Background radiation here, so close to the sun, with no atmosphere, is screaming high, plus there's also constant exposure to nasty toxic metals, in the form of dust that gets everywhere. That's what they call radzundslag—the mix of radiation and poisons that they live in from the moment they're born, and that they're all dying of, all of them, all the time. Even if we do stop MLB, we will barely have touched a tenth of a percent of what's wrong with this place."

Shadow said, "But we will have touched that. Hard enough, I hope, to end it. Like most invasions, evil is best defeated in detail."

Dujuv made an unhappy noise. "Weehu, I almost forgot to thank you for sticking up for me in there. I appreciate it, Shadow."

"I was glad to do the service, but truthfully, I was also just annoyed at the slight to our honor."

"It's good that you were," Jak said, "because I never know what to say when people treat Dujuv that way."

"There are two expressions in your language," Shadow said, "which you might try for such occasions. If they begin abusing your friend, say, 'That's not true.' If they persist, say, 'Fuck you, asshole.' "

Jak and Dujuv both started to laugh; Shadow said, "I was not aware that I had said anything funny."

Smiling and shaking his head, Jak said, "It's just that the first of those expressions is moderately rude, and the second is spectacularly rude. It would upset people."

Shadow set his reader down and looked at Jak long enough to make him uncomfortable. "I fancy I know humans rather better, and like them much better, than most Rubahy do. But every so often I am reminded, somehow, that you are absolutely aliens. Why should you care about showing courtesy to someone who has insulted your friend? Why worry about offense to one who has revealed himself as at best a lout and at worst a declared enemy? Yet most of you will not give the lie to, nor call out, someone who insults a whole breed of human, or a nation or a faith or any other group to which your friend belongs, even though you know full well that the insult cuts your friend as deep as a personal one would. Human courtesy seems to require that you sit and listen and nod, or even chuckle as if it were an inept joke, if someone says that panths are stupid, yet you would start a brawl that instant if they were to say that Dujuv specifically is stupid—but how much difference can it make to Dujuv? Now, I know, it's in your Nakasen's Principles, it's 56: 'Courtesy has no logical basis but practice it anyway,' and perhaps you are not supposed to question or argue with a Principle—"

Jak's purse said, "Urgent message from Greenworld Intelligence, via back channel."

"Put it up on the screen for all of us."

The chamber lights dimmed. The projector's white square formed on the wall. The person looking out at them was not Mattanga, but was sitting in her not-yet-redecorated office. "Hello, this is a response to your query.

We have no information on why former head of security Mattanga did not acknowledge information received from stringer agents, but in any case, while we are forced to agree that it would be to Greenworld's advantage to suppress the activities of MLB and return the situation to the *status quo ante,* we cannot see that the advantage is so great as to warrant our sending an armed force. We do not feel it is even enough to warrant the retention of two agents in place. The two of you, Jak Jinnaka and Dujuv Gonzawara, are therefore discharged from Greenworld's service, *in situ,* and will have to make your own arrangements for transportation to any other location, or seek employment where you are. You can expect no further support from us and we request that you do not contact us. If by any chance it should happen that you are able to take effective action against MLB, that you take it, and that it succeeds—entirely on your own initiative and without making any use of Greenworld resources—we would be happy to consider reinstating you with our organization." The message blinked out.

"Well," Dujuv said, "I think I dak what you mean about how things can always get worse, Shadow."

CHAPTER 13

"There's Things Worse Than Being Broke, or Dead"

This is your rocable," Kyffimna said. "Don't hesitate to use it if you need it."

The rocable strapped to the back of your pressure suit; it was a twenty-five-kilometer-long monosil cable with a rocket, transponder, and grapple at the end. Monosil, the same stuff used for sunclipper lines, could hold against tons of force, but a twenty-five-kilometer length of it massed less than a kilogram. If you were in real trouble, you fired the rocable. Trailing the monosil, the rocket and transponder climbed high into the sky, and, in Mercury's low gravity, fell back slowly; if any craft was nearby during that long fall, it grabbed your rocable and hauled you up.

With so many small taxi and freight rockets in service, plus a large number of low-flying satellites and other crewed and uncrewed spacecraft, rescue was more likely than not.

Of course, one dirgey tune that Reedjox, the simi who played accordion, had wheezed out interminably last night, had been about two "poor stranded miners," surrounded by rising magma, watching as their rocables fell slowly but inexorably back to Mercury:

No ship above, no rocket near
No friendly satellite
And closing 'round their island drear
The magma hot and white.

Jak remembered from ethnography class that people in dangerous occupations often had a rich folklore about accidents; he wondered if the "Bil Balee" and "Kei Sijoniz" ballad was toktru. When "and now the rocket's fallen and the time is all run out" would anyone actually say:

Bil, we're gonna cook here,
And suit-steamed we shall be.
So the com log ought to show you've been
A toktru tove to me.

Today they were substitution pumping for aluminum. Dujuv would be operating the portable slagger (a big positron laser) melting a medium-sized hill of fused metal; a mix of iron, copper, silicon, and general junk, to provide the heavy magma that would force the valuable stuff up. Shadow would be jocking remote slagger two kilometers down in the ore pocket, via telepresence. Jak was to be flowmaster, making sure the heavy magma flowed down the two-meter tube at an acceptable rate, the light melted ore flowed up through its narrow heated tube, and the flow was delivered at the proper temperature to pour across the tunable-matter plates of the separator. "That's the only piece of equipment we rent," Kyffimna said, "so if you gotta lose anything, don't lose it."

Jak looked at the separator thoughtfully. It was about sixty meters long—more than half the length of a soccer field—by twenty-five tall by forty wide. The outer casing was bright chrome steel, formed and extruded here in the vacuum of Mercury and therefore never tarnished. On each side of it, the catchers (for no reason Jak knew, he had heard some people call them the "washboards"), great racks of many thousands of thin metal rollers running the width of the separator, sat waiting, their empty bins below. To move the separator, Jak knew, would require raising it on jacks and lowering it onto a linducer track built out for the purpose.

"It looks kind of big to lose," he observed, "but I guess we can tie a string on it or something."

"I mean lose it to a magma flood or from overloading or any stuff like that," Kyffimna said. "You sure you're not the panth in the crowd?"

"Uh, I said something dumb, but is that a reason to insult my tove?"

There was a long silence, and then Kyffimna asked, "Dujuv? Why didn't you say something?"

"You'd have just thought I was humorless, like all panths."

She left in silence.

The work was not complex or demanding, and they had soon settled into the rhythm of it. The sun, two and a half times as wide as it was seen from Earth, the Hive, or the Aerie, bathed the landscape in fierce light. Though the brightness was filtered by Jak's faceplate, the stark contrast and pallid grays of the land around him still demonstrated the fury of a nearby star. The short horizon—just three kilometers away—gave a strange, foreshortened feel to the view, as if it were a stage set or a photo backdrop.

Jak hadn't realized what "the busiest space in the solar system" could really mean until he looked up from the Mercurial surface. Always at least fifty satellites, local rockets, space stations, ferries, longshore capsules, and interplanetary spaceships were within fifty kilometers of the surface, all in the dead silence of vacuum, moving at six times the speed of a bullet, so that they shot from horizon to horizon in no more than four minutes.

Now that he was getting a little accustomed, Jak took a moment to watch the separator. On one end of the huge machine, there was a blur in the air, like a hummingbird's wings if a hummingbird were made of silver, extending almost the length of the machine itself beyond its edge, an oddly rectangular cloud of blurred shining metal. Those were the heart of the big machine, four hundred plates—sheets of tunable matter, thinner than tracing paper, more rigid than reinforced concrete, the surface of each covered with more than 10^{25} pseudoatoms—flying in and out two to five times a second.

Each pseudoatom was a complex knot of a few hundred ordinary atoms, essentially a molecule configured so that an electronic signal on one end of the molecule changed the effective valence on the other end. Ordinary chemical atoms cannot tell the difference between a pseudoatom and a real one; both have the same electrons in the same orbitals, and the fact that a pseudoatom has no nucleus and is tuned to imitate a particular atom is invisible to ordinary matter. The pseudoatoms on the separator were tunable to be pseudofluorine (the strongest oxidizing atom), pseudofrancium (the strongest reducing atom), or pseudohelium (the most inert atom). Behind each pseudoatom sat a molecule-sized NMR detector; as hot magma poured over the plates, the pseudoatom switched to fluorine. If the NMR detector registered aluminum, the pseudoatom stayed fluorine and retained it; if the detector registered anything else, the pseudoatom switched to helium, let it go, and then switched back to fluorine to try again. That process could be repeated many thousands of times per second; in a mere hundred iterations or so, faster than one can speak a single syllable, the tip of every pseudoatom would be occupied by an aluminum atom, and the sheet would shoot out to deposit the aluminum onto the rollers of the washboard; wipers moved the aluminum continuously off the rollers and down into the bin, and the now-blank sheet of pseudoatoms flew back into the magma to collect another load.

Every stroke of a plate represented a little over four hundred grams of aluminum, they had told Jak, allowing for leaks and wastage; in six hours of working flat out today, the 383 separator plates tuned for aluminum would pull out about ten thousand tonnes of pure aluminum.

Aside from watching the pumps for trouble and monitoring flow rates, Jak was to watch the NMR indicators for any good quantities of anything resalable. Right now, after all the aluminum had been captured, nine of the other seventeen plates were capturing oxygen for the krilj's own use, and the last eight were capturing nitrogen, which was the most abundant stuff in there that could currently be sold for a profit.

Anything that it didn't currently pay to smelt went off the tunable-matter plates and into the heavy slag that Dujuv was pumping down. (Because they were mainly extracting light elements today, the residue was much heavier than the raw stuff coming out of the ground.)

An hour went by, and the only event of any interest was a spike of molybdenum in the mix. Per instructions, Jak reset three plates to capture moly instead of nitrogen. This was a matter of pointing at options on a screen, and took less than a minute, but at least it felt like work. Jak watched as the newly assigned plates began their too-fast-to-see dosi-do in and out of the flowing magma, each exiting plate wiping off two kilograms of moly dust onto the rollers—nothing like the tonnes of aluminum and oxygen shuffling out, or the dozens of kilograms of nitrogen, but still, according to the rolling util meter, every forty seconds the quacco was earning the price of a big sack of potatoes.

Kyffimna came back shortly after to ask, "How's it all going?"

"Dull but fine," Jak said.

"Dull *is* fine."

"Can you stand another stupid question?"

"I live for 'em."

"Well, then why don't you just split up all the rock you run through? The tunable-matter plates can extract any kind of atom, and every atom is salable at *some* price, right, even if you aren't going to get much for it."

Kyffimna chuckled. "How many years of school have you had?"

"Uh, four years dev school, eight years gen school, and two years at the Academy—uh, fourteen."

"At least they taught you to add. Must've skipped some economics. A plate can only extract one element at a time. If a plate is extracting something cheap, like silicon, so that it passes up extracting something valuable, like thorium, you lose money. You want to get all you can of the highest-priced stuff, so you take that out first and allocate as many plates as it takes to get it all. Then you extract the most valuable stuff that's left in the slag, then the most valuable after that, and sooner or later you're down to something marginal that you don't take all of."

"But there's stuff like gold and uranium in there—not much, but the NMR shows it."

"A plate doesn't cycle till it's full, and you have to have

enough of whatever you're extracting in there to support at least two cycles per second or you run the risk of cooking the plate in the heat."

Jak looked again at the immense tank, half the size of a soccer field, and the blur of plates flying in and out of it. "Not a dumb question this time, I hope. I bet there are a lot of accidents around anything that big, moving that fast."

"Not dumb at all, and the answer is yes. Don't be one of them. Precesses the hell out of your pizos and their production goes way down for days afterwards. Not to mention that if there's anything left of you the rest of us have to clean it up."

Jak shuddered, then realized. "And I see what they meant in all those songs about getting slagged. That molten rock would dissolve anything in a pressure suit, and the suit itself, masen? You'd end up in solution in it."

"Sort of. First suit cooling would fail, then the temp would go way up inside so you'd, um, steam, basically, in your own juices—half a minute to turn you into Jak au Jus—then in another minute the suit would rupture."

She wandered off to talk with Dujuv. Jak noticed that it was much, much easier to concentrate on his job than it had been. The blur of the separator plates continued, and the flow of molten rock never slowed.

She spent a while with Dujuv, and then with Shadow, and seemed happy enough with both. Before going, she stopped by Jak again and said, "You all are doing fine as far as I can see. I'll stop by at the end of the shift and see how things are going, and just look over your shoulder while you walk through shutdown, but that's pretty much a formality. Pop wants to have another little talk tonight, he and some other older heets think they have some ideas. You haven't heard from your uncle yet?"

"No, which is unusual. Usually when I ask that heet to talk, I don't get another word in for hours. And I've never known him to be at a loss for an idea." Jak added mentally, *as long as quality of the idea is not an issue.*

"All right." She seemed to be about to get back into the little five-wheeler and take off, but then she said, "Uh, can I ask you something?"

"Sure."

"Um, your friend Dujuv. Does he have a demmy?"

"He's kind of, well, carrying a torch for someone, but she's been all done with him for a long time," Jak said, figuring the truth would be the simplest.

"Oh. And, uh . . . what does he like?"

"Well, I've known him a long time," Jak said, "and, uh—most of his demmies are kind of tiny. Little bitty girls, all of them."

"Oh." Kyffimna sounded very sad. "He's a really nice heet. I was . . . oh, weehu, Jak, I'm no good at the discreet stuff. Of course I was sounding you out—"

"I hadn't noticed."

She laughed and swatted his arm; it was like being batted playfully by a gorilla. "Well, anyway, I was just wondering if he was slow to pick up a hint or something, or if he was mad because of some of the stupid things I said. I mean, I know you all won't be here long. Just . . . while you're here . . . you know, he's good-looking and he's one toktru nice heet."

"He's about as good as they make," Jak agreed, not sure what else to add, or whether that was just making it worse. "I don't like to carry bad news, but he's pretty good about hints and things. I speck he probably got it. Probably it's not anything you said, though, if that helps you feel better. Masen?"

"Toktru masen. You're blunt, Jak, but I needed it. Thanks." She got on the five-wheeler and drove away.

At lunch break, as they ate in the cabin of the five-wheeler, Jak recounted the whole conversation to Dujuv, specking he'd think it was funny that the big, strange-looking girl had taken such an interest in him.

After listening, Dujuv shook his head, wiped more sweat from his hairless scalp with a rag, and took another bite of his sandwich. "Jak, you didn't have to be *that* blunt with her, it probably hurt. And she'd have specked, eventually, pizo."

"I'm just trying to help. I know she's not attractive to you and you need to get some distance—"

"Jak, the only thing she's done is like me. It's not her fault that I don't like her back the same way. It's gonna hurt her no matter what, and I'm sad enough about that without having you hurt her too."

There was a crackle and bang overhead on the five-wheeler cab's speakers. "Mayday, all channels, Northeast Caloris Territory, Mayday, all channels. We've got a magma breakout in the southwest section of Crater Hamner, crew isolated from a vehicle and in danger. All aid requested—"

"That's over by the MLB facility on the opposite wall," Durol Eldothaler's voice said, in the speakers. "Move, people."

Dujuv was at the controls in an instant; Shadow and Jak barely had time to belt in before the five-wheeler was spinning across the waste country. Jak pulled off his suit glove and spoke directly to his purse. "Order everything into emergency shutdown at the site we were working at," he said. "I don't know if we'll be getting back there today, so shut down all the stuff that was on standby for lunch."

"Main separator chamber will be drained in ten minutes, shafts will be cleared in twenty minutes, and all above-surface slag will be cooled in three hours. Subsurface magma may remain liquid for up to six days but is not estimated to pose a hazard."

"Good." Jak pressed the reward spot; his purse cheebled, indicating it felt rewarded and would try to do similar things in the future. Then Jak pulled his glove, and then his gauntlet, back on over his purse. He looked around.

They were just passing the central pinnacle, joining a dozen other vehicles with Eldothaler Quacco insignia, all racing and bouncing over the shattered, partly melted land. The combination of low gravity, loose light dust, and slick melted surfaces meant that traction was sporadic and unpredictable. Dust flew away from the tractors in parabolic arcs, not sticking to itself and unslowed by the air, a stream of tiny streaks like illustrations in a physics book. The five-, ten-, and fifteen-wheelers bashed over the rough and lumpy ground, wheeled arms flying up and down as needed, sometimes skidding sideways or bounding high on their legs like a hand flexing on a tabletop, sometimes running on only three legs with the other two raised high, almost fastidiously, as if to step over a dirty spot. They were about halfway there.

Dujuv was on the com, getting directions, and he took a moment to say, "Helmets on and suit up. One of you do me, please. We'll probably have to pop the cabin open as soon as we get there. Sounds like they're going to need lots of hands outside."

Jak and Shadow closed suits and checked. Luckily, Dujuv had only removed his helmet and sweat cap to eat.

Still, the cab was about as stable as skateboarding on an airplane wing. Fitting the sweatcap onto Dujuv would have been easy if covering his eyes or folding his ears down had been all right, and getting his earphones on would have been a cinch if they had ignored his cries of "Ouch!" and "Careful!" Shadow and Jak really only struggled in getting his head into the helmet, straight, with the helmet locked down. (It would have been easy enough if Dujuv's skull had been soft and flexible.) As it was, however, it was a challenge, and they were less than a minute from arrival when a green light in Dujuv's heads-up display told them that he was okay to step into vacuum.

From the top of the next rise, the jagged rock wall of the crater, like the brutally twisted lower jaw of some ancient leviathan, lunged up over the horizon.

Dujuv stopped behind the other vehicles, saying "Go to general freq twenty-two, that's what everyone's using," popped the door on the cab, jumped out, and ran up the line of parked vehicles, Jak and Shadow racing after. Clearly their tove had heard something during the drive here that precessed him pretty badly.

Over the next low rise, they found a lake of magma, at least four hundred meters across as they faced its narrow side, slightly more than a kilometer long, glowing white everywhere with just occasional red and yellow scum at its very edges. Almost in the center of the lake, at least 150 meters from shore, was a small island of still-bare ground, no more than twenty meters across, and on it, two human figures standing as close to the center as they could manage. At first Jak thought he was seeing them waver from the rising heat between him and them; then he realized that that doesn't happen in a vacuum. The two workers were weaving as if drunk; the cooling systems on their suits must be close to overload.

"Where are their cooling fins? And why aren't they

using their rocables?" Jak asked, barely aware that he had spoken aloud.

Kyffimna answered, moving next to him and putting her helmet against his, to talk via conduction so that valuable radio-cellular communications channels could be kept open. "They don't have any of either and MLB wouldn't have given them to them. MLB goes into Bigpile all the time and just grabs up drunks and druggers for day labor. If you don't have equipment of your own, you work without it—they're *toktru* nonunion," Kyffimna explained. "We're going to try for a rescue, but we need a creeper bridge, and that's coming as fast as it can, from the Thomagatz Quacco, they had one and there was a big freight rocket available, so right now it's all a race against time."

"Who's winning?"

"Us, barely. That island is sinking because it's melting; there's no more magma coming in. So as the magma cools, the island should sink slower and slower, and maybe not sink all the way at all. That ought to give us time enough— if everything else goes perfect and those two heets can keep standing up and stay in the middle of that island. Especially with this many hands on the job—creeper bridges are one of those things where the more people you have, the faster it goes. And the Thomagatzes are sending along four experienced techs to supervise."

"Who's paying for this?"

"Us and the Thomagatzes, for right now. Then we'll send MLB a bill, which they'll fight in court, because the only courts around here are private, and they'll eventually get it into some court with some judge they can buy or threaten, and they won't pay. And you'll notice we don't have any workers from the MLB side out here helping; because this is going to be a little scary and dangerous—we'll all have to work less than three meters above the magma, and if you take a dive into that your name is sizzle-sizzle-pop. So the MLB heets are, let's say, being a little shy about coming out to join us. So we're losing a pile of money and risking our lives, masen? Dak it now? But—look at that white-hot shit, Jak. Think about what it would feel like to cook in your suit like a potato in foil. We can't leave two living people in the middle of a rising magma lake, without trying. We'd have to look at ourselves in the mirror afterward. There's things a lot worse than being broke, or dead."

"Rocket coming in, clear the area, five-minute warning," came over the general freq. Everyone hurried back to their vehicles for shelter from the sodium exhaust.

Since the door was pointed opposite the landing point, they left it open and did not bother to pressurize the cabin for the short wait. They saw the white flare overhead grow bigger and bigger, then clearly head for the field behind them. Jak looked out from the cabin window and saw the silent shiny shower, a perfect parabola of millions of silvery dust motes, glinting in the sun like a wispy steel rainbow, arcing down to spatter the ground around them. It was the sodium condensing out of the exhaust.

In the vacuum, it was soundless, but Jak felt a heavy vibration for just a moment through his feet as the rocket touched down and shut off its engines. Then everyone ran to it.

Passing pieces of the bridge to each other, they had just removed it from the cargo hold, and the people who dakked the djeste of the bridge were arranging the parts, when the general freq crackled. "This is MLB Operations. Anyone working near the accidental magma pool, please be aware that to save vital facilities inside the structure we will be dumping additional magma in five minutes. Magma level will rise about a half meter. Everyone clear the area. Dumping in five minutes."

The voice clicked off.

Durol's voice on the radio was frantic. "Hailing the controller inside the MLB facility. Hailing the controller inside the MLB facility. There is an emergency in progress with human life at stake and Treaty Law prohibits turning off your radio."

The silence continued.

"Hailing the controller inside the MLB facility. You have two employees stranded on an island in that lake and they are much less than a half meter above the magma. They will not survive if you dump more magma." He clicked to the group frequency and added, "Keep working on the bridge. They can't do this. We're going to get to use that bridge, so get it ready."

All the workers scrambled, following the directions of the Thomagatz technicians, linking strut to truss, frame to brace, and piece to piece. Jak had no idea exactly how this thing would do it, but it was a bridge that could reach those people, and he did his best to follow directions as quickly as he could.

After almost a minute there was a scratchy sound on the emergency frequency. "This is MLB central. Please repeat."

Durol did, carefully.

"Our records show that all our employees are inside, safe."

"These are contract workers, I'm sure! They don't have rocables and they're in regular pressure suits without gauntlets or therm boots. From the way they're staggering I'd judge they already are near heat prostration, and I speck their cooling systems may fail at any moment. We will be

ready with a creeper bridge in just a couple of minutes. If
you wait another fifteen minutes before dumping that
magma, then—"

"Thank you for advising us of the situation," the voice
said.

On the work frequency, a cry. "They've dumped it!
They've dumped it!"

Some evil streak in human nature—a streak which is its
own punishment—compels us to see the worst. The crowd
ran to the ridge top, just in time to see the thick red rolling
wave of magma sweep across the island. It was only about
waist height, but being many times denser than water, it hit
with overwhelming force, and the two pressure-suited figures were thrown headlong into the magma. One lay still;
the other struggled for an instant, then seemed to stop like
a running-down movie of a swimmer. A moment later, one
suit, and then the other, burst open, and the distant moun-
tains wavered, refracted by the briefly rising column of
steam.

Shadow rushed by Jak and Dujuv; both of them cried out
for just an instant, on the frequency they shared with him,
but a moment later he was coming back from the lake. He
seemed to have run down to its very edge, bent over for one
instant, and come back immediately. As he returned, they
could see that he was holding a sampling bucket. "We
ought to see what is in this magma," the Rubahy said. "If it
is what I fear and hope, we have a real crisis here—opportunity and danger." He glanced back toward the lake of
magma, in which the shapes of the two bodies were still just
barely visible. "Over on one of the other channels, I heard
that they dictated their wills and then turned off their trans-
mitters, not wanting to burden their friends and relatives

with the death cries that your media would surely have picked up and broadcast. They died with honor."

Jak shuddered. He was mostly remembering Principle 116: "The dead can have honor, but *they* can't eat it, either."

Kyffimna said that Durol normally prohibited business discussion until the dishes were cleared away and the last of dessert was eaten, but tonight at dinner in the krilj the whole quacco watched as Bref and Shadow walked through a set of graphs, showing what had been in the magma. The first surprise was that it had been unexpectedly radioactive, not at all common with any material with which they would normally work on Mercury. Even the isotopes used to tag metal were usually either stable, or, if radioactive, had such long half-lives that they were barely even detectable in the trace quantities used. "What does this mean and why did you look for it?" Durol asked.

"Well," Shadow said, "my friends, a thought crossed my mind. Before they dumped the red, almost-cool magma, that lake was white-hot, and there was barely any trace of surface cooling—only at the extreme edges, where the liquid was very shallow, am I correct?" They all nodded, and then the implications sank in. "So if that second wave of magma had started off white-hot, they'd have dumped it, not waited for several minutes, and anyway they appeared to be able to contain it . . . so it wasn't the heat that was the problem. That meant there was something dangerous about it otherwise—toxins or radioactivity. So I thought we'd better grab some of the material before it was mixed and diluted by other things, because it might be our best chance to find out what they were doing. Well, material at that temperature, highly radioactive, means just one thing—"

"They lost containment on a hot-metal, liquid-mix reactor," Durol said. His heavy gray eyebrows shot far up. "That's the only thing that would do that. Those things are basically just a big tank of mixed fissionables and moderators in solution in liquid metal, masen? So if they lost containment, or maybe if it overheated and breached, you'd get a lake like that, till it spread out enough to be in a geometry where the neutrons escaped enough to take it below criticality."

"Uh," Narav said.

Durol looked at his youngest son. "Told you to keep up with schoolwork, even when we can't afford the good stuff. Look, nuclear reactors run on neutrons; if lots of neutrons get out, it cools off and stops, if most of them stay inside, it heats up. Neutrons escape through the surface area, and a sphere—which is the shape of the container for those things—has very little surface area for the volume it encloses. Now, when it spreads out into a big old molten pancake, like this did, it's the same volume (because it's the same amount of stuff) but far more surface area. So eventually it cools off. What Shadow is saying is that they needed to hide the fact that they had a huge reactor there—what, probably half a million cubic meters in volume?—and then had an oopsie with it."

"I have already reported the 'oopsie' to the Duke of Uranium," Shadow said. "Unfortunately, he seems to be sequestered for the next four days—revisiting at Greenworld, for some reason—and he won't hear of it till he is done with whatever he is doing there. There are people at Fermi who can start all the preparations for an expedition to come here, investigate, and shut them down, but it will be a matter of several weeks, at least, before any such effort gets here. And in that time, given that they have that isotope separator, the MLB people can remove most or much of the evidence. After all, very likely that reactor itself was legal, and I have no doubt that the facility built around it was designed for quick concealment whenever an inspector from the Duchy of Uranium popped in."

"What is that facility?" Dujuv said. "Shadow, you have me talking like you. I just mean, so what were they going to do with this thing?"

"Well, first of all, power for the isotope separator, of course," Shadow said, "because the solar array they would need for a really large separator would be very conspicuous, and someone would ask what they needed all that electricity for. But secondly, those hot liquid metal reactors are extremely good for producing isotopes, as well. Very high neutron flux inside and you can lower materials in a thermos basket, or just dissolve it in the reactor and pull it out with tunable-matter plates. Then run it through your separator, throw the short-lived radioactives somewhere (in this case, apparently they flowed right into that molten lake) and you have all you need to dope lots of metal with false IDs, in quantity. And my offhand estimate—Bref helped tremendously with this—was that the amount of metal they were planning to reprocess, redope, and thus label for resale without having to pay the miners any of what's legitimately theirs—would be right around ten percent more than what Mercury currently produces. Oh, yes. They are definitely in it for the long haul and for a full conquest."

Durol was grinning broadly, now. "More opportunities."

Dujuv bolted an unusually large bite—which, for him, meant practically as big as his head—and said, "Opportunities? I'd say this sounds like a disaster."

"Only if they win," Durol said, grinning. Jak realized that even though Durol Eldothaler's face was a record of all the poisons poured into him, radiation shot through him, and burdens imposed on him since before he was born, it had the kind of character that you saw in medieval Italian paintings or movies. And somehow, his very facial deformity, the record of his murderous environment, enhanced the effect of his confident tone. "But they're in motion, and I seem to remember that they teach you in the Disciplines that 'to move—'"

"'—is to be vulnerable,'" Jak finished. "I see what you mean. They also teach that 'to stand still is to be defeated.' So I hope you have something in mind."

"Not yet," Durol said: "I'm going to have to spend a while in multiple conference messaging tonight. But I know there's much more to work with now than there has been. The isotope separator makes MLB a threat to everyone, first of all, so a lot of people will take it more seriously. And when someone comes galloping in to overthrow the Treaty; and the first thing they find a way to go after is one of the few things that protects the miners in any way at all . . . well, that doesn't look good.

"And it happens to happen that we have some recordings of that incident this afternoon. Dumping that second load of magma was pure murder, and if they had done it to shut those men up it would have been damning—but you know, I really don't think they did. I think they were just that indifferent and just that careless. Or in short, as the saying used to be back on Earth where I grew up, 'They're just not from around here.' Nobody who was would have done that, at least not the way they did.

"So I'm going to start messaging everyone I can, and see how they all react to this." He leaned back, his eyes seeming to search the ceiling for his memory. "Oh, yeah, there are plenty of people out there who I've heard begin a conversation with 'What kind of bastards . . .' and end with

'MLB.' They always came to me to complain because MLB is right here in Crater Hamner, but they never wanted to get together and do anything when it was just that we didn't like MLB and they'd got bit once.

"Well, now I can remind 'em they got bit, and then show them that MLB plans to go right on biting, and show just how bad they bite. And get them all talking to each other. This is looking better than things have looked in months. Just have to remember everyone who has some fresh grievances against MLB."

"Norinez Quacco, Dad," Bref said. "MLB underbought them last week, three days short of their final payment on their drilling gear."

"Oh, yeah," Durol said, making a note in his purse. "Something about having everything you own grabbed, getting Invisible Thumbed deep as it goes, just when you were about to get yourself clear of debt, probably precesses you pretty good."

Kyffimna nodded. "Thomagatzes were there for the mess this afternoon, but remember two months ago, that split-off quacco they were just launching, the Melozjians?"

"Oh, yeah. Thomagatzes and Melozjians need to be among the first I call," Durol said to his purse. "A brand-new quacco with three pregnant women in it, and MLB leased them a chamber for a new krilj, over in Crater Jiang, and never mentioned it was crawling with cadmium and radiophosphorus."

Within twenty minutes, he had a list of more than a hundred quaccos to message, all with one awful story or another. He got up with a strange smile, saying, "Lots of messaging to do. Take it easy on the wine, those of you that want to find out how this comes out, 'cause I'll be up late on this one. But I think with all this, plus what happened this afternoon, plus what we found out . . . well, we'll get some action. Not necessarily effective action, these are Mercurials after all, but at least action."

No one was in much of a mood to tell stories or sing, with the fate of the planet being discussed in the next room; everyone had long been in bed, and the Eldothalers, Dujuv, Shadow, and Jak were sitting around drinking coffee and not bothering to talk any more when Durol returned.

"Not the best idea we've ever had," Durol admitted. "But the leaders and elders of lots of different quaccos have been talking, and a lot of the little guilds and cults and families in Bigpile, and we've settled on at least trying to make our voices heard and trying to make the outside world aware of what's going on. So there will be a one-week strike, all over the northern Caloris Basin and the rim and scarp around it, against any activity for export—we can't very well make it a general strike, we want the power workers and the heets that make air on the job!—and everyone who's taking the time off will be going into Bigpile for a week of demonstrations in the public areas—well, actually, every square centimeter of Bigpile is privately owned, and we can expect that MLB will keep buying the ground under us and ordering us to move, but that, too, ought to do us some good if it gets in front of the cameras.

"We'll also be picketing the offices of the big offplanet companies, and we think most of their local workers won't cross our picket lines. Plus there's five sunclippers making a pass by the Bigpile loop in the next few days, and with the loading crews on strike, they won't be able to do cargo switches. They can divert to other loops, offload, and get other cargoes, and they all carry strike insurance, we checked that, so they'll be okay, able to pay off everyone whose loads they don't pick up, but since a sunclipper can't turn around, anything that doesn't get picked up at Bigpile has to wait for the next one. Deliveries will be months late for metals to all kinds of industrial plants all over the solar system, and even though they'll get cash to cover from the insurance, mostly the businesses in the upper system don't *want* money, they *need* metal. So that should get a lot of attention."

"Is it going to get sympathy?"

"Hell, no, not at first. The sunclipper crewies will be mad at us, and the industrial companies will hate our guts, and our own unions aren't authorizing this—most of their members aren't here, they're in factories in the Hive and on Ceres and so on, and we'll be throwing a lot of members out of work. But it means they'll all be paying attention."

"I see all kinds of risks," Dujuv said.

Durol shrugged. "There's risks either way, so you might as well pick the way that leaves the person in the mirror more attractive. Did you see those two heets this afternoon? No doubt they didn't want to risk another day without a job, so they took that one."

CHAPTER 14

A Principle 4 Case,
if Ever There Was One

The strike would begin at noon, General Solar System Time; coincidentally, it was almost noon by local solar time anyway (and would be for some days; Mercury's day is one and one-half times as long as its year).

No one would come back from lunch. Instead, they would all meet in Bigpile that afternoon, to be assigned locations and places for the picket lines and demonstrations. The objective was to make it impossible for offplaneters to move through any part of Bigpile without running into protests, to flood the solar system with messages that there was big trouble here.

But to make an impact, it was thought to be better for it to appear suddenly, in the middle of the day. That also gave all the quaccos a chance to get some last-minute essential work in before they would have to start clearing it through the central committee.

Jak's morning job was to move probes. About as tall as his knees, and very light, they looked like chicken wire teepees. The chicken wire was both the solar collector that powered them and the antenna by which they talked to the base station about what they found. Each probe gradually pushed a centimeter-wide spherical bit, made of tunable matter, down through the crust of the planet, sometimes going to a depth of ten kilometers. Inside the bit, NMR probes read the composition of the surrounding materials. On the face of the bit, pseudoatoms flipped through their phases from fluorine to francium to helium, forming a pattern without moving like a crowd in a stadium doing the wave.

The pattern was two parallel helixes—a double screw—one of francium and one of fluorine, microscopic in width, separated by an equally narrow band of helium, turning thousands of times on their way up past the wide part of the sphere. At that wide point, the fluorine helix ended in a band of helium, which deposited a mixture of metals that formed the electrically conducting wall of the shaft; the francium helix continued up into the center of the tube, releasing oxidizers (mostly gases) into the same slender hose that carried down the power lead from the surface. The oxidizing gases rushed up the hose into the vacuum of space, the metals were deposited in a dense layer on the side of the shaft, and the ball sank steadily into the earth, needing only its little trickle of power to keep going.

In about forty days of sunlight, each little station could drill down to ten kilometers, mapping everything it encountered with millimeter accuracy. Since on Mercury the synodic day (the actual time from sunrise to sunrise) is 175 Earth days, this meant that in each synodic day there was time for each sampler to check two sites. It was close to Mercurial noon, so it was time to move them all; if they waited till after the strike, precious data might be lost.

Since the machines told Jak, via his purse, what to do, the job was barely more complicated than watching the readouts the day before had been. Jak drove to each sampler, detached the old hose and bit, and left them in the ground, put the sampler on the five-wheeler, drove it to its new site, put on another bit and hose, and told it to start. He was certainly learning how to follow directions on this mission.

He was just placing the last one, running way ahead with more than an hour to go in his shift, when a five-wheeler leapt over the horizon and headed straight for him. It wasn't carrying either the MLB or the Eldothaler insignia, so it was odd that it was in Crater Hamner at all, and it was being driven badly, with lots of unnecessary bounces and spinning out, moving like a drunken mechanical spider in a hurry, so that Jak realized after a moment that it couldn't be a Mercurial driving.

The suited figure climbed awkwardly down, falling from the tire before getting up and hurrying toward him. There was something about it—

"Jak Jinnaka," a voice said in his earphones, and he realized.

"Mreek Sinda," he said, "I heard that you were here on Mercury."

"Well, yes, I am. Still pursuing the story that happens to have you in it. Much to my regret because you're not cooperative and animation is expensive. And before you check, no, that didn't go out on general frequency. I'm here to present you with an opportunity. MLB has just opened an office in Bigpile to recruit 'security people.' Which some people might call 'goons.' Looks like they're getting ready to play rough."

"Thanks, I'll pass that on to the strike leaders." Jak didn't know why she had driven out to tell him this.

"I *said* an opportunity." Sinda was petite and her pressure suit carried no extra supplies or rescue pack—another thing no Mercurial would have done—so she looked preternaturally tiny. But she stood up very straight, hands on her hips, as if prepared to defy him to the death if need be. Whatever argument she thought she had, she thought it was a good one.

Jak sighed. He had to know. "All right, what is it?"

She put her helmet against his so that he could hear by conduction, the almost-unbuggable way to talk. "MLB doesn't know you from anyone and you haven't yet put Eldothaler markings on your pressure suit."

"Yes, and?"

"So pretend to be a stranded crewie (that happens all the time if a longshore capsule isn't fit to fly back just as the ship is moving out of range) and go to the new MLB office in Bigpile and see what happens if you try to enlist in their goon squad. I'll wire you with so many cameras and mikes that someone could open the Jinnaka channel. See what MLB's pitch is to the hired thugs. If you're actor enough, maybe suggest that you'd like to rape a prisoner or interrogate young children in front of their parents, your standard evil-tyrant's-henchman behavior, and see if they start nodding and promising that you'll have a chance to beat up old people or batter orphans or whatever. Anything like that you can get them to say will be terrific for both of us."

"Suppose you explain that part."

"Well, when they strike, the miners are going to be everyone's whipping boy. The media are owned by the same people that own the factories, masen? And the miners aren't exactly photogenic. But if you can provoke MLB into saying some really outrageous things, *they* get some bad coverage and they'll have to cut back on goons. That's good for your friends. Plus this will tie the story of the miners and all that esoteric stuff about mineral prices and working conditions and people getting hurt and all that boring,

boring, boring stuff into a story about a beautiful young princess and her man of mystery. You see? No one gives a shit if MLB burns a miner alive every day before breakfast, Jak. That's not news. But if *you're* involved, dragging along the Princess Shyf story, then it's interesting. Suddenly my little backwater oppressed-miner story is an important public issue, which is good for me *and* the miners."

"Hunh. You're right, I think. I'm going to call back to the krilj. If they say okay, I'll do it."

"Jak, the krilj is bugged so heavily that MLB probably knows which side you sleep on. My own smart bugs walked in there—how do you suppose I knew so much about the strike?—and found at least two MLB bugs in every room. I don't speck anyone will place you, but if they have a voice-print file with a quick-access search, you might get caught. I guess I shouldn't have concealed that from you. But if you call home to tell them what you're doing, you *will* get caught."

Unfortunately, it sounded like she was telling the truth. He could explain things to his toves afterward, easily enough, and he wasn't due anywhere until thirteen thirty; there would be plenty of time. "All right, let's go," he said.

As he drove toward the point where Sinda's rocket had landed, he watched her five-wheeler ahead of him bounce all over the broad, switchbacking ledge cut into the crater wall at a low spot, perhaps by the Eldothalers, possibly by anyone in the last twelve hundred years, for without rain or wind, every surface stayed the same forever, and it all looked as if it had been done ten minutes ago. The burned and melted floor of Crater Hamner spread out before him in sharp-edged contour lines marking where past magma floods had spread out or been dumped. As Jak reached the top, the central pinnacle looked more like a necromancer's tower than ever.

During the long climb up the side of the crater, Jak touched the communication spot on his purse so often that it finally asked him if he was thinking of sending a message; a little curtly, he told it to mind its own business, and then a moment later realized that he might be alienating it, and ended up spending most of the rest of the drive trying to explain to it how to tell when he was thinking about talking but toktru didn't want to.

Jak had only passed briefly through one small corner of Bigpile before; this time they had grounded at a rocket port on the periphery, on the westernmost of the outer corners of the rough, lumpy Maltese cross that formed the shape of the city as it spilled around the intersection of a wrinkle ridge and a fracture fault. It would be about a three-kilometer walk to the central area where the Bigpile Marriott was. Unfortunately, one of Bigpile's several distinctions was that it was the largest human city without Pertrans service.

"Is it always like this?" Jak asked.

"Usually only in the central shopping areas or around a shift change at a factory," Sinda said. She whispered to her purse for an instant. "Thought so. About twenty percent more people than usual in the city, this morning. Mostly in from the kriljs. So it looks like your side is doing all right for mobilization." She raised her left hand to her face and spoke into the purse. "What's the difference between a cheap sprite and an expensive one?"

"They're all expensive," her purse said, in its resonant baritone.

"Are there differences?"

"None, really."

"Get me one from the middle of the alphabet."

A moment later a sprite appeared, and she turned to follow it. Jak asked, "This place has different sprites?"

"Competing sprite companies. No public utilities here, remember?" She turned and plunged into the crowd.

Jak simply couldn't go through the thick, milling, buzzing crowds in the rock-blasted corridors as quickly as the tiny woman. Her sprite had to pause every two hundred meters or so and dance around, waiting for Jak to work his way through a knot of people or out of a blind corner. The closer they came to the center of the city, the tighter people packed, and the more a tense electric connection seemed to fuse the crowds together. Miners in pressure suits, workers in coveralls, gamblers and hookers dressed up in their best clash-splash-and-smash, mercs in the uniforms of half a dozen units employed by the corporations, children in school uniforms, and drunks in whatever they'd slept in, all pushed and tried to ease themselves through the city in one direction or another, all apparently feeling that if they could only get to somewhere else they could be where something was just about to happen. The air was dense; the CO_2 and water scrubbers must be having a hard time with the extra load.

The thicker, more contentious crowd near the Marriott slowed them, but they made their way through the big doors into the lobby, among a mob of people pouring in, apparently hoping to be safely behind the Marriott's security perimeter if trouble started, pushing through a lobby crowded with people wandering in little circles around their piles of luggage, talking to their purses, scrambling to find passage on any outgoing sunclipper.

"Travelers," Sinda said, shaking her head. "As soon as anybody mentions that some politics might happen and there might not be ice for the drinks, they fill a suitcase and go stand around in the least comfortable area they can find, asking questions nobody can answer and demanding that somebody do something. Three-quarters of them not in a pressure suit, so if any real trouble started, they'd be dead anyway. This way up to my room."

Sinda had done this many times before, and it only took her a few minutes to put microcameras and concealed microphones onto Jak's pressure suit and cap them with metal to make them look like rivets.

At the downtown offices of MLB, ropes were up to bend a long line of applicants back and forth in the front lobby, several times. The line seemed to be moving, so he got into it; within minutes, there were many people behind him. From halfway up the line, Jak looked around. *Either this job has fabulous pay and benefits, or else there just aren't too many other positions open for big thugs.*

Jak put in an earpiece so he could listen and keyed a question to his purse, his fingers dancing over the little spots of the keyboard.

"Yes," the purse said in his ear. "The unemployment rate on Mercury is high, it's higher in Bigpile, and seventeen percent of Bigpile's new immigrants are convicted violent felons from somewhere else, traveling on an exile ticket. In fact four percent of the total population arrived in the max security brigs of military vessels."

Jak keyed "Done," and touched the reward spot; the purse cheebled in his ear and added, "Be careful." As Jak retracted the earphone into the suit collar, he felt oddly touched by that; he'd never had any machine reach the point of feeling any concern for him before.

There really weren't as many heets in line as it had looked like, Jak realized after a while. It was just that most of them sized each other up and decided to allow a lot of personal space.

When he went through the door at the end of the line, he was already cutting it close for getting to the demonstration on time, but there was still some time to do some good here. Then he saw that the "reception desk" was just a camera and mike set hooked to an AI; he would have just left, but he was at the head of the line, so he walked up and answered the standard questions—name, occupation, and so on. There was no way to probe for any good quotes, for Sinda.

"How long will I have to wait to be interviewed?" Jak asked, looking at the dozen or so goons roosting on the bench along the back wall of the waiting area, bodies bent forward because most of them were too large for the narrow bench.

"Wait your turn. Your name will be called in the order in which you arrived. Next."

Jak sat and keyed his purse to time the interval; after a minute or so, another heet was called in. It was ten minutes and seventeen seconds before he emerged and the next one was called. There were thirteen heets in front of Jak, now, he realized, counting. About two and half hours, far too long. He got up to go, and was actually walking through the door when the voice said, "Jak Jinnaka. Jak Jinnaka, please come in for a special interview, proceed directly to the president's office."

Maybe they wanted him for an executive position or something. Jak turned and walked back, past the bench of goons, and through the small door that dilated at the end. It slammed shut behind him in an emergency seal, and reflexively Jak grabbed for his helmet—normally that sound meant a major pressure breach somewhere—so Jak was reaching back over his shoulder and bending down when a thrown knife rang against the door behind him, right where his head should have been.

Jak looked up. Bex Riveroma, the man he had the most cause to fear anywhere at any time, was coming at him.

Jak had studied the Disciplines since before he could remember, and he had practiced even more ever since Riveroma had beaten him so thoroughly on Earth. He sometimes practiced with an image of Riveroma's face on the viv attacker. The situation was surprising, but familiar; Jak did not hesitate.

Riveroma lunged for a grip. Jak sank, swept Riveroma's hand away with a left block, caught the hand, and pivoted into the body drop, jabbing sideways at Riveroma's temple. Riveroma hip-blocked and ducked, freeing his arm, his hands trying to slide into Jak's collar, and Jak followed the motion, folding around the big man, hooking a leg and rolling it.

His blood screamed through his veins, the world was rimmed in red, and a rough tornado howled in his throat. He wanted to attack, but in a sustained fight, Riveroma, master that he was, would surely win. So as Riveroma rolled, Jak kicked the tall, muscular heet on the top of his bald head, then threw himself back against the light partition wall.

The wall went over as a unit, and there were shouts and bellows and the odd sensation of sliding down a wall under which several heets were trying to stand up. Jak had crashed back into the room with the long weaving line of applicants.

As he bounded for the door, over the heads of the con-fused crowd in the middling grav, Jak shouted, "Police sting! Big bald pokheet in there! They're checking records and executing fugitives!" He charged through the door and down the corridor.

Behind him, slug-throwers popped, and a fighting laser hissed, amid screaming and shouting. Someone must have believed him.

Jak dodged at every corner, in the direction of less traffic, stopping for breath when he could no longer hear the uproar. He had his purse shut off Sinda's mikes and cameras, ran through a few more corridor intersections, and took the time to pry them off and crush them under his boot. No sound of pursuit.

So Riveroma was president of MLB. It made sense. A heet with many different prices on his head, all of them large, couldn't hide anywhere forever. And fearsome as his skills were, he was becoming a liability to hire. Probably like many people before him, finding that he could not get hired to do what he was good at, Riveroma had gone into business for himself.

His choice was bold but offered a real chance of success. While he was starting out, Mercury was as safe a place for an outlaw as one might find in the solar system. And if Riveroma went on to gain control of Mercury, he would be too tough ever to dislodge. Every international expedition ever sent to Mercury to put down a revolt had taken months to ship troops, bring them down on the loop to a loyal city, and then move to take back areas in revolt. And in more than fifteen hundred years of space travel, no one had ever successfully invaded an armed, hostile planet. In the Seventh Rubahy War, the Rubahy attempt to storm Mars, and the human counterinvasion of Pluto, had both failed miserably, and nothing had changed in the seven hundred years since; a planet gave too much cover, and space was too exposed. Trying to storm a planet from space was like trying to take a medieval castle atop a perfectly smooth glass mountain on a bright sunny day.

So, if he got control of Mercury . . . Riveroma could proclaim himself whatever title he wanted to take, emperor if he liked, and make it stick by the traditional right of conquest. And in a few hundred years no doubt his bloodline would be as honored as the Karrinynya.

Jak shuddered. He splurged on a confidential, untraceable sprite to guide him to the rally. The strike leaders needed to know what was going on.

As he neared the rally site, the flow of the crowd became against him—sad, grim people walking away from the space where the rally was to be held, rather than toward it. Then he saw the little knot of the Eldothaler Quacco coming on, Durol at the center of it talking with Kyffimna, with Dujuv and Shadow walking a little farther away—*No, Dujuv at point guard, Shadow at rear,* Jak realized. He pushed through the crowd to join them

"What's going on? Where's everyone going?" Jak asked.

"Where have *you* been?" Dujuv sounded angry.

"I got a chance to check out something about MLB. Bex Riveroma is the president of it—"

Dujuv looked stunned. "Weehu. Well, I guess that explains a lot." He never took his eyes off the crowd, and Jak realized that his tove was not just angry at Jak, but also alert and psyched and expecting an attack at any moment. "Well, great, we can use that later to get some bounty hunters in here after him. For right now, listen up because there's a lot for you to catch up on. Watch my left rear for me while I talk, okay, and keep a general eye out in all directions.

"Now, while you were off playing detective or playing media star or whatever your game was today, MLB bought the public space we were going to demonstrate in, revoked our permission to use it, and sent the pokheets to arrest the whole demonstration. So all these people are going to walk a kilometer and a half out of the big doors on the south side of Bigpile, to a mine that belongs to one of the quaccos that's with us—we're hoping that doing this as a march, even an illegal one, will keep enough of our people together so that the pokheets will be too scared to try to break it up.

"Now, why we're guarding. A heet tried to stab Durol Eldothaler, as we came out of our rocket, and there was a dud bomb thrown at the feet of the leaders at the start of the rally."

"It wasn't a dud," Kyffimna said, behind them. "*Somebody* grabbed it and stuffed it into a hazardous materials chute so that it went out onto the surface before it went off."

"Kyffimna, I'm trying to keep you and your father safe," Dujuv said, impatiently. "We can cover exact details *later*. It was no big deal. I need to brief Jak right now. Anyway, one pokheet shot at Durol—and Shadow shot back, which made the pokheet think about another line of work and hurry off to apply. So besides opposing scum we have to watch out for police scum. Durol is listed as a ringleader, and Shadow will probably be wanted for assaulting an officer soon, so they both have to be hidden out in the kriljs somewhere. And they're *so* inconspicuous.

"So while you were off doing all that doubtless fascinating stuff, and yes it's good that we know that it's Riveroma, old tove, we just developed a few little problems, which are kind of urgent, and if you're not doing anything else, and can take time out of your busy schedule, maybe you could help Shadow and me guard the leadership, because you might have noticed this is a big crowd, and there's only two trained fighters to guard Durol, with thousands of people all around, and I'm normally only this nervous during urological surgery."

Jak didn't blame Dujuv for sounding angry—Jak was late, he'd been needed, it was justified. He did dread Dujuv's finding out he had been late because he was dealing with Mreek Sinda.

Well, time enough to explain everything later. Meanwhile, he moved into the position where Dujuv wanted him, and put all his attention into being a guard.

It became more of a march as they went on. People pulling on pressure suits joined them; shopkeepers stood at their doors and cheered them on; there was a crowd along the streets, and Jak caught sight of Mreek Sinda, over to the side in one of the large spaces, talking to one of her drones while a dozen of them buzzed around the crowd. As the side walls came to be lined with spectators, the miners packed closer together, and as Bigpilers who had run home to grab their pressure suits rejoined the march, it became still more compact.

Jak was at right rear, Shadow at left. The back of Shadow's pressure suit, where there were small pockets to accommodate the rage spines, had an odd bubbling motion that indicated that at the least, Shadow on the Frost was getting precessed by the number of places that had to be watched for a threat, and the number of people moving through them.

Dujuv, up ahead, working point, was better at this. His level, even voice—"Keep back, please, clear the way, please, sorry, security, I need you to move back"—cut right through the crowd noise, and people seemed to comply with his directives as if he were the voice of authority.

At the center of the group, Durol had his head down close to his daughter's, talking fast and low; from the few words Jak caught, he gathered that they were replanning the program—conducting it outside in vacuum, some things like group singing had to be omitted, and they urgently needed to assign radio channels for each function, and to work out contingencies for things like radio jamming.

By the time the marchers sealed helmets and walked into the big airlock, things were in at least some sort of order. Without a pressing crowd around, the march widened and slowed, like a river coming out of a narrow canyon into a broad shallow valley.

The south side of Bigpile fronted on a long, boulder-covered slope, and going around the larger boulders further divided them into small groups. They were a straggling rabble by the time they reached the outer rise of the small, round crater and passed through a narrow tunnel into the inside.

The crater was perfectly round, with very high walls that rose almost to the vertical, jagged-topped and very narrow. Durol and the other quacco leaders would speak from a ledge that had been excavated across the foot of the crater wall, standing in front of an ore separator that was still finishing the day's run in a blur of plates and catchers. There was no sound, of course, in the vacuum, and it seemed to Jak that it was sort of a waste that everyone would hear perfectly anyway due to digital radio; if there had been air, this crater would have resonated beautifully.

Shadow's voice crackled in Jak's ear; the yellow telltale on Jak's helmet faceplate display told him that this was private channel and that only he and Dujuv were hearing it. "Here I am being a guard in a Bombardment crater. I'm not sure whether this qualifies as your human idea of irony."

"It'll do," Dujuv said, and Jak agreed. The Bombardment—the initial Rubahy attack, a thousand years ago, when they had tried to conquer the solar system—had been made up of many thousands of quartz balls, about the size of coffee mugs, arriving at more than ninety-nine percent of the speed of light, aimed at the four lower planets, about fifty a day for about fifty years on each planet. The Bombardment was the reason why Earth, north of 21° S, was dotted with tiny circular lakes, and why Mars now had a dense atmosphere after the release of deep frozen volatiles deposits north of 23° S. But on Mercury, the craters of four billion years had never eroded, and a mere million additional kilometer-and-smaller craters had been barely noticeable. Nonetheless, Shadow was right—the steep high sides, indicating very fast liquefaction and very great recoil forces (more energy released in a smaller space than ever occurred with a natural meteoroid)—meant that this had to be a Bombardment crater.

When everyone had come into the crater, Durol announced, over the general speech channel, "We're going to start now."

It was impossible to find a good place from which to guard the people speaking, and anyway the speakers had not consulted their improvised (and desperately under-manned, and underRubahyed) security detail. Durol El-dothaler, with his row of about ten supporters and other speakers behind him, stood directly in front of the body of the separator, which provided a plain white-and-black backdrop. Someone had hung a banner, "Strike Against Tyranny," on the side of the separator's main tank, about two meters off the ground. Dwarfed by the four-story-high, sixty-meter-wide tank, it looked pathetic.

He was wide open to any shot coming out of the crowd, and anyone in the front row might have tossed a grenade or a bomb in among the platform party. For that matter, there were excellent sniper positions all around the crater rim, and in the low gravity a man with a club or an ax might pop out of the crowd and be in among the speakers in three hard bounds. Worse still, Kyffimna caught them and said, "Pop wants you well out of the way. He says having bodyguards makes it look like he's done something wrong."

Dujuv whined in his throat, for all the world like a frustrated German shepherd, but Jak realized that it was on their personal channel. "That's what I feel too," he said to Dujuv, as they meekly followed Kyffimna.

"If that sound means *This whole situation is dreadful, but I don't know what to do about it,* then I must learn to make that noise." Shadow on the Frost added, also on private channel.

Kyffimna led them up onto the ledge the speakers stood on, but they were at least two hundred meters from the platform party, too far away to do more than be witnesses if anything happened. She left her brothers with them as well. Jak sourly muttered, "So all us embarrassments are together," on the private channel.

Dujuv hand-signed, *Absolute maximum affirmative.*

Over the public channel, Durol said, "Make sure your neighbors have Channel Nine on, that's the one we'll be using for the main event. All right, friends, we know why we're here, but we ought to say it again, just for the record. We are here not because we're greedy, not because we're complainers, not because we can't cope with what Mercury does to us. We've been had by every crook in the solar system and we've eaten *radzundslag* till we glow, and we still bring in metal when they need it and as much as they need it. But when we get one terrible abuse after another, when we see nothing but worse conditions and eventually our planet being turned into a giant slave camp, by a company whose only purpose seems to be complete tyranny, it's time to say enough is enough.

"So let me just lay out the facts here. The solar system lives by what we do here on Mercury; without us there wouldn't be half the human settlements, they'd never have dug out from the Rubahy Wars, neither the Hive nor the Aerie would exist at all, and in a thousand ways they'd all be poorer and colder and less numerous. They owe their existence to us, and they are more than welcome to that, but in return we are owed some measure of protection, if not from the ordinary thieves and dullards they send to exploit us, then at least from the worst kinds of pirates, thugs, and goons—which is what MLB is. To begin with, they imposed a contract on us that—"

A white-hot spot appeared on the side of the separator; Jak, Shadow, and Dujuv were bounding toward the platform before there was even time to think, *Laser.*

Not even Dujuv could have been fast enough. The bright spot whirled out a circle two stories high, on the side of the separator tank. In seeming slow motion, due to the distance, but actually with terrible speed, the circular piece fell out, and a flood of white-hot magma dropped out and splashed over the group of speakers and leaders.

Durol had only time to say, "What—" Then there was a deep bass howl of pain and a hissing sound, and the public address channel went dead. The flood of magma poured over the ledge toward the crowd below.

In less than fifteen seconds the three toves reached the edge of the stream of magma; by then, all there was to do was to help Bref and Kyffimna hold Narav back from rushing into the magma itself, trying, in his confusion and panic, to rescue Durol. Unfortunately the delay meant they were all still close to the magma, close enough to feel, through their feet, the *whump-thud* of pressure suits bursting under the magma. When Narav stopped struggling, Kyffimna rushed to the side of the separator and slammed the red "close intakes" button, shutting off the flow of fresh magma from the heated well under the ground.

Below, the crowd scattered and fled from the white-hot flood; fortunately there wasn't enough of it to flow all the way across the crater, and soon the assembled thousands were packing and clogging the tunnel like a wad of bran flakes in a drain, getting through but not quickly.

On the general speaking frequency, Riveroma's voice said, "Return to your kriljs and await orders. Return to your kriljs and await orders. This is the Provisional Government of the Republic of Bigpile. We have taken control to restore public order and to prevent further deterioration of the economy. Return home and resume work. Everything is being taken care of."

"This is a Principle 4 case," Jak said, "if ever there was one. MLB could very well be ruling this planet in a short time."

Dujuv was angry but still listening. "Go on." Kyffimna nodded through tears. Jak looked around the big common room of the krilj, at the blank faces of the Eldothaler Quacco. He was being listened to, but the only person who looked normal was Shadow on the Frost, who never had any facial expressions.

"Well," Jak said, "like I said, Principle 4." One of Nakasen's most important insights was that "the other bastard can't win if you can kick over the table." He drew a deep breath and said, "Toktru, I would be glad to never see Mreek Sinda again. Believe me, or don't, but it's toktru. But she wants to talk to me. If I dump the whole story to her, Riveroma at least will have to run for it, because his cover will be blown, and he's bait for every bounty hunter in the solar system. Not only will that get rid of MLB's leader, but (since I bet none of Riveroma's business associates are any more savory than he is), aside from the bounty hunters going after Riveroma, there will be thousands of them going after most of MLB.

"If I talk with Sinda, I know she'll do one of her stupid bloated puff pieces about me and make me out to be the hero, and it's embarrassing and I'm sorry and I wish other people *would* get the credit, or the truth would get told, but at least MLB will be on the run, and off the miners' backs. So I'm going to, and you can hate me if it helps.

"I'm afraid that Bex Riveroma will find a way to take a hard kick at everything he can while he's on his way out. So I speck that the quacco should evacuate, right away."

Kyffimna looked up, wiped her face with her hand, and took a couple of long deep breaths. "You're right, but as soon as we leave with work under contract, we forfeit, and MLB can salvage all our equipment."

"Not if you can prove they were stealing from you with that metal-relabeling operation," Dujuv said, looking at the wall, avoiding seeing Jak. "If you prove that, you get back rights on everything they stole, and reclaim whatever they claimed salvage on, and their insurance company will have to pay you plenty."

"You're right," Kyffimna said, "but how do we prove—"

"Got it." Bref looked up from his purse; he had been working quietly in the corner ever since Jak and Dujuv had taken him aside and explained things, just before the quacco meeting began. He looked around the room in mild surprise at how everyone stared at him.

"Well," he said, "obviously that was the very first

issue—how we were going to prove what MLB had been up to. So I went looking into that. We knew they had to be changing isotope tracers, which meant they had an isotope separator. Well, those are pretty big and have a major energy demand, and they're not easy to hide—we already knew it had to be in those big chambers in the crater wall over on the other side—so I'd been processing all our old records, and I've got it.

"There's one chamber over there that would be right next to where they were running the reactor, with an easy pathway to good surface positions for solar collectors, that would be big enough for the isotope separator and the several months of metal they'd have to warehouse until they got it relabeled. If anyone was to investigate that chamber, they'd find a whole lot of ingots that we'd sold too low, and a whole bunch of new ones marked to sell too high, and the machines to turn one into the other. And just possibly some records about it all, too, for that matter. Or in short, that big chamber contains all the evidence you'd need to shut down MLB and get every member of it erased and sold into a labor brigade."

"So if I spill the story to Sinda," Jak said, "will they be able to hide the evidence after she accesscasts?"

Kyffimna visibly brightened. "Maybe if they blew it all up with an atom bomb. Otherwise, no. My little brother's right. This is it. We get everyone we can out of here, we leave behind just enough people to jam it up for Riveroma and MLB if they try to destroy the evidence, and Jak runs and squeals like an informing rat-fink son of a whore to that media bitch, and after all this is over, just maybe we'll win. At least we take one more good kick at their heads, eh?"

CHAPTER 15

Nobody's Going to Blame *Me*

I don't like you at all," Jak said.

He was sitting in the conversation pit in Mreek Sinda's hotel suite, in Bigpile, and she was sitting across from him. He was trying hard to pay no attention to the cloud of camera drones around him. He was not succeeding. "I know you can make me say anything you want by the time you put it out on to accesscast, but just now I want you to hear that. I don't like you at all. I don't trust you. I loathe what you do for a living."

Four of Mreek Sinda's drones positioned themselves at forty-five-degree angles to her face, creating the corners of a square, and focused soft warm lighting on her; it made her look perfect, so that even the traditional helmet-hair looked comfortably natural. "Then why are you even bothering to talk to me? You know your family has money. And this is Mercury. You and your two friends could be on a ship out of here in no time. No one would stop you."

Jak stared at her. "We must see the world completely differently," he said at last.

"Yes, well, the difference is, the way I see the world, and what I choose to see, is the way everyone will see it. So my view of it matters, unlike yours. Now what do you want to show me?"

She lowered her gaze slightly; her cheeks came up as she parted her lips in a smile.

She thinks she's getting to me. He felt amusement and rage and swallowed both. "Well," he said, "here's a story for you. It even ties everything in to the previous series you did about me."

Quickly he told her about Bex Riveroma: that a crime syndicate might soon control the richest mines in the solar system. "So if they let him get away with it, it's war, runaway inflation, letting a thug create the richest single fief in the system and run it as a slave camp, most likely all of the above. And right now a battalion of beanies from anywhere could stop it cold. But there is no battalion of beanies. Just a bunch of broke, hungry miners who won't take it anymore, on strike for their lives, being murdered and tortured by Riveroma and his MLB goons. How's that for a story?"

"And are you here to do something about it?"

"I came here not knowing what was going on. I'm going to do my small part to stop it, sure, but others will pay higher prices and accomplish more.

"What's important is for people to know that the leader of MLB is Bex Riveroma. Somewhere in the solar system there must be some honest pokheets, and every one of them will want a shot at Riveroma. If anyone takes a good look at MLB's isotope-separating facility in the southwest of Crater Hamner, which they're using to starve miners and raise metals prices at the same time, they'll see what's up and put a stop to it." Jak hesitated, and as foolish as he felt trying to appeal to Sinda's better side, he added, "Please accesscast at least those sentences. Please. It would make such a difference if you did." She nodded and gestured for him to continue his statement. "I'm asking everyone who has the power to do something about this." He could think of no more to say.

The drones turned off their lights and flew back into Sinda's bag. "Well," she said. "Weehu. Tense stuff there. I think that's going to sell. You'll be surprised at how much makes it into the accesscast unmodified. Of course, there's a lot of stuff to be generated before the accesscast, and you've already made it abundantly clear that you won't co-operate with me in producing the prefatory material I need. So I will have to generate all that prefatory material by an-imation. That will take at least six or seven days to get the minimum scripted material into place. So I hope that your miners can hold out for those six days—plus whatever time it takes the politicians to negotiate an international inter-vention, and whatever time it then takes the nearest war-ships to get here to participate in it, and then there's some planning time but they may be able to do that on the way—"

"You're talking about a month."

"Easily. Just tell your miners to hold on that long. Or a little longer. Things can take that long."

"You could accesscast what I just gave you and then make up more." Jak felt as if the room were slowly turning, screwing its way down through the floor, down through all the *radzundslag* of Mercury, right down into the iron ball at its core.

"I could." She was more businesslike than he'd ever seen her. "But it blows a major punch line and loses much of the interest. And if I wait, nothing bad can happen, be-cause even if Bex Riveroma slaughters half of Mercury, the story will only get better, you know. A bigger war, and a bigger scandal, and I can make it all look like you could have stopped him and sat on it. Nobody's going to blame *me*. So the sensible thing for me to do would be to sit on this for the forty days or so until I have the generated parts that I want, making you say the things that I need for the broadcast, that you won't say for me.

"Luckily for you, there is a solution available. I will accesscast absolutely everything about MLB, Bex Riveroma, the falsified metals claims, all the things that will have the League of Polities meeting tonight, and troops headed this way in two days. I'll use it all, uncut and unmodified, right away. *If.*"

Jak almost said *If what?* before he realized how obvious it was. He felt as if a snake, with a texture like fine chilly leather, were trying to find its way upward through his bowels. "And if I say what you tell me to—"

"And make it convincing." Her jaw was set and she looked ready to slap him. "By the way, I hate and despise you too. For saying the kinds of things you have said to a person in my position. For mocking me and my job. For deliberately acting as if I didn't matter. You don't *ever* look away from a camera, old *tove*." The tone would have been more appropriate to her calling him a child-rapist or a torturer. "So let me just add—*make it convincing.* If it's not, the deal's off."

The snake's head reached into Jak's heart and paused there, flat expressionless eyes looking into the dark of each chamber, venom oozing from the fangs into his bloodstream. "You'll accesscast the material I need to get out there, if I cooperate, and not if I don't?"

Sinda smiled, not a smile he'd ever seen on any accesscast. "Results soon are much better than results later, silly boy. If ten minutes from now I have the stuff I need, and it takes twenty minutes to edit it, then thirty-one minutes from now it will be out there grabbing audience."

"The parts about MLB—"

"All great, toktru, I wouldn't cut it for a billion utils, because it'll make that much. But I'll hold it till I can frame it as I like. If you give me what I want, *right now,* I can frame it as I like, *right now*, and it goes out, *right now*." Anyone looking in at that moment might have thought she was flirting with him. "Now, Jak, do I get my interview with the answers I want? Before you're even back at the krilj, or wherever you're going next, it will be all over Mercury and on its way to everywhere else. You are right. Once this is accesscast, Riveroma's little scheme will be over."

"Well, then," Jak said. "Well." He swallowed hard. "And you won't give me any evidence I can take with me, about why I actually said these things?"

She laughed. "Do you know how much you could sell that for, to a competitor, as an accesscast? One second after you say it, I'll be denying everything—and I intend to be in a position to make those denials stick."

He stared at the situation. He preferred his friends alive (and wrongly hating him) rather than dead (and rightly trusting). "All right then."

"Full cooperation?"

"Full."

Drones flew from her bag, and surrounded Jak in a mass of tiny lights and cameras. "Now," she said, "start with explaining how the whole purpose of this is to win back Shyf Karrinynya's heart, and how you'll do anything for her. Then slide into how angry you are with Dujuv Gonzawara for screwing everything up and for being a big stupid panth. Stress how much he lied about you and what a fool he is. Remember, be convincing."

*   *   *

Just four people remained in the krilj when Jak returned: Dujuv, Shadow, and Bref, who had to be there, and Narav, who wanted to be everywhere his brother went. With Durol dead there was no one to tell Narav no. Shadow looked up from his diagrams and said, "No doubt my tove will explain that accesscast, and apologize later. Right now we have a plan to carry out and I cannot be sure how much time remains to us. Bref's data penetrations show that MLB knows what is going on, and we have to worry about the possibility of the rest of the quacco being held as hostages, either by capture or by some weapons being sighted in on their ferry. So we need to move fast and decisively. Therefore I am going to tell you all what to do; I have some experience at this kind of thing. Please accept any offense to your customs as a matter of pure necessity.

"Here's what we're going to try." He talked quickly to his purse; maps and diagrams danced across the projected screen on the wall. "That's it." He made each of them review his part. "We're ready. Any serious reason to delay?"

Four human heads shook in unison. The Rubahy nodded once, gravely, and said; "Sinda's accesscast will bring help, but if the evidence is destroyed, this will all just have to be done again, when all the rats come back after the cat is gone." He raised his head and looked at each of them in turn. "I derive great honor from being permitted to direct an operation with four very brave people in it. I thank you for the honor. This is not the time for the discussion of any other points of honor."

Jak said, "I do have an explanation and an apology, the moment that there's time."

"Of course, you would," Dujuv said. He pulled his helmet on and closed up for outside work. The boys, then Jak, closed up and com checked.

Shadow closed up last. "Now, my friends, quiet and quick, and let us see how much honor we can wrest from so estimable an enemy. Shut off your default sends—I think it best that we maintain radio silence."

"Tell me, again," Dujuv said. "And don't tell me like I'm stupid."

Jak hoped his nodding would show through his pressure suit: "All right, then. First team on the surface, that's Shadow, Narav, and Bref, scoots for cover. Second team, me and you, activates the dead man trigger on the slagger. Each of our purses checks with us and sends the dead man switch a signal every twenty minutes, via the *Spirit of Singing Port,* which will be in orbit overhead, where it's line of sight from us, for about two hours. Phrysaba and Pabrino will be monitoring com links the whole time, too, so if things go badly there's at least some human judgment in the loop."

"That makes *me* feel better," Shadow said dryly.

Jak went on. "If it doesn't get signal from any of us, the dead man switch starts a clock. If we still haven't called in six minutes later, it turns on that slagger Kyffimna planted earlier. The slagger sprays the upper part of the west wall of the crater, where MLB is, with positrons. That will trigger a big, fast flow of magma down onto the crater floor, and it will keep doing it until the flowing magma overruns the slagger itself. Check your rocable, because that's how we get rescued if we get trapped outside with a magma flood."

"I can't wear one because they haven't made them for anyone with rage spines," Shadow said, "so I will either have to die with great honor or be extremely quick and clever. Either way, actually, will get me great honor."

"All right," Jak said. "Now, the objective is for Shadow

and Bref to get across there, to the main storage cave, and hack the recordkeeping system so that it will upload everything to general access, along with any pictures they can shoot. Everything else is just a diversion from that. But if we're all captured before we can get there, then the flood of magma will keep them pretty busy, and seal over the outside of the cave. That will tie everything up in dozens of courts until they can excavate and confirm that Kyffimna was telling the truth, and, uh—just possibly kill those of us who don't get to high ground fast enough. So let's hope Plan A works."

"All right, everything's what I thought it was," Dujuv said. "Sorry to make us all review."

"Dujuv Gonzawara," Shadow on the Frost said, "a human of your honor and accomplishments is entitled to as many reviews as he wants. Now let's move. As Duke Psim often says, plans are like fresh mayonnaise, best used just after they are made, dangerous if the least bit old."

They used only passive infrared to guide them through the old tunnels.

The Eldothalcr boys needed no navigation device; Bref would simply pop up into a shaft and begin chimneying up, Narav would follow, and Dujuv, Shadow, and Jak would turn to each other, shrug, and follow. Or Narav would inexplicably veer right or left as they walked down a dark tunnel, its walls a mess of confusing shadows in the infrared, into what had seemed to be a big spot on the wall; Bref would stop to guide them into the spot, and they would find that they had entered a different tunnel.

All around them the surfaces gleamed in weird shapes under the infrared, reminding them that many times they were walking through a tunnel that had been bored through a chamber that had been filled with melted waste from yet another chamber, which might itself have been carved into a big vault that, after the slaggers it housed had been removed, had then been filled with melted tailings from a surface operation. There must be rocks around here that were on their tenth human melting.

After a while Bref gestured. The five of them bent over at the waist, helmets together, to hear each other by conduction rather than risk radio. "Up this chimney, about twenty-five meters." Bref shouted so that they could all understand him clearly. "Opens in a cluster of rocks; should be invisible except overhead."

"We don't want any sensor pointing toward the main party," Shadow said. "So Jak and Dujuv, whichever of you gets to the surface first starts the dead man. Six minutes after I'm out of the hole, get going on the diversion."

"From the time you pop, six and go," Jak said.

"Got it," Dujuv added.

The vertical tube was narrow enough to chimney. Jak put his back against one wall, his feet against the other, and walked and humped his way up. It had probably been an outlet shaft for substitution pumping, Jak decided.

Jak noticed a slight pittering sound on his helmet; tiny pellets of metal were falling off the walls from the three climbers above him. The walls were peppered with metal droplets no bigger than a period on a page, which showed as dark spots in the passive infrared.

The dark dots became "stars" sporadically; some visible light was coming down into the shaft. A little higher, and there was more light as Bref climbed out, up above, and then Narav, and finally Shadow. Jak saw a few bright stars in the tunnel mouth. He started the clock and chimneyed up farther.

At the top his helmet adjusted to the brilliant glare pouring into the top of the shaft, and the stars were lost in that. Another heave and kick, and he lay on the surface on his back. He rolled over, staying low, set the dead man, checked his time, blipped a com check through a rerouter to the *Spirit,* and heard Phrysaba's voice murmur in his ear, "Com check successful, we're here, good luck."

Two more minutes till go time.

Beside him, Dujuv thumped onto the surface, rolled, and put his helmet to Jak's. "Just wanted you to know that I know you have a dozen good reasons to accomplish the mission, so I'm sure you'll do it, but I also know it's got nothing to do with your personal honor or your loyalty to a friend or anything like that. You're a useful bag of shit, but you're still a bag of shit. Masen?"

"Toktru. Ten seconds to go. We'll talk later."

The little red bar in Jak's helmet display winked out. Jak and Dujuv leapt onto a boulder between two spires, then down a long slope covered with the black carbon tailings, trying to stick out like a head of cabbage in a banana split.

Dujuv unslung his flash bomb, set the timer on the blasting cap for ten seconds, and tossed the bomb down the slope. It was a flask of liquid oxygen packed into a metal toolbox full of powdered aluminum, with the blasting cap's timer sticking out through a hole on top.

Even on a slope bathed in Mercurial sunlight, the flash was bright, and would have alerted any sensor pointed this way.

Jak and Dujuv ran across the carbon slope. When they were about a hundred meters from the gully on the other side, Jak said, "Purse, execute cover noise."

His purse switched through two general frequencies several times, to help MLB's sensors lock on. He played back the recording Jak and Dujuv had made back in the krilj—

neither of them was much of a playwright, but perhaps audience interest would make up for it:

"Dujuv, you complete idiot, how could you have done that? How are we going to accomplish our mission without that bomb? And you set it off right where they'll see it!"

"Yeah, well, who's broadcasting open channel with power and volume all the way up?"

"Whoops!"

That was the curtain line. Jak followed Dujuv into the gully. The panth was bounding along easily ahead of him, kicking up sprays of carbon.

His scanner was picking up plenty of encrypted noise, but his purse wasn't having much luck with decrypting it. Once he heard the high beep-squeak of Duj squeezing off a message to Phrysaba and Pabrino, in the *Spirit of Singing Port*.

The whole plan depended on Jak, with that sliver in his liver, being a bigger draw to Riveroma than anything else, and on Riveroma's being completely in charge. If everything was working right, Riveroma's scanners would have identified Jak's voice pattern and linked it to the suited figures and the flash bomb; Shadow on the Frost, Bref, and Narav would have gone undetected; and a mass hunt for Jak and Duj, over here on the wrong side of the crater, should be starting.

Jak and Dujuv scurried down the long gully. The surface here was probably aboriginal, pitted and rough, but without melting or flows. In the long dark shadow, Jak could see that he was mostly kicking up white regolith.

Dujuv motioned for Jak to hold. High-pitched squeaks in Jak's scanner—some message from the *Spirit,* or a relay from Shadow and the boys? The panth hesitated, then made an overhand gesture, and bounded directly into the sunlight and down the slope.

Jak swallowed hard and followed. His purse said, "I have a request via scrambled text channel for you to say something loud and rude to your friend, on Channel 87. You should specifically sound very angry."

"Set 87. Dujuv, you idiot, get out of the sunlight, they'll see us for sure."

"Get off open channel, asshole," Dujuv replied. Jak thought his acting might be a little too convincing.

"Now who's on open channel?"

"Get into the shadow over here, dumbass," Duj said, "follow me to it, haven't you heard me all that time asking you to get into the shadow?"

"There's lots of shadows around here, I don't know which one you mean, and don't call me a dumbass."

Jak saw Duj flash his helmet lamp on and off in the deep black shadow that hugged the north side of a bedroom-sized boulder; on airless Mercury, with its harsh bright sunlight, shadows made things nearly invisible to the naked eye. "Oh, *that* shadow. Okay, coming down to you." He bounded down the slope in the bright sunlight, kicking up more gray-white regolith.

Jak guessed that Shadow and the boys had had to make some use of radio, and Pabrino, monitoring from the *Spirit*, had found the word "shadow" in decrypts of the malphs' communications, which would imply that the malphs had heard and decrypted some of what the other party had said. On the chance that MLB hadn't heard too much, and in the interests of keeping them preoccupied with hunting Jak, Dujuv had contrived a situation in which the word "shadow" would go out from his suit a couple of times, hoping to confuse the other side's analysis.

Or it might be something completely different.

Dujuv leading, they broke from the shadow and bounced back down into the steepening gully. A hundred fifty meters farther on, the gully ended in an enormous pile of white powder, perhaps fifteen meters high and stretching half a kilometer across their path, that must be some sort of tailings; Dujuv tried jumping up onto the pile but immediately rolled back, scrambling, flinging the powder everywhere. Jak could see him shrug even in the pressure suit, seeming to say, *Oh, well, old tove, the point of this was to attract attention, masen?* Except that Jak was not sure that Duj would ever call him "old tove" again.

They dashed around the dark side of the pile. Jak was following Dujuv when he disappeared. A moment later the ground opened under Jak, and he plunged into darkness. Barely over a second later, he thudded, hard, into a pile of sand or dirt.

He rolled over and looked up; he had fallen into a pit which faced away from the sun, and its mouth was completely within the shadow of the old bit of crater rim, so the slice of sky he could see was spattered with stars. He let his helmet's passive vision adjust to the sudden change and looked around. Dujuv was just sitting up, pounding the soft dirt in frustration; though it was hard to tell in the starlight, probably this was the same white stuff that formed the huge pile outside. Dujuv ambled over and put his helmet against Jak's. "You hurt?"

"I'm fine. Are you okay?"

"Other than a bad case of the frustrateds, I'm great. I guess we climb out and get moving again."

"Yeah," Jak said. "Well, at least we suddenly vanished; that should make us harder to find."

"Not necessarily." The panth's tone was oddly tense and quiet. "Look up."

Ten people in pressure suits stood at the mouth of the pit, blotting out the stars. A floodlight clicked on. The pit was shallow, blind, completely a trap. In the harsh new light, Jak could see that each pressure suit bore an MLB logo, and each person was carrying a military laser.

A tall one stepped forward. Though Jak could not see through the faceplate, the way he moved marked Bex Riveroma.

The tiny blue bar to the left in Jak's vision showed that Shadow and the boys still had almost thirty minutes to go; maybe no one had seen them yet—

A harsh scream filled his headphones, and all except the life-support displays on his helmet faceplate went out. They had tried to grab control of his purse, and it had self-erased to prevent that. A voice in Jak's earphones ordered him to put his hands behind his back.

As someone back there tied his wrists, Jak winced with grief. He had worked with that purse for two years, trying to coach and encourage it, and it had gotten very good at knowing what he needed and wanted. Now it was gone, just as gone as a dead person; he could restore from a backup, of course, but somehow a purse was never the same after that.

The MLB men tied their prisoners to the railings on the platform of a big fifteen-wheeler. The driver got into the cabin and headed the big, spidery vehicle down the slope toward the central pinnacle. "Now," Riveroma said, in a warm conversational tone, "what would two little boys be doing out on a mountain slope with a bomb that was barely big enough to hurt anyone?"

"We weren't out to hurt *people*," Jak said, hoping to sound petulant and whiny.

"Well, with that bomb you couldn't have hurt much of anything. The instruments got a clear fix on it and the temperature and energy output weren't more than what might be used in a big firework. So that's what I think it was. Probably to get my attention, so I would come out and do what I'm doing. Now since I can't imagine you wanted to be captured, my fine little boys, and since I don't think that Jak wants me to remove his liver, particularly not with him alive and unanesthetized, and most especially since Dujuv is surely aware that I have no reason to keep him alive, it seems to me that trying to attract my attention is a very odd behavior. This makes me think, in turn, that if you want my attention drawn to yourselves, there must be something you want attention drawn away from . . . and I'm having the whole crater searched."

The fifteen-wheeler lurched over the rise and came down a gentle slope toward the base of the pillar. Jak had no idea how his hands were fastened together behind his back, and nothing to cut with even if he had known.

"Now, Jak," Bex said, "the real question is whether you are going to be cooperative, in which case the sliver will come out of your liver in a relatively gentle fashion managed by a professional surgeon, or uncooperative, in which case I shall simply lop off the parts of you that are hard to fit into a storage canister—that would be your head and limbs—and hand your torso over to qualified personnel for disassembly at some more convenient location. Dujuv, I'm afraid all that I can offer you is your life. If you should tell me what is going on, and where I should look for what threat, right away, then you will get to keep it. For either of you, the answer to that set of questions—'what operation is this a diversion for, who is involved, where are they, and what do I need to do to foil it?'—is all I will be interested in.

"Now what I propose is this. Whichever of you takes my very generous offer first, will get the full benefit. Going second will do no good; once I have the information from one of you, I will dispose of the other."

"I'm not stupid enough to fall for that trick," Dujuv said. "It's the prisoner's dilemma problem. You study that in school when you're, what, ten? It's not even a very hard one."

"Oh, on the contrary, there's nothing harder than a dilemma. By definition, it's a situation where there's no good solution. Of course, one man's dilemma is another man's ironclad guarantee. I'll let you think about which man is which. Don't overtire that panth brain."

"Can we make you a counteroffer?" Jak asked.

Riveroma waited a few seconds before answering. They were almost at the central pinnacle now, a massive tower of broken-faced rock perhaps eighty meters high. There were crevices and chimneys enough, Jak realized, so that in the low gravity he could climb it easily—if only he were there and if only his hands were untied. Well, the former was happening pretty fast; the fifteen-wheeler was now less than half a kilometer from the dark broken cathedral of melt-glass.

"If you have a counteroffer to make," Riveroma said, "I suggest you talk fast."

"Untie my hands first."

"Tell me everything I need to know, and then I certainly will. You'll need your hands free to carry Dujuv's body."

Jak said, firmly, "If I talk we both live. You have no reason to let Dujuv live, I understand that, but you also have no reason to kill him. Untie my hands, let us both live, and I'll talk."

"Is that the best offer you can make?"

The fifteen-wheeler rolled into the flat area that had been glazed into a parking lot. Two ten-wheelers and a little five-wheeler sat on the lot. No sentries or guardposts; must be robot guns in shadows somewhere. The main door stood to one side of a tall outcrop; on the other a dark zigzagging line up the cliff face marked a crevice. There would be lots of handholds in there, and it ought to take them at least twenty minutes to get him surrounded and pinned down and force him to surrender. . . .

If Shadow and the boys had been caught already, and had talked, Riveroma would just have killed them and taken the parts of Jak he wanted. If they had accomplished their mission, Riveroma would be running. But if, as seemed most likely, Shadow and the boys were still at large, more delay—besides, if Riveroma only held Dujuv, he would be safe until Jak was recaptured. "Uh, yeah," Jak said. "Those are my conditions. Untie my hands and let us both live."

Riveroma leveled his laser at Dujuv. "Suppose I shoot him now and then we'll only have to discuss untying you."

"No."

"You see how it is. I just don't think that helping me— much as I truly do need the help—is really your priority." Riveroma poked Duj's belly with the laser a couple of times and said, "Now, how do you feel about that, Dujuv? You could go on breathing, you know. And I have rather a better record of keeping my word than your ostensible friend does of keeping his."

"Up yours."

"Touching. A historical quotation. Who'd have thought a panth had that in him?"

Riveroma was trying to infuriate them. What could he get out of that? Uncle Sib—who had known Bex Riveroma for more than a century—always said that though Riveroma was an amoral butcher, he was also a complete pro. He never did things just to be nasty, unless you counted existing.

So there was some reason he wanted them both angry and not thinking straight.

"I don't see why you balk at the cost to get everything you want," Jak said. "Our other team was only about five minutes from their objective when you picked us up. If I tell you about it, you might have to scramble, but you could probably still undo what they've done, as long as you act within—well, weehu, my purse went and suicided when your heets tried to hack it, you know, so I couldn't exactly say how long you have. But knowing where the evidence was, either for the burning armchair case or about *Titan's Dancer,* ought to be worth taking off a pair of cuffs." Jak was gambling that Riveroma couldn't afford to have his past crimes discussed with fifty MLB malphs listening in.

"Perhaps we should work something out," Riveroma said, his voice slurring slightly—was he furious? Or was he laughing at Jak?

The fifteen-wheeler was slowing to a stop at the main gate to the central pinnacle.

"Look," Jak said. "My Uncle Sibroillo always said you were a man of honor and reason."

"He *did?*"

"I speck because he always admired your skills and your record, sir." Best not to lay it on any thicker than that. The two men despised each other, but each believed that the other one was secretly in awe of him. That had led Sib to do some stupid things in the past; Jak just had to hope that

Riveroma would prove equally susceptible. "Anyway, sir, here's what I was thinking. We do it in a series of trades. My arms really are killing me, so you could undo my bonds. As soon as you do, I tell you what the main party has done, and how you can undo it. Then you release Dujuv. Then I let you knock me out to take the sliver, and trust you to take it in the way that lets me wake up afterward—which you do, and then wake me up. You go on your way having gotten everything you really want. We get to keep our lives. Everybody wins, except these poor stupid Mercurial bastards, who neither of us cares about anyway. And chances are that neither of us sees the other one for a good long time, which I bet you'd like as much as I would."

"That begins to sound like a deal," Riveroma said. "Now, how does either of us know that the other will keep his part of the bargain?"

"We don't, toktru. But if you untie me and I don't tell you the truth, you tie me up again. If I tell you the truth and you don't release Dujuv, I fight you for the sliver and you take your chances it gets damaged. Like that."

Riveroma leaned back against one of the guardrails and looked around. The harsh glare of lights and darks, and the weird jagged landscape of pits and spires, piles and smears, reflected from the gold of his faceplate; his silver pressure suit was a zebra pattern of light and dark wrinkles. "Worth a try. All right, unfasten his hands."

Some flunky moved behind Jak, and he felt the release. Not even drawing a breath first, Jak jumped as hard as he could over the rail, and ran. A laser spot flared on the rock ahead to his left, leaving a blue dot in his vision and a drooling red spot on the parking area.

Over the general frequency, Jak heard a scream of "No!," a crackle of shattering locks and seals, a dull *foom!*, and a brief harsh whistle of air. Riveroma had forced the man's helmet off, killing him with explosive decompression.

"I'll uncap any man who uses a weapon, is that clear?" Riveroma said. "Now catch that asshole. *Alive.*"

Three hard bounds took Jak to the crack in the pinnacle. He grabbed a handhold and started up; unfortunately, a long fall and a suit rupture wouldn't harm the sliver at all, despite their consequences for Jak, and therefore he needed to get to someplace where lassoing him or just knocking him down from the wall would be difficult. He climbed as fast as he'd ever climbed, taking chances he'd never have taken, and all the while he listened to MLB's open channels. In the low gravity, wedged far back in the dark of the crevice, he could move quickly but many of the moves were mistakes, and as he scrabbled upward he showered the ground below him with rocks. He had no idea how much more of the clock he would need to run out, but he thought this way he'd be able to run out plenty. He grabbed, pushed, and pulled, as hard as hc could, as fast as he could, and when he next looked around, he saw that he had at least reached a point where, even in Mercury's low gravity, a fall was apt to be fatal.

CHAPTER 16

The Master of Principle 204

Jak scrambled and climbed inward and upward; the farther back in the dark crevice he was, the harder he'd be to see, and if he was far enough up in a tight enough spot, he could surely keep them busy until Shadow and the boys did the data dump, or until the slagger went off.

Presently he came to a corner; to his right, a wall rose up toward the patch of sky where he could just see one star glittering in the blackness. There was a dark patch on that wall about a meter above the level of his feet, and turning his head to make out its shape in the dim passive infrared, he concluded that it was a shallow depression in the wall behind a narrow shelf. It seemed as good a place for a stand as any.

In the moderate grav, it was easy to jump up the distance sideways onto the shelf, but in the dark, twenty meters up, it was a nervous business. Gravel kicked out from under his feet and he went to his knees, deliberately falling forward into the shallow cave. With his head all the way inside, the passive infrared adjusted, and he could see that what was in front of him was a flat steel door.

He turned back for an instant, looking out toward the rise of the crater wall in the distance, up along the slope of old melt and tailings. Why would there be a steel door here?

It couldn't be an escape route—he was more than high enough for a fall to kill anyone.

It did have a good view through the mouth of the crevice to the surrounding plain. A gunport or sally port, then.

A big rock dropped by the cave mouth, with a cry of "Sorry, heads," through the headphones. Another party, hunting Jak, was descending the crevice from above. He was pinned between the two.

He felt the thud at the same instant that the figure silhouetted in front of him. His hand grabbed the first rock that it came to, a big awkward one, and he shoved it in the general direction of the man in front of him.

The heet had just landed, and the lip of the ledge was narrow and slippery. The rock, too big and too awkward to be much of a weapon normally, took him squarely in the crotch, and he fell backward into empty space. An alarm scream on the radio announced that the man's rocable had activated, and a moment later a "Gotcha!" suggested that they had been able to catch it from the tower top and save the man—though he'd probably take a hard swing against the wall before he was hauled up.

Jak snatched up a fist-sized rock and whipped it at the next man onto the ledge. It went high and caught the man in the faceplate; he fell after the first, possibly unconscious, for this time there was no rocable alarm. Jak snatched up another rock.

He felt a rumble in his feet, turned, saw the airlock door open and two heets in pressure suits coming through, continued his turn, sprang, and bounded into the first one, driving the rock into his front life-support pack, which flashed red. The heet fell over, twitching, and Jak brought the rock down on his second opponent's helmet. It didn't break, but it must have been like having your head inside a bucket when someone whacked it with a broom handle. The heet staggered, and Jak pushed past him into the airlock.

The door entry box was pulsing with green lights. Jak hammered on it with the rock. It fell off the wall, and the emergency override slammed the door shut. Jak was alone in the airlock and with the control for the outer door destroyed, it would take them some time to get at him from that side.

He switched on his helmet light and saw a big Makita hypervelocity gun, the size of a dining room table. Hypervelocity guns threw a half-kilogram slug at around twelve kilometers per second, more than enough to wreck any vehicle up to and including small spacecraft; in the Military Basics course at the PSA, Jak had had a total of forty-five minutes on one of these, and it hadn't been this manufacturer.

At least it was easy to find the main power switch. The gun came alive with lights and began powering up. The plain old optical site on the thing must mean there was a way to fire it manually. Jak looked it over and threw every switch marked "arm" and pushed every dark button that said "power." All the lights were green.

He took a moment with the rock to hammer out the other door-opening control, the one for the inner door; he hoped this would mean that they'd have more trouble getting in, but probably there was a central control that could bypass the wall box, anyway. Well, all he needed to do was use up time.

Now that there was air, his external suit mikes could pick up banging and thumping against the outside door. On the radio, a bunch of heets were all interrupting and shouting at each other about whether the airlock door that the central operator had just opened was the same as the airlock door that the pursuit party had wanted opened, or whether the pursuit party had asked for the wrong door.

Jak decided not to wait for them to figure it out. He pointed the gun toward the center of the outer door, punched BURST and TEN HEX, hoping that those keys meant what he thought they did, made sure it was set to FIRE ON MANUAL, and hit FIRE.

He remembered on Earth, at the Duke's private preserve, he had once done some plinking, shooting old bottles and cans with a slug-thrower (it was an aristocratic activity he would never understand), and he'd shot a can that had turned out to have a lizard hiding in it; the can had flipped over a few times in the air and thudded to the ground, and the lizard had appeared to break the light-speed limit getting away. He'd felt really sorry for the lizard.

Being in a small closed room with an operating hyper-velocity gun, firing a burst of ten, made him appreciate the lizard's situation much more than ever. At least his ears were covered by the suit, and the mikes had cut out, but what conducted through his helmet was plenty.

In front of him, the outer door now had ten doorknob-sized holes, their edges still glowing, forming two hexa-gons joined on a side, across its middle. The voice on the radio—faint in his deafened ears—demanded to know what the fuck had happened and why nobody was answering.

Jak tried to rotate the gun with the idea that he might be able to do something similar with the inner door, causing more havoc and delay, but the gun would not swing any far-ther than the edges of the outer door, and whatever stops or intelligent controls blocked it, they weren't visible or ac-cessible. He tugged at the gun, yanked, pushed and kicked it, but it swung no farther.

Riveroma's voice spoke in his headphones. "So, now

that you've killed five men and badly injured three, and established that I cannot trust you under any circumstances, perhaps you'd be willing to just sit still until we get you out of that airlock. We have you under surveillance and we can tell whether you move or not, so I would advise you not to. One of my clever technicians figured out we could use your dead purse as a null connection, and he has hacked into the life support and other controls for your pressure suit. By way of a demonstration—"

Jak doubled over in agony.

"You see? We can give you a pretty good shock anywhere you're catheterized. Don't worry. It does no permanent damage. I might yet decide to release you, and you can go back to amusing the princess with that. But meanwhile do keep in mind that I can make it feel as if you would rather lose it. Also—"

Jak's ears hurt, his eyes felt sore, he was choking and could not breathe. He thrashed around the room, crashing against the gun and back against the wall, before falling sideways to the floor.

He could breathe again. His eyes and ears felt normal.

"*That* was the argument that persuaded your friend Dujuv," Riveroma said, very casually. "Just turning off the air supply for an instant and power-venting the suit. And I'm still exploring other unpleasant things I can do. Now, are you going to sit on the floor, with your legs extended in front of you, perfectly still, with your hands away from your body?"

"Yes." Jak had complied with each direction as Riveroma spoke it.

"That's a good boy."

Presently Jak felt a heavy thump through the floor plates. They must be mounting a temporary airlock on the other side. When the door opened, two men came through, grabbed him, forced him to his feet, frog-marched him into the airlock, and pressurized it. One of the men removed his own helmet, then grabbed Jak and tore the helmet off him.

The man said, "You killed Preal Shafaritz with that stupid stunt. Remember that name, Preal Shafaritz. Repeat it."

"Preal Shafaritz."

"Thank you. He was my brother."

The man hit Jak, hard, in the face, the rough suit glove scraping his cheek and his head slamming back over the mounting collar. He hit Jak four more times, taking careful aim each time, making sure that he was hitting fresh skin, and spat on Jak's face. "Put his helmet back on him," he told his pizo.

The other heet yanked the helmet back onto Jak as if dressing a mannequin.

As soon as the helmet was on and the pressure came back up, Jak tried to switch on the face wipe. It didn't work. "Hah," Riveroma said, in his earphones. "You can live with that on your face for a while."

The two heets conducted Jak down a long corridor to an airlock elevator, shoved him into it, and took him all the way to the top. The doors opened on the treacherous, deep-pitted top of the central pinnacle. From here you could see all the way to the crater walls, five kilometers in all directions, and even a little beyond. They led Jak to the edge of a steep drop; Riveroma stood there. Beside him, Dujuv knelt at the very lip of the fifty-meter drop.

"Kneel beside your friend and make sure you're at least as close to the edge."

Jak did. He felt coldly certain that each of them was about to receive a laser cut across the back of the neck, and he was miserable to think he'd gotten Dujuv into this.

"Well," Riveroma said. "Well, well, well. Very impressive. You know, Jak, if I were Dujuv, I don't think I would like you. He's been taking a beating on your behalf more or less continually since you pulled your stupid little pointless stunt. And I think he rather believes you were just trying to save your own hide. Now that he's seen you as you are—and since your entire record shows you don't care in the slightest for or about Dujuv—this whole process will go so much more quickly."

Bex Riveroma is a slick liar, the master of Principle 204, Jak kept reminding himself. *He always tells the lie that gets in under your skin and that's hard not to believe. He gives your own worst thoughts back to you and makes you believe them.*

He hoped that Dujuv was remembering that too.

He looked down. A simple roll forward would send Jak into a long enough fall to die instantly on impact.

"Are you listening, Jak? Are you listening, Dujuv?"

They both agreed they were.

"Well. I'm going to make use of my control of your suits. And I'm going to do things to each of you. Either you can endure it or you can say the magic phrase—Jak, for you that's 'Do it to Dujuv,' or Dujuv, for you that's 'Do it to Jak.' Then while I do, you will tell me what your friends in the other party are doing, and what I need to do to stop them.

"You will tell me what I want to know, while your friend endures whatever it was that bothered you so much. Then I will kick your suffering friend's back, hard, and he will fall to his death, and you will live because I will decide to let you.

"You might notice, Jak, that although it's not ideal for the sliver to undergo a heavy impact and sudden decompression, it is very conveniently safely wrapped in a few kilos of meat—that would be you—and is likely to survive the process. Not that I actually expect any noble self-sacrifice of you, and I don't think Dujuv does, either, but it did seem like something that ought to be pointed out to you, just in case you have some tiny saving moment of decency and loyalty right at the end."

Jak looked down into the drop again. It must be at least fifty meters. In Mercury's gravity, that would take more than five seconds to fall, and there would be a horrible first second in which you didn't fall much farther than your own body length. The miners called it the "wake-up second," when you had time for a last look at the place where you had been safe, a moment before.

But at the end of fifty meters, with no air to slow you, you'd still hit at eighty kilometers per hour. In the back of his mind all of his math instructors seemed to gabble together in a nightmare of precision; doing ballistics in one's head was normally a skill anyone who worked in space needed, but just now Jak would have been happy not to have it.

Riveroma tried a big jolt of pain, like a roaring flame, through the urinary catheter, first. Jak managed not to roll forward into the chasm nor sideways into his friend.

Abruptly it stopped hurting. He sucked in a good, sweet lungful of air before his chest exploded with pain; Riveroma must be messing with the cardiac stabilizers. Another interval of almost-comfortable almost-sanity; then his guts roiled in brutal cramps.

Uncle Sib said you could always sow some confusion—"Do it to Jak," Jak said.

Riveroma laughed. "Oh, Sibroillo, Sibroillo, Sibroillo, the stuff you teach your nephew. Jak, I know where the transmission comes from, it's right there on my display. If you were trying to save your friend, which I very much doubt, it was a nice little thought, I suppose, but I would bet you were just trying to sow confusion because that is what your uncle taught you to do whenever the situation was hopeless. He always had such faith in—*What?*"

The "what" was shouted on the general channel, probably in response to something Riveroma had heard, but Jak couldn't stop to analyze yet; he was too relieved by the sudden, complete cessation of pain. After a few deep breaths, without thinking, he triggered his face wipe. To his surprise the soft sponges moved across his face in the familiar, comforting way. He could hear Riveroma and the others all shouting at each other as he scanned frequencies.

His face and faceplate were clear and, since no one seemed to be paying any attention to him, he stood up, moved away from the cliff, and looked around.

Dujuv raced past him. Obviously no one was watching them.

Still trying to get oriented, Jak looked in the direction Shadow and the boys had gone. Motion in the shadows all along that side of the crater—a vast rockslide, at least two kilometers wide, was pouring down the inside of the crater. The dead man switch had turned on the slagger. Shadow's group had been captured too—or they had lost their tight-beam link to the *Spirit of Singing Port*—or for some reason they had decided to let it happen. There was no way of knowing which.

Jagged rock along the crater edge began to tumble inward; the slope itself exploded with puffs of steam from frost deposits, which had lain under boulders for gigayears, vaporizing as the positrons heated the rock around them.

Half a kilometer of the upper crater rim glowed dull red,

then sagged like butter in a microwave. The glow turned orange, and a white line appeared at the base of the bulge. Along that half-kilometer section, the upper third of the crater rim fell inward, and white-hot magma was now pouring over the still-tumbling slide and flooding onto the crater floor. The wide pool was already half a kilometer beyond the edge of the slide, racing across the crater floor.

Jak's scanner was overloading as it hopped from channel to channel, picking up various radio alarms, artificial intelligences giving warning, people calling for help, and sheer terrified jabber. Jak turned off his radio, just to be able to think.

Men were rushing around the top of the pinnacle like hornets around a burning nest. A long tongue of the magma had raced ahead of the swelling flood on the crater floor, and was now lapping around the base of the pinnacle. The surface carts parked there exploded as their fuel and oxygen tanks melted and mixed. Even with his faceplate set for 95% darkness, it was getting painfully bright out here, and when Jak checked his faceplate display he saw that his surplus cooling capacity was dropping rapidly toward zero.

Something moved beneath his feet. The men around him, still rushing from one side to the other of the great stone tower, stopped and raised arms over their heads, as if trying to balance on a tightrope. In the heavy heat-resistant pressure suits, it looked like a sacred dance of bears.

The ground moved again, hard enough to knock him to his hands and knees. For no reason, as he got up, his rocable went off; perhaps the heat, or perhaps an environment in which so many machines were screaming their deaths over the radio, had set it off.

He didn't suppose it would hurt anything; not much could hurt or help now. Jak realized what the motion of the central pinnacle had to be; the pinnacle had been hollowed out to make it into a combined office building and fort, and though its walls were thick rock, there were doors and openings everywhere along ground level, closed only by ordinary steel doors. Those were now giving way. Air was rushing out, magma was pouring in, internal walls were dissolving, heat was setting off explosives in the magazines and flammable materials everywhere. The violent thuds in the ground were explosions and collapses below.

With a hard lurch, the whole pinnacle slid sideways, and Jak was flung out into space, above the boiling magma. In the low gravity, he didn't seem to be falling at all. He had a glimpse of the crumbling pinnacle falling away below him, and of a white sea of magma, now beginning to spot with yellow-orange. It seemed, impossibly, farther below him than the pinnacle had stood above it. Probably the explosion that had taken down the pinnacle had thrown Jak upward, and so he might be saved for as much as half a minute, but falling from this height, with nothing to land on but boiling rock, he was surely not saved for long.

CHAPTER 17

An Opponent Fully Worthy of Our Considerable Skills

The pool of boiling magma receded rapidly from his feet. It must have been quite an explosion to have thrown him this high—no, to get thrown this high, even in Mercury's low gravity, the acceleration should have mashed him into jelly.

He was now at least a kilometer above the lake of liquid rock, and apparently still rising. Surely at any moment he would begin the downward drop into it?

But the magma continued to recede, and now he saw craters beyond Hamner, then the dark ground beyond the terminator line, and finally the black curve of the horizon. He was still rising; the magma pool was now just a red eye on the planet's face beneath him.

He became aware that he had turned his suit radio off. He jaw-clicked twice, so that his scanner would look for friendly transmissions.

"—radio must be out," Dujuv was saying. "He looked fine to me when you grabbed his rocable."

"His suit telemetry's good," Phrysaba agreed. "I guess we'll just have to wait till we get you heets hauled in."

"I'm here," Jak said. "I had my radio off and forgot to turn it back on."

"Oh, am I going to *enjoy* giving you a safety lecture," Pabrino said. "Right now, we just have to reel you and Dujuv in, and then head out to rendezvous with the *Spirit*. Just sit tight and we'll have you on board in about—um—"

"Seventy-three seconds," Phrysaba said, "give or take a tenth or so."

Not knowing what else to say, Jak said, "Thank you."

Phrysaba laughed. "I'm doing the easy part. Just routine flying on this little tub. We took off as soon as we heard you get captured for the second time—it sounded like things weren't going very well and sometimes it's useful to be closer to the problem. The hard part was cracking the code so that we could go in on top of what Riveroma was doing and access your rocables. If Pabrino hadn't done that in record time, I don't think we could have done this. Once he did, it was really all just a textbook exercise—a little tricky keeping the lines from going down into the soup, but otherwise it was like a piloting problem in the beginner class. So no making a big deal out of it, masen?"

It occurred to Jak that he was dangling from a cable attached to a small, dodging, jinking spaceship in a low eccentric orbit, and that the pilot was spending a lot of time talking to him. "Uh, don't let me distract you from flying."

"Oh, don't worry about that. Soon as we had you, I put it back on autopilot. The machine flies better than I do, anyway."

Jak looked at the serrated, rough, burning hot rocks now far below, and tried to borrow as much of her attitude as he could.

"How long have you had your radio on?" Dujuv asked.

"The first thing I heard was you saying my radio was out," Jak said.

"Good."

"Why?" There was a long pause while Jak turned slowly on the cable, and Mercury fell farther and farther away from the soles of his boots. "Why was that good?" Jak repeated.

"Because," Phrysaba said, "your friend is still furious with you, as well he should be, about everything you said to that Mreek Sinda. But when he thought you might be dead, he was beside himself with worry about you. He didn't want you to hear how much he cared, because he'd also like to break your neck. Which, I might add, is a very healthy impulse and one I fully support."

"Me too," Pabrino added. "We can discuss that once we get you both reeled in, which will be less than a minute now."

Phrysaba added, "Pabrino is trying to get a good cable speed, ship acceleration, and trajectory match so I don't slam you against the inside of the cargo hatch. Actually, to be fussy, I'm trying not to slam Dujuv against the inside of the cargo hatch, and I'm trying not to slam you *too hard.*"

"We'll talk to you again once that's done," Pabrino said. "Always assuming we don't concuss you, bringing you in."

The bone-colored curve of Mercury, with its brightly lit sprawling cities and black ore roads between them, fell farther beneath him, the planet rapidly becoming a sphere rather than a plane. The dark shadows of the cuts and ravines between the scarps of Caloris turned into a mere pattern of irregular black razor-cuts, and the scarps themselves blurred together into a thick dark curve. Jak hung high above the little planet, suspended between the launch over his head and the ground far below, and waited while Phrysaba gently accelerated the launch and Pabrino slowed the winch.

He saw a suited figure near him in the sky, drawing ever closer—Dujuv. It had taken a long time for the lines to bring them together, after snatching them out on slightly different trajectories. The suited figure folded its arms and twisted to face away.

They drew closer, moving in odd arcs, whirls, and tugs that must mean they were now being guyed and snatch-lined, to keep them from banging into each other.

The cargo bay doors slid past them, and for an instant, Jak was blind in the dim of the cargo bay. When his face-plate adjusted, he saw Dujuv swaying beside him. The doors slid closed.

With a click and whir, the rocables uncoupled and re-tracted, leaving them floating free in the empty metal box of the cargo bay. They pushed off and glided into the air-lock.

Emerging, Jak managed, but only just, not to say "You look like hell" to Dujuv, whose slick, hairless face could not have been more drenched if he had just plunged his head into a bucket of sweat. The dark circles under his eyes looked as if he'd been on the losing side of a brawl, and his lips were tinged blue—the panth gasped the relatively clean, cool air of the ferry through his open mouth as if he'd just run ten kilometers in high grav.

Dujuv looked at Jak. "You really look like hell."

"I thought I might," Jak said. "Did you know anything about getting rescued, in advance?"

"I had no idea. You?"

"Not a clue."

"Are you telling me the truth?"

"Yes."

Dujuv nodded, warily, but appeared to accept it.

The door to the crew space slid open, and the two of

them airswam through it. Phrysaba was sitting at the control chair, leaning over toward Pabrino in the second seat. He had just set up the vector for a quick burn to put them on the minimum-energy ballistic back to the *Spirit of Singing Port*. Checking it through local traffic control, Phrysaba waved distractedly.

Pabrino said, "System communications dialing through—we're going to put you in touch with Shadow on the Frost. He's been worried about you."

"And we've been worried about him," Dujuv said.

Shadow appeared on one of the cabin screens; some of the feathers on his face looked charred. "Jak! Dujuv! You're alive! This spares me the effort I might otherwise have had to put into avenging you!"

"I'm glad to see you alive, too, Shadow on the Frost," Jak said.

Dujuv blurted out, "Are you all right?"

"Better for knowing you're all right, and still better for your asking, my oath-friend. I will recover. After the magma started to flow, I fled to high ground. We had a close one as we were running; Narav fell and slipped back. I got there and pulled him back, but his foot touched the molten rock. I guess they will grow him a new one, or so the doctors say. Kyffimna is absurdly grateful, but truly, it was something anyone would have done. One does not leave a friend in danger of pain and death."

Jak said, "So, where are you now and what are you doing?"

"I'm at the Uninsured Charity Hospital at Bigpile. After I was able to reach high ground and call in an ambulance for the two boys, I tried to locate you and Dujuv and could find no beacon for either of you. I was very sorry for the loss of an oath-friend and contemplated scarring myself. I am glad I waited.

"There is also news which is bad for our cause but good for our honor. Riveroma found a rocket to grab his rocable. My purse traced him as far as the Chaudville loop station, and since several ships are passing in the next few hours, I have no doubt Riveroma will get away. That's sad on the one thumb, but the thumb that meets it makes me over-joyed. We're not done with him, Jak Jinnaka. He is an op-ponent fully worthy of our considerable skills, I have great faith that he will be back to do battle with us again, and we may yet taste his blood in our mouths and claim his corpse as trophy. It would have been such a pity to lose him to the magma; he merits a far better finish, for he is a fine enemy indeed."

Jak had enough trouble specking his own species; Rubahy esthetics were likely to be forever beyond him. "I am glad my oath-friend is pleased."

"And I am sorry that he is crazy," Dujuv whispered.

They closed up after some pleasantries; Shadow would be joining them back on the *Spirit of Singing Port* within a few days, as soon as he was sure that Narav was out of dan-ger and would be taken care of. "I have heard too much about doctors and insurance companies," he explained.

"Will you be able to do anything about it if they do mess around with Narav's treatment?"

"All I need to do is find the right person to bite," Shadow said confidently. "I will talk to you again soon, oath-friends."

When they turned back from the screen, the ferry was in free fall, headed on its intercept course to the *Spirit,* and Phrysaba and Pabrino at last had time to talk.

"I don't suppose this gadget has a kitchen?" Dujuv asked.

"No, but I packed a big lunch," Phrysaba said, "knowing I'd be feeding a panth who's been working too hard." She opened a storage compartment and pulled out a hot-cold box, then passed it to Dujuv like a basketball. "Didn't know exactly what you liked, and the ship's galley records said 'everything', which wasn't very helpful, so there's a couple kinds of soup, five kinds of juice, and about a dozen sandwiches, all different kinds."

"Perfect," Dujuv said. "And your ship's records are fine. 'Everything' is my favorite flavor."

When Dujuv had finished off a few of everything, and therefore was slowing down, he paused to ask, "Are you all still flying off cargo? Can I take a longshore capsule down to get back to Mercury?"

"We've got several days of loading yet to do," Pabrino said. "You can be back to Mercury within a day. Set it up for you then?"

"Yes, thank you."

"You can be there for eight days, if you like, before the last scheduled cargo flight, and even then you could come up with a load of construction materials for another few weeks; we'll be here for a while during refit."

There was a brief pause while Dujuv folded a whole sandwich into his mouth and swallowed it the way a boa does a hamster. After a gulp of juice, Dujuv said, "Naw, I'm going to be staying over for a year or so."

Everyone stared at him. He looked back calmly and said, "Well, those people trusted me. Someone has to make sure that there's nobody left from MLB. And you might recall we slagged a big share of their mining gear—it might help them to have me there to testify to insurance investigators, or even get it covered out of some Hive or Greenworld gray budget. But one way or another, they shouldn't lose half the machines they make their living with, just because they happened to get in the way while we were chasing malphs. And I do care about them. So there's all kinds of reasons. Really, nothing's done, down there, yet, if you see what I mean. It might take a year to straighten it all out and do the job right."

"What about the slamball team?" Jak asked.

"They can get along without me for a year; they did before I got there, they will after I go. This is more important."

"Duj," Jak said, "you can write them a letter! They were lucky that you turned up and helped out! The insurance company will only need some recorded testimony to justify paying for the slagged equipment! I don't understand."

Dujuv shrugged and went on eating; after a moment he said, "I don't speck that whether you understand, or not, is going to be very important to me, anymore."

Jak asked, "So . . . do you think I should go back too, and take care of things there until everything's all right? Do you think that I owe that to them too—I mean, do you expect me to do that?"

Dujuv thought for such a long time that Jak thought he had just decided to ignore the question, but then he said, "No, I wouldn't expect that of you. I guess I never *should* have expected anything of the kind of you."

Phrysaba pulled herself back into the pilot's chair and said, "Strap down, boosting in forty seconds." Jak hastened to fasten his lap belt; Dujuv managed to do his one-handed without letting go of the food; Sib and Pabrino checked theirs. The engines thundered and boomed, there was briefly gravity toward the back of the ship, and then silence again. "Next boost in about fifty minutes," Phrysaba said, to no one in particular, unstrapping and letting herself float up for a better view out the front window.

None of them spoke to Jak again for the rest of the flight back to the *Spirit of Singing Port,* and Jak was afraid to try to start a conversation.

CHAPTER 18

Nothing Personal

Actually," Myx said, "I haven't seen Shyf myself for days." She stretched and rolled over; Jak admired the job the reconstructors had done. Not only was Myx's new left leg as functional as the old, it was as pretty and as pleasant to the touch, and having thoroughly explored, Jak could attest that the attachment was seamless. "Are you still brain-locked on her?"

"Yes," Jak admitted.

"I don't suppose I can get your mind off her for a few minutes, since you can't get your body onto her?"

"I'm still a little tired from the last time," Jak said, "and besides, I speck maybe I should get dressed, and get up, and go sign up for some shifts at the barracks."

Myxenna rolled over onto her belly and pushed up onto all fours; Jak admired the sway of her full breasts. "Hunh," Myx said. "I wouldn't have thought you'd be interested enough to do that. The ship leaves in two weeks, and nobody's going to care if we just hang around and party, masen? I only put on the fancy dress and go up to court and do the lady-in-waiting thing because it's fun."

"And her little night activities—"

"She still wants some of us to watch, now and then. She gave me to Kawib as a present for a while—I think in her weird mind she wanted to try to cheer him up—but of course he wasn't interested, and I certainly didn't want to press things. The main thing she uses me for is a crying towel."

"For what?"

"Oh, for Seubla, of course. That poor girl tried so hard to be Shyf's friend—not that I blame her, how else could she hope to stay alive?—and it looks like, now, looking back, she *did* become Shyf's friend. So now Shyf is lonely and doesn't have anyone to talk to or argue with, and she spends a lot of time telling me about that. Which I avoid whenever I can. Life, like me, is short."

"And can be delightful."

"Oh, there's the difference. I am, life can be." The blue starring in her green eyes twinkled, but she put on a serious face and said, "Now don't change the subject. Why would you be going back up to the barracks to rejoin the gigolo corps?"

"Maybe I just like the fancy clothes," Jak said.

"They don't make me do military drill when I wear mine."

"Well, yeah, but I look like crap in a long gown." Jak sat up and reached for his underwear.

Myx sighed in frustration. "All right, pizo, I admit it, I feel like I really want to dak what you're up to. Especially because, if you haven't noticed, I've been trying to tell you that Shyf is crazier than ever, more cut up inside into more weird sharp nasty little pieces, and the worst possible thing you can be is someone she likes. It's like being the pet bunny of a sadistic ten-year-old boy; he wants to wub his wittle face on your soft fur, and he's wondering what it would be like to hang you. If you had any brains, you would *stay away from her.* What's this sudden attack of a sense of duty about? Did you bang your head on the headboard while I was too busy to notice? Or is it something left over from the conditioning? I thought that had faded."

"I think it has. I'm not sure I could explain it myself."

"Well, then," Myxenna said, "will going tomorrow morning, instead of this evening, make any difference?"

Jak shrugged.

Myxenna wet her lips and smiled that smile. Jak started to see her side of the argument, and it became convincing when she stood up and pressed herself against him.

The next morning, while Myx was still asleep, Jak got up and walked to the RPG barracks. He was carrying his uniform slung over his shoulder in his jumpie, and he might have been anyone with any minor errand to run.

There was no way of cutting through the Palace grounds faster; the interwoven canals, tall hedges, ponds, gardens, and thickets meant that you pretty much had to stay on the path, even in one-third g, unless he wanted to try jumping a hedge at the risk of landing in a slough.

Ahead of him, a low-flying hawk—the things weren't the smartest creatures that the genies had ever made— stalked Jak's sprite, and he laughed as it swooped down twice, obviously puzzled by the moving object that became just a spot of bright light when it got near.

He had been back in Greenworld for ten days and this was the first real walk he'd taken. He loved the winding grassy walkways between the hedges. He liked ambling slowly through the narrow thoroughfares with their dozens of little shops, each selling some single highly specialized handicraft. Complex reversed curves at a lintel end echoed the transoms over the windows and facades, so that the whole effect was fractal and swirly and intensely alive.

Down another street, he found he had walked into a promenade, and he politely moved to the right, walking nearer the shopfronts, to leave the center to the passing young men and women, for he had no intention of participating in the mutual inspections himself, and anyway he was dressed more than a few levels too informally. He noted, though, just in case future reference would be useful, that he saw no military uniforms or court livery; whether it was a whole street of republicans, or mufti was always expected, Jak didn't know, but he made a note to his new purse to learn something about the customs.

Clearly the ethnographic stuff was taking hold. He winced at the self-teasing.

As he walked the last greensward, between the cascading fountains, to the barracks, the perturb alarm hooted, and he crouched low, letting the brief moment of lightness and heaviness pass. All around him, fountains crashed and passersby whooped; it was a nice day to be splashed with cool water.

Kawib Presgano was behind the desk again. "Jak Jinnaka. Congratulations on your successful mission; I understand they reinstated you with back pay after your success?"

"They did," Jak said.

"I wonder how old I will be before I get to do anything."

Jak didn't know what to say, so he just watched as Kawib made some more notes. "So," the thin, pale young man said, "you do realize that you are utterly mad." He seemed to try to force his old sardonic smile back on; it didn't look like it fit anymore, probably because he couldn't help meaning what he had said.

"I'd like a regular watch assignment."

"I was told that when you came in, I was to give you all night watches. Doesn't that make you think about going back to your hotel and staying there?"

"It's what I want."

"I don't want to know what that's supposed to mean." The two shook hands like thieves who hope never to meet again.

During his first night patrol, Jak alternated between rehearsing the things he needed to say, and experimenting with how silent and alert he could be as he followed the gray-white cross. After a while, he stopped rehearsing, and just followed the cross. His own inward silence matched the dark silence of his surroundings.

Soon he could comfortably hear every crunch of his boots on the pavement, then the hiss of his every breath, and finally the low deep pulse of every slow heartbeat, in the state of total awareness that the Disciplines sought to achieve.

After leading him aimlessly around the maze for hours, the sprite went to the Heir's Palace by the shortest and quickest possible route. Senses up and heart quiet, Jak followed.

Sesh liked drama and surprises. He had half-expected to find her naked. Instead she was sitting, fully dressed, at a writing desk in the center of the room. She gestured for him to take the seat opposite her, and he sat, hands on his knees, as if she were interviewing him for a job, or explaining his algebra grade.

She hesitated. In the instant before she spoke, Jak let his eyes enjoy her gracile lines, perfect thick crimson hair, and rich soft brown skin.

"Well," Sesh said, "remember that at the time that you received Riveroma's false message, there was a real one diverted? I told you what was in it. Do you remember?"

She stretched and turned, balancing and aligning that dancer's back with the grace of a waking kitten. When she turned back to look at him, head turned a little to the side and face partly blocked from his view by that curtain of soft crimson curls, the eyes that looked straight into his were the color of clear Martian twilight, dark as night yet purely blue, like looking a hundred kilometers down a well into a running reactor. "Well," she said, "I'm waiting for an answer to my question. And princesses are not supposed to be kept waiting. Do you remember what was in that letter to you, from me, which you never got?"

"You were getting rid of me."

"Right." She sighed and brought her hands up onto the desk, resting them there with arms crossed; he admired the flat, chiseled muscles of her bare arms. His gaze drifted up to her chocolate-and-coffee tanpatterned shoulders, so vivid against her soft, cream-colored tunic. Sesh sighed again, and her fingers rolled in a little arpeggio of frustration and impatience.

"Now, you see, things are different. Oh, not that different. There would still be excellent reasons for getting rid of you. You are still, of course, not much more than a lively boy in bed—real talent there seldom goes with a knack for heroics. You are still republican at heart—you don't properly appreciate that I am a princess. But you are more interesting now. You're a perfect addition to my media image; a dashing heroic commoner lover is an asset beyond price in the battle to stay popular. I'd never have thought you would be willing to step all the way into the image. I would have marked you down as a naive boy, based on your devotion to all these 'toktru toves' of yours. I'd have said that you would never betray a friend, but, well, I was wrong."

"No, you're wrong now," he said. "I treated Dujuv and Shadow like that because it was our best chance to beat Riveroma."

"I'm sure that's what you told yourself," she said. "Jak, there are senior operatives who haven't half your sangfroid. You left Dujuv to be tortured while you did a pointless stunt—killed what, five heets? Just somehow or other, co-incidentally, that happened to make a fabulous climax to Sinda's new series about you. Well, such men are useful. And very attractive. Like the Hive itself—apparently big, warmhearted, forgiving, not too smart, way too sincere; actually with a black hole for a heart. You might have made a prince of yourself, back in humanity's glory days—you could have slaughtered a million people to get a crown, and then afterwards firmly believed it was for everyone's good, and enjoyed the slaughter and the crown alike.

"Well, now that I really *know* you, my only problem is securing your loyalty. So here you sit, Jak, bathed in my pheromone mix . . . given a view that makes me nearly perfect . . . listening to a voice cadenced for hypnosis . . ." She beamed at him, and then gave him her Sesh-giggle again. Jak had never felt so in love before. "Undress," she said. "I haven't been a delicate little virgin in weeks."

Afterward she breathed "Calm love" in his ear, and he lay holding her, happy and at peace, until she said, "Now, something is bothering you a lot. Tell me all about it."

He adored her; holding her was the greatest peace he had ever known. The words he had rehearsed seemed a million years in the past, in some other language entirely. "You and Mreek Sinda set me up. You really did record that message I got. It took me forever to realize how much it costs Sinda's company to make even very short, semi-convincing viv animations, which any code-breaking AI can tell from the real thing, even if her nitwit audience can't. And your message was twenty minutes long and perfect. The way you did it was, you recorded that message, probably three or four times, cut it all into samples, and averaged it. That way it looked extremely real, because it was, but the cutting-and-averaging process was just detectable at the limits of what analysis can do, so when Mattanga looked into it, it looked like the best fake in history. It all makes sense, too. Sinda really did need a new story, and you really needed to be a celebrity—being a princess just gets you into the club, being a celebrity gets you a chance at going places, masen?"

"Toktru," she said.

"Did you always plan to send me where Riveroma might capture or kill me?"

"Oh, no," she said. "Sinda did. That was irritating, that she didn't tell me, but toktru, Jak, I'd have sent you anyway. Not because we needed anything done on Mercury—it didn't matter whether Riveroma ran that. Suppose he had won? He'd have had to sell metals at pretty much the same rates as the quaccos do now. If he'd tried to push metals prices much higher, the resourcers on Venus and the aster-oid miners would have expanded and beaten his prices down. Whether Riveroma or the corporations or the miners' union controls Mercury, the only difference is who cashes the checks, not how much they're for, and I suppose whether some very ugly people with very dull lives live longer or shorter. But at least it is turning into lovely pub-licity, and the Greenworld and Uranium troops that went there to 'restore order' are doing a nice job of getting some schools and hospitals and so forth put up, and making things just enough better so that Psim and I will have the miners' loyalty for a generation or so. Many thanks to your toktru tove Dujuv, by the way, who is very good about talk-ing us into things we were already going to do anyway; it makes everything so much more credible."

"The miners really need—"

"The miners really need a media consultant. They'll get their schools and health plan and so forth out of this, but they should be sitting at the table as one of the players in the solar system, and once again, they're shut out. Too bad for them they didn't have a real hardcase bastard like Riveroma take over. He'd have gotten them somewhere."

Jak discovered that the "calm love" command precluded arguing; he specked that was one of Sesh's favorite things about it. "Well, if you didn't intend to send me after Riveroma, what did you intend?"

"I thought I could bend you and Dujuv, and maybe Myx, into a fatal fight with some of the Royal Palace Guards. Ideally I could have provoked them into an attempted coup and the three of you could have foiled it, and several RPGs and ladies in waiting would have gotten dead—I'd have rigged things to make sure it came out that way—and I'd have had several fewer problems to worry about, and a lot of favorable coverage because Sinda's story about you was bound to reflect well on me.

"Instead, that stupid half-animal, your tove, bonded right to the ones I most wanted killed. So Sinda wanted to send you to Mercury, and Mattanga came up with a way to get you out of Greenworld—only Riveroma failed us, too. One of Mattanga's best schemes ever, too."

"If she's so good, why did you fire her?"

"I didn't. She suffered an accident."

Jak froze; he knew the game, he knew the rules, but he remembered Mattanga's kindness to him, her gratitude to Dujuv—

Sesh sat up in bed, sucking in her gut, sticking out her breasts, and putting on a pouty face. "Now I know you're angry; it's just the 'calm love' that's keeping you from being able to touch the feeling. That's why you feel weird and disoriented and numb."

He nodded; that was what he felt.

"It was nothing personal. All right, it's soundproof in here . . . let's have some excitement and danger. When you were a well-intentioned goof with a nice body, you could be fun in the right mood, but now that I know the devious treacherous bastard underneath, I'm toktru hot for you. Release rage. Hard."

Halfway through, he looked into her eyes and knew that apart from the speed and force, what she was really enjoying was his self-disgust.

When it was over, she put her arms around him and murmured "Calm love, calm love, calm love," until he fell asleep with her lying on his chest, breathing the dense synthetic pheromone mix from her hair, warmer and happier than he'd ever felt before.

Until the ship left, he did his Disciplines practice, enjoyed Myxenna's body, wandered around Greenworld seeing the sights, and made his nightly patrols. Always, while he watched the sprite, he willed it to turn suddenly toward the Heir's Palace. It never did.

When the time came, he packed his jumpie and, along with Shadow and Myxenna, boarded the *Ceres Throne,* a quarkjet liner; the Princess was generous about that. *Ceres Throne* had no need to run dark, like a warship; her quarkjets supplied a steady tenth of a g, exactly what passengers tended to find most comfortable, and the 258 million kilometers from the Aerie to the Hive was a nearly straight line, clipping well inside Venus's orbit and taking only twelve days. Liners actually spent much more time having their thrusters rebuilt and their Casimir volumes retuned—a necessity at every stop—than they did en route, but from a passenger's viewpoint, it was great, assuming you could afford a ticket that cost as much as large home on the light decks of the Hive. Jak didn't expect he'd be getting too many more rides like this one.

At Greenworld, on shipboard, and once he was home, Jak recorded and sent a message to Dujuv twice a day, giving him the same story and explanation over and over; about every two weeks, Dujuv would send a short, curt note, text only, telling him what he had been doing (mainly recording testimony, arguing with lawyers and agents, and occasionally working out in the field), about his new hobby (Dujuv had gotten bitten badly by the ancient languages bug, as had Phrysaba, and the two of them were now pen-pals in three dead languages), and about his political activity (Dujuv had joined the United Breeds, an organization that sent whiny, hectoring letters to the media about stereotyping and tried to make breed children feel special—at least that was as much as Jak could speck). No note from Dujuv ever referred to anything about their friendship or Jak's behavior.

While on *Ceres Throne,* Jak did his CUPV duties mostly around the reactor and synthesizers, and started to learn a little astrogation from Shadow. He saw little of Myx; turned loose among fashionable young rich men, she was nearly always busy.

On his off shifts, he sat in the observation lounges, beside Shadow. Occasionally he listened to the strange, violent, seemingly aimless stories of the Rubahy. Mostly they just sat facing outward toward the dark dotted with stars.

*   *   *

"Well, what an interesting year for you," Dean Caccitepe said, meeting Jak as he airswam through the dilating door. "Probably most interesting because you've seen so little of me. Grab a seat, we've a little talking to do, but I don't think any of it will be unpleasant, or at least I have nothing unpleasant on the agenda." He airswam back to his own seat, behind the desk, but then popped over the desk and perched on its edge near Jak. It was much more informal but it also put the tall ange into a position where he loomed over Jak like a vulture, sitting reared back with his long legs and arms tucked in close and looking down his long nose. But the Dean's smile seemed kind and genuine. "Not only did you start off with a brilliantly completed Junior Task, but you also did better in all of your classes than you'd ever done before in your life—I know students hate the expression, but you lived up to your potential."

Jak shrugged. "Everyone keeps telling me what a success my Junior Task was for the Hive, and I know that I learned a lot." It seemed like a safely neutral thing to say.

"And," the Dean said, "I would have thought it was impossible, but I have not had you in here all year, this year, though in your previous two years you might as well have had a cot in the waiting room. I have had no disciplinary infractions of any kind to deal with. Now, though I am forced by circumstances to believe that Jak Jinnaka can go a year without getting caught, it is beyond my power to believe that Jak Jinnaka can go a year without doing anything." The Dean cocked his head to the side as if to get a better angle on a worm. "So, what's going on? Is it that Dujuv is on leave, and you don't have anyone to do things with?"

"Um, no."

"Is it that he was always the least adroit liar of the team and often got you caught?"

"It's nothing to do with him."

"You have lost your taste for pushing your luck to see where it breaks—"

"Not a good guess."

"You no longer enjoy getting caught."

Jak was about to deny that he had ever enjoyed getting caught. But the Dean would be pleased with himself, and therefore pleased with Jak, if one of the guesses proved right. "I was going to try to convince you that that one isn't true, sir, but I *have* learned to really enjoy not getting caught, and . . . well, I guess that's all. I don't like being a bad boy anymore. I really like being a successful sneak."

Dean Caccitepe smiled as if he had just killed something. "I have no doubt that someday you will be one of the Hive's finest operatives. We worry about such things. There are, unfortunately, people who are masters of deceit but cannot leave their good work alone. Some of them—it's all too common—are obsessed with truth, and that is *why* lies fascinate them. Indeed they become such proficient liars *because* their minds are constantly nattering on, in the background, about the issues of truth: what *should* it look like, how does each individual tell truth from lies, how can all the different kinds of truth-filters be spoofed, are there any that can't be, how does the fit between the true part and the false part make a lie more or less effective. But they are people who should be philosophers, not operatives.

"I have an acute interest in this myself, you know." He wrapped himself in his own arms and stroked his long-fingered hands down his own long, lean triceps, unconsciously preening. "If you check the library you will find three monographs of mine on just that personality type. Furthermore, I shall authorize you to access the fourth one."

Jak at least had learned how to recognize a completely unsubtle hint, so he said, "Well, I'll read all of them. They sound interesting. If it's okay to ask, though, the classified one sounds like the most interesting, so what's it about? Or do I need to read the unclassified ones to dak it toktru?"

"It isn't classified, Jak. It was conditionally suppressed."

This was beyond strange; conditional suppression was the category the pokheets and courts used for heresy and for peaceable sedition.

"But," Jak said, "you can clear me to read it?"

"The work is about a century old, Jak. So in the eyes of the law there are two separate Caccitepes. There is Caccitepe who long ago wrote a scholarly study that was ruled heretical and conditionally suppressed, and who also long ago served his sentence. Then there is Caccitepe the distinguished scholar with forty years in Hive Intel, who is now the Dean of Students at the Public Service Academy. And that latter Caccitepe has the power to authorize any student to read any suppressed work.

"Now, as for why it was suppressed, I say with some pride that my heresy was not just any heresy. We were just discussing those talented-but-oddly-handicapped liars whose propensity, proficiency, and perspicacity in lying all arise from their fixation on the truth. They very often, you see, later in life, change overnight to rigorous truth-telling.

"This is so common that for millennia the secret services of every nation have been bedeviled with people who keep deciding that 'the public must be told.' I argued that just such a personality—the truth-obsessed liar—was evident in the historical record of Paj Nakasen. Mostly back when he was plain old Bob Patterson and the Wager's naming convention had not yet taken hold."

Jak winced at the mention of the forbidden name. And

why was the Dean telling him so many things it was dangerous to know? This game was clearly far more than just recruiting talent for Hive Intelligence. Well, as Uncle Sib said, when in doubt, sow confusion, and as Nakasen said in Principle 212, "If you are thinking of changing the subject you already should have."

Jak said, "Mreek Sinda and Princess Shyf wouldn't have been able to pull that hoax on me unless they had someone helping them in the Hive. That had to be my Uncle Sib, whom I know it wasn't, because I checked—or Dujuv, who wouldn't do it in a million years—or you. I can show you the evidence, if you're interested, that it was you. You were in it with them all the way back to composing that phony message. Bex Riveroma was as surprised as anyone when I turned up; you people put me within his reach. Now I know that Sinda did it because it was good viv, and Princess Shyf hadn't actually planned on it . . . but why did you? Were you just shopping me freelance for the money?"

Caccitepe smiled, pleased that his pet had just executed a trick flawlessly. "Think, Jak. Yes, I did conspire with a few people to put you where Riveroma could get at you. It was nothing personal, and I did rather hope that you'd come back alive and successful. But it was neither my intention that you should live or that you should die, and it was only of passing interest whether you succeeded or failed on the mission. So why would I shop you? The PSA and the Hive would have to know. Why would they let me?"

"Because you don't like me, and neither do they?"

"I don't, and they don't, but that's not the reason."

Jak stared into space. "Does this have to do with the problem liars you were talking about before, and how happy you are that I don't seem to be one of them?"

"What do you think?"

"I speck that your job is to turn out what the Hive needs. And for some jobs, the Hive . . . just like Greenworld or any other serious player . . . has to have some real rat bastards. People who will stab a friend in the back without even remotely thinking about it, people whose only loyalty is to themselves—"

"And who does the Hive have who is like that?" The Dean got up to show him out. "Congratulations and welcome. You and I will doubtless have much more to do with each other, without enjoying any of it, for I very much doubt that we will ever become friends. So rather than spend time in each other's company before we must, I suggest you leave now."

Jak airswam out of the office, his mind utterly blank. As he descended a rung tube into the main part of the PSA, down where the grav would be too heavy for airswimming, he remembered to check, and locked his legs around a rung before bringing his purse up to his face. "Time check."

"You have sixteen minutes. Estimated time there if you take Pongo and pay premiums for speed is fourteen and a half, if you go to the nearest station."

"Do it and direct me to the nearest station."

"Down this rung tube, nine more levels. You can drop it if you don't mind a disciplinary infraction."

At least his restored purse still was willing to help him break rules. It was good that he'd made two real friends in the last few years, even if one of them was a blue glove and the other was a feathered lizard.

Jak kicked off and let himself fall; it wouldn't do to be late. When he swung through the door, he could see a couple of campus pokheets just turning to walk toward where he was emerging—they'd have him marked and ID'd anyway, so there was no point standing around waiting for them to lecture him on safety. He bounded hard to where his purse directed, a siding that he wasn't authorized to use. Pongo was just grounding, its canopy already sliding open.

Jak popped inside and belted in as the canopy irised over him; then there were several minutes of violent jerks and sudden accelerations as the purse and Pongo's own nav equipment found the fastest possible way through all the available Pertrans track. Lights from the ports in the tunnel walls flashed by, forming mad hyphens and streaks; grav must have hit three g's a couple of times; but with just over two minutes to spare, since Pongo had outdone itself, Jak was dumped out at the receiving area for the big docks, deep down in the Hive, where warships came in and locked down for maintenance and repair.

The *Hope of Peace,* on which Dujuv was a CUPV, was just docking; Jak intended to be standing in the receiving area when his old tove got off it. "Message from Shadow on the Frost," Jak's purse said.

"Display on the palm screen." He held it up to his face. The tiny image of Shadow whistled a greeting. "Jak, my tove, I can think of no way in which I can help matters by being there, and several ways that, through ignorance of your customs, I might damage things. And I am afraid that on a project as honorable as repairing a friendship, and as important, it is best for you to act alone. But the moment you can, please call me and tell me how it went! Your oath-friend—and Dujuv's—cares very much. I hope we will again be able to watch him, together, as he stuffs an entire plate of beefrats into his face."

"Thank you, Shadow," Jak said, "I'll try."

"Honor reclaimed is the finest kind," Shadow said. "Good luck, tove and tove-of-my-tove."

When Jak looked up from his purse, they had already

connected the flextunnel to the *Hope of Peace,* and the crew were just coming down the ramp into the receiving area. Jak moved forward toward them.

Dujuv came through the door, saw him, vaulted the side of the walkway, and bounded to Jak in three big leaps, like a mad kangaroo. As he landed in front of Jak in a deep crouch, he said, "You came down to meet me. Thank you. I wasn't expecting anyone." He was grinning already.

Jak grabbed Dujuv's outstretched forearm, felt the panth's big powerful hand close like a vise around his own slender arm, and said, "Welcome back. I've missed the hell out of you, pizo, and we've got to go have some fun." Jak hoped to Nakasen and all the gods that Duj could tell that he meant it.

ACKNOWLEDGMENTS

As always, there are people besides me whose effort and intelligence was important to the completion of this book. These include: Betsy Mitchell, who guided me through the process of creating this series with a very large number of suggestions that proved invaluable, and whose work on the first book, *The Duke of Uranium* helped me find out what I wanted to do; also, whose sure eye was invaluable in developing this world and these characters: Jaime Levine, my editor, for support and extraordinary patience; Dave Cole, for a very thorough and intelligent copy-edit; and Ashley and Carolyn Grayson, my agents, for encouragement, support, patience, and keeping the business side under control while I dealt with that art thing.

There's also one special acknowledgment. This book is dedicated to Jessica (Jes) Tate, who I sometimes describe as the other half of my brain—the half that works. Some years ago, Jes showed up at an audition for *Oh Dad, Poor Dad, Mamma's Hung You in the Closet and I'm Feelin' So Sad*, which I was directing at the small college where I taught, and took on the job of being the puppeteer who operated Rosalinda the Fish, squatting under a fish tank for two hours, in a role in which the only visible part of her was a large piranha-shaped mitten and her only lines were "gloop" and "gleep."

She turned out to be capable of more.

Later, when she transferred to a bigger university with a much better library, Jes began doing part-time research work for me, at which she excelled, at first for academic projects (she deserves a sizable share in the credit for my fifty-three articles in *The Oxford Encyclopedia of Theatre and Performance*), and later in assembling the background research for novels.

Jes has always delivered more and better work than the contract called for. In the past couple of years, as I have returned to full-time writing, she has made herself absolutely indispensable, not only as a research assistant, but as a thoughtful critic and listener, and a loyal supportive friend.

Unfortunately for me, but fortunately for the world, bright students do graduate, sooner or later, and get jobs for which they are paid real money. There are still some projects ahead of me for which I have Jes's characteristic neatly stacked and categorized piles of complete and thorough research ready to go, but those are the last such piles there will be, at least until I train some mere mortal to take Jes's place. As I write these words Jes is finishing her last major research project for me, and will be done in less than a month. Shortly after, she will be turned loose on the world. If she has any effect on the world like she has had on my office, it is about to become a considerably better place. For its own good, I advise the world not to argue.

Having done most of my theatre work backstage, I have always enjoyed that moment in the curtain call when the follow-spot swings around to give the invisible people their well-deserved acknowledgment. So before you go, Jes, this time, climb out of the fish tank, wave at the people, come all the way to downstage center, collect your roses, and take a bow. Applause, people. This is someone special.

ABOUT THE AUTHOR

John Barnes lives in downtown Denver and writes full time. At various times he has worked full time as a gardener, systems analyst, statistician, theatrical lighting designer, and college professor. More than fifty entries by John Barnes appear in the 4th edition of *The Oxford Encyclopedia of Theatre and Performance.* His most recent books include *The Sky So Big and Black, The Merchants of Souls, The Return* (with Buzz Aldrin), *Candle,* and *The Duke of Uranium.*

1198

VISIT WARNER ASPECT ONLINE!

THE WARNER ASPECT HOMEPAGE
You'll find us at: www.twbookmark.com then by clicking on Science Fiction and Fantasy.

NEW AND UPCOMING TITLES
Each month wc feature our new titles and reader favorites.

AUTHOR INFO
Author bios, bibliographies and links to personal websites.

CONTESTS AND OTHER FUN STUFF
Advance galley giveaways, autographed copies, and more.

THE ASPECT BUZZ
What's new, hot and upcoming from Warner Aspect: awards news, bestsellers, movie tie-in information . . .